FORGE SORCERER

BRINDOLLAN AFFAIRS
BOOK 1

CHRISTOPHER JOHNS

MOUNTAINDALE
PRESS

CATCHING UP

Sometime long ago…

Well, not too long ago, really. More like a stone's throw on the timeline of things that recently took place—okay, got it. I'll shut up and just get on with it.

Brindolla was in danger and there was little-to-nothing the best fighters that we had at the time could do to stop this galactic entity called War from taking over other than to keep him and the rest of his horde out. For a while, things were bad. Generals and minions who served him slumbered as the gods gathered what little strength they could spare to call forth beings from a neighboring planet called Earth, just across the veil from us.

Eventually, they willingly answered the call for aid, and the gods whisked away their souls, allowing them to choose living avatars here on Brindolla so that they could grow stronger and level up to fight back against War's band of miscreants. There was controversy about it, sure. Some didn't like that these Travelers had come to interfere, and thought that the fate of the world should instead depend on the true sons and daughters of Brindolla. The gods knew that their people stood no chance, so they ignored them and blessed these beings as much as they could.

With these blessings, Zeke, Bokaj, Balmur, Jaken, James, Muu, and Yohsuke were able to slowly but surely foil attempts to distract the gods, and eventually faced the malformed avatar of War himself in a battle that nearly brought the void into the world in a way that could have eaten the continent. They weren't aware of it at the time, but it did almost happen.

But before their brawl with the big bad, there were tender moments. Love blossomed and vows were spoken and, from that love bloomed the lives of two very special children. And it is these children that I have been tasked with watching over, as an impartial overseer of sorts. I am to record their lives as a favor… in hopes that someday there will be someone who wants to know. And this is where the story begins.

Though, it does seem like I will have trouble reading the boy, he seems… odd. Something is wrong with him. It's like I can see him and catch glimpses of what he's possibly thinking, but it's all weird. I'll show you what I can, but it will not be everything it seems. Sorry.

CHAPTER ONE

"You are certain this will work?" I was careful to make my voice as icy and terrifying as I could before it echoed across the frozen hall toward the woman shrouded in a long, green flowing dress. Four tails stuck out of her backside and all of them whipped back and forth, but my guest dared not speak as to what forced them to move so frivolously.

Rather, she bowed her head and simply stated, "Yes, Queen Maebe. Your children will remain under the spell until I unbind them again when you feel they are responsible enough to control themselves and their powers."

I, Queen Maebe, the Lady Darkest and the Void of the Snow, watched her from my throne as my oldest living companion Winterheart stared down at the bundles next to me in an icy cradle. The two slumbering children cuddled together in warmth and comfort. He hadn't let the two of them out of his sight in the weeks that they had been alive, he wasn't about to begin now. Luckily, I had been able to convince Vrawn to go and rest to recover herself from her latest bout of depression at the loss of our love and her daughter's brutal birth, but this woman's presence was a blessing more than the nuisance I allowed it to seem.

"It will not bind their magic, just their ability to shift their form?" I watched my visitor with interest, my blue-gloved hand rising to support my chin in an effort to suppress my desire to touch and coddle my—our—beloved children.

At least, more dangerous physically. I could ruin someone's life before taking it a thousand years from now, where she would just kill them outright.

"Correct, your Majesty." Farin F'arine bowed her head once more. "This will be but two more of the hundreds I have done already. Provided they do not grow strong enough to break the binding themselves, they will not be able to change form, and their magic will remain intact."

I allowed myself to remain in thought for a time, unusual for someone who had almost always been as swiftly decisive as she could be, but this concerned my children. *Two more of hundreds? Does she not know that these are my children? If it were not for the fact that they cannot control their physical shapes already, I would slay her where she stands for the insolence of that statement.*

I stared down my chest for a moment, hoping to rein in my anger at her negligent wording and began blankly noting my dark skin, offset by the dots of silvery white on my body in the shape of the constellation in the skies above. Over the light blue dress I wore, the contrast was stark and lovely. As a celestial elf, I had grown up with these markings and was used to them. The only times I had ever marveled at them had been when I had first seen them take over my husband's body after giving him my blood and the Rite to allow him some of my strength and shadow magic.

And that had been one of the best choices of my life. My heart ached fiercely for the man. His smile and happy nature. His antics that made me laugh. His friendship.

I stared down at the children bundled in the cradle next to me and smiled, seeing the same familiar markings on their skin as well. Though one of them was not my own, I treated her as a daughter out of love for her father and mother.

So it was for the Queen to decide on whether this was the best avenue to follow in their upbringing.

"This is a common act, this binding?" She had said this, but for my vengeance to come if she made a mess of it, I needed her to confirm it.

Farin ducked her head. "Yes, it keeps the children safe from being hunted or getting lost on their own." The kitsune druidess clenched her hands together and wrung her fingers before adding, "In fox form, kitsune children are at their most agile and mischievous, and while I am certain they are well behaved now, soon their personalities will begin to show and they will be able to make off on their own. The binding is a common way for them to learn how to be responsible and safe until they can manage their powers and use them wisely and safely."

Winterheart's head rose from where he watched the children and he spoke carefully so as not to wake the slumbering infants. "Do I look like the kind of loving grand-uncle to lose his most-treasured babies?" His teeth flashed as he glared hatefully at her. Slowly his mass grew, his head towering over her, looming so that his impressive shadow covered the now-cowed woman. The temperature in the room dropped several degrees and I had to intervene with a soft wave of my hand to keep him from freezing her on the spot. Instead of lunging forward to bite her in half, he growled, "Tell me."

"I wouldn't dream of implying that you would lose anything, oh Great Wyrm." The kitsune woman bowed her head reverently. "Only that it would potentially be easier to keep them from sneaking off as most kitsune children do. We are a… mischievous sort of people."

"I know that." I grinned, remembering the pranks Zeke would play on his friends and how it delighted him to tease them. "Very well, bind their ability to shapeshift for me, and I will take the forest of your city into my protection from the Seelie, I swear this on my power."

This was a costly thing, but seeing as though she had come to make the request while I had been home before going to find Zeke after losing contact with him on the Continent of Beasts, it was good to know I was gaining more. The court would be able to use their territory as a stepping stone in the coming war between the Unseelie and the Seelie. With the treaty ending, the likelihood of a fight continued to build and build as the two of the Courts continued to posture and peacock.

I glanced over toward the children and where they lay, thinking of all of the work I would need to do if I was to prepare myself and my Court—leading them into battle against our most despised and loathed enemy would take all of my focus and energy. I would do my best to be available to the children, but I needed to ensure we were ready so that they had a future.

Fury rose through me as I remembered the words of the gods that took my husband and love from me—from my children. They would not defend him despite his heroics and they stole him from us. If he were here, the preparations would have been infinitely easier than they would be now, and the gods themselves were at fault for my inability to be there for everything with my children.

Farin lowered her head for a final time, then stood fully and walked toward the throne and the children asleep next to it.

Winterheart's irises became slits as the kitsune woman moved closer and the cold around him intensified to the point where even my own breath became visible and ice gathered on my visitor's clothes and fur.

"Winterheart, she came here by *my* invitation and is under *my* protection." My voice was soft, but my tone firm. He was dangerously close to breaking the law of hospitality. "Go and get yourself something to eat, and check on Vrawn for me."

Winterheart, the great white dragon—Hoarfrost with wings —whined like a child told to leave his favorite friend's home to do his chores. "But the children…"

"Are with me." I turned my face up to glare at the dragon. "Do you doubt my ability to keep them safe?"

He said nothing as he fled the room, his massive bulk skulking away until he had to get through a smaller door, then he shrunk down to become a humanoid of some kind. It looked to be a mixture of dragon and human but the proportions were off, somewhat.

Once he had left the room, Farin moved closer to the children and this time it was I who stopped her. "I know that you want protection for your people from what seems to be coming, but I need your word, sworn to me three times, that you are *only* binding their shapeshifting ability."

Farin could have told me that this was the four thousandth time that she had done this over the span of her lifetime. She could have just rolled her eyes like I knew she was apt to do from watching her for a time, but instead, she just hung up her pride and gave in. "I swear on my power and position as High Druidess of Terra's Escape, that I mean only to bind the kitsune ability to shapeshift so that they look no different than they do right now, until such a time as they are mature enough to handle the responsibility of shapeshifting, or they are powerful enough to break the binding on their own. I swear, I swear, I swear."

The oath slid from her chest where it coiled like a viper and fluttered into me, the notification screen reading me the same, and that if she bore any lies or ill will, it would strip her of her power and give it to me. Then I would kill her in the slowest, most gruesome way imaginable.

She closed her eyes and reached out to touch each child after I stepped back.

After ten minutes of focusing, checking, and rechecking. "The binding is in place and reinforced to the point where there is no way anyone would be able to break it until these two children are truly meant to be able to control themselves and their power." Farin stepped back, sweating and huffing, but bowed anyway. "It is done, my queen."

I reached out and carefully lifted the two children from the cradle, one of them a dark-skinned elven boy with cute pointed ears and specks of white and gold scattered all over his body. His hair was black, but there were little specks within it as well. The girl, her skin as dark as my own, her brother's, and likely her father's, wasn't elven but orcish. More orc than she should have been with her father's blood running through her veins. To most, I knew she appeared to be bald, but there looked to be a soft brown down on top of her head that would grow to be her hair, and I relished running my fingertips over it when she was sleeping as she was now.

"They appear to be well. Thank you for your service to the crown." I smiled down at the children and replaced them in their cradle. "I will remember this, and know that even now, my people come to secure your own. Thank you. You may leave."

Farin did well enough to hide her joy from me, but some of it bled through into her words. "Thank you, your Majesty. May both of your children grow stronger than anyone before them."

My smile widened and warmed as I stared down unblinkingly at the babies before me and replied, "They will."

————

AZLO

"Come *on*, Uncle Thogan!" I groaned exasperatedly, the stone-skinned dwarf staring at me in disbelief. "Just one more round, please?"

Thogan Swiftaxe knew better by half that delaying my magic studies would see him confined to the Fae Realm far longer than his supply of mead would last; I knew because mother had threatened him with it before.

"Later, lad." Thogan growled, failing to hide the mirth in his voice as I hung my head in sorrow. He muttered to himself, like he did at times without realizing I could hear him, "Eight years old, an' strong as some would believe a dwarf to be, though not nearly so stout."

The compliment made me smile. "But I was just about to beat you!" I growled and hefted the small hammer in my hands so that it rested on my shoulder. It was something that Thogan felt comfortable giving to me as a weapon, since I wasn't too good with swords and the axe being his preferred method of dealing death and all. Hammers hefted kind of like axes to him, and he figured it was close enough. "I still don't understand why you won't just give me an axe but Nadir can use one."

"It ain't me place to give it, Prince Azlo," he snarled back, likely more upset than he meant to. It was common for me to push, but when I brought up my father this way and the weapon of Thogan's people, Thogan's mind and purpose of action were clear. "Asides, she were the one to choose it with her ma's blessin'. Again, you ain't her and she ain't you. Yer yer own lad, be yer own lad."

It wasn't his place. It was my father's.

Bringing him up was a roulette for me, according to the dwarf. He wasn't quick enough to answer my questions without confusing one or the both of us, and every time he failed to at least explain something well enough, it made it hard to care about the lesson. Or I would grow so upset that I couldn't keep my hammer from trying to crush the dwarven man.

"He's gone, Uncle Thogan. He can never give me an axe." I tried to make my voice sound more sincere, but I didn't know if it was coming through correctly. "I don't know if I'd want one from him anyway. I mean, he's a hero sure, but I'm my own person. I don't need his approval or anything. One day, the realms will know my name and fear me just like they fear my mother."

I hefted my hammer and stared at the head of it before picking it up to swing it a few times in front of me with more intense focus. "Maybe I'll go to the prime realm and make a name for myself there as well? Explore and get out from the shadow that everyone constantly hauls me back into."

The dwarf whistled at that and quickly, Thogan offered, "A compromise then?" I raised an eyebrow at that curiously. "Ye come back later, once yer lessons be done, an' I'll show ye how to swing that hammer for somethin' other than a fight. How's that?"

My eyes widened and I nodded hard enough my brain felt jostled. Just as I started to leave, I remembered something and ran back to Thogan. "The hammer falls."

Thogan chuckled and rubbed my head affectionately. "And rises again." He pinched my cheek threateningly before swatting at my behind. "Go on an' get ye to yer next class, Highness, afore I pay the price."

I took off, swift as I could, Thogan chuckling behind me.

———

My turn? Finally! I'm not telling you my name yet, so chill, just know I'm watching and relaying things to you, okay? And yes, I can kinda read minds, just a little. So don't think on it too much. Cool? Time to see what's poppin'.

Thogan's sigh after the boy scampered off made me tilt my head and then I saw a shadow extricate itself from the wall. It was the Queen. I settled into my perch and watched them, carefully hiding my presence as the dwarf spoke.

"I think he means to leave one day, Highness." He pulled out his pipe and packed it tightly before lighting and taking a pull thoughtfully. "The boy wavers from lovin' his da an' bein' curious, to despisin' him and wanting nothin' to do with him or his legacy."

Maebe nodded once as she listened and spoke softly in return. "This is to be expected, despite not liking it. I wish there was a way to tell him everything without making it sound patronizing, but at least he does not yet know more."

Thogan cleared his throat and muttered, "He has plans to leave, it seems, Highness. Wants to make a name for himself outside o' what he has as prince. I think if you ain't careful, he may want to take off some day."

Maebe grinned. "This is good news, then. I am certain while exploring the Fae realm, he will strike fear into many."

"Prime, Maebe." The use of her real name drew her focus as her head snapped toward her champion. "He mentioned the prime realm specifically. Unless ya want him to go, I'd make sure you dissuade that. Things there are nay what was an' what had been known, and things are changin' fast. It's no place for the boy."

Maebe clenched her fist and turned toward the shadows of the wall. "Thank you for your wise council, Thogan. I know you love our children as if they were your own family. Please, continue to monitor and guide him." She stalled and closed her eyes. "Both of them."

The dwarf dipped his head as he puffed on his pipe, standing to turn and watch her walk into the pool of waiting darkness. "Aye, Majesty."

"Good day, Master Thogan." Nadir's voice drifted toward Thogan from over his shoulder, the girl stepping from the shadows in the doorway of ice into his training grounds that had true dirt and grass, though not much. He hadn't been able to tend it as he wished to with his duties to his growing clan and watching over both children as he'd been expected.

He took one last puff of his pipe before he turned and addressed her.

"Princess Nadir." The child always seemed odd to him. Muted and proper. She reminded him more and more of her mother than Zeke, but she was a brilliant girl and she was every bit the fighter her ma and da were. "Healer."

The brownie slunk from the darkness after her, his fur-covered body moving slowly with his mounting age, the graying of his bear-like muzzle another sign of his coming end. He turned his beady black eyes to Thogan and grunted. "Feh. Get on with it, we have better things to do than watch you swing that over-sized axe."

Thogan's eyes closed and the wooden haft of his axe groaned under his clenching grip. *Nay the girl's fault her master is more stubborn than a troll an' 'bout as ugly as one.* "Princess Nadir, I think today we should work on your form. You have the strength to wield an axe well. I know that your ma gave you one of your father's, an' I seen ye practice with it."

She did that weird thing where she would acknowledge him, but just played his observations off with more bearing than the soldiers of his former clan could have ever managed, and Thogan hated that. It was unnerving to know that a small child such as this would just be as emotionless as possible.

Is she like this when the old coot is nay there, I wonder? Thogan shook his head and stood, a sip of mead passing through his lips from a ladle he had dipped into the barrel to drink from. "How far have ye gotten with yer ma?"

"She's been teaching me the sword and spear, but the axe is my true interest." A small bit of emotion there, a flare of excitement and a soft smile.

Maybe there be hope for her yet? Thogan stroked his bearded face. "Aye? Good choice, that." He stood up and brushed the dirt off his cloth pants and stared at the child. "How much of a handicap ye need?"

"None." The brownie yawned. "She learns this as she learns all things—the hard way."

"I didn't ask yer opinion, furball!" Thogan roared, dropping his attempt at politeness with the old thing before leveling his axe at him. "Queen Maebe asked me to teach the lad an' lass me way with battle, an' I mean to. But it be *my* way. I rule here, nay yer self."

The brownie looked bored, then addressed Nadir, "End him quickly."

The wood stool that he'd been seated on splintered to Thogan's right as the girl hefted an axe that he recognized right away—Stormcaller. It had been one of her father's favorite weapons before something had happened to it that made it inert. It was no more than a normal axe—well-crafted and beautiful to boot.

She was fast. Thogan had no idea what kind of training she was enduring under her mother's watchful gaze, but she was much faster than her brother. Thogan's axe lifted and he kicked out at her, his foot catching her in the hip and shoving her backward.

She let the momentum carry her to her back, then shoved her legs into the air over her head and was back onto her feet and rushing forward in the blink of an eye, axe swinging for his head.

Thogan ducked and struck her in the solar plexus with his fist, then walloped her in the side of the head with the haft of his axe like it was a stave. Any other child would have been sprawled out from the attack, even if it hadn't been half-strength on his part, it should have put her down.

Instead, it fueled her and made her stronger. Each swing of the axe was crude and rudimentary, but it felt like he was just metal being hammered at an anvil. Finally, after three minutes of back and forth, Thogan decided he had to start truly fighting back or she would overwhelm him.

With a growl, he swept her feet from beneath her and chopped with the head of his axe rocketing toward her shoulder. With the healer so close by, he would be able to keep the wound from getting infected and then heal it in the blink of an eye.

Her eyes glowed crimson and she snarled, her foot kicking straight up into Thogan's bottom hand, shoving it and the axe aside so that her own haft rocketed into his throat. He coughed and sputtered as she launched herself back to her feet, then spun the axe so that when it connected with his ribs, it was the blunt side that hit.

His vision swam and a heartbeat later, he was on a knee fighting to get any kind of air into his lungs. The girl swung with the intent to kill, 'bout as surely as a dwarf whose cup was spilled at a party would.

He felt a cool touch on his throat and air—sweet and deli-cious—gusted into his body. His vision cleared and there she stood, with her hand on her throat and a sweat-covered brow.

"Thank you for teaching me, Master Thogan." She bowed her head to him and turned to her master. "Can we work on healing bones today since I won?"

The brownie Healer just laughed and nodded before leading the little girl out of Thogan's training grounds, the dwarf still on a knee, wondering how to explain this to the Queen and the girl's mother without worrying them.

CHAPTER TWO

AZLO

The moon showed high overhead in the dark sky above our icy fortress home, and I watched the banks of snow listing to one side before they fell and formed a smaller hill. That looked like it would be fun to play on. I was ten now. The day had been eventful, certainly, and the classes were never ending, but I was hoping that Nadir would be able to slip away from her own duties and studies to see me. I missed her.

She was always gone with Healer, his title all any of us save my mother called him and that was all. He hated that she would sneak out to see me sometimes and if he caught her, there would be hell to pay.

It had gotten so bad that I had made a game of having to go and see him a few times a day because I wasn't *minding* my surroundings and getting hurt. The one that came to mind most readily was the last time, and mother herself took me to his tower, where Nadir's room was just above the room he took patients. As soon as the door opened, the wizened old brownie growled, "Let me guess—Prince Azlo and his intrepid nature once again rule over his ability to keep his balance and he scraped his knee, hmm?"

I smiled to myself through the pain, since this time I had actually broken my arm in a fight with one of the human children who was older than me in training. They were the only ones allowed to actually hurt me if I attacked them, because they were doing it in defense and it was good training for them too.

"Not this time, Healer, and I would remind you to maintain a modicum of respect for one of my children." Mother's voice was frosty as she swept into the room behind me. She had known my game and had Thogan intervene. "There was a training incident."

The brownie's sagging furry eyebrows just bobbed as he tutted and called, "Apprentice! Time for a lesson in setting bones!" Nadir raced down the stairway behind him, and I caught a glimpse of her for the first time in weeks. Each trip he had been careful to ensure she wasn't there, claiming she had already learned how to heal this kind of injury. "Grab the two bars there, and a set of strips of cloth. We need to ensure the bone is set before applying healing magic to it."

Mother watched her cautiously, careful not to make it seem like she was here to see the young orcish girl as well. When Nadir had done as she was told, she joined me and I whispered, "Hello, sister."

She frowned at me and said nothing, only going about her business, but Healer joined us and grabbed both sides of my arm, the bone having slipped through the flesh painfully. Even at the age of six, pain had little grip over me and my bearing. To show weakness was to invite doubt and potential threats. Mother had taught me that personally.

"Now, with a break of this magnitude, we have to pull the bone back into the skin carefully, and make certain that the wound is set." With that said, he held my wrist steady on his table and then gripped my forearm near the elbow and yanked the appendage back toward himself painfully. It made me grunt and he grinned, his sharp teeth and whiskers near enough to my face to bring me a bit of a start. He whispered softly, "You constantly coming in distracts your sister, and I cannot have that. Your games are juvenile and could get someone else hurt. Are you certain you can handle the pain my next unnecessary healing will cost you?"

I took a steadying breath and looked to Nadir and there was genuine fear in her eyes. She mouthed, "Please. Stop this."

My mother bent over the brownie's shoulder and hissed, "Any pain you cause *any* child in this Court had better be necessary, Master Healer, or I will find you out on your ear—or worse. You might have been promised an apprentice of your choice, and your choice of Nadir—while lamentable—was your own. You cannot blame him for wanting to see his sister."

The brownie growled, motioning for the girl to splint and then wrap my arm. She did so while he responded to the Queen, "And though I cannot blame him for that, I can blame him for his recklessness and his wild abandon for the charges *you* swore to protect. How many has he forced into this very room because he wants someone to injure him? How many times must I pause the girl's lessons for the petty whim of a child not yet responsible enough to know better than to sate his own selfish needs?"

Mother remained pensive at that. Few told her she was in the wrong and lived—it was why she was so feared—yet the Healer did not care. "You cannot force me to give up my apprentice because it would damage your husband's memory and reputation for having gone back on his offer of an apprentice of my choice. Nor can you order me to allow her the distractions you so desperately wish because she is yet still bound by that same oath. I cannot train her if I have to take care of your daring, demented little spawn."

Mother was across the room with him in the palm of her hand so fast that it frightened the two of us, her face was icy and her eyes were wide as she spoke clearly, "The *prince* may be in the wrong, but it is my duty to show him the way. Not your own. If you ever refer to him as anything so disrespectful again, I will know and I will kill you. I swear that upon the very Court itself. You might be able to hide behind a misspoken oath now, but there will come a day where she is free and you are no longer needed. Keep that in mind."

She threw him away from herself, wiping her hand on her platinum dress as Nadir finished, and said, "I am sorry, my love, but I cannot force him to loosen his reigns. Are you well?"

Nadir nodded, answering, "Yes, my queen." She turned back to me as she finished her work and said, "Please don't do anything so reckless again. I miss you too, but I can't do what I must if I have to worry for you."

We had left the room after Healer had cast a minor healing spell on my arm that would see to the wound's closure and the bone setting, but the damage would need to heal as it would for now. He would do no more for me. As we stood there in the dark hallway looking outside over the Court and our courtyard, she looked pensive. Enough that I thought I would be able to sneak off without punishment.

"Your father gave his word, and I cannot override that even though I am the queen," she said, this tense look of worry on her face that made me pause my flight and return to her. "I will ensure that she is being treated well. You should rest. Your classes are growing harder, you know."

They always were. To the point where I had to block everything else out sometimes. Between training to fight, training with my magic, learning history of the Fae realm and the Prime Planes, there was ever more to learn. But being prince was like that, wasn't it? It was my duty to become the very best at everything so that I could protect them when I ascended the throne someday.

Them. Our people. I looked at the stacks of maps in front of me that showed where our interests were, both here in our home realm and on the Prime Realm. There was Sunrise, Djurn Forge, all of these places that the Unseelie had interests and places to bring us raw materials we might not have here. Places like the Continent of Beasts.

I was to be their king someday, and protect them. Bring them power as well as myself.

What's the point of power if I can't even protect my sister from that nuisance of a healer? I growled to myself in frustration; she wouldn't be coming if she wasn't here by now. I didn't need as much sleep as she did, so I was allowed four hours of time to study that wasn't during classes.

Study. I chuckled to myself and wound my way behind my bookshelf with a huff and into the passageway there. I had built this at eight years old so that I could sneak around the fortress, playing jokes on the staff and the like. It had taken some time; with my magical abilities and some training weapons, I had hollowed the area out.

What I didn't know then was that I could take it a little further and get into Thogan's storeroom of mead. And by extension, the city of Sunrise by way of portal hidden behind a large rack of barrels.

He had taken me there once after a few months of practice smithing so that I could see the Dragon Forge, but my sight had been bound by a thick cloth. The city was beautiful. But every time I went there, it felt like it was trying to talk to me. Lately, I'd taken to sneaking out of my study time to practice my favorite hobby there because the place had become a second home, and escape.

I stepped through the portal into the forge, the air still warm from the day's work. Tools and anvils were clean, the floors neatly swept and all was as it should have been. The scent of metal in the air was enough to make me smile on its own.

Smithing was unlike anything I could have ever thought of. It took skill and talent, certainly, but the best part was that this was something I could do over time and perfect as I went. No two pieces of ore or bars of steel were the same. Since I was only half Fae, working iron was easier for me.

Cold iron made me uncomfortable, but not nearly as much

as it made people like Xiphyre and the other elves that weren't born here.

His enchanting lessons were irritating, but I did like him. His children were nice to me, as well. Watching him and Uncle Thogan bicker was a sight to behold, and I adored it when I was able to be there.

Rowland's forge had been redone over the years, an influx of apprentices and dwarves from the dwarven city of Djurn Forge had come to the city to assist in building the place up and to visit the monument to their clan and the lost clans of old like Thogan's.

As the village had grown and become a town, and then later a city, the forge had been upgraded and enchanted to keep the noise down for his neighbors. Though many of them were dwarves in this portion of the city.

I pulled my own tools from the small enchanted bag on my hip. Since I wasn't yet of a level of any sort, I couldn't access my inventory, and it was irritating to say the least. This had been a work around for me of sorts, seeing as it was the best I could make without master Xiphyre's assistance.

But just because his classes were annoying didn't mean that they weren't informative, or that I didn't pay attention. I just didn't want to waste my time with the craft, so I could focus on smithing.

I also took the time to pull out some metal that I would be working with for my time here. It wasn't too long that I had, but it would be long enough. Having spent the last couple years working the forge at home with Thogan, and taking weekly visits here to hone my craft, had taught me much of what I needed and now it was all a matter of putting it to use.

The massive ingot I pulled from my bag was steel, a simple metal that my strength would allow me to beat into shape faster than most others except the dwarves. Even Rowland had gnashed his teeth and tugged at his beard when he had seen me working metal. "No elf should be tha' strong, Thogan, not a one! That be Zeke's blood, sure as me beard!"

As if summoned by the statement itself, mother appeared in the shadows on the far end of the forge and the dwarf sore vehemently as she asked, "What was that?" He went to speak until she walked over to the far wall and chose one of his thickest swords from a rack and bent it in half in front of him, smiling as she said, "Not just his father's blood flows through his veins."

Rowland had howled with laughter and delight that she was so strong

That made me chuckle as I tossed some wood into the forge, the flames inside rolling into existence hotter than they had been. It was made to run on mana and fuel, the Dragon Forge, the attachment inside to the plane of flame where the primordial fire resided stronger than anything known to Brindolla or the other realms.

As soon as the fire was kindled and stocked, the whispers began again, but I shut down my mind and focused on what I had to do in front of me.

I stuck the ingot into the flames where it sat for only a few seconds before it was cherry red and hot enough for me to begin shaping with my hammer. It would take a while to do what I wanted to with this—years, maybe—but I would do it.

———

I blinked and looked up from the wall of text that I had been trying to make sense of for the last half an hour when mother's presence wafted into the room.

She's always trying to sneak up on me, but she never really seems to realize how adept at reading the shadows and movements in the air I am. I greeted her calmly, "Good afternoon, Mother."

She smiled at me, her wide grin making me smile back.

"Good afternoon, my love." Mother returned the greeting and touched my chin as I looked up at her. "I know that today is your thirteenth birthday, and there is someone I think you would like to meet, who I know would like to meet you."

Ever curious, I perked up and nodded excitedly, then paused. "Will Nadir be there?"

She frowned softly. "I requested that she be able to come, but you know how master Brogden can be about her missing any kind of training for what he deems frivolous things."

"I don't understand why you cannot just make him release her for an hour." I scowled up at her, though I didn't have to look very high. By now, I was only a couple of inches shorter than she was.

"Your father made a promise, and that promise must be kept." Mother closed her eyes and sighed as if even talking about it again pained her. "Any interference from me could put him in danger."

"But he's not here right now," I retorted, growing steadily angrier as I spoke, at her, the situation—my absent father. "He hasn't been here since before I was born, and she needs her family now. She needs us!"

"She needs to perfect her training so that she can be rid of her master's influence, Azlo." Vrawn joined us in the hallway to the library after we had walked out, her hand finding Mother's and holding it comfortably. "You know as well as we do that the sooner she's out from under his thumb, the more free she will be."

"Hello, Vrawn," I greeted the other woman sullenly.

Vrawn leaned down and scooped me up onto her shoulders with a soft *hup* that made me snort. She always made me feel tiny. "Hello, my love. She said she misses you, and she's asked me to give you something."

"What is it?" I asked excitedly as I looked around her, but found nothing. "Can I have it now?"

"Later, I think, would be better for this." She smiled up at me and my joy and excitement barely contained as I bounced excitedly as she walked with Mother and I outside and into the frozen courtyard where Winterheart had taken to haunting sullenly.

The massive dragon was inside today, but the outer and

upper level of the garden in the courtyard held something else that I had only ever heard about in the stories that Mother and Vrawn told from the time I was a child.

The gargantuan mass of azure and light-blue feathers had yet to realize that we had arrived. She was larger than the ancient dragon and then some, and her wings spread out and blocked the sun from the sky.

"Kayda!" Mother shouted and the bird turned to regard her happily, her head cocking to the side as she looked at all of us. "We brought Azlo, like I said I would."

Lightning arced in the sky and a thunderous peal echoed through the entire area for what had to have been miles around as the bird cried out. Her head lowered to the point where her man-sized eye stared at me curiously, her excitement charging the air around all of us until it was almost painful.

She cooed and clicked her beak at me, and though it looked like she was trying to be gentle, it was still loud due to her size, but when the feathered tip of her massive wing gently rested against the back of my arm, I smiled. It felt good, like a cool charge of something stingy and powerful was rifling through my veins. An odd sensation, but nothing so strong or painful that I wanted to break the contact.

"Here." Mother reached into her pocket and pulled out a single azure earring with a small blue feather dangling from it. "This is for you—a gift for your birthday from me."

I took it and pierced my ear with it, the sting of that so much less than any of the myriad wounds I had collected fighting and learning for as long as I could walk.

Feather Brain
While worn, the wearer can speak to and understand the bird whose feather this earring bears.

Earring made by ...

I stopped reading the notification as the legendary Storm Roc, Kayda's voice reached me, "Tiny one?"

She sounded so... uncertain. Almost like she was afraid to hear my voice in return, but I wanted to talk to her. "Kayda?"

She reared up and screamed, the lightning flashing above them deepening and the thunderous crash of her voice mixed with her howl of joy. I laughed and covered my ears, squinting, but she was back down in front of me and prodded me with her beak softly. "How are you? You're so big, but still a hatchling, how is this possible? I love you. I love Father. I miss Father so much. He loved you too."

Extreme sadness and loss fell over me then, *Why could no one just want to see me for me? Why does everyone bring him up so much?*

"Were you there with him?" Kayda cocked her head at me and my soft question and blinked twice before I added, "When he was here, were you with him?"

"Yes." Kayda nodded emphatically, her beak scraping the ground and leaving a huge gouge in it. "I was mainly kept in a bauble to stay safe while we were here, but I was here."

"Do you still have the bauble?" She shook her head. "Would you be my friend?"

"I love you too much to be a mere friend—you are family to me." She butted her head against my chest, the stinging sensation returning so much that I couldn't help but laugh as she said, "And I will always be here for you as much as I can. Though I know not much of what I can do or become, I feel more alive than I ever have. When I find a mate, you will be bonded to one of my eggs, and they will be your sibling and love you as I loved our father."

"You can do that?" I asked, unable to contain the wonder in my voice. "And why do you call him your father?"

"He helped my mother give birth to me when she was dying." Her eyes flicked to Mother. "Your mother is far too strong to be defeated by someone the way mine was. As was our father. When she passed, I stayed with him as his protector and guardian. We traveled the world together." She laughed, her feathers ruffled and she added, "The stories I could tell you!"

"Were they funny?" Yet again, I couldn't hide my excitement. The funny stories that Mother and Vrawn told had always been my favorite, even if thinking about Father hurt sometimes, or made me feel… off. I especially loved the ones of the times father would shout, "Pie!" then do something that made people question his sanity.

"Oh, so many." She snickered and lowered her head some more, then asked, "Have you ever heard of your uncle Goblin?"

My knees buckled as a gout of uncontrollable laughter tore from my mouth while Kayda regaled me with stories of Muu, how they had met, and all the funny things he would say and do. It was like listening to the stories of a jester, or watching Mother's shadow goblins wrestle over food.

It's me again! Did you miss me? … fine. Be that way.

Above, high in the tower that Nadir was forced to live in to be closer to her master, the young girl watched forlornly as her beloved brother was able to meet the Storm Roc who even her master stared at in awe. She looked once more as if she wondered what sort of stories Kayda had to share, and what insights she could offer someone like herself.

If Kayda would love her as much as she wanted to be.

Your mother loves you, Nadir, you selfish girl. She put down the book she had been reading for her own pleasure and learning. "The Dichotomy of Orcs and All Others," by a name she could hardly pronounce. *If Father were here, he would likely feel the same based on the stories you've heard. All you have to do is keep getting stronger and smarter until the master passes. Then you can go into the dungeon and finally be close to Azlo. Like siblings should be.*

She stared down at the painting that was on her wall. Her small room was austere except for the books that she was both forced to have and those she couldn't bear to part with. Other than her bed, the small desk, and the wardrobe for her clothes, there was nothing as far as decoration or comfort were concerned or considered. Except the painting of her and Azlo slumbering together as babies.

She could still feel his closeness sometimes. His scent still lingered on the blanket she had on her pillow. She missed it. Before she had been old enough to be taken as an apprentice, the two of them had been inseparable. Playing together all the time, telling each other secrets, making mischief for the servants and their parents. Bending the shadows to their will together to make funny shapes on the walls. Teasing Grand-uncle Winterheart and sliding down his tail like it was a slide while he tried to flick snowballs at them.

Those fond memories had been enough to get her through the years of harsh tutelage from her master. He wasn't cruel, but he expected more than she could give at times, and when she failed to perform to his standards, his punishment was to take the little free time she could manage from her. She failed less often now, but her free time was used to ensure that she never failed like that again—the cycle repeating.

And now, watching her brother be the child that he was allowed to be, that she yearned to be, Nadir was bitter. She felt so alone now. Only really seeing anyone else when she had her lessons with her mother, and yet there she was with the queen and her brother and her father's first bonded companion. The legendary Kayda.

Master never allowed her to see anyone else, outside of the times that were for training, because any interaction outside training was a distraction. So everyone else got to be with their loved ones and peers and family and… She whimpered once as the thought threatened to crush her and her resolve to dust.

And here she was learning about the people that not even her mother had ever met. Why? To go and meet them some day? Other than the dungeon, she would never leave these walls. She was to become the Healer. She was here to ensure the royal family had their health.

The burning anger within her seethed and writhed until finally it was too much and she roared in anguish, the enchanted lights in her room guttering and flickering before finally they went out.

Again, girl? her master muttered through her mind, making

her shiver. He knocked just to be polite but opened the door anyway, before he spoke to her in person, "Come, there is something I would like to show you concerning that little stroke of power that you have little control over."

Nadir hung her head for just a moment before she straightened and muttered, "Yes, master."

CHAPTER THREE

AZLO

The hall was quiet for a time as I walked past yet another shining surface meant to act as a mirror. It was difficult not to notice myself in it. Now, a little taller and broader through the shoulder, making it a tad more difficult to sneak through crowds like I normally might have when I was younger and smaller. Not that the room was empty, or dark, I just preferred not to talk to the subjects who milled about and politicized amongst themselves. It was my sixteenth birthday now, after all, and it was the first time in three years that I would be able to see Nadir.

Mother had insisted I wear the outfit that Svartlan had put together for me. The shoulders of it had been padded slightly with extra cloth, but otherwise it fit comfortably. The jacket that went over the plain, frost-blue shirt was a vibrant blue that, as you passed through various sections of shadow, would glow with an eerie, almost-ghostly glow. The same for the matching trousers. The orc always did have a good sense of fashion, but this was new even for me.

So many people tried to catch my attention, some even so bold as to clear their throats in my general direction, but I just smiled and nodded them away. An excuse here, a tasteful disengagement there, and eventually I stood alone next to the icy throne while all the nobles and guests of honor watched me with as much tasteful disinterest as they could feign. Well, as much as they could get away with feigning, that was.

The room darkened and suddenly Mother sat on her throne with her shoulders high and her chin lifted. The entire room went silent, and everyone there took a knee.

The door at the end of the hall opened, and in swept Vrawn with Nadir at her side. Nadir dressed simply for her status, a simple deep brown dress that showed off her musculature, but still somehow managed to look feminine and inviting to the eye.

My, how tall she's become over the last few years. She towered over me now just like Vrawn did—the two of them almost equal in height, and she was only sixteen years old. Her shoulders were still a little narrower than her mother's, but the muscle that was there was nothing to be taken lightly.

Her hair, shaved at the sides like her mother's, was a ghostly white with deep crimson streaks through it.

As she stepped through the shadows, the dress she wore shimmered with a red radiance that looked similar to her hair. "She's beautiful." Queen Maebe smiled, and glanced my way. "You've both grown so much. You both have."

The fact that she had repeated herself was odd, and as I turned to look at her, the tears welling in her eyes as she stared from Nadir to me became evident. Both Vrawn and Nadir walked to the throne and Maebe stood to give the larger child a hug, levitating to touch her cheek and stare into her eyes. "You're beautiful, Nadir."

"Thank you, my Queen." Nadir curtsied and lowered her head.

Mother looked hurt, but said nothing more; she would likely ask her to talk later. As it was, she needed to address their people, but she simply said, "Both of you stay with me once this is all done. I will have something for both of you that you have a right to once they all leave."

Both of us nodded, but it was hard to not try to speak to each other. It had been so long since we had seen each other, even in passing, and yet here we were in the same room.

Mother squared her shoulders, stepped forward, and raised her chin in a way that made her appear larger than she was for her short stature. "Unseelie Fae, before you all gathered today, stand the hope of our people. My son, Prince Azlo, and his sister, Princess Nadir." At our names, we both stilled and stared out over the people who watched with apparent interest and some of them even hunger. "They work tirelessly to prepare themselves for the arduous task of leadership, and soon, they will face the dungeon for their right to be considered rulers of the Fae someday."

She smiled, her eyes sparkling. "Though we all know that it will be a *long* time before I abdicate my throne, I have nothing but the highest faith that these two are the future we need."

"Here here!" someone in the crowd shouted. A human boy, possibly no older than we were, looked embarrassed to have not been able to keep himself contained.

Mother just chuckled to herself and nodded. "Yes, Varil, this is a cause for celebration. Today, among the Fae and the Orcs, both Azlo and Nadir are considered adults, though young as they are. Today, we celebrate their birth, and with that, the prosperity that has come and will come for generations. Please, line up to bring your gifts forward so that the prince and princess might thank you."

They obeyed, then lined up and brought up various trinkets, both enchanted and not, but all of them garbage compared to what we had access to thanks to Xiphyre, his children, and Thogan. I smiled, thinking, *I'm not too terrible with a hammer either, according to the old dwarf.*

Tediously, time trickled on, those presenting their items and gifts tried to do their best to make their names known, and all I could do was file them away for later remembrance. Though I could seem casual and disinterested with the best of them, I would not forget a name. It was how I was raised as Fae and as potential ruler.

Finally, the line was done, and it was time for the gifts that our parents had gotten us.

The gift to choose who we would become and how it would be that we would advance.

Queen Maebe stood from her throne and stepped to my side as Vrawn took a step forward and stood next to Nadir. Both raised the hand closest to their respective child and put it on our shoulder, before Maebe spoke, "To this child I have raised and protected for these sixteen years, I relinquish all the experience and levels that you have herein acquired under my care. Release."

Power flooded into my body in a way that I'd never felt before. It was so much that it arched my back and nearly put me on my knees. All those classes, all those training sessions with Thogan, Winterheart, Mother, Vrawn, all of them had been flooding me with experience and at the culmination of it all, it was here now. Finally *mine*.

The sound of a cane tapping along the floor interrupted Vrawn beginning the ritual to relinquish Nadir's strength and power to her. Everyone turned to see the old, gray brownie wobbling toward us.

"This is highly irregular, master Healer." Queen Maebe growled as her head listed to the side a bit. "You assume a great deal due to your usefulness to this court."

"Hush, child." The brownie growled, his cane still assisting him with loud clicks as he continued to march forward. "My time is come. As her mother releases her owed power to her, I will add my magic to it and the new Healer will be born. To stop this by any means is to make false the word of your husband."

My eyes widened as Mother's jaw audibly clacked shut and she raised her hand and clenched her fist, the shadows below the insolent creature coalescing over his body before spitting him out just to the right and behind the girl, opposite her mother. He grunted and breathed a sigh of relief. "Thank you."

He looked up at the girl and she blinked down at him, a single tear running from the rim of her eye down her cheek as he reached out and tapped her arm in a way that occurred to me as affectionate.

By the looks of it alone, he was old. Tired. Hanging on by sheer willpower alone, and he could have given her his power any time before her coming of age. Mother had muttered far more of those when she had assumed she was alone for me not to know that this was a bid for Nadir to win the credence of the court to wield his power and access it properly from the start, lest she be turned down the wrong path.

He hung on for her. Because she deserved to have someone there, among the faceless many who knew nothing of her, who had watched her struggle and rise to who she could now become. Who knew her better than anyone, even if it had been for selfish reasons like his.

She deserved to have him be proud of her. As he stared up at her and said, "I am," another tear fell and she just nodded once and turned back to the crowd.

Vrawn lifted her voice, a touch angry. "To this child I have raised and protected for these sixteen years, I relinquish all the experience and levels that you have herein acquired under my care. Release."

The old brownie muttered under his breath and the pleasant chill in the room became a sweltering heat that raged to the point that it began to melt the ice. Mother's power flared and kept the building from falling down onto all of them as the heat continued to climb higher and higher. Eventually, it was all anyone in the room could do to stay standing, the only ones able to stomach the heat being Mother herself and Winterheart, who had barged into the room to help keep the castle stable.

After a few moments, the power flared one final time and the brownie faded from view in a wash of ash, leaving a sweating and huffing Nadir behind. Burns radiated down Vrawn's arm where she had been in contact with the heat and Nadir reached out to touch them, the marks fading as swiftly as they had been raised.

I breathed heavily for a moment as I stood to my feet and watched her. Mother grunted and blew her hair out of her face before she shouted, "Ladies and gentleman of the Unseelie Fae, I give you, your new Healer!"

The crowd, all of whom were in various states of shock, gasped and spoke to each other in low tones. Finally Vrawn had enough and bellowed, "Why are you just talking to each other? Go! Spread the news to everyone that a new—*stronger*—Healer has been born."

They stood and didn't move because they had never really been addressed by her before, but Maebe's cold fury building and the look on her face said it all: Obey.

The Fae fled the room in whatever ways they could, the more humanoid on foot, those who were strong enough were allowed to flee by teleporting, but would not be able to return in such a manner unless summoned.

The queen uttered a long string of unintelligible words under her breath and an army of Fae creatures rose from the shadows in various forms. Large cats, the most popular among them, though some of them chose more grotesque avian forms with misshapen wings and cruel-looking beaks under intelligent eyes.

"Go, and spread the word of my children's ascensions and their impending quest within the dungeon. They will have one week before they go, as is custom." As soon as she finished her explanation, they all took off in different directions and faded from view almost immediately. The queen turned to her children and lover with a sigh. "That was interesting, to say the least. Nadir, how do you feel?"

Nadir glanced down at herself; her clothes were slightly

singed, which was a shame because the dress had been lovely. Physically, she looked fine to me, but I could see there was a hint of something more hiding behind her eyes. Something I was used to seeing as we got older. Something she wouldn't share. "I feel better, your Majesty."

"Nadir, please, call me Maebe, if you will not call me Mother." Mother reached up and put her hand into the young woman's. "I was there the day you were born. Your mother and I love each other."

Vrawn reached out and put a hand on her lover's shoulder in support. "We do."

Nadir just bowed her head. "I know. It's just difficult to speak so plainly with you now after everything I was taught. Please, don't take offense to it."

Mother eyed her for a mere moment before she offered the younger woman a soft grin. "Very well. Your mother and I have gifts to give you, come with us."

She turned and we went to a small sitting room just down the hall where she entertained visiting dignitaries from the Unseelie's holdings and allies in the Prime Realm. Inside, there were two large books.

"Inside these tomes are the combined histories of the dungeon that you are to enter and defeat, who defeated it, and how far they went through it together." Mother touched one book, sliding it to me, then the other to Nadir. "Familiarize yourselves with it in the time you have to prepare before entering the dungeon."

"Yes, Mother." She turned and faced me, then looked to Vrawn before looking at Nadir. Something was going on. "What's wrong?"

Mother's brows knit together, then she sighed. "We do not know what your statuses will look like, nor what classes will be available to you. That not knowing has been eating at me for all of these years and now that they are available to you, I am curious to see what you will become. Forgive me, I am unused to this level of impatience."

"What we have to give you is here in this room, though." Vrawn walked over to the couch in the corner of the room and lifted it to pull out a bundle of items that sounded heavy, but didn't look like it in her massive hands.

Mother waved her hands and a large wooden table formed from nothing, likely summoned from her room, giving Vrawn a place to set the items in her hands. "Thank you."

"Of course." Mother smiled at her before turning back to us. "Your father requested that we give these to you when we thought you ready for them."

Nadir held her hand out and a weapon appeared in it, the yellow and black great axe with a head shaped like lightning shimmering in the light. "I have this already."

Mother turned, looking askance at Vrawn before Vrawn offered her daughter a soft smile that flashed her tusks. "We know, but this is different. These items were enchanted by him specifically and left to us so that you could have them."

"Nadir can have them." I spoke softly, my heart sinking as I stared at the bag. Mother frowned and stepped toward me, but I shook my head.

"Azlo, I know that this is all very much to take in, but this was his wish for you both before he left this existence." She pursed her lips and looked like she was trying to decide if she wanted to speak and say something I had likely heard dozens of times before.

Finally, sixteen years later, I had heard enough and couldn't keep it all in anymore. The small remarks and cutting jabs that had been stated by me through the years were never enough, never heard. I would no longer be ignored or placated.

"So what?" I bellowed back. My mother, the most powerful being of the Unseelie outside of Samir himself, flinched and looked stricken. I repeated, "So what? He was too afraid to stay here himself? To give it to us himself?"

"Azlo, please…" Vrawn began, her bulk moving closer, but Nadir held a hand out to stop her, keeping her away from me as I breathed through all of my thoughts.

"Azlo, your father and his friends *saved* all of us." Mother tried again and this time when she stepped forward and I looked up at her sharply, she did not shy away. "You would do well to remember that and honor his sacrifice." She again stopped as if there was so much more she wanted to say, but she didn't. She never did.

"He made his choice, Mother." I growled, seething now. "All our lives, we've been made to look up to someone who isn't *here* because of a choice that was made outside our control. Forced to live in his shadow without knowing him ourselves, and only having stories to try and learn anything about this *stranger* who left us here without him."

I motioned to Nadir and fought not to raise my voice any more than I had already. "Someone who unwittingly sold my sister to a creature who forced her away from a family she needed as much as I did, and we're supposed to just accept these gifts from him and that makes everything okay?"

"He didn't know that master Brogden would choose me." Nadir spoke softly at first, then stared at me and frowned. "But you have a point. I lost everything, was given everything, and then lost it again today. Though I love the man in the stories, I can't take his things and just call it good."

Vrawn looked uncomfortable, then cleared her throat and said, "We were also going to take you to see him."

If I could have seen myself in one of the mirror-like sections of ice in the hall, I would have probably appeared dumbfounded. He was here? How long had he been here, and why had he not shown himself? Nadir looked the same way I felt, though her mask of stoicism returned faster than mine did.

"Take us," I ordered softly, the need to please my mother and mind my manners fully gone now.

She stared at me, hard, and when I didn't look away or back down, it took Vrawn pulling her into her chest to get her to relax, before the orcish woman muttered, "They have gone through much more than we thought, my love. They are owed this. Let us take them."

Mother stared at me a moment longer before she nodded once, ever so slightly that it would have been easily missed by any who didn't spend time with her. I'd angered her. I knew I had. And I didn't care. I was about to meet my father for the first time.

CHAPTER FOUR

It took only so long for us to wind up in the most heavily guarded part of the fortress that I had never been to in my sixteen years, and I was grateful that I had never been here.

There were at least ten red cap guards, all of whom were plainly visible to me and my True Sight, six sylvan guards with crossbows, and one surly-looking mage who read from a tome as thick as my leg as we walked by.

None of them paid any mind to my mother or Vrawn, but upon seeing us, there was a distinct feeling of unease in the air from all of them. It was hard to put into words what I was feeling and thinking from all of them, so I focused on what was in front of me.

Mother took her gloves off and raised a hand in front of the brown door. As I looked closer, I could make out small, thin slivers of silvery scars crossing her palm as it faced her, but she drew a blade from her waist to draw across it. Her blood flooded forward readily and she didn't even hiss at the pain of it, just rubbed the blood onto the stone.

Stone, I muttered to myself mentally. The door in front of her wasn't stained brown because it was wood, it was stained brown with her dried blood. *How many times over the years had she come here? Had he always been here?*

My questions dried up as the door slid inward and my mother disappeared into the darkness with Vrawn motioning that we should follow.

Once we were inside in a small reception area, the door closed behind us and flames flickered to life above our heads, feeding light into the room.

Mother didn't turn around when she spoke, but the gravity of her request was such that I couldn't question it. "Before I take you any further, you will swear on your true names to never speak of this place to anyone but each other, Vrawn, or me. Anyone involved with it has been placed under a geas to forget about it until such a time as I bid it important for them to remember. I do not wish that to be the case for you. Swear it now."

"I swear on my true name that I will speak of this place with no one but those here presently." I worded it that way purposely but she didn't make me change the wording before the oath gripped my heart and made me grimace at the immensity of the weight of it.

Nadir swore a similar oath, and Mother finally nodded once before walking on, the path ahead lighting as we moved. The walls of the hall we crossed burst into life with multi-colored runes and sigils that reminded me of things I had seen in my enchanting classes, but it was far too advanced for me to know the slightest bit of what was going on here. The hallway opened into a wide room and before the lights brightened here, a tidal wave of magical energy so intense and strong washed over us all and took my breath from my body.

Six massive elementals surged from chalices on the walls at once and prepared spells that could have leveled an army if sent flying; instead, they saw my mother and Vrawn and backed down with bows. The lights flickered to life above the room, and I noted that there were several crystalline structures with fluid in them that had a slight blue hue to it, but the fluid was unimportant.

It was the men floating within who garnered a gasp from both myself and Nadir.

"These are the members of Storm Company who gave their everything to the cause." Vrawn spoke hoarsely. Looking at her, her gaze fell on one structure in particular. "Their sacrifice secured life for all of us."

Numbly, my legs moved toward what occupied her vision and found a kitsune floating there with his eyes closed in simple clothes, black fur covered in sparks and spots much like what covered Nadir and I, like constellations in the night sky. He looked so real.

Like he could open his eyes at any moment. As if, when my hand touched the crystal, he would raise his hand to mirror me and smile. Say he was sorry that he missed so much, but he was here now.

But as my fingers touched the cold crystal, the only warmth that flooded me was the tears that spilled painfully from my eyes. He wouldn't wake. My hand slowly closed and became a fist, my shoulders shaking as my breath came in heaving sobs of anguish, and the only thing I could do was scream.

Scream my frustration to the cosmos at having given me so much, but taken what was most important. What *should* have been most important.

Hands touched my shoulder and my first thought was violence. To lash out and crush this place. To destroy the monument to my loss. But I knew nothing.

"They could return some day," Mother whispered. "It is why I gathered the strongest, most creative minds in the world and the realms to build this place. So that they would have bodies for their souls to return to."

I turned back to find Vrawn clinging to Nadir as the larger woman wept and Nadir just stared into the structure.

"If he could return some day, how is it that we are allowing him to return to a world with the Seelie planning war?" Nadir asked softly, surprising all of us. *The Seelie had plans to march on us?*

"There is still time yet before the peace we have will reach its end," Mother explained and sighed. "I know how and why you know that. I wish only that I could have shielded you from it for a few more years."

It finally occurred to me how sheltered a life I had lived.

"Mother, I cannot go to the dungeon as I am now." I turned to Nadir. "I don't know that it would be right for either of us to go."

"What do you mean, Azlo?" Vrawn sniffed and rubbed her nose on her forearm once before looking up at me. "You have to go. It's your duty."

"I have a duty, yes, as we all do." I looked down at my hands before looking back up at the husk of my father. "But having seen all this, I still don't know who I am. Our father is right there, so close I could almost touch him, and yet we have only stories of him told to us here in the safety of these walls."

Both Mother and Vrawn stayed quiet, but Nadir seemed to get what I was saying. "You wish to have time to go out and figure out who *you* are, and prove yourself against the legend of our father." *I almost wouldn't say that last part,* I thought, about to say as much, but she continued on, jutting her lower jaw forward, saying, "I feel the same, both of my father and my master. If I am to prove myself as the new Healer for this court, I must challenge myself." She glanced at me and nodded once, correcting her statement. "*We* must challenge ourselves."

Queen Maebe frowned at me. "I cannot simply have you running rampant in the Fae Realm with the Seelie plotting war."

"Then they can go to the Prime Realm," Vrawn interjected, surprising all of us. Before Mother could reject it, she hastily added, "We have allies there. People who will know of Zeke and Storm Company. Who better to see them safe than the ones who knew their father best?"

"Me." Mother growled sullenly, then sighed. "I will think on this."

She said no more on the matter, turning to stare forlornly at my father, any attempt to garner her attention met with stoic staring that started to strain my soul. Eventually, I just gave up and headed out of the building, all of the elemental creatures watching me curiously as I strode by.

Once I was outside, I decided to take a look at what I was working with, "Status."

Name: Azlo Erebos
Level: 10
Strength: 17
Dexterity: 21
Constitution: 12
Intelligence: 21
Wisdom: 14
Charisma: 16
Unspent Attribute Points: 30
Unassigned Chaos Points: 10

I blinked at all of the stats and smiled. My strength made sense, for my build and swinging hammers all the time, seventeen was a good number. Dexterity and everything else seemed normal for me as well.

I touched my class options and was flooded by notifications.

Abilities Unlocked

Kitsune Shapeshifting — Take the form of an anthropomorphic fox, elven with similar features, elven, or a fox as your natural shape. Transformations are indefinite until the Kitsune chooses to change forms. Each of these forms is considered a natural form, as all are the Kitsune.

That was interesting, and as I felt for the ability, it was like a dam broke in the base of my neck and I could suddenly *feel* so much more around me then I had before. My vision shifted and sharpened. I could smell that the old man reading the book hadn't bathed in a week and was in dire need of a change of socks.

I blinked away the discomfort as warmth flooded me and suddenly I felt *different* but somehow more me than I had ever felt. Looking down at myself, I found my arm covered in fur, my nails had grown in length and sharpness to the point that they had become claws. I reached up and touched my nose, finding a snout.

"First change?" a soft voice asked quietly behind me. I turned to find Nadir watching me quietly from where she leaned against the now-closed door.

"Yes," I answered. The voice was mine, but the movement of my mouth felt off to me. She smiled. "What about you?"

She shook her head. "I broke the binding for our racial inheritance years ago." She stretched and as she did, her whole body shimmered and changed. Suddenly, she was two feet taller and looked more lupine than anything else. Her eyes remained the same color as they had been before, but her fur was ebon save for the tuft of white and red on the top of her head. "Somehow, I think I collected more of Father's wolf than his fox, like you."

We stood there awkwardly for maybe a moment before the shadows pooled on the ground between us and a massive panther of shadows with golden eyes sprang forward, looking around wildly. The mage stood with the warriors from the other places and began to cast spells as the red caps tromped forward, but the creature shouted, "Queen Maebe!"

"Mother is inside the building there, who are you?" I no sooner had the words out of my mouth than a blood curdling shriek of grief and rage shook the building, the temperature dropping so sharply that my body began to shut down. Nadir strode forward and touched me, my muscles warming and releasing from the cramp-like sensation the cold had been enacting on me.

The door slammed open, Mother shouting wildly, "Search the grounds for a mage, my husband's avatar is gone!" Her wide eyes alight on the creature before me. "Servant? What happened to my husband? Why are you here?"

The panther became a man and knelt on the ground with his arms spread wide. "I failed you, my queen, but all is not lost."

The queen was across the distance between them before I could even think to blink and had the man in her grip, choking him as she screamed, "What happened to Zeke, Servant?"

The man called Servant choked and sputtered, "He lives, Majesty." He managed to look our way for just a moment before he could say, "He has awakened on Earth, and reclaims his strength as we speak."

She dropped him onto the ground as Vrawn came to her side and fell to the ground in a heap with her, the orc growling softly, "Speak plainly, Fae."

He bowed his head again, and this time tears streamed down his face, his voice rough but the joy and elation in it were enough to stop my heart from beating for a moment. "King Zeke is awake at last. He's trying to find a way home to you." The Fae turned and smiled at my sister and I sadly. "To all of you."

CHAPTER FIVE

Mother watched the creature with more slowly building rage than anything else, and even before she could open her mouth, the bowing creature said, "I swear by my very existence that he has awakened at long last."

"How…?" Mother started to speak, but stopped and turned to stare at the tomb behind her. "Why did his avatar disappear, Servant?"

"It's tied to his soul, my Queen," Servant explained gently, much to my confusion. "As such, when his memories returned, his body returned with it."

"He means to return?" Vrawn's voice was almost a bare whisper.

"Yes, Lady Vrawn." Sergeant bowed to her. "My sister is with him as we speak. He searches for a way to get home."

Mother frowned, her eyes closing as she seemed to break. This was the first time that I had ever seen her drop to her knees and break.

Queen Maebe, Lady Darkest and the Coldest Embrace, openly wept in front of everyone. She sobbed in such a heart wrenching and crushing way that even Vrawn looked concerned.

"My love…" she heaved, her hands clenching into fists over her chest. Her eyes looked almost welded shut as the tears fell from the corners of her eyes. She whimpered and finally looked up at Vrawn. "Our king will return."

Mother held her arms open and the larger woman went to her to hold her. Together, they shed tears of emotions I could hardly recognize as I'd not seen either of them really display them before—least of all like this.

After an uncomfortable amount of time wallowing together, Mother stood and cleared her throat, some of her composure returning.

She stared at the two of us for a long moment before stating calmly, "The two of you are going to the Prime Plane in order to explore and become stronger. You have one year of Fae Plane time before I have to force you to go into the ancestral dungeon in order to cement your claim to the throne. I fully expect you to become strong enough to succeed me in that time."

She lifted her hand and flexed her fingers, magic washing over us and a timer flickered into the edge of my vision that had a current count down of the date from one year. "This is a spell that will return you here no matter where you are, so be conscious of it." She stared at both of us and added, "It cannot be dispelled by any means other than a god's interference, and they would not deem it necessary, so do not fret."

"Do you have other expectations of us?" Nadir asked calmly.

"Do not break any of our current treaties, children are to be protected, and do not allow each other to fall." Mother looked thoughtful, then a small smirk made a chill run down my spine. "If you come across any Seelie on the Prime Plane and they attack you, kill them. Do not be above goading them either, if you think you can handle them. This is an issue I would person-ally love to see fixed before your father returns, but that would also mean potential all-out war. So in this, you must be cautious."

Nadir closed her eyes and nodded. "Which is why you need us as strong as we can be before we return to delve into the ancestral dungeon."

"Exactly." Mother stared at Vrawn for a long moment before stating, "Three days. Allow us three days to collect the things we would like to give you before then. If you have weapon needs, or need to have things enchanted, please let Thogan or Xiphyre know and they will see to it."

I lifted my eyebrows. Xiphyre was a particularly mulish creature who hated doing things like this, though he was my enchanting instructor and loved Uncle Thogan like a brother, his services offered up like this was new. I would have to see about that.

"Mother…" I spoke softly and her gaze turned to me. "I still have yet to receive any insight into what class I can take up."

Vrawn and the queen both gasped audibly, even Nadir stared at me with concern. "You're certain?"

I nodded at my sister and her question then hung my head. "Am I fit to be royalty without a class?"

"Leave it with me. Allow me another day, and I will look into it along with some of my scholars." The queen stood as she spoke and came to me, Vrawn following closely. The large green woman's hand alit on my cheek as she kissed my forehead and rumbled at me with her chest. It was something she had loved to do since I was a child and it had always been comforting. "There is much to do, but I assume you mean to go and forge as you have been over the years when you have free time?"

I tried to school my features to keep the shock from finding out she knew from her, but she smirked anyway and laughed at me. "You had to have known I knew everything going on in my lands. I allowed it. I used to sneak out and hunt creatures as a child. It was therapeutic with the pace we are expected to learn."

Mother turned to look at Nadir, who was much more

guarded. "Unfortunately, your master saw through all of my attempts to do the same for you, my heart. I would give anything to have afforded you more chances to just be a child."

Outwardly, nothing changed on my sister's facial expression, she may as well have been a statue for all she gave off, but it was that particular lack of change that made Mother wince.

Queen Maebe's head hung in moderate defeat. "I have asked forgiveness fair few times in my lifetime, long as it has been, but this is one of those instances where I will not waste my breath." She lifted her face to stare into Nadir's face and stated softly, "I know that no words I say can return to you the losses you have endured and the time that was stolen from you by an unknown promise. I can only swear to you with all these witnesses here, that if I could have spared you without doing irreparable damage to our court and your father…"

The words hung in the air as Mother made to finish the statement. I could feel the ether building like a tidal wave, the chaotic energies of the Fae realm swirling around our feet in nebulous strides, like an overly eager dog nipping at my heels, ready to jump at the smallest sign of attention.

Nadir stood even straighter and blinked once before breaking the silence. "No." She continued to stare ahead of herself, as if she were staring past Mother. "Forgive me, my queen, but there are preparations that need to be made if we are to carry out your will. I will also check my maste—*my* library to see if I can cure the Prince's class issue. Good evening."

With that, she bowed at her waist and hurried from the courtyard, Vrawn's bellow of her name just rolling off her shoulders and broad back. Vrawn put a comforting hand on Mother's shoulder. "I'll go talk to her."

Mother put a hand on Vrawn's and shook her head. "No, she has every right not to hear me out, or accept any word from me. If it were anyone else, I would have supported the training with my whole power, and I think that also bothers her. Leave her to her way, and we will focus on what we can do for her moving forward."

Mother looked at me and just made a shooing motion. I took it and took off for Thogan's courtyard, following the labyrinthine halls to it by memory and knocked. There was no answer, but I knew he wouldn't mind my entrance so long as I had a good reason. The need to forge that I had at the moment would have to be good enough for him.

Once I was inside, I found my way to his not-so-secret portal to the city of Sunrise and the Dragon Forge.

Hammering made me flinch and I walked into the next room to find Rowland working at the anvil, his back to me.

He sniffed at the air. "That Thogan I smell?"

He shoved his work back into the forge to heat, huffing, "Listen, I told ya I wouldnae do it, even if ya brought me all the sweetest dwarven ale ya could find. Ain't right, that." He turned and found me standing before him and tugged his beard. "By the Dwarven God hisself, boy—coulda said somethin'."

"The hammer falls, Rowland." I bowed my head in his direction and he just stared at me for a moment then heaved a sigh.

"And rises again. Come here, lad. I can see ya got the itch about ya, sure as the beard on me beautiful face." He noticed my raised eyebrow and snorted. "Ya gonna gimme what I oughta get for that, or are ya itchin' too bad?"

"I'm a little…" I grinned boyishly and motioned to him and said, "Well, not as little as you, but I'm out of sorts, and this is where I go to when I need to get my mind off things."

He roared and leapt at me, grabbing me around the neck and rubbing his knuckles on top of my hair, the roar of indignant hurt turning into a burble of laughter. He snorted and smacked me in the face affectionately. "Better an' better all the time, boy. Come on, ya got anythin' in mind for the forge today?"

"Nothing really. I could use the space to just forget." He nodded sagely. "Do you get this way?"

"Me?" He snorted and shook his head, then grinned. "All the time, why I have me Mini. She helps when ol' Rowland gets in his head an' cannae escape. Her an' her wee fox kits keep me company sometimes as I forge aimless-like. Ain't their favorite place to be in the heat unless it be winter, but they like me fine enough to stay an' keep me company."

He grinned a little wider. "'Specially when Vilmas and the twins be off."

He went over to where he kept some of his better materials and hummed to himself for a moment before bringing me some mithril ingots. "Here we be, this one calls." He looked at me and flicked the metal, no pain on his face, just a serenity as he listened to the small chiming ring that the metal gave off. "Hear it?"

I nodded; it was a pure note. Not the discordant sound that one might hear when working in a smithy, but a piercing one. As it moved through the space between us, it resonated with the ingots he had in his hand under the ingot he'd flicked.

"I do." He stared at me for a moment before I touched it and the sound stopped from all of them slowly. "I know what it wants to be."

"Can ya handle it?" I nodded at him and he smiled, pulling his hammer from the small pouch in his apron. "Ya can use me lucky hammer then. I'll stay and offer advice for ya if ya need it, but I'll be an ear as well. Never hurts to say what's on the heart aloud."

"Thank you." I took the hammer, gray with use and black on the head, the worn wood of it comfortable in my hand, though my fingers didn't quite fit the grooves where Rowland's fingers would typically grip.

I put the ingots into the flame as Rowland took his own project out and went through my normal ritual before smithing. I took off my shirt, the material too light and flowing to be useful near flames, more of a hazard really, and then found my apron. It had been a gift from Vilmas; it was resistant to heat but wouldn't affect the heat of my projects. I'd thanked her for days and weeks for it. To the point that she shouted, "You're welcome, lad!" any time she saw me.

Now the thought of it made me smile. I grabbed the tongs I would use and set about my work. These ingots wanted to work together. They *needed* to harmonize and create something dense. Something strong that would strike and ring true.

Sweat beaded on my brow as my hammering became a thrum of background noise. This was where I wanted to be. No. This was where I was most comfortable.

I could see the will of the metal I worked, as it sang to me. I was never really all that great at singing, so I kept the beat of the song with Rowland's hammer and allowed the sweet symphony we created to swell, growing and growing until it crescendoed and then died down as the metal had cooled too much for me to shape it. I reintroduced it to the heat and as I stared into the flames, I noticed that the whispers that were normally there were quiet, even as I fed more fuel to the flames.

I dipped my head to the side and when I did, I found something that made me pause. "Rowland, what's this shape in here? It looks like a crown?"

"Flame Primordial's blessing on the forge, lad." He cleared his throat. "A gift from yer da that cost him... Well, it cost him his arm."

I blinked and as I focused on the mark, it swam in my vision, flickering. Still no voices though.

"Metal's ready, lad."

I grabbed the tongs and pulled out the forming metal and began the hammering process again, renewed vigor flowing through my veins. Had my father been interested in forging as well as enchanting? I hated enchanting, not as passionately as I had before when I was younger, but it just wasn't what I wanted to do.

Enchantments didn't tell you what they wanted to be, they just laid there and did what you told them to do and that was it. There was no nuance to them. At least none that I could find.

But he lost an arm for this place. For his friends. That was stupid on top of the fact that was a princely sum to pay for the glory that was this forge, right?

I wouldn't have done that. Though I would have researched the proper enchantment and materials necessary. Father had never been one to do that, from the stories I had heard. Xiphyre called him a trashy prodigy, that his imagination and creativity gave him an edge where many enchanters would have otherwise failed or fallen flat.

I could only hope that I was better with my hammer than he was at getting himself blown up.

The metal was cool again, so I grabbed it and stuck it into the flames. It was too late—lost in thought as I was—that I realized that I had done it with my bare hand, but the flames didn't burn me. They were warm, and lapped at my flesh like they should have, but there was no searing pain or agonized loss of feeling.

"Oh, for fuck's sake, lad!" Rowland howled. "Bucket! Bucket for the forge!"

The glow of the forge radiated outward and finally the whispers returned, only this time, they were clear as the ringing chime of the mithril's song.

We've been waiting for you, Prince Azlo. The spectral voices sent a chill down my spine as the words came from everywhere and nowhere all at once. Finally, after moments of nothing and pregnant silence, there was a crackling voice that spoke to me, *Finish your work, and then come to the place your father fought in twice, once to grow, and once more to recover his friend. We will meet you there.*

With that, I checked my project and saw it wasn't ready, but Rowland stood by me with shock on his face. "Y'alright lad?" Someone hauled a bucket of water into the room and he hefted it toward me. "Don't need this?"

I nodded and showed him my arm, how it was pristine, and quickly asked, "Father fought somewhere near here twice, somewhere that he ended up saving a friend from—where is it?"

"The ol' ruined fort?" He scratched his head and frowned as he explained, "East o' the city. Yer da an' his friends went there at first 'cause it was somewhere they could test their mettle an' their teamwork before movin' on an' hunting for their enemies. Then they went back when a lich threatened Sunrise."

"Thank you for that." I went to turn back to the heating metal in the forge and Rowland sidled next to me cautiously, looking at my hand as if in shock. When he saw nothing, he peered up at me with amazement on his face.

"Since when can ya just pick up cherry metal, lad?" I blinked at that and just shrugged. "Fuckin' magic kids an' their magic bodies an' shite."

With his head still shaking, he left me be with my work as he left the room. Without him here to distract me, the next few hours passed in a blur until my hammer head was finished and sitting in the oil bath, cooling. I would pull it from the bath and then treat it soon.

It was nearly perfect. The head was about as broad as both my hands palm up side by side and squared, but the edges were rounded slightly so that if I used it to hammer metal, there wouldn't be any kind of dents or marring from them. The opposite side of it was a spike-like pick that I could use to fight with, almost like a pick axe.

"What do ya think, Sarah?" Rowland's voice startled me as I stared at it.

I turned to find Rowland and his daughter. She was a nice-looking woman in her late thirties who had a small, half-elven child on her hip. She eyed the hammer critically and frowned. "I'd say it needs better wood than what I have at the moment, Da. Maybe better off with a metal core, with how dense and heavy it looks to me from here. Is that thing etched?"

I shook my head. "I had planned to etch it in an acid bath."

"I'll do it." Rowland went and grabbed a crystalline bucket and put it onto his workbench where he poured a vial into the mouth of it and then a bucket of another reagent. The two of them were rather noxious together so he had to open a window, the little child making noises that made her mother and grand-father chuckle.

Rowland took his tongs and lifted the hammer head, grunting with the effort. "Boy, you were using mithril! By the gods, how is this so dense?"

I smiled and winked at him. "A little trick that Uncle Thogan taught me." He frowned at me and I pointed to the fire. "I overheated it a lot."

"Ya *what?*" His shout was enough to make the little girl on Sarah's hip flinch and set her lip to quivering. "Forgive yer grandaddy, wee Whimsy, me beard got the better o' me, I promise."

He sighed as he slowly dipped the head of the weapon into the acid bath and left it there. "Ya left it in the flames for longer than necessary?" I nodded at that and he frowned. "Because that's somethin' that Thogan showed ya? If ya had left it in too long, it would have been too hard to work it."

"I know, that's why Thogan showed me how to do it, and then made sure I knew by continuing to do it for a while." He frowned at me and I smiled. "Elves like me aren't weak, Rowland. We can take a heavy weapon. To be honest, I prefer it."

He seethed silently, gnashing his teeth and tugging at his beard as he thought, then decided on something before spitting and saying, "I'll be beatin' Thogan for that. Why did he nae teach me that?"

"It was a gift for reaching my majority." Rowland blinked at me howled as he kicked his anvil in a fury. "What?"

"I forgot ya were that old!" He pointed at his daughter. "Let's get to work, we need to get the hammer done up proper for him."

Sarah grinned and looked to her daughter. "Whimsy, did you want to stay here and watch your gran-daddy work, or did you want to come and curse with Mommy?"

"Can I curse with Grandaddy?" The girl's voice was all innocence and it made me smile at her from where I stood. I'd only met the little half-elf a few times; her father was an older dawn elf who had come here from the High Elven city in the north, and when he and Sarah had met, it was a whirlwind of drinking, making, and—to Rowland's disdain—marrying.

But his little Whimsy was his pride and joy, and he boasted about her often.

"Ya bet my beard ya can, girl. Come over here an' sit on yer grandaddy's bench here. I'll show ya what ya do to keep a hammer this heavy swinging right."

"Yay!"

Rowland turned to me after collecting four more mithril ingots and growled, "Show me."

CHAPTER SIX

"Prince Azlo!" A hoarse whisper reached my ears and I opened my eyes from my trance.

I blinked and stared at Rowland as he held a thick finger to his lips, then jerked his head to his left. Whimsy and Mini laid together with two brownish-red kits snuggled over them, sleeping peacefully.

He grabbed my bicep and pulled me along until we stood outside and closer to his house. There was a table with biscuits there and some jam with knives to spread on them. The biscuits were warm and the jam melted on them as I smothered them, and Rowland took a swig from the mug on his side of the table. "Vilmas says hello, an' that she hopes yer life is fruitful, yer beard long an' thick, an' that your arm never falters."

"Tell her and your sons that I hope the same for them, and that should they ever need help, I am able and willing." I bowed my head as I spoke and made sure he knew I was serious.

"Ya know, I consider ya clan, lad." His voice was soft. "Watchin' ya grow big an' strong like this, did me ol' heart good. Knowin' ya donae care for talkin' o' yer da, I won't bore ya with how he should be givin' ya an axe like he had."

"Thank you." I tried not to sound overly grateful, but he was keener than most and the wry grin on his face said it all. He knew more than he ever let on, but still respected my wishes.

"That said, this weapon an' the materials it was made with be a gift, from a doting uncle and clan elder." He glared into my eyes as if daring me to tell him no, but I just bowed my head and he smiled. "Good lad."

He reached behind him and lifted the weapon he spoke of onto the table and set it down before taking out his pipe, packing it and lighting it with a few thoughtful puffs before speaking on. "Made with fine wood, that was. Oak heart, treated with a lacquer that will withstand some of the most common spells. This goes over the metal core you created with the head to give it the best durability."

I lifted it and appreciated the craftsmanship of the haft. It was well-made and the leather grips were light but had good friction with my hand. It was amazing. The acid bath that the head had been in brought out the folding that I had done with the mithril and showed the layers beautifully, with slightly darker lines in the lighter blue metal. The head of it was broader and tapered into the body and on the other side of it there was a pick, standard for a war hammer, but that I would use this as a smithing hammer meant that I would need to be cautious of it coming back at me or flying from my grip.

"Weapon like this should have a name." Rowland was gentle with the suggestion but I knew from experience that he was right. This was a well-crafted weapon and it deserved that level of respect.

"I'll call it Shaper." As I said it, the weapons statistics populated in front of my vision and I smiled.

"Shaper?" Rowland snorted. "Why is that?"

"Whether it's shaping metal or skulls, it will mold what I want to happen into reality."

Rowland whistled at my answer and let me look at the stats.

Shaper
+5 damage.

Weapon can be used as a smith's hammer as well.

With little more than a swing of this dense monstrosity, the wielder can forge their own path ahead, in metal—or blood.

Hammer crafted by Layman Smith Azlo and Master Carpenter Sarah Dathir.

I smiled, so I was a layman smith now… "Wait… if I'm a layman smith, that means I get an extra level added to my original level, right?"

"When a master smith recognizes ya as one, yes." Rowland grinned and winked at me. "Smithing works differently sometimes, lad. The one who teaches ya most, or the closest one to ya typically gets a notification that their pupil has reached that threshold, and if we think ya ready, we allow it."

"Am I not ready?"

Thogan's voice rumbled from behind me and made me jump to my feet. "Yer as ready as any, my boy." I grinned at him and he pulled me into a fierce hug and shook me. "Let's see her, lad. Come now."

I handed him Shaper and he whistled. "Made it dense like I showed ya, this is a good one, this is." He glanced around me at Rowland. "Want the honors?"

"Wouldn't dream o' takin' the pupil of a legend like that, Thogan." Rowland winked and I received a notification.

Congratulations!

You've reached level 26 Smithing, bringing you to the rank of a Layman Smith!

Level up!

I smiled, knowing there were even more points that I had yet to spend. Granted, it was only three more for me to spend as I would, but that was still more than forty points total.

"Thank you both." I turned and reached down to grab another biscuit before clearing my throat. "I have somewhere I need to go."

"You don't want that weapon of yours enchanted?" Xiphyre's voice floated over Uncle Thogan's shoulder.

"I was going to come and see you later, Master Xiphyre." I bowed my head respectfully and the Ragalfr actually *snorted* at me!

"Give it to me now, and tell me what you want, Prince Azlo." His appearance had mellowed slightly from the time that I had first met him. Now his hair was a particularly vomit-colored monstrosity, and his massive wings fluttered beautifully behind him. Some would mistake him for a pixie if it weren't for the fact that his head was proportionate to his body, unlike his counterparts.

"I would like it to be able to be any size I want it to be, from just a normal smithing hammer to a great hammer." Xiphyre's tight, angular features showed surprise and that was enough to make me smile. "I want the density to remain the same for when it's smaller, and if it can grow by about half as it gets bigger, I would appreciate that."

Xiphyre actually smiled at that. "And here I thought you were going to do something boring." He held his hand out for the weapon and as soon as he took it, his wings had to work a bit harder to keep him aloft. "Oh, this is going to be *fun*."

He flew into Rowland's shop and then came back out onto the street a few moments later with the hammer in his hands and held his hand out. "Blood please."

I frowned at him and narrowed my gaze. Both Rowland and Thogan stepped closer to the Ragalfr and the stone-skinned dwarf asked softly, "What did you get me for my last birthday?"

Xiphyre looked hurt for a moment, then cleared his throat and looked away. "I had my wife knit you a very nice blanket and I enchanted it for you."

Thogan's eyes narrowed slightly, but it was Rowland who asked, "And that enchantment was?"

Thogan's eyes widened and he started to wave the answer away when Xiphyre smirked and said, "To feel like a hug every time he uses it."

"No!" Rowland chortled as Thogan just hung his head with embarrassment.

I put a hand on his rough shoulder and muttered, "I think that sounds rather nice."

He just swatted my hand off his shoulder and muttered, "It's him, lad, give him the blood if you want."

I held out my hand and he pricked my finger, then smeared my blood from the haft of the weapon to the top of the head and it glowed amber before going back to its normal color. There were symbols on the head that made sense for growth and shrinking, but I couldn't tell why he had needed my blood.

"I've only done an item like this once before, so I will need you to keep me updated with it from time to time, but this is now a growth item." I frowned at him a little deeper and he smirked. "You can't see the engraving for that one, boy, it's embedded in the core of the item and hidden away. As you grow stronger, it should theoretically grow with you, though it will likely be slower. It's taken years of work and study for this to come to fruition, so if you lose this weapon, I will…"

His hands shook and he tried to smooth himself out with one hand but lost it and snarled, "I'll die trying to murder you, do you understand?"

Uncle Thogan had his hand on the smaller man's shoulder and fingers around his throat so fast that I wondered if my own mother could have moved that quickly. His grating baritone voice rumbled with barely contained malice as he growled, "Did ya just make a threat to the crown prince o' the Unseelie Court? One o' the living heirs to Storm Company? My beloved nephew?"

Xiphyre choked out a simple, "A little?"

"I understand the sentiment and significance, Xiphyre. You can let him go, Uncle Thogan."

The ancient dwarf stared at the smaller man for a moment longer as his face turned an ugly mottled shade of blue. "I don't care for that, Xi. Do it again, an' I will kill ya. Friendship or not. Ya know where my allegiance will always lay."

Xiphyre nodded and dropped my hammer to the ground with a heavy thud. As soon as Thogan let him go, the man took a breath and ground out a meaningful, "Sorry." Then disappeared.

Thogan took a couple deep breaths before turning to me and sighing as he fought to rid himself of his rage-thickened accent. "I am too, I should go and ensure that he knows the depths of his folly. Gods forbid this get back to the queen before me."

"Thank you, Uncle Thogan." He nodded and headed back inside the smithy to go back to the Fae Realm. I collected my weapon, and it felt better than before. I confirmed that what the Ragalfr had said was true and focused on it becoming as small as it could become. There was a dim radiance around it, and then it was the size of a small setting hammer that a jeweler would make, only a little larger than my finger.

It felt just as dense as it had when I carried it at full size, but the weight was gone. Rowland whistled. "Looks like a fair way to carry it in secret, if ya pleased. Could always have it on yer person an' not a person with any reason would pay it any mind."

I nodded. "I can appreciate that." I willed it to grow to its largest form and grunted as it was too heavy for me to lift with the amount of strength I had at the moment. "I can appreciate this as well. He does great work."

Rowland nodded and took another puff of his pipe. "Aye, that he does." He stared at the weapon for a heartbeat and closed his eyes. "That place is dormant for now, lad, but I donnae know what is likely to come of being there. If ya must go alone, I would ask that ya be careful, please. If not for yer sake, then for mine an' yer uncle's, aye?"

I gave a curt nod. "Aye." I patted him on the shoulder and stopped beside him. "The Way is long and winding."

A soft smile tugged at his beard and mustache as he looked skyward with closed eyes. "But never are we alone. Go with the grace of Fainne, lad. And fight with all the strength of your adoptive clans."

I nodded and was on my way to the edge of the city.

The large gathering of homes, the mixture of both beast-kin, dawn elves, humans, and dwarves was always bewildering to me. This was a great place to live—a truer melting pot of what it meant to live here in Brindolla if I had ever seen or heard of one.

If it hadn't been for the constant reports of growing unrest in some of the factions on the continent, I would have been able to just assume that the world was a better place now than it was when my father and his friends had been here. But the unrest was there.

Even in the whispering around me, as I walked the streets with people staring at me with both open confusion and mild curiosity. There were some who recognized me for my trips here with chaperones and Mother, and then there were the ones who spoke to each other in hushed tones.

"Zeke's son…?" They would stare at me as I continued to walk on and ignore them, though I returned nods and greetings to be polite.

Once I reached the true edge of the city and found the wall, I exited it by walking up the ramp to it and jumping over the side. It was no more than a forty foot fall that I could easily survive with a roll at the bottom and as the guards knew me from knowing Vrawn, it was simple to ignore their shouts to come back.

I sprinted through the open area into the slowly thickening trees east of the city toward my destination and rather than cause myself to be potentially noticed by anyone, or any of the bears that patrolled the area thanks to their treaty with the city, I shifted into my fox form and ran on all fours. It was so freeing to run in the warmth of the early morning light, the wind in my fur.

It was hours later that I finally found myself staring at the ruined keep that I suspected to be where I had been invited. There was a strange mixture of scents.

The scent of the overgrowth surrounding the area, the darkness inside the walls having long since been eroded by the touch of countless dawns and the lich's interference and dominion over the area waning. Even that scent still lingered. But as I watched it, I could see clearly that there was a beaten path to the front gate, as if this place was traveled to often.

It had been blasted inward, and the footsteps were both fresh and old here. The massive courtyard was covered in rusted and decaying armor and arms, weapons of times past. How many of these undead warriors had Storm Company laid waste to? How many of them never even stood a chance? I could imagine it was left to commemorate the battle or the metal just wasn't worth collecting to reuse, but there was much of it.

"Welcome," a voice called to me from ahead, their shape hidden in the shadows of the wall to the north of where I entered on the south side.

I was still in fox form, so it couldn't have been me they spoke to. I glanced over my shoulder and my tails and saw there was someone else there, but it wasn't a someone so much as a some*thing*. An elemental made of winds blustered in the entrance to the compound.

The strength of the breeze coming from it whipped toward me, rustling my fur and it carried words to my ears. "They speak to you, son of the hero."

I blinked and frowned, taking my elven form. "What did you want of me?"

"To speak with you," a different crackling voice called from the eastern wall, a bright towering flame in the shape of a humanoid stepped closer. "All of us are here as proxies for our masters."

"Why?"

My question gave them pause and the flame elemental flickered before answering, "Did they tell you much of your father's bond with nature?"

"I know what was regurgitated to me many times, yes." I tried not to sound tired of being constantly forced to relive his absence. "He had bonds with many of you."

"And even more, beloved." The speaker from the shadows

took more of a shape and stared out at me with white eyes. "As we loved your mother, we love you."

"You always sound so creepy when you speak like that." A burbling brook-like voice crept toward me and I noticed a water elemental in the western portion of the yard where puddles of recent rainwater gathered.

The air in front of me shimmered and a bright elemental that looked like spun sunlight opened its arms. "We are here to bring you to our masters so that they might speak to you."

I frowned. "Do I have your word on your powers that you will not harm me?"

"We will not harm you, prince." The light elemental spoke readily. "As to our power, it is not ours to give."

I knew that to the best of its knowledge it believed that. "Fine, how do I do this?"

The flame elemental spoke softly, cracking sparks and burning in its voice. "Sit where you are and open your mind to the elements. We will take care of the rest."

"We will guard your body as your spirit ascends to the medium they wish to speak to you in, we swear on their power." The water elemental's word cemented it and I did as I was told, though I had my shrunken hammer in my hand to ensure I was ready to fight if I needed to.

I took a deep breath and the world around me darkened, then lightened, warmth flooding over me in a breeze that brought the scent of earth and fresh rain to me.

"He joins us at last." I opened my eyes and found myself in a room that reminded me of a courtroom. There were chairs placed around me, six of them on raised pedestals in the color that most accurately represented the element that sat on the chair at the top. Each of them was in a human-like form and watched me with interest.

But the interesting thing was that there were other, smaller chairs placed around the room. Some between the main ones and then outside that further away. One between the red and green of fire and wind, respectively, had someone seated in it, the yellow chair had a man that gripped a lightning bolt as if it were a weapon. His eyes glowed as he watched me curiously, then he winked and the light around him darkened so it was harder to see him.

"Please, attend us, Prince Azlo." A woman's voice reached me, coming from the direction of the lapis chair pedestal. Atop it sat a woman who appeared to be no older than how my mother looked. She was beautiful, with blue-hued hair and her smile was genuine. "We have much to discuss and precious little time to do it in."

"So eager to offer up the lives of children, no thought." A larger, more rotund man with muscle in place of anything that could be considered fat grumbled. His was the mud-colored chair. "The shifting plates of Brindolla move slower than this."

"That's the point, you tectonic twit—we need to hurry because there's a lot more at stake than just one life." The green chair seethed. This one had a man in it that was rakish and his long hair seemed to float and whip around his head dramatically as he glared around the circle at the others gathered. "There are people hunting down those we've blessed—*again*."

"While some of us are used to the persecution and hunting of their own, some of us are not." This time it was a woman in light robes on a blindingly-white pedestal. "The void and I are those two and it is most disconcerting."

An oddly echoing voice spoke behind me, opposite her. "The shadows are constantly persecuted against, but none dare lurk in us too long. Now, they have no such qualms."

"So what is it exactly that you need of me?" I glanced around at the ones who had spoken so far, but it was the one on the red chair and pedestal who stared down at me.

He spoke softly, "Nothing like your father." That gave me pause and it made him quirk his lip in a saddened smile. "He would have helped, but it would have cost us dearly like it already had. Some of us dared to call him friend. Can we trust you to hold our needs in a similar regard?"

"So then, that would have to make all of you the Primordial

elementals." I glared at all of them. "Some version of you was at my birth, my sister's birth, and yet here you remained silent until I could serve you."

"Not by their choice," a soft voice whispered to me from over my shoulder and I turned to find a woman clothed in a starlit robe with it over her head standing behind me. "Hello, little prince."

"Who are you?" I had nothing to defend myself here, and it was difficult to imagine that someone able to butt in on a meeting like this wasn't powerful enough to not care for the word of others given.

The figure chuckled. "I am Seraestar, Goddess of the Cosmos and Magic." I could hear the mirth in her tone as she spoke on. "I am here with these beings to offer you a deal."

Deals were huge to the Fae. A massive amount of my kind collected power through deals, both kept, broken, and brokered. A deal with a goddess could make or break my power and my ability to operate in this realm as well as home against the Seelie.

I did the smart thing and took a knee, though I didn't genuflect the way a servant might. I wasn't one.

"A group, sect, clan—something—has begun to actively build itself up and now hunts down those who have been practicing magic." Her voice took on a softer tone. "Our casters are slightly better prepared for them than they were, but with their fervor, we worry it won't be enough."

"So you want my sister and I to hunt them down and stop them?" The goddess was considerate for a moment, but I added, "I don't even have a class right now. I'm too weak to do much for anyone, let alone hunt those who can kill mages."

"Because with your skills, and their backing, I will offer you a special class that has not been offered in centuries." She raised a hand and motioned to the elementals above me. "And they mean to offer you strength, as well."

The one that had spoken of my father elaborated with a raised hand to keep me from interrupting. "Your father's bond with us all yet lives, so we cannot form another bond, however, we can impart secrets to you to ensure your success."

The large one laughed loudly, then smiled down at me. "Secrets you already touch upon. You bend the minerals that come from the ground, the spine of the earth, to your will and hammer impurities from them. I will give you knowledge of them, and ensure that you know where to find more, and that their properties will be more easily viewed."

"What he means to say," the one with flowing hair on the blow pedestal growled, then cleared her throat, "is that, with our assistance, you will be able to combine the spirits of elementals with the weapons you forge, and form pacts with them."

I frowned. "So, does that mean it won't be with any of you? Or like my father's power?"

"It will be wholly your own, and as you learn aspects of your smithing, and how to form pacts with the elementals you find, you will grow stronger still," Seraestar assured me calmly.

I blinked at her, then at all of them. "Find? There are elementals out in the wild on Brindolla?"

"We have been reintegrating with the realms after the threat of War and his minions was taken care of and, to be frank, even our elemental children have begun to fear these hunters." The wind primordial seethed for a moment, then ran his hand through his hair with apparent frustration on his oddly human features. "Our slowly building numbers of summoners and elemental mages have been attacked. Few have been killed, but it is enough to reach out for aid on their behalf."

"Where is the quest?" I stared at him and he blinked back at me. "Where do we begin?"

Seraestar spoke this time. "There is a city that bans magic. It was left in ruins, and now it is used as a stronghold for these factions after the avatar of War arrived." She turned her back to me and continued to speak with her voice raised. "You would do well to find some leads first, but collecting your class and sub-class would be the best place to start."

I frowned; this was a good place to start. And with having a class that was all my own, and access to more power with the assistance of elemental pacts… what could be my limits?

"How do the pacts work?"

The water primordial laughed, a burbling sound welling out of her that was disconcerting. She wiped her eyes and pointed at me as she looked around the room. "Smart. Very smart."

She shook her head and held out her hand, making an elemental appear. It was made of water and was misshapen and only about the size of a small child. "This is one of the basic elementals, the weakest variety of elemental you will come across. As of now, you could form a pact with him based on your level and skills as a smith."

There was a rumbling shift in the ground and behind me a large, almost-golem-looking elemental with steel, iron, and copper veins running through the stone, it was still lumpy and misshapen, but vaguely humanoid-shaped. The larger man on the mud-colored pedestal explained, "This is one of the warrior elementals, the weakest of them is the shield caste and the next strongest is the sword caste."

The one that came out now could pass for vaguely human from a distance if it weren't for the mithril, platinum, and silver veins apparent along the body that appeared to be dotted with precious gems like rubies and diamonds. There were even some sticking out of the hands, like fingers but sharper.

"After that we have the guard caste, and that has three itera-tions that you can learn more about later." The big man rubbed his chin and glared down at me. "With your smithing skills, you could possibly make something worthy of a shield caste elemen-tal, but you lack the mana and stats to control them."

"How do I bind them, and how does my class work?"

Seraestar chuckled again. "You will find out should you accept our quest. Do this, and you will be rewarded greatly."

"And if I refuse?" It wasn't difficult to put doubt into my tone. I knew I would accept the quest only because the benefits were too great to ignore.

Seven voices in unison replied, "You wouldn't."

Seraestar added, "Here, think it over if you feel so deeply about potentially denying it."

There was a snap of her fingers, and I sat in my own body once more and opened my eyes to see the various elementals watching me with interest.

The shadow elemental had come out into the light and looked uncomfortable in the sun. It touched me and said, "This is where you may be able to find more pertinent information on your quest, and they all asked that we tell you this: if you decide to say no, that is fine."

The light elemental spoke this time, adding, "Another champion will rise if you are not strong enough to stand for your kind."

The crackling voice of the flames spoke next. "But that does not mean there is not someone, or something, out there that won't hunt down your kind, or your allies next."

"First magic users, then magic beings," the water elemental whispered, like raindrops on sandy beaches. I could barely tell where the eyes were meant to be on the thing, but it felt as if it stared into my soul as it said, "Never too late for the problems of the Prime to reach the outer realms. Soon, this will be *everyone's* problem."

I frowned at that statement. That meant that the mortals who hated magic could try to come for my family, right? But this didn't make sense. "Why would you come for me? Do you think that my father's freakish aptitude for the elements is my own?"

The flame elemental snickered. "No. But our masters sent proxies to your births. The elements have an interest in your bloodline, child. Not all blessings come with the bonds that others laid the groundwork to."

Finally, it was the earthen elemental who rumbled, "And you will stand on shakier ground and fight anyway."

"Better to be rewarded for fighting first and protecting your future." It looked skyward and began to dissipate and its final wisps carried a breezy, "All our futures."

A map populated in the upper right hand corner of my vision and then a green blip began to pulse as the quest notification populated before me.

QUEST ALERT!

Rumblings of Magical Malfeasance — The Primordial Elementals and the Goddess Seraestar have requested that you investigate a series of deaths believed to be linked to various individuals or organizations with motive to hate magic users and beings such as elementals. Find them and either figure out their motives, destroy them, or hamper their ability to do what they do. Reward: 30,000 EXP, further support from the goddess herself, and possibly untold aid from the elementals. Failure: Nothing aside from what may come from inaction.

Will you accept: Yes / No?

That was rather annoying, basically preying on my conscience as if I were a child. Though the possibilities and implications of the Fae being targeted if these people gathered too much power and resources was even more annoying.

And there was nothing mentioned about the class I was supposed to receive if I accepted it. I rolled my eyes, thinking to myself, *Because I have to accept it.*

Heaving a sigh, I accepted it and the fanfare of it was irritating, but it was the notification that was surprising.

Class Unlocked!

Sorcerer — The magic of this world comes to you as naturally as breathing, and as you go along, you'll be able to coax it into doing what you like. Good luck with that!

Elemental Manipulation (Minor) unlocked — Your will and connection to the magic around you manifests in the ability to affect (in a minor way) the very elements that make up reality. Cost: 3 mana per second up to ten feet around the caster.

And that was all it was. I didn't *feel* any different, not really.

But what I needed most in order to truly use my class to the greatest effect was going to be a forge and anvil.

"And elementals." I frowned and thought about it, the only lead that we had being north of me and the city. With nothing more left for me here, it was time to return to Sunrise and bother the smiths and Xiphyre.

And report to Mother that I had my class now.

CHAPTER SEVEN

By the time I returned to the Fae Realm, I had only been gone half a day at that point, so I found Thogan and Xiphyre bickering in the courtyard I used to play with Winterheart in.

"Are you serious with that request?" I nodded at them and they both frowned at me, Xiphyre narrowing his gaze at me. "You seriously intend to try to have us make you a portable forge big enough to create full-size weapons?"

"I wouldn't come to you like this in order to tease you, I swear it on my power." He frowned as my word bound me. "I need this to practice and ply my craft. I'm serious about growing my skills and in order to do that, I have to have a forge and anvil that I can carry with me."

Thogan held up a hand and grunted. "Aye, I agree." He turned to glare at Xiphyre and rumbled, "Least you could do for that stunt you pulled outside Rowland's forge."

"If I can be there when you enchant the forge itself?" Xiphyre looked exasperated and I hurriedly explained, "I wanted to use some of the fire from the Dragon Forge to see if it would help make the one I carry with me any better."

The Ragalfr stared at me with evident disbelief on his face, but answered, "You want the work of an amateur to be used on an item enchanted by a legend?" He shrugged. "Sure, less work for me on finding materials to add to it."

Rowland's face began to glow an ember red until Thogan put a soothing hand on his shoulder, sliding the winged man a knowing look before he agreed to work on the things I would need right away to ensure I had what was necessary before I left, then I went to find my mother.

———

For *hours,* Nadir sat and poured over her extensive library that her master had left behind for her to read over. There were books on the classes, and how to obtain them based on one's statistics that she pulled out, but there was nothing to show how one could gain a class when there were none offered.

"I genuinely hope the queen was able to come up with something where I failed to." She left the books on her study table and pulled a few extra copies of books on herb craft from the shelves where the Prime Plane was concerned. They would be useful to her there.

She also pulled books on the various races, maps, as well as notes on the various cultures within certain cities too. And then there was a well-thumbed and dog-eared tome that she pulled out. How many times had she read this very book even though she knew it by heart?

It was the book of her ancestors.

"Do you mean to go and find them?" Vrawn's voice made the younger orcish woman flinch before she turned around. Nadir knew better than to hide the book, but had to fight the urge to anyway.

"Maybe, if it means that we might be able to become strong enough to help fight the Seelie and prepare for the King's return."

"You can call him your father, Nadir," Vrawn urged gently. This wasn't the first time that she had told her that, and she certainly wouldn't stop. "I know that things were really tough on you, but he would love you as deeply as I did."

"Would he have allowed me to be taken to become this if he had been here?" The question caught Vrawn off guard as Nadir glared at her mother. At least, it was as close to a glare as she would come with all of her extensive training to control her anger.

"I... don't know," Vrawn answered honestly. "He would likely have tried to find a way to get you out of it. Taken the training himself to save you, if he could have. Combed the world for a better-suited candidate so that he could be with you."

"But I would have had to do it anyway." There was no hiding the accepting hurt in Nadir's tone. She had long since come to terms with the fact that her father was dead. The heroes were gone. Had been.

Now there was no telling what was going to happen and how they were going to come to terms with what went on. Would she be able to face the man who abandoned her and her brother to a life of duty and no father?

Vrawn would have said more, but Nadir shook her head. "I have much to prepare for with the coming months away from home as they are, and time shift as the realms ebb and flow toward and away from each other. We must cram as much growth into ourselves as possible in that time."

Nadir piled more onto her bed to take with her in her pouch of holding and inventory before Vrawn finally spoke with a soft edge of defeated reality in her tone. "Please don't do anything rash."

Nadir stilled and frowned, then turned toward her mother and surged across the room in swift strides. Vrawn almost prepared for an attack, but Nadir only hugged her and muttered against her shoulder, "I know that you've been trying to be a good mother. I know you wish things were different." The younger orc leaned away from her mother and smiled sadly. "I do too. But I wish that, instead of lamenting the daughter you never had the chance to have, you would just get to know the one standing in front of you."

Vrawn's mouth opened and shut as tears filled the corners of her eyes and she wept as her little girl proved her wisdom. Wisdom that she should never have had, but there it was.

"I forgive you." Nadir spoke sweetly, but firmly. "I need to be ready for what is to come."

Vrawn nodded once, hugged her daughter and said, "I love you with all that I am. I am proud of you and who you are. I hope that one day, we can grow together."

Nadir smiled, her tusks flashing. "I would like that very much."

Vrawn left her daughter to return to her duties and preparations and wept the whole way back to the Queen's private study where Maebe attended her and listened as she explained as much as she could.

While Azlo had made requests of Thogan and Xiphyre, Nadir had not. She had her father's weapons, or at least the ones she liked, and weapons of her own to use. Maebe wished that Azlo would have taken anything his father had made, but the boy was staunch in his annoying and misguided loathing of his father. That was beside the point now, as she combed through book after book. The only thing she had to worry about now was finding a cure for what ailed her son.

––––––

AZLO

There was no finding Mother, so I just focused on preparing for the coming journey into the unknowns of the Prime plane.

I prepared clothes, rations, and even a few pairs of sturdy boots and socks. Never knew when you would need to change your socks on a walk.

I frowned at that. If I was to walk, there would need to be something to ride eventually, right? I also needed to collect components for the weapons I would be making in order to bind elementals to them.

I wondered if Kayda was still visiting her nest here with Grand-uncle Winterheart.

With that, I tapped my earring that I never took off and bolted out of my window and down the icy lattice that led to the part of the castle that most people tended to avoid for the simple fact that both the ancient dragon and Storm Roc enjoyed playing too rough and had a bad habit of accidentally killing servants.

I made it to them in record time and found the two of them cuddled up together for a nap, the large bird resting her head on the back of the dragon's broad, white neck.

Both of them still cut a terrifying image to those who didn't know them. To me, it was just my family cuddling and having a solid snooze. I whistled and both of them opened a single eye to regard me, all lethargy fleeing from them as they scrambled to alertness.

Grand-uncle Winterheart blustered first, clearing his throat. "Are we under attack? Where are they?" He raised up to his full, massive height and roared violently, ice crystallizing from his very breath and dropping to the floor. "I'll kill them all!"

Kayda spread her wings and a storm cloud began to brew over her head as she cawed, "Death to all!"

I laughed until a particularly nasty freezing bolt of lightning struck the ground near me, forcing me to call, "No one is dumb enough to attack us with either of you here, let alone both of you!"

Both of them considered the area around them and then huddled their heads closer to me. "What do you need, hatchling?"

"I wanted to see if you would be willing to share some of your feathers with me as components for my smithing?"

Kayda screamed, rising to her full height as she called out, "Yes! I am proud to offer myself for you to have a strong weapon."

Grand-uncle Winterheart nudged his way forward and asked, "Can I give you some as well? Why didn't you ask me too, my boy?"

"You're an ancient dragon, Grand-uncle, I thought that asking that would be rude and beneath you."

He hefted his large head and stared down at me as if I had stabbed him with his favorite sword. "Rude? I am a doting family member for you, my boy. I have watched over you your whole life!" He lowered his head. "Who was it who taught you how to show your fangs?"

I had to lower my gaze to keep from laughing at his mock hurt. "You did."

He puffed his chest out a little and bellowed, "I did! You have the most fearsome fangs for a dragon to witness now, you are welcome. And who taught you to preen your scales?"

This time, I did laugh. That had been a very interesting bath, the massive dragon telling me to lift my leg a little further to get to my haunches. Mother had come in and chased him out of the room as I came out of the water with my tongue out and leg raised. I kept laughing and answered him, "You."

"Exactly!" His voice was raised now, full of indignation. "You should be asking me for my scales, claws, fangs to be a part of whatever it is that you make!"

He lowered his head and his voice softened, "I am old now, Prince Azlo, my beloved little dragon." His large eye was almost as wide as I was tall as he blinked at me. "I am not long for this world, and when I go, you will need to guard my hoard and tell my stories to your hatchlings."

He frowned and turned to Kayda. "Listen to me, I've begun using words you use. This is unacceptable. Is that a tail feather? Really?"

Kayda dropped the heavy feather beside a growing pile of her other types of feathers. One from her wing, a chest feather that was a little more crystalline than true blue. One of her talons sat in the pile as well. She quirked her head at me. "Do you need blood too?"

I shook my head. "This will be plenty!" I glanced over at the ancient dragon. "I'll accept anything you're willing to donate, Grand-uncle."

"I will give you two of my teeth if I can get a scratch on the left side of my head, right behind my horn?" He sounded as if he was uncertain that I would fall for it. He did this to Mother often.

I rolled my eyes and motioned for him to come closer. He growled in delight and dropped his head so fast, the wind almost gave me frostbite. He craned his head so that I could reach the spot and as soon as my fingers touched his scales, his tail slammed onto the ground in sheer happiness as I scratched futilely on his scaled head.

"Winterheart!" My mother's voice caused both of us to jump, straightening and turning toward her. "This is no time to be enticing a scratch you old, scaled... shit!"

The audible, thunderous gasp from the dragon was telling that she had never spoken to him this way. "Queen Maebe, language!"

"Oh stop, he has no class, and here you and Kayda are making the whole castle feel like there is about to be a battle, what excuse have you for this?" She had her hands on her hips and glared from him, to her, and then finally at me. "And you. Why are you out here and not trying to figure out what is wrong?"

"Because nothing is wrong anymore." I smiled at her and her confusion. "I have a class now, it's sorcerer."

I reached out to the ice around us and made it kick up a little bit. I'd never really been all that good with water; it was a little more difficult when it was harder and more dense as ice, but it wasn't impossible.

"I've never heard of that class." Mother narrowed her gaze at me and her eyes flashed in the light. "Why did you come out here to bother them and not come find me first?"

"I couldn't find you." It was a simple omission. I had chosen not to look in certain places that she was most likely to be if she wasn't in the main library or the throne room.

"You didn't look hard enough." She smiled and pulled me into her embrace. "I am glad you have begun to forge your own path. I have heard of what you asked Xiphyre and Rowland to make for you. Are you sure you wouldn't rather take money with you to rent a forge?"

"It wouldn't be the same as working with something that is meant for me." I hugged her back and pulled back slightly. "Then there will be no true way of knowing how often we mean to be near any kind of city or town with a decent enough forge for me to borrow, let alone rent."

She nodded once and rubbed her fingers into my upper back slightly. "Good thinking. Your glamour is good as well, so I know I needn't worry about you on that front."

That sparked my interest. "Is it a good idea to be using glamour in the Prime Realm?"

"Yes." She frowned down at me as if she were questioning my judgment on asking the question. "Especially if you mean to try to disconnect yourself from your father's legacy and develop yourselves into your own people."

That made sense. I just didn't like using the glamour even if I was adept with it, because it felt like I was wrapping myself in a blanket and hoping that no one could see me peeking out of it at them.

"You could always stay and prepare with me for a year," Mother offered softly. She frowned at the air in front of her as if she were seeing something no one else could. "Even your grandmother would love to train you before you go into the ancestral dungeon."

I laughed. "Grandmother dislikes Father almost as much as we do, do you think it a good idea if we spend more time with her before he supposedly returns?"

She smirked, clearly thinking better of it. "No, likely not." She let me go and sighed. "I wish there was some way I could prove to you that he didn't want to leave."

"The burden of his defense is not yours, Mother, it will be his." Her head whipped around so that she could look me in the eyes, a question on her lips, but I knew she knew the answer. "You taught me that. As a ruler, we do not defend the people who make the mistakes, they do so themselves. It is our burden and purpose to decide if that defense and reasoning is sound enough to risk the kingdom over."

I extricated myself from her slowly tightening grip and collected the items that both Kayda and Grand-uncle Winter-heart had offered, his being scales, the teeth he promised, and even a small chunk of one of his horns.

I slipped those into the pack I had on my shoulders and they fit, though snugly. It was too small for the feather on top of the other items. I stood next to her for a moment, then asked, "Would you like to have dinner later together? All of us?"

She nodded woodenly. "I would like that very much." She stared ahead and waited a moment before breathing out. "You may go."

I bowed my head respectfully and left as she bid me. It would be a while before I was completely packed anyway, and I needed the time.

CHAPTER EIGHT

The days after that dinner were tense to say the least, and though I could tell that she wanted to spend more time with us before we left, a queen's duty never ended.

Mother's spies had put in long hours within the Fae realm and the others to ensure that the likelihood we went to face off against something we weren't prepared for with the Seelie was as mitigated as it could have been. We even had the time to go through the gifts that the court had brought us.

Most featured notes of hopeful admirers or those who wished to curry favor with us, mainly me, but I just ignored them. Mother had read them all anyway to ensure there were no threats.

Nothing of any great interest was among mine, but from what I could see of Nadir's, there was a bag that was designed to bring the perfect book for a situation to her hand. So long as the book was in the bag, it only ever felt like she carried two books.

It was the final day, early in the morning, and as we finished breakfast, Mother and Vrawn both looked as though they'd had little to no rest the last few days.

Finally, Vrawn asked, "Do you have mounts?"

I shook my head, fully expecting to need to buy a horse or something from the city once we arrived in Sunrise.

"We will acquire them as we can," Nadir assured them as Vrawn reached into her pocket, the younger orc waving for her to stop. "Any more assistance than has already been given will negate the wish for independence that we have. Thank you for doing all you can for us, but it is time for us to leave and make our own way forward for a time."

Vrawn looked defeated and Mother reached over and put a hand over hers, nodding once. There was this unspoken conversation between them and before I knew it, we were up and walking to Thogan's courtyard.

They walked with us through the portal into the smithy and then into the forge area itself, where Thogan and Xiphyre both still worked.

"Yer Majesty!" Thogan called, stopping his work to bow before his queen. "We've still got some more work to do on the forge and anvil, I fear. Would ya be willing to spend another night here in the city?"

Rowland offered his place, they had room to spare, but part of this experience was getting away from them all to be ourselves.

"We'll stay at the inn for the evening," I assured them and though Rowland understood, he was a little deflated. "But we would love to have you and Vilmas join us for dinner. The children too."

"The lads would like that." Rowland thumbed his chin and beard thoughtfully.

Nadir nodded to the men in the room and turned to Mother and Vrawn. "Good luck with all of the preparations for the war, and if you need me, you know how to summon me."

"I do." The queen stood before us both and stared from her, to me, and then back to Nadir. "You will both make a name for yourselves, but do not do so at the expense of our people. I will not make you swear it, but know that the Unseelie are counting on you to become your best selves."

Vrawn spoke next. "And kill any Seelie who try you." She looked like she had more to say, but refrained as she stared at her daughter, simply adding, "Be careful. You never know what you might find out there, or what might find you."

"We will." I spoke with confidence and when they both stared at us for far too long, Xiphyre growled and shoved me. I turned and looked at him. "What?"

His eyes narrowed as he held up a small box. "For that alone, young prince, you will be putting the finishing touches on your forge—come." I hesitated and he growled, "What did I say?"

"Yes, master Xiphyre." Pulling the hammer from the small cord I had fashioned for it fastened to my neck, I willed it to grow to the size of a smithing hammer.

Rowland pressed the item he'd been working on back into the flames and winked at me. "One o' the four walls to it. Right now, I'm just straightening it out an' makin' sure it can withstand temperature shifts when yer forgin' out in the elements." He pulled it out for me and placed it on the anvil. "Need to make sure it be up to spec, then weld it to the other three walls to get it going. You got it?"

I nodded once. "Yes sir."

I glanced at the design he had in mind while he hammered on the wall a bit, then allowed me to take over. Once the wall was to the size and thickness it needed to be, I stuck it back into the forge while I went to go and collect the other pieces.

The bottom was bowed downward and had a retainer that looked like it would hold the fuel I would use for the flames to devour. This was the right side wall that I was adding. I stuck that into the flames as well, but the open side down so that the weld would stick a bit easier.

"Here, I've been usin' a small rod of this to help the joints adhere a bit better, make 'em stronger." Rowland pulled out the some-overheated mithril and winked at me. "Thanks for teachin' an ol' dog new tricks, lad."

I pulled both the mostly-finished section and the new wall to be added and pressed them into place and Rowland tapped the mithril onto the inner seam. I did the same on the outer seam, making my hammer smaller so as to get a finer control of it and let the density work for me.

When we finished up, it was a rectangle with a small lip sticking out of it on the front side.

"Stand aside!" Xiphyre barked and made the two of us move as he fluttered through with his own tongs. He shoved our work back into the forge and waited a moment before pulling it out and glaring at it, then shoving it back into the flames.

Another tense few moments passed and he grunted. "Sorry for threatening you, Azlo."

I shrugged. "It was a first for me, I will admit."

He glanced over his shoulder at me. "Me too, though with your mother imprisoning me with a deal, I thought about offing her often."

The clang of Thogan's hammer hitting the anvil and not his actual work made the hair on the back of my neck rise as the stony dwarf turned a near-murderous glare on his friend.

Xiphyre rolled his eyes. "Oh come off it—acting like you didn't feel the same when you were just a sideshow to her rule before becoming her champion. I know you thought about fighting your way to freedom, so get off my wings, you sullen old shit!"

Thogan's hammering could have shaken the whole place if it hadn't been for the fact that the place was on the ground level.

"Acts as though policing thoughts is something that should be done, bah!" Xiphyre adjusted the item in the forge and then stared at it. "I'll admit, I am happier now. Children have their dad, I get to teach them as is proper, and the line carries on as it did for generations before me. That's something to be proud of."

He fluttered and pulled the item from the flames and set it on the anvil we were working on, with the front facing down to the cool metal. "My only regret is that you chose this barbaric beating practice over the elegant art of enchanting."

He looked up and his eyes met mine, his tone a growl. "But you were terrible at it anyway, so it's not too terrible of a loss." That made me laugh and he cracked a smile as he pointed at the forge. "You'll need a back, and this is going to be it. Hold it steady, Azlo, and watch closely."

I did as he asked, donning thick gloves to hold the cherry-red metal steady as the Ragalfr readied the other item—a thick slab of diamond engraved with some symbols I didn't recognize. He pressed it onto the back of the small forge-to-be and muttered something as he pressed around it like a potter would knead clay. The metal covered the corners of the diamond backing and dulled immediately.

He took a deep breath and brought three more items out of his inventory, one of them an engraving brush that ate through almost everything easily. His movements and strokes were honed and well-practiced as the brush made sections of the metal disappear in beautiful flowing lines. He hummed as he worked and smiled as he finished.

As he worked, my skin began to prickle and warm as whispers began to come from the fires crackling inside the forge. Inside it, I could see eyes, warm as coals, looking out of it.

I stepped closer and realized that inside the heart of the Dragon Forge, there were several elementals watching what was happening, curious and interested from the safety of the structure.

"Hello." I spoke softly so that the others might not hear me. When the elementals realized I could see them, they ducked down and hid away from my sight. "It's alright, I wanted to talk to you about something."

One of them stuck its head back up over the lip of the forge and stared at me, so I spoke again. "We're making a forge for me to take as I travel around the world and make weapons. Do you like being a part of this forge?"

A crackling, wispy voice came from the watcher, there was an almost metallic cast to it as it spoke, "Yes. They feed us good food, make us feel stronger with the primordial's blessing."

"If I gave you good food, would you help me?" They were quiet, almost contemplative as I added, "I'm going to be on a quest for the primordial elementals and I'll need all the help I can get."

The elemental considered me for a moment, then disappeared, "No."

I frowned. "Oh, thanks for considering it then." It was hard to keep the bitterness out of my tone.

"Who're you mumblin' at, lad?" Rowland stared at me with open concern on his face.

I frowned. "Just talking to the fire in the forge, you know how it can be." He blinked and stared some more then turned back to the action happening at the center of the anvil he stood next to.

A small voice, barely a crackled whisper, tugged my attention back to the forge. "You mean it?" A tiny elemental stared out of the forge at me as he stood on the rack to get a better look at me. "You talked to the Primordial Flame?"

I nodded. "I swear it on my power."

It blinked and looked down at all of the rest of the elementals. "Can I come with you? I don't get much to eat here."

"Are you sure you can handle being away from your family?"

It frowned at me and spread its misshapen arms. "I am only me." The flames around it guttered and lessened. "Will you feed me? Help me grow?"

"I will, so long as you can pull your weight and help me forge items and weapons." I held my hand out to it as it considered the weight of my offer. "Can you do that? In return, I promise to feed you as well as I can."

It let its arms fall down and then nodded. "I will do my best as long as I am fed."

"We have an accord." I reached out to it and it touched my hand. There was no burning sensation, just warmth. It crawled into my hands, the warmth coming along with it.

"Time to add the fire to it." Xiphyre turned with the now-cool object in his hands, only to jump and lose his grip when he saw me with a portion of flame burning in my hands.

Luckily, Rowland was able to catch it on his foot, but the howls of his ire and frustrated pain made that streak of luck more like an accident than any sort of skill.

I quickly lifted the object after palming the flaming and guttering elemental flame with my right hand, then said, "This will be your new home, should you so choose. What do you say?"

"We have an agreement, and though it is small, I will still grow stronger with better and more food." The elemental clambered into the small forge with my assistance and then immediately began to burn brightly. "Could I have some food now? I'm very hungry."

I blinked in surprise and turned to Xiphyre. "Is there more that you need to do to this, or can I start using it now?"

He just lifted his hand at me and pointed at me, then the forge, then my hand. "What? How?"

"My class allows me to handle and manipulate the elements a little." Not an outright lie, but enough of the truth to throw them off asking too many questions I didn't know the answers to just yet. "But is there anything else?"

Xiphyre blinked and then took the small forge back. "It's warm, but not really." He frowned and took it back to the bench where he began to add mana and components to it before there was a final flash. He turned back to me and stared at me openly. "You cannot lie, I know that—so what does 'forge sorcerer' mean?"

I blinked and a series of notifications populated in front of me.

Congratulations!

Class Specification Unlocked!

Forge Sorcerer — This sub-class of the sorcerer focuses on creating items, weapons, and armor that will house elementals in order to augment their abilities. This class is not the normal mage type class, and is one that is meant to be the go-between for the elements and the world by creating items of great power in a time where mages are persecuted.

There was a whispering of air along the back of my neck and I could hear Seraestar speaking. "This subclass was made specifically for you. Congratulations on exceeding your father's legacy so young." The breeze left and then came back. "As you did not choose it, I will send a harbinger to teach you about it. Go to the tavern where it all began."

I could feel my hackles raising at her mention of my father, but I decided to just wait and pass judgment later. For now, I had real questions to answer.

"Me, I am the forge sorcerer." Xiphyre stared at me with open curiosity and I cleared my throat. "I don't know everything yet, as I just learned that, but it is something I mean to explore. Once I know more, I can compare notes with you, but suffice it to say that the elements and I will be working as closely as can be allowed for the foreseeable future."

He looked like he wanted to ask more, but I bowed my head. "If the item is ready, I have an errand I need to run for now." Thogan still beat on the anvil beside Xiphyre and though he was interested, his work carried weight, as a proper anvil was needed to make any reliable weapon, items or piece of armor.

Xiphyre just passed it over and let me go. I ignored the information that came from the forge in my hand for the time being and nodded to them as I headed toward Hero's Tavern with mounting trepidation. I thought about feeding the little elemental, but figured I would do so later when I had the time to watch and talk to it as opposed to being out in the open like this.

The place that had once been a tavern had turned into a guards barracks, and then an inn where the majority of the visitors to the city came when they wanted to feel close to the heroes who had saved Brindolla. It meant that there was no end to the tourists and pilgrims who came to this place to ensure that they could either pay their respects, hear tales of their adventures, or just get some plain old good food.

As I prepared to walk through the front door, I had to make a decision. Did I allow myself to remain the prince? Or did I use a glamour and try to blend in?

I heard someone inside hollering, "To Zeke!" I rolled my eyes and decided, *Glamour.*

Focusing on my magic, I wove it over my skin in a netted sort of way that covered my skin and the silver and gold stars, shortened my ears slightly, and then dulled my eyes. It was annoying, because it felt like I was covered in the world's wettest blanket, but it would at least assist me in keeping a lower profile and not being subjected to strangers trying to talk up my father to me.

Or worse—use me to get to my mother or him. It was better this way. I would have a lot more freedom and be able to move without being seen like this.

I walked into the room and looked around, expecting to find my sister, but I couldn't see her at all.

I walked to the bar and sat down, the dawn elven woman behind it chipperly asking, "What can I get you, good sir?" She stopped to look at my darker skin and ears, likely seeing a dark elf, but her smile only slipped for half a heartbeat.

"What would you suggest?" I smiled as she thought and I raised a hand. "If there's something popular with the dwarves who visit here, I would see that as a boon."

"Oh, you want the good stuff? Sir Dillon keeps that in the back, gimme a second?" I nodded once in her direction and she hurried off while throwing her towel over her shoulder.

"Dwarven drinks already?" Nadir's voice came from my right at the bar and I just glanced at her with my peripheral vision. She looked to be a near-spitting image of her mother, green skin and all with her own glamour. "How was the forging process? I take it the Queen and Mother didn't stay long?"

I shook my head. "They didn't. They left shortly after there was talk of me needing to help forge things, and I haven't heard anything from them for a time. What about you?"

"I secured us board here for the night and I have a meal ordered for us as well." She took a draft of her mug, a frothy beer from what I could glean, and grunted. "We need to talk about what we plan to do from here."

I agreed. "We do." I stared after the bartender, where she had gone was seemingly taking her quite some time to return from. "I have a quest of sorts. It's clearly defined, but is vague as well."

"Can you share it with me so that I might be able to look at it?" I nodded and thought about what I wanted to happen. She blinked and hit something, and as soon as she did, I knew that she had accepted the quest as well. "This is… irritating."

I raised a brow and actually looked at her, noting that she was looking into the polished mirror as some of the more boisterous and drunken rousers raised their glasses and walked toward the bar. They didn't look like they were in foul moods, just that they were coming straight toward us.

One man was elven of some variety, not Unseelie. We had a certain darkness to us that all of the other Unseelie could see even under the guise of a glamour. Just as the Seelie had a certain lightness about them. It was difficult to explain or encapsulate in words so much as it was just instinctive that I could tell this man wasn't friend or necessarily foe.

The other man was human, his skin kind of sagged off him in places and his middle was paunchy, like he drank too much.

"Another round, my fair temptress!" the elf hollered. It had been his voice I had heard outside toasting to my father. "Where did she go?"

I pointed to the doorway that was still empty and she finally came back with a medium-sized barrel on her shoulder. And the man behind her carried a much larger one with moderately more trouble.

I knew who this was and while I wasn't too familiar with him, I did jump the bar and catch the other side of the barrel to assist him.

The wizened but still deep voice that came from him was as comforting as the first time I'd heard it. "Thank you, lad."

Sir Willem Dillon bowed his gray, pony-tailed head in my direction as I walked out from behind the counter awkwardly. His stern, fair human features had softened with age, even his formerly frightening physique had diminished, though he was still strong enough to contend with a barrel of ale. He wiped his hands onto his trousers and offered a placating smile to the men that stood a bit too closely to Nadir. "How can I help you gentlemen?"

"Another round, if you would please, sir." The elf sighed dramatically. "How can we celebrate our friends' compromising quest without imbibements and libations?"

I hadn't heard the word used that way before and almost laughed aloud. Rather, I just accepted my drink from the dawn elf and smiled. "Thank you."

Nadir and I stood to go back to the table that she motioned to and the elf glared at her. "Orcs like you should know better than to come so far south as this." His drunken gaze slid off her back but his insults didn't stop with her disinterest. "You think you're too good to talk to me?"

I rolled my eyes. How many books had I read that started in a bar with someone making an imbecile of themselves?

The owner of the tavern rumbled, "Sir, you will not make a spectacle of yourself in my tavern."

Sir Dillon's voice was firm and broached no response, but the human just waved him off. "Orcs don't have no right to a spectacle, old timer. Ones up north kill our folk all the time. Don't matter that the land is treacherous and the animals up there ain't tame no way, no how—they'll kill ya soon as look at ya. Specially if ya got magic."

That caught my attention, but the man's glaring at my sister as she stilled made me pause and consider my options. If he touched her, she would kill him. I had not a single doubt about that, as she had never had to train with Uncle Thogan again one day. Said she'd nearly taken his head off when she was just a little girl, and I had since then fought her *once* because it was expected that we be able to fight anyone at a moment's notice if they challenge us. I had challenged her to a duel to spend the day together.

I still couldn't recall how she had beaten me, but thinking about it made my head ache.

Nadir turned her head slowly and cast one eye back at the speaker. "Do you have it?"

The man blinked, clearly startled as she turned the rest of her body with her head to look at him, he stammered, "W-what?"

"Magic." She leaned closer and sniffed him theatrically, but I knew she was memorizing his scent profile. I'd begun doing it as soon as my sense had grown sharper with the release of my kitsune form. "Do you have magic?"

"I…" He looked at the elven man and back to her before backing up a step. "No. But we're members of Storm Company!"

"*What?*" Sir Dillon's shout was filled with so much malice and anger that it was hard to fight the shiver that almost traveled down my spine. "How dare you!"

"He's not lying, old man!" the elf barked and I could taste it.

I raised my voice slightly so as to be heard and said, "They think they're telling the truth, Sir Dillon."

"Think?" The elven man stepped closer to me and breathed his rank breath into my face. "You *think* you want to start a fight with someone who's a part of one of the greatest fighting forces on this world?"

I rolled my eyes and fought the urge to give in to my mother's oft more… brutal lessons and urges. Her voice chided me even as I stood in front of him and stared into his bleary hazel eyes. *"All it takes is one person to make an example, Azlo. A precisely placed heart frozen in someone's mouth sends a* very *clear message, wouldn't you agree?"*

I had since I had seen the still living, frozen Fae who had irked my mother enough to elicit such retribution. Even Father, from the stories Mother told me, had ripped out a heart or two. Though what he did with them, I didn't care as much.

"They're dead and gone, fallen in sacrifice to keep War and his horde out of our world forever." The words tasted bitter on my tongue, and I hated myself for saying them as they were technically true and also a carefully curated lie. Just saying it made me feel filthy. I hated lying. It left you open to the laws of the universe.

"They're stronger than ever with new leadership while the original members are gone." The elf lifted his chin and again, I could taste no lie. "The children of the group lead the organization now."

I blinked at that and let my gaze slip over to Nadir whose face was carefully blank. How could that be possible? Curious and angry, I asked, "Who are they?"

The elf actually scoffed in my face. "Like we would tell just anyone about our leaders."

The human cackled. "Tryouts to join are closed for the year, as well."

"I find it hard to believe that the prince and princess would want anything to do with reviving their father and his friends' party, especially all that's happened and is currently happening in the Fae realm." Sir Dillon stood on this side of the counter now and narrowed his gaze at the two unruly patrons. "You've insulted my patrons, and my friends. Leave and never return, you or anyone who claims the false Storm Company name."

They just rolled their eyes and stared at him. "We weren't done with our drinks."

"Sir Dillon, would you like the assistance in getting rid of this rabble?" I asked calmly, carefully turning my back to them.

He laughed, and it was a hearty one. "No, my apprentice will be delighted to though. Agatha!" The young elven woman behind the bar perked up at her name and he jerked his chin at the two men and their three friends who stood and made their way closer slowly. "Don't break what you can't fix or pay for."

The bartender grinned wildly. "I've been saving for this for *years!*"

She was up and over the counter so fast that I thought she would knock me off my feet with how excited she was to get to her prize. Both the elven man and his human friend snickered as she came upon them like a charging Belgar. But rather than horns and a thick hide, she carried only her hand towel and somehow a barstool.

The stool raised and the towel whipped out, snapping the human in the cheek painfully, the welt forming almost instantly. The barstool crashed down onto his neck and shoulder, leaving a single leg in the woman's hand like a small wooden sword that she used to slap him on the other side of the face.

She bellowed, her whole body covered in a red aura that shimmered like a ruby, "Come and fucking get it!"

"Language!" Sir Dillon chided her, but the woman was already shrieking like a furious banshee and crashed into one of the three unknown drinkers who had come with the human and elf. She and the larger man went to the ground as she beat him around the head with her makeshift weapon.

The other two imbeciles got their wits about themselves and started to loom over her when I decided to step in and assist anyway. A large hand rested its palm on my shoulder and I saw Nadir shake her head, then Sir Dillon tipped his head back to the fight.

Agatha beat the man beneath her until he was unconscious before one of the others managed to grab her, but that just served to make her fury even worse. She roared and the space around her *warped* slightly and the hands that were on her suddenly weren't and she turned on him with eyes glimmering golden. Her hair whipped behind her and she lashed out with her foot, catching him in the gut and sending him flying into a table that shattered and crumbled like only so much lumber.

Her gaze shifted to the elven man and she snarled, "Get the hell out of my bar!" She seethed as he had yet to move in three breaths and howled before springing at him. "Now!"

He ducked her and Sir Dillon caught her before she could turn and make her way back at him.

He leaned down and began to grab his human friend to drag him out before his other still-whole friend helped. He had the poor state of decision-making to threaten us. "You'll regret this! This whole place will burn if our leader doesn't like our treatment!"

Sir Dillon just made the same shooing gesture that I would have and they were all gone.

Agatha's breathing slowly steadied and she glared around the room. The patrons who stayed cheered when she smiled and she turned to Sir Dillon with a sly grin. "Looks like I haven't spent all my savings with this one."

CHAPTER NINE

Clean up wasn't so bad and when Sir Dillon bowed his head to us, he smiled. "Thank you for assisting us, and for wanting to come to our defense and the defense of my friends. I cannot believe that someone out there claims their party name for their own use."

I bowed back, careful not to reveal that I knew him. "We would have been happy to have been of assistance regardless."

"How generous." He smiled at me and looked to Nadir. "You look just like your mother, Princess Nadir."

To her credit, Nadir only blinked at him. "Thank you."

He glanced over at me and his smile never faltered. "And Prince Azlo, your looks are close enough to how they would be that I don't need to see your real skin to know you're Zeke and the Queen's boy."

I frowned at him and asked quietly, "What should I change?"

He patted me on the shoulder. "Nothing, son—nothing at all. Most people who met your father wouldn't know what to look for in near-human or elven form, and those who know your mother wouldn't dare stare at her too long to get an idea of what features could carry over."

I nodded to myself, but still decided to change some of my features with my glamour to make sure this didn't happen again.

"It was me who gave it away, then." Nadir spoke softly but watched the man intently.

He didn't deny it, but instead said, "I'm so glad you're here. Based on your being here, I can safely assume it isn't you besmirching your father and his friends' good names?"

"You would be correct," Nadir stated as we continued to our table. "Do you know any more on this matter? It is sorely irritating and is something I would like to look into while we are here."

I shot her a look, but her disinterest in me meant two things, either she didn't care about the quest we already had, or the two could be related.

"This is the first I'm hearing of it, if I'm honest." He sighed dejectedly as he motioned to a chair and I nodded, allowing him to join us. "I will be looking more into it, however. I cannot abide them disgracing their good work like that."

He could clearly tell that we weren't willing to discuss it more and settled for speaking softly on his own. "I won't try to explain away what happened, or what you've been through."

"Thank you," I said abruptly, wishing to save us both from this same speech that everyone seemed so Hells bent on giving us. He looked my way, startled, so I smiled at him. "We've heard it so often that I think I could tell you what your next thought is."

"Forgive him, Sir Dillon, the prince has a hard time with people who mean well." Nadir's soft words held a steel whip of correction in them as she turned to stare into my eyes with a disapproving glare.

Sir Dillon chuckled and shook his head. "Very well, I mean nothing ill, as I am certain you know." He patted the table and stared at the wood with eyes that focused on nothing. "I am here, should you have need of my wisdom, or an ear to listen. I am here."

Nadir inclined her head and said, "Thank you, Sir Dillon."

"Willem, princess and prince—I must insist."

I leaned back and stared at him with a soft and apologetic smile of my own. "Then I am afraid that the formality of titles chafes us as well. Azlo will serve just fine." He frowned and I grinned a little more before adding, "I must insist."

Barking laughter caught my attention as Agatha brought the food out to us and grinned. "They got you there, boss."

"And what would a youngster such as you know about being caught?" He playfully raised an eyebrow at her then motioned to the table. "Bring them more food. And something warm to drink as well. This is on me, of course."

"We cannot accept that." I waved his rebuttal off and he just took my hand in his larger one, forcing me to still and listen.

"I am christening a new friendship, and all the best ones start with food and drink enjoyed together." His eyes sparkled as he smiled widely. "I am your friend now, Azlo and Nadir, and I will honor you with my presence."

That made me laugh, and even Nadir cracked a smile and said, "As you wish."

More food came and as it did, we ate and were merry. At least as merry as we could be with the circumstances of our being there, but it was still a nice time. The food was delicious, and we learned more about the state of the city, and even Agatha.

"She's a zealot, an odd form of a Paladin that relies on righteous fury to attack," Willem explained as Agatha cleaned up the mess that she had made. "I know a thing or two about it, so she is here with me as she comes to terms with who and what she is in service to our goddess."

Could she be the one Seraestar meant to send? I wondered as I watched her moving through the room, sweeping shards of wood off the planks below.

After a couple of hours, Nadir excused herself. "We have travel ahead of us, and I wish to be fully rested before then, no matter what it may mean. Thank you for your companionship tonight, Willem. I wish you the best."

He nodded in return and stood as she did. "And I wish you the same, Nadir. May your way always be lit, and the knowledge you hold tempered by wisdom—your own or divine."

She smiled and left at that, allowing me to stay for a tense moment with Willem before he sighed and ducked his head toward me. "Sadly, there are some duties still this evening that I must attend to, and I fear I must excuse myself as well. Thank you for allowing an old man the pleasure of a new friendship, Azlo."

I stood and bowed my head in return. "And thank you for allowing a young man the honor of yours, Willem. Thank you for everything. I must say it was a fine meal, and finer company." I pulled out four gold coins and he shook his head. "If not for the meal, then for the entertainment before the meal, and allow what isn't used on repairs to go to Agatha, I believe she earned it."

He chuckled and took the coins, pocketing them with a wink. "I'll be certain that she gets it, thank you."

With him gone, I was alone with my thoughts. I could have gone to the bar, or to the room, which was likely what I was supposed to do if the furtive looks coming from Nadir before she'd left had been any indication. I just didn't want to turn in quite yet.

I decided to walk out of the dining area and into the back area where there was a garden and training area for the guards. The night sky here in this realm was so peaceful, and with nothing actively trying to kill me or claim my power or time, it was lovely to just sit and stare up at it.

"It's such a miracle of the work that can be done by the gods—those stars," said the soft-spoken visitor who would have startled me if I hadn't felt them moving through the shadows cautiously. "Don't you think, sorcerer?"

So here they were. "I do." I sat up fully and shifted where I sat to look at my god-sent visitor. She wore simple platemail with a crest on it that I didn't recognize, but what I did see was that she was a kitsune. Her auburn fur looked soft and there was a bit of white trailing down her throat into the breastplate. She stared at me with interest and when she said nothing, I skipped the preamble and stated, "Seraestar sent you."

"My goddess did, yes." She stared at me for a moment longer, then came to join me on the wooden picnic table I sat on. "She wished that I impart some things to you about your class, and how you would do best with it. My name is Dawnstar, but you might call me Dawn, Azlo."

I sat in excited silence, eager to learn more but not knowing what to expect as she gathered her thoughts until finally I offered a greeting. "A pleasure to make your acquaintance, Dawn."

She nodded and said, "Your manipulation skills already exceed what should have been possible thanks to your lineage. Part of your father and mothers' bonds to the elements is your own by the blood in your veins. That said, you can do more than we had thought and will likely soon pick up the next rank of Elemental Manipulation on your own, we just cannot be sure."

"Why not?" I had to try harder than I would have to keep my voice quizzical and not accusatory as I added, "She is a goddess. Her whim rewrites the laws of the world all the time."

She shook her head. "She can only work with what is there already, as the system is in place by *all* of the gods together, not just her."

That was interesting to learn. "So then I am bound by the will of the other gods who might oppose her?"

She nodded once. "We have much to impress upon you, so please allow me a moment." She took a deep breath once more to gather herself then spoke, "Your class and subclass focus on your natural affinity with the elements, but as you need to work on the pacts you form with the elementals, there is a social aspect to it as well. Charisma, believe it or not, is how you will accomplish much, and as a caster class like a mage, you will want to spend your proficiency points that are in your weapons tab on wands."

I followed her and opened my status screen, looking into what she was saying as she said it.

With the weapons tab open, I could see that I had six points to spend on whatever I so chose, but wands? "Dawn, I don't use wands."

She scowled at me, her lips pulling down and her muzzle wrinkling with disdain. "I was getting to the reasoning before you interrupted me." She sighed and clarified, "Wands and staves are how many magic users cast their spells, or through other means, like a holy symbol. For a sorcerer like you, your likability is what will help you cast spells."

She pointed to Shaper on my neck and said, "And as a Forge Sorcerer, the very weapons and items you make will allow you to cast spells, or affect the elements as if they were a wand; this works to your advantage."

"Is that fair?"

She shrugged. "It is within the confines of the system put in place by the gods themselves. If it works and fits their needs, I wouldn't question it."

I almost grunted and just left it at that. So I could use these points with wands and be proficient with more weapons? At least, those I created.

"What else is expected of me? Do I need to pay fealty or homage to your goddess?"

"No." Dawn snorted. "Seraestar only seeks those who seek her. She saw something in you that could bring about change, but that was nothing that would not have happened without her intervention anyway."

My eyes narrowed in her direction as my mind reeled. *So I had been played? Was this goddess just pulling me into this to ensure that the Fae would be interfering here as a means to keep things confusing?*

"Other than that, you have the opportunity to form a pact

with any elemental you find." She thought about it for a moment, then frowned. "That's not good."

Blinking, I stared at her as she hung her head as if listening. "Your ability to actually gain spells is inhibited. You won't gain spells like most classes on Brindolla, through study or even by tricking elementals or others into teaching you."

"Then how am I supposed to use my magic?" It was difficult to keep the fear out of my voice. There was a good deal that manipulating the elements could do, but without a flat cost to cast specific spells for specific situations, the cost would be prohibitive at the kindest of times.

Unless I put almost all of my points into Intelligence, I would never have the mana needed to affect anything at a distance efficiently.

Not unless I learned how to throw knives or something inane like that, or a bow.

"She is working on a means." I frowned and she just sighed. "I swear to you on my power, bequeathed to me by the goddess Seraestar, that I speak truth when I say that my goddess is working to find the means to allow you at least a small amount of spells."

I nodded, her word cemented in a notification and the taste of purity in the back of my throat at least confirming she believed what she said.

"Fine." I shook myself out. "Is there anything more that I should expect for this quest she has me on?"

"Go where you have been pointed to, and keep a low profile." She stood up and reached out her hand. In it, there was a small stone with runes and symbols carved into it. "This is a calling stone. Should you ever need aid, push mana into this, and I will know where to go. I will bring friends."

I nodded once. "Thank you for your assistance in the service of your goddess."

I stared down at the stone. "I do hope that this would go both ways. While I am young, I am able and the Unseelie do not abide debts long."

She chuckled to herself. "No, they do not."

She turned without another word and left me there to stare up into the night sky alone.

CHAPTER TEN

Nadir's brother slipped into the room well after she had thought that he should have returned. With the ability to enter a trance-like state to rest, he wouldn't need much to stay healthy, though he could technically sleep like a normal being.

"I take it your meeting went about as well as one might expect?" Nadir didn't need much sleep either, but that was thanks in part to her mastery of healing magic. Taking fatigue away from those they took care of was a massive boon, but only when there was reason to take it.

Sometimes allowing the body to rest and recover was as necessary as the healing itself. Not just for the body, but the mind and spirit too.

"I was being schooled in my class and subclass by a cleric of the goddess who contacted me with the elementals." His explanation was adequate. It meant he didn't know exactly who she was or what she was in the grander scheme of things, but Nadir did only because she had read everything she could find about the groups connected to the gods around four years ago.

Dawnstar of Simioln was no mere cleric but *the* cleric of Seraestar. The goddess had a select following and those in her care were the best of the best. A member of the Braves of the Thorn, and a founder of the Church of Magic, she was a force to be reckoned with.

Someone to watch and keep at a distance, or closer than Nadir would care for.

"Do you know enough to make an educated decision about how you will spend all of your points and arm yourself?" He nodded once and Nadir grimaced. "You're quiet, why?"

"My subclass and class mean no spells until the goddess can figure out a way for me to get them."

Nadir didn't wait for him to finish his thought, already keen on what that would mean. "That means you will be primarily fighting from close range for now, unless you start using ranged weapons like knives, darts, or a bow."

He nodded once and the young orc actually smiled. "You won't be doing that though, will you?"

Azlo returned her grin ruefully. "No. No, I will not be."

She laughed softly; it was nice to be back with her brother again.

"Have you thought of where you wanted to go?"

His sister's laughter died a little and she cleared her throat, hopeful. "I was hoping to go north, further north than the quest marker, to find something out." She looked uncertain, the first time in many years that she had ever felt self-conscious. "I want to find my people."

The prince, not stupid by any means, reasoned, "Orcs." She tilted her head forward and he frowned. "You think Vrawn's tribe was up that far north? How would she have been found by a human and raised by her?"

"After a battle, I think, but regardless, they're the last bastion of true orcs out there and I want to get to know that part of myself." She frowned to herself as Azlo watched her quietly. "That part that Mother never even knew."

He watched still, even less animated than before, the stillness of the normally-full-of-motion young man before her would have been unnerving if it were it not for her being able to see him breathing.

"Do you think it will give you some kind of closure over the life you've had?"

A simple enough question with implications unknown.

Nadir straightened and answered, "I'm not foolish enough to hope. But if there is more to me than being the Healer and the daughter of a missing hero, then I would know it."

Azlo shrugged. "Very well."

Nadir started to speak, then paused and stared at her brother in disbelief. "What?"

He blinked at her and motioned at her. "You have a chance to learn about yourself, and I have to get better materials for smithing eventually. Why not learn something along the way for both of us? Who knows? Maybe they have some ancient orcish smithing techniques that I might be able to learn."

Nadir stared at the boy in disbelief and shook her head. "Thank you."

"Of course." He was quiet for a moment, then asked, "Were you serious about wanting to figure out who was behind the whole Storm Company business?"

"Yes." All measure of uncertainty and girlish charm was gone and in her place was the Healer. "Those people call themselves their children. They make themselves a banner they did not earn, and they pretend to be us. The implications of that are far reaching if you are to obtain the throne and lead our people."

"I see." Azlo turned on the chair he sat on and focused on the wall. "We will see what they hope to gain, then destroy them if we can't bend them to our use."

"Yes, my Prince."

He turned his gaze to her without moving his head. "Nadir, please. Don't call me that. Not while we are away if you can't avoid it at all."

She stared at the boy and just watched him for a time, then

he decided that he was done speaking and slipped into his trance state to rest.

Nadir reached into her small book satchel and pulled the worn copy of her book on orcs, lovingly spreading her hand over it as she allowed her eyes to unfocus as if she could see herself there with her people.

Would they even accept her? She would have to find out. She would have to try.

———

Rowland glared at Xiphyre, staring at him as if he were a devil, but the only thing he would say was, "Be safe, lad. And come back." Likely because he wasn't able to come and eat with us due to injuring his foot. I could see that it was still bandaged.

Nadir reached down and touched it, her hand glowing slightly as she did so, and his face went from bitter anger to relieved anger. "Could've done that from the beginnin'?"

Nadir smiled softly and just answered, "Had I known it was that bad, yes."

He grumbled and hobbled away because the bandages wouldn't allow him to walk well.

Xiphyre snorted and rolled his eyes and Thogan held out his work for me while the Ragalfr spoke, "This and the forge are both designed and enchanted to grow to the desired size you need to accommodate whatever project you might be working on."

Thogan held out a small bag and grunted. "This be a gift for you. Odds and ends of materials that most smiths would have if they had the means. Make something worthy o' our admiration, lad."

"Thank you all." I smiled at them and gave Thogan a firm handshake, a nod to Xiphyre, and then a call of, "See you around, Rowland!"

He bellowed something and I just smiled wider.

"Be safe, lad," Thogan ordered, and finally said, "Remember the tenets of The Way, and follow them."

I bowed my head before turning and walking off. We had plenty of money to go and buy horses if necessary, but there was nothing here that would make it easier to travel in the woods than being who and what we were, so for the time being, we would move on foot.

Once we reached the gate to the city, Sunrise at our backs, we moved off into the dawn of our own adventure.

In the woods, Nadir turned and asked, "Are you ready?"

I grinned. "Yes, I am."

With that, both of us shifted our form and ran north as star-covered foxes. It seemed like no matter how swiftly I ran, Nadir was always ahead of me, leading the charge through the brush and trees. Competition brought innovation and drive, so I pressed myself harder, trying to gain the advantage on her, but failing miserably.

For hours, we ate up ground, resting as we wished and just enjoying being able to be free at long last.

It would be days still before we made it to a city or town, and we still had to venture over the mountains on our way there.

The forest was so alive and it was just fun to run as we were. Eventually, the stones dug too hard into our paws to make climbing the mountains in our fox forms effective, so we shifted to our more normal forms, neither of us bothering anymore with glamour.

"Have you spent all of your points yet, Azlo?" Nadir stared up into the mountainside and I shook my head. She responded, "You should. It's part of why you were slower than me."

Acquiescing, I opened my status screen and looked over my options.

Name: Azlo Erebos
Level: 11
Strength: 17
Dexterity: 21

Constitution: 12
Intelligence: 21
Wisdom: 14
Charisma: 16
Unspent Attribute Points: 33
Unassigned Chaos Points: 11

I blinked and added ten points to Charisma out of the gate, since it was how I would be able to form my pacts with the elementals.

Once I did that, I added five to Constitution, Strength, Dexterity and Intelligence, with the final three going into Wisdom.

Once I made the selection that spent all my points, the other eleven just disappeared and my stats were completed.

Name: Azlo Erebos
Level: 11
Strength: 28
Dexterity: 26
Constitution: 17
Intelligence: 27
Wisdom: 17
Charisma: 30
Unspent Attribute Points: 0
Unassigned Chaos Points: 0

That seemed like a decent spread. It was annoying that I couldn't control where they went, even knowing what Mother had said about the Fae having a chaotic assignment of their points, but this time it had worked in my favor somewhat with the added points to Intelligence, Strength and Charisma.

I stretched as the changes rushed through my body uncomfortably. Muscles tightening and then leaning with the improvements to my Strength and Dexterity, then it felt like my face glowed uncomfortably for a moment. Then it stopped, and I was myself again.

My mana bar grew as well, so that was a blessing as it gave me 270 MP to use.

"All done?" Nadir's question made me grin and I nodded. "Good, let's go."

And on we went. Up into the mountains and onward. Aside from the occasional mountain lion that stalked up until it got an idea for how strong we were, there was nothing following us or close to our level here that could have been a threat.

"I can't recall, the ruins of where War's avatar was summoned are close, aren't they?"

Nadir nodded and pointed further north. "We will pass by it on our way to the quest destination." She was quiet for a moment. "Did you want to go there?"

"We can't." She frowned at me and I said, "Mother told me that the place has been put under a barrier placed by servants of all the gods. To try to keep anything from slipping into our world from elsewhere."

The silence between us was almost palpable until I smirked and muttered, "Doesn't mean we shouldn't stop and look in it though."

She smiled and, with that, we jogged up the mountain path until we decided to rest for a time and eat on top of the plateau. Our lunch consisted mainly of small meats and cheeses that we would easily run off once we could get over the side of the mountain.

"Do you think we should have gotten mounts?" I chewed in thought at Nadir's silence and asked, "What would we even ride?"

She swallowed her food and pondered for a moment before saying, "My people have been known to ride massive wolves." She shrugged. "Do you want to find something to tame and make a mount? You're abysmal with horses."

"It's like they can tell that you think they are beneath you." She laughed at that, she knew that I found most animals like horses slightly intimidating. It was like they could smell my fear. "Maybe I can make an item that will allow me to fly, or something?"

"Could be an interesting item to make, but I don't know

that an elemental would want you to be able to do that, or that it wouldn't be mana inefficient." Nadir was right in that aspect as she stared ahead and in the direction we needed to travel. "Had we gone into the ancestral dungeon, we could have maybe found mounts there. The queen did."

"I heard there were dungeons all over this world; do you know of any that we would be able to go into and try to see if we can't find one?"

She frowned and pulled out a book from her satchel. "Give me the night. We should rest here if that's the case, so we don't get closer or further from any potential ones."

I nodded. "Fair enough."

I reached into my inventory and pulled out a tent that had been enchanted long ago that Mother had gifted to me. It folded itself out and up, creating an almost villa-like structure on the inside. The spatial crafting of it made it valuable to us because it allowed us to forgo the elements of the outdoors, have a modicum of privacy inside, and a bit more luxury as well.

There were two mounds of lavish and fluffy pillows that would be our beds, changing partitions, and there was even a tub on each side of the room made of copper that would heat up and warm the water as we bathed.

Shadow goblins exited the sides of the 'walls' inside the tent and attended to our every desire. They even brought food directly from the palace on platters of gold as my sister had inherited Father's lycanthropy.

She bowed her head. "Thank you. Please, take this as my gratitude."

She reached out and swiped a portion of the food onto the floor and the shadowy servants screeched in sincere delight at their prize.

They devoured the food and stared at her with clear adoration. I loved feeding them personally as I ate, so it felt like I had someone eating with me. Mother had always tried to discourage that, but once she was gone, they would return and eat with me.

Three of them, the boldest of them, waddled out of the shadows around me and smiled their oddly creepy, but charming smiles at me. They had no teeth or eyes, but they looked genuinely happy to see me.

"Gentlemen, how are you?" They produced food for me. A casserole directly from the kitchens that they knew I loved. They loved it too. I cut sections of it and served them, then served myself. "Thank you for bringing this. Let's remember to give your friends some too, yes?"

They nodded and I knew they would leave only crumbs, but such was how they chose to dote on those they liked. I would always share my food with them so long as they at least tried to share.

"I'm happy to know I wasn't the only one to have figured this out." Nadir watched them eating with me slowly, relishing each bite as if they might never get the chance to eat again.

"Figure anything out about the dungeons yet?" The casserole made me feel warm and fuzzy inside, like I was home and eating at the dinner table with Mother all over again.

"Somewhat, but this is more the theory behind finding them and how they are created." She frowned and flipped the page. "It's not terrible to read all this, but there are a lot of technical elements to being able to find them that I need to focus on."

I nodded my understanding of her unstated request and just focused on eating. Where we were, there was a good deal of earth around us, so this could be a perfect place to try and reach out to an earth elemental.

But what could I make that would entice one of them into being in it?

That gave me pause and I looked into my proficiencies and made it so that all six points that I had went into Wands. It made me smile to know that I could be proficient with any weapon I made.

But did it have to be a weapon? The description had said that it could be anything that *I* made. Or if the forge was to be added to that, helped make. But even with my level in smithing, creating something like a ring or earrings would be more of an annoyance than a good practice of my skills.

Deciding on an odd, but reasonable plan of action, I finished my dinner and allowed the goblins to take the plates back, and I even left more food for the others so they could eat. Once I was cleaned up, I went back outside to a partially windy evening sun and stared around me.

There was nothing but rock and stone all about and that was what I needed.

I took a knee far enough away from the tent so as not to disturb my studying sister and put a hand on the ground. There was nothing there. Not a thing.

"Hello?"

Still nothing came and I frowned to myself. This was the perfect place for there to be an elemental of earth?

Rather than dwelling on it, I pulled the forge out and activated the runes on it, making it grow to the point that I needed it to. For the style of fighting I had in mind, I needed to have light armor that was tough. Probably tougher than I could manage, but I would try for it.

I pulled out my ingots and glared at all of them, trying to decide which one would go best for what I wanted. Chain mail would be light, but would take a serious amount of time, and a breastplate would be heavier and harder to don and doff on my own.

I could do a half plate, then attach it with chain mail. Thinking like this was a little dangerous, but it was the only option I had at present and it would still be a while on the chain linking. I did have a quicker way to make the links themselves, but it would still require me taking the time to piece all of them together individually and then attach them to the breastplate. *Make the plate first, then a couple of the chain links to get that started.*

I chose two metals that I thought would work well together, the alloy that they would make was light and durable, and then I would pair that with mithril links to make a good match.

The metals were copper and Fae iron. I'd discovered this

mixture by accident once, but the resulting alloy was not just light weight to the point of near cloth-like levels, it was sturdy. Nowhere near what mithril could reach, but still reliable enough that it was worth making.

Because the amount of mithril needed to make a breastplate exceeded what I had, I would have to be satisfied that the links for this would be stronger than the plate itself.

I put the Fae iron ore into the smelting chamber that Thogan and Rowland designed into the forge so that I would not have to worry about heat constantly.

"What's that?" the fire elemental asked from inside the heart of the forge. It blinked at the bucket in the chamber and rubbed its wispy hands together. "It smells good. Can I have some?"

"You'll eat metal?" It nodded, and I frowned. "Will you eat the impurities?"

"If I can, sure. It all burns sooner or later." I pulled out some coke, coal, and a few small pieces of a higher density wood, and it paused. "Is all that for me?"

I smiled. "I told you I would feed you well if you did as I asked, but to do that, I think I have to offer you a good meal first, do I not?"

I pressed the coke in first, the warmth that took it from me building as I added in the coal around the outside then the wood in the middle with another layer of coal over top of it. "You can start wherever you please once we get this ore liquid, okay?"

The little elemental ignored me for only a moment as the last of the coke burned and became a part of it. "As you will it, master. How hot do you want it to be?"

I smiled. "*Hot.*"

CHAPTER ELEVEN

Once the smelting process rendered the Fae iron into a pool of liquid green that glowed cherry while molten, I added in the copper ore and a sprinkling of sand to help them adhere. The heat of liquid metal alone would be enough to make the copper melt, but I still had the elemental warming it to keep it liquid. I checked the progress of it all with a rod that was enchanted to match the heat from the metal around it, then pulled it out and tapped it on the side to get the molten metal off.

I pulled my gloves on and poured it into an ingot mold then did the same thing five more times to make six ingots total. I did it this way to keep from being wasteful if I over-poured or didn't pour enough, and it was a helpful way to get myself ready to make the armor.

The small acts of getting ready for the piece allowed me to really focus and build the image of that I had in my mind out.

Once all of the ingots cooled, I pulled them out and slowly began the process of heating them and combining them through hammering and folding. Then, after all of the ingots were folded together, I drew the combined metal out until it vaguely resembled a body that was larger than mine. This had taken several hours already, and I was good where I was for now.

But as I wasn't done heating, shaping, or tempering it, and I didn't put it into any oils or quenches, I simply put it straight into my inventory. There, the state of the item wouldn't fluctuate, and I could still work on it as I wished without too many worries of breakage or weakening it.

This wasn't the preferred method of working on it, but it was what I had. While I had been working on that portion of the armor, I'd been melting down mithril ingots to make the links to my chainmail.

This was going to be a little more annoying and much more time intensive, so I began setting up right away. I had a mold already made for links, painstaking as it had been to make and annoying as well, it had worked the last time I had made them and it was faster than making each individual link by hand.

I laid out the mat that had a set of ring-like layering to it before going to get rocks that would keep it on the ground and level for me, then gloved up and began to lightly pour the molten metal into the shaping below. This would have the rings connected to each other almost like chicken wire, but this was thicker and the shaping was a lot more symmetrical than most wire molds as well. All I had to do was take diamond shears to them to cut the shapes I wanted, heat then treat them, before clipping and affixing them together, and then I would have the chainmail I wanted.

There was a prickling at the nape of my neck and I stood, looking behind me. Nothing there. I glanced over at the entrance to the tent and found nothing yet again.

Sighing, I spoke softly, "If you watch me out of curiosity, do not interfere, as this is important work." Then I spoke with a bit of a growled threat in my tone, "But if you mean harm, show yourself so that you are not the coward you were raised to be."

Goading someone into an attack was less likely to work, but

insulting someone could lead to a mistake, and I was okay with taking advantage of that.

Nothing appeared or came at me, so I just took a calming and cleansing breath before returning to my work. I poured until the mithril I'd melted down was gone, then let it cool for a bit before gently tugging it out of the mold. My shears' diamond edge easily cut through the metal and separated out six pieces that I could easily work with while walking the following day.

"Did you have a good meal?" The elemental inside the forge still ate and I smiled. "I'll leave you out of my inventory tonight so you can still eat if you like?"

"That is fine." It almost sounded like it was trying to just get me to be quiet so it could eat in peace but when I was about to shrink the item down, it spoke. "A name."

I blinked at it, but it spoke again. "You should give me a name."

A sense of unease came over me as I knelt where I was and carefully explained, "I am Fae. Specifically, I am Fae royalty. If you have no name, and it becomes how you are referred to in this realm, I could hold a sway over you that is wholly not what you wish. If you choose your name, I will have less power over you and this will be a pact of mutual creation and comfort."

The little elemental stared at me for a long while, so I added, "While it would benefit me greatly to have access to all of you, I don't wish to make our previous pact one that forces you to be mine and mine alone. If someday you wanted to leave, I would happily let you go. But if I name you and it binds you to me, I could force you back. I don't want that for you."

The thought of my mother knowing my own true name was alarming enough that she could call me back at any time she so pleased even more so.

"I have many names already. I wanted to be referred to as something by you so that I can call to you as well." The popping and crackling sound in the forge continued for a moment, and the elemental stated, "Call me 'Pop,' for the sound I just made."

I grinned. "Happy to meet you, Pop. I am Azlo, please, call me that."

"Azlo." He'd said it as if the name felt funny. "Did you know you were being watched by something?"

"I felt something was amiss, yes—did you see anything?" He was quiet and after a time I asked, "Was it another elemental?"

Pop shook his head. "No. It was bigger."

I dwelled on that for a moment, then nodded. "Thank you. If you notice it again and you can, would you tell me so that I can address it?"

"It heard you, but it fled." That was a relief, so I just thanked him again and shrunk the forge so that I could carry it inside without it being too much of a burden.

When I came into the tent, Nadir glanced up at me, then back at her book and I just laid on my pile of pillows before entering my trance-like state for rest.

———

How the boy had noticed my presence was beyond me, but the fact that the elemental had noted my watching was also concerning. Was I losing my ability to watch them as they grew more powerful?

I shook my head. *No, that can't be. The girl is much stronger than the boy and I can read her mind.* I stared at her as she read her book, flicking the pages until she got to where she wanted to be, then read some more. *Could it be what makes it so that I can't read his mind that alerts him to my presence? It could be possible. Unlikely—but not impossible.*

I would need to lay low for a little while, and truly shore up my skills to keep out of their sight.

Another page flipped, and I noted a word on it that made no sense. It looked to be scrawled onto it in ink that had been dried hurriedly with sand.

Nadir stopped and touched it, muttering the word when a

large creature appeared in front of her. This one looked like it could easily swallow her, but the problem wasn't its proximity to her, it was what she had said.

She scowled and motioned toward the door, the creature going out before her, but having to shift its shape in order to do so.

It changed back as soon as it came through the door and backed away so that she could step into the dark of night.

"Who are you?" Nadir spoke calmly and the creature just watched her. "What are you doing here?"

It motioned at her with a massive paw, then dropped the appendage to its side and waited. While it was in the light of the waxing moon, I could see it resembled an Ursolon, but had a set of antlers almost like a moose, each of the points coming to an almost metallic, spear-like point.

"Me?" Nadir pointed to herself and the antlers dipped. "So that was your true name that I spoke."

The creature continued to watch her until Nadir spoke again. "The book I found your name in was one that I was reading to find out more about dungeons. Do you know about them?"

The creature considered her for a short amount of time and then nodded once.

"Can you tell me how to find the closest one?" The creature stared again then she lowered her voice. "If you will allow me to bind you to myself, I will strike your name from that book and only utter it in times of true need, unless you have other stipulations you wish to provide."

The creature huffed and knelt down, a baritone voice so low it resembled more of a growl than anything else. "I serve the Healer. If the Healer needs a dungeon, then I will find one for them."

That was it. That was how I would be able to make my presence known while being able to maintain my vigil! Oh, this was going to be so much easier now.

Just had to find the right time to place the 'name' that would summon me.

With that, I just grinned to myself and watched as the creature Nadir had summoned disappeared with the wind and she returned to her reading.

CHAPTER TWELVE

I came out of my trance to find Nadir sleeping on her pillows, surprisingly, so I simply pulled out the links and shears and began my work in silence. I clipped them for a time, but once I was certain she would stay asleep, I went back outside to make more since it was quiet still and only in the early morning hours.

I was able to melt, pour, mold, then cool another set of links, and then began melting another portion of mithril before my sister woke and joined me outside. She stared into the sky for a long moment before muttering something to herself and nodding. "I found one."

I turned to her and frowned but she corrected herself. "Several, but the closest one to here is newer. I think that something happened here that made a lasting mark on the land and that mark grew into one."

"So where do we go?" She pointed to the other side of the mountain and I frowned. "The eastern side of the mountain? Isn't there just another plateau there?"

Her head dipped and she looked toward the tent, then

frowned. "And a former village of sorts, yes." She walked back in, then poked her head out. "Breakfast is here."

I grunted and poured the last set of links I would make for the day before I went inside and cleaned my hands to eat.

"Do you think we will be okay going into it?" My question made her pause her chewing and think. "You said it wasn't that old, so that means it hasn't had the time to really grow all that much, right?"

"I think we will need to exercise caution, but we should investigate it, certainly." She frowned and finished the food on her plate before adding, "Just because it isn't ancient doesn't mean that it's necessarily weak. From what I read, dungeons grow stronger when the creatures they create manage to kill whatever enters, or for being left alone for long periods to absorb ambient mana in the area around them."

"Okay, but there aren't many people up here who could go into it, right? So that's a non-issue."

Nadir shook her head and stated, "Monsters can go into them as well. The book said if the monster is of a certain level and stays there for a time, then they take over the dungeon and can repopulate the dungeon in their image around their level, and the environment of the dungeon changes."

I grunted again and ate some more of the eggs on the platter in front of me before tossing a bit to the shadow goblins and sighed before speaking, "So we go in cautiously and if things are too tough, we leave?"

She thought about it, then nodded. "I can agree to that. I will be able to keep us healthy and strong, but we cannot throw ourselves into too much risk."

"With the power you inherited, you're stronger than me. I don't think we need to be overly cautious." She narrowed her gaze at me and I just shook my head, trying not to sound overtly chagrined. "I was there, Nadir. I saw his power transfer to you."

"I only have so much access to it." That was all she could say and I just shrugged. Finally, she said, "I know I'm stronger than you, Azlo, but you didn't have to say that."

I stood and brushed my legs off to rid myself of crumbs before coming to where she sat to flop down next to her. "I don't say it to deride, or mock you. I don't want to be on your good side to curry power or favor. I know you don't want that with me. I just want there to be honesty between us about this."

"I kept it to myself out of habit." She ducked her head and heaved a great sigh before adding, "I'm so used to having to do it all myself. It's hard to confide in people who have to rely on you."

I nodded. "I know. Every maid, guard, being in the Court had their own goals in interacting with me all the time. The only ones I could truly be myself with were you, Mother, Vrawn, and the dwarves." I put a hand on her shoulder and squeezed gently. "There's no need to worry about that. Out here, we're just siblings. So please, let me help you."

She nodded, no words coming to her, and we just sat there for a time in silence and enjoyed each other's company. After half an hour or so, she cleared her throat. "We should move on. The sooner we conquer this dungeon, the easier it will be to do more for ourselves."

"Agreed." I smiled and helped her to her feet. We gathered the items we wanted to keep on ourselves and ready before leaving the tent and I willed it to return to its folded-up shape before stowing it away for safekeeping.

Moving around the mountain was a little more difficult, so I began to train myself in the uses of my manipulation skills, taking the stone and trying to make better pathways for us to follow.

It was nearly impossible for me to do so without almost bottoming my mana out to make the smallest amount of headway. To experiment with it, I found some actual grass and loose dirt that grew on a slope and worked with that. It moved and shaped as I wished for it to.

"So that means that stone itself is outside your reach?" Nadir crossed her arms and stared at the shapes I made for a moment, then nodded to herself. "Good to know."

"Annoying, to say the least." It was hard to keep the sullenness from my tone. I could only manipulate loose dirt? How was I supposed to make stone spikes burst from the ground and gore my opponents, or throw rocks as big as my head by just thinking about it?

If all I had was my hammer for now, I would be severely limited in what I could do even if I was faster than your typical frontline fighter.

I decided that with this experiment a failure, I would dedicate time to working with my manipulation skills to find, at a minimum, what I could and could not do. It would take time from my craft, but an hour or two would be negligible in the grand scheme of things if I had more control.

What I needed was another weapon.

Thinking about the materials I had, it was daunting, for certain. The mithril I had was slated for my armor. I didn't have much Fae iron left and it was highly conducive to magic and mana. There were other types of metal I could use, but that was assuming I could find them.

If only I could do the things that Anisamara did with beast materials. Would Kayda count as a beast? For now, I would keep the things I had been given and see if the dungeon gave me anything.

We made the trek to the other plateau, clambering over the stone-faced mountainside with hands and feet gripping the rock for purchase. It wasn't the easiest thing, but we were strong enough to make it.

True to what she had said, there was an entire village around a stone structure that looked to me like it was some kind of temple.

Nadir stared at it just as I did and muttered, "That has to be it."

"I don't think it could be anything other than that." I grumbled to myself and stared into the village. "I can't sense anyone. The shadows here feel barren."

I continued to glare and finally decided that it should be safe and stepped forward into the unknown that lay before us.

"You can relax slightly," Nadir whispered to me, a slight glint of amusement in her gaze. "This place has been empty for a long time if the state of disrepair is to be believed, that and the significant lack of any sort of scents."

I lifted my nose, nostrils flaring as I agreed with her; it smelled dead here.

"Okay, let's go ahead and get inside to get this over with." She nodded at my statement and we were on our way cautiously through the village.

The houses around us still succeeded in making my hair stand on end, as the eerie silence and breezy air carried many sounds from the world below toward us.

Inside the stone structure was an entrance built into the ground with the bones of a massive avian creature standing sentry above it, wings sort of out in a protective manner, but it didn't move and the bones themselves looked more stone-covered than actual bones to me now.

Sighing, I jabbed my thumb onto my pocket knife's tip and smeared my wound across the door at our feet. The door released a rather large cloud of dust into the air before dropping inward to admit us to a set of stairs.

"Royalty first." Nadir smiled at me when I turned to glare at her briefly before walking down the stone stairs first.

The first floor of the dungeon was empty, nothing there except a high ceiling in a sky-painted stone. There was plenty of room to fly, and I wondered if Kayda would have been able to move freely here, but there was nothing to find.

There were only rocks taller than a man and thicker than Winterheart's massive head.

It was just too hard to keep the smile off my face as I muttered to Nadir, "Odds are good there are enemies behind those stones that mean to ambush us."

"I would take that action." The rocky ground around us had plenty of stones for one of us to pick up, and she did. She hefted a large one and when she heaved it toward the large rock on the right, it cracked against it and a medium-sized bird-like creature jumped out with wings aflutter as it screeched and realized there was nothing there.

If it weren't for the three others that joined it, I would have lost all my bearing and heaved myself to the ground with how hard I wanted to laugh. It had clearly been waiting so long that any noise it heard prompted a response.

Instead, I chuckled to myself and willed Shaper to grow to the size of a slightly larger-than-normal battle hammer and launched myself forward.

The stones were only forty feet from us, so crossing that distance was easy when I pushed myself toward them. The three that berated the one who gave away their position had their backs to me for only a second before my hammer crushed one of their skulls and the body crumpled to the ground.

The three remaining turned and screeched at me in unison, their wails painful to my sensitive ears.

Wailing Believer Lvl 7

The name drifting over their heads made me pause. Were those what they were called? I'd never seen anything like this before.

I blinked and threw myself to the ground as a wing slashed toward my head, the feathers there slicing into the stone near where I had been. Glowering at them, I kicked out at their legs before two of them jumped and I hopped back to my feet while swinging my hammer at the one still trying to slash at me.

I shrank Shaper and pointed the top of the head at the Believer before willing it to grow again. It sprang forward and slammed into its chin, knocking it backward and onto the ground where I stomped on its throat. Experience rushed into me and I smiled.

The hammer was a great hammer at this point and there was no way I would be able to reach the bird creatures where they were now, with them fighting more than twenty feet in the air.

"Would you like some help?" Nadir's call was unassuming enough that it didn't feel like it was a jab or a barb, just matter of fact. Like she was perfectly willing to step in and assist me if I asked.

"No thank you. I want to try something, though I think it will be a little mana intensive, so could you make sure nothing sneaks up on me?"

"Alright."

———

Me again! You missed me, just admit it.

Nadir watched as Azlo lowered his weapon and took a deep breath. The girl could easily see the mana around him shifting as his will gathered inwardly and then crept forward. His range with Manipulation spells was somewhat limited, but he could still use it.

The air in the dungeon floor suddenly shifted and the bird-like humanoids shifted as well, the wind swept from beneath their wings. One of them plummeted to the ground where her brother waited with a lopsided, triumphant grin on his face as he swung his hammer as hard as he could.

The Believer above the falling one used that time to attack, dropping into a dive that would have been dangerous even if Azlo hadn't been distracted by the first one.

Nadir's heart pounded as she watched her brother kill one, but took a hit from the other on the shoulder that could have been avoided.

She knew. She knew that he needed to make these mistakes to learn from them and that it was her job to actually heal him when he needed it, but it was still hard to allow it to happen. Learning to fight together could wait until he was a little stronger, so for now, she would observe and take notes on how he liked to fight and adjust her fighting style to his where she could.

He took the slash and hissed before twisting and lashing

out with his left foot, catching the recovering bird-creature in the hip. That slammed it against the rock behind it, blood flowing from a cut on the back of its head as he loomed over it.

Azlo hefted the hammer and swung it down as the creature slashed once more with an oddly sharpened wing. He took the hit on his hip, but managed to crush its skull before it did much else.

He heaved a sigh and looked back at me. "I suppose this is where you tell me what I did was dangerous?"

Nadir smiled. "If you are asking me that, then I suppose I don't need to."

He grimaced as the young orc waved her hand in his direction and the wounds knitted themselves back together, his health points climbing back to full with them. "Thank you."

"I find no fault in your reasoning, just your range." She nodded to the fallen enemies. "They were able to fly over you, but you had to dip into your mana just to make it so that they couldn't fly. That had to be hard. How much mana did you use?"

He glowered and replied, "More than I would have wanted to."

Nadir nodded. "Very well. I will take care of any avian opponents who happen to go into the sky out of your reach, and you can take care of land-locked ones. Is this acceptable?"

Azlo nodded to her and she smiled. "Thank you. Should we form a party?" Nadir shook her head at his question, so he asked, "Why?"

"All of the experience is wasted on me, so I will just force them down, and then once they are within range, you take care of them." She stilled, thinking about something for a while and finally decided on saying, "My master's power augments mine and makes me stronger. I would like you to experience the gains of this venture for now."

He accepted that explanation for now, and grunted, "Fine."

Nadir shook her head, her brother's nearly-dwarven

mannerisms making her think ruefully of how formal he would one day need to be.

"Come, let's collect what we can and then move on."

Azlo bent and began to look at the wings of the monsters as his sister did the same. They were sharp, sure, but they were still flimsy to the touch if you were to touch anything but the edges.

Nadir stood and began to walk the room, looking along the walls to see if there was anything hidden, but found nothing.

They went into the floor boss's room only to find another one of the Believers in there, but this one could actually cast spells which made Azlo's attempts to get to it more annoying for him. Nadir thought it good training, as it would cast one spell to buffet him backward when he got too close, then send waves of air at him that cut at his clothing and skin with a dagger that looked to Nadir like it was carved with wind symbols.

He took a couple such cuts before getting irritated and throwing his hammer up above the creature. It merely side-stepped and slashed the air with a dagger that sent another air slice as it landed harmlessly next to it. He ran straight at the wave and then disappeared for a heartbeat.

He'd changed his form! His claws as a fox skittered over the stone underneath the attack as he shifted back in time for the monster to try to shove him backward. This time, his mana aura whipped out and sloughed the defensive maneuver off to the side, leaving him charging forward with a roar.

His hand found his hammer as the Believer tried to fly up into the air, but he managed to grab it and yank it back down as it screamed. Once it was on the ground, he beat it with the hammer until it was a bloodied paste smeared against the stones in a way that reminded Nadir of a child playing with their food.

He huffed, angrily pulling his weapon from the creature's splattered gray matter and flicked his wrist. Gooey, wet, crimson rain shook onto the ground and left the hammer almost pristine as he glanced back at Nadir.

"Well?" His gaze was steady, curious.

Nadir cleared her throat and, with a smirk, stated, "Clever

with the shifting, the boss didn't expect that at all. Neither had I. Throwing your weapon like that was a poor choice, but getting closer to it did have a requirement, and distracting it with a lost weapon or a missed attack worked nicely." Nadir tapped a finger on her hip and added, "I think having an off-hand weapon for that would prove a better strategy than throwing the only one you have."

He nodded and reached down toward his heel before standing straight and grinning as he waggled the dagger that the boss had been using. "Looks like that's taken care of for now."

He glanced over it and grimaced. "This has to be dungeon-made, but it's poor quality for certain. The edges are barely even sharp? This wouldn't cut a fly!"

Azlo sat on the ground and pulled out a small stone and some cloth, then spat on the stone and began to run the edge of the blade over it.

While he was distracted, Nadir went to the body and took a bit of the blood to wipe on the door that led further down.

It opened and she waited as her brother tended the weapon he had just collected. It only took ten minutes for the budding smith to finish his self-imposed task but when he was done, it was clear that he was happier with it.

He twitched his wrist and the wave of wind that surged from it was faster and sharper than it had been before. It gouged the stone and sliced the remains of the boss on the ground quite easily. A weapon with an effect like this would be very nice.

He smiled. "Lovely." He switched it for the knife he carried in his belt and put that one in his inventory before joining her. "Ready?"

She just nodded and onward they went.

CHAPTER THIRTEEN

At the entrance to the next floor, there was something carved into the door that I noticed right away, but it was confusing. All it appeared to be was a name.

I muttered it to myself under my breath as I read it, "Arimat?"

There was a fluttering as the door opened and just inside it stood a single raven, watching me.

"A Fae creature?" Nadir asked me and stared at it. "Did you summon it?"

I blinked at it and the bird opened its mouth. "He did!" The voice was much smoother than what I imagined a raven sounded like. "And I'm glad you did. This floor is going to be a bit of a doozy for you alone."

"Why?" I lowered my voice and put a tone of command in. "As holder of your true name, I demand the truth."

"I couldn't lie to you if I wanted to, *your Highness*." The raven cocked its head to the side in an almost sort of bow before answering me, "The creatures here are stronger than those above and use better magic and teamwork."

"Okay, so what do you suggest?" I tilted my head in a mirror of what he had done. "Should we run off?"

It shook its head. "That's up to you. I'm only here to serve the one who spoke my name."

"Very well, do you have a battle form?"

"I'm more of a watcher?" the raven retorted and hopped up onto my shoulder.

"You aren't bound to me." I flicked the creature off my shoulder. "Why would you be so familiar?"

All Fae creatures who served the royals or those they felt worthy of their time and service were bound to them by an oath of service and when this was given, it was okay to let your guard down around them; only a little though. And the more this one spoke, the more I got the feeling something about it was off. It was too friendly. Too eager to tell the truth, as if it was omitting things.

"I'm just an observer of sorts." The raven sounded like it was meant to be a jovial statement, then added, "I find creatures I think are interesting and go along with them."

"So wait." Nadir frowned and stepped forward to kneel in front of it. "You put your name there?"

It nodded. "After you did something so interesting fighting up there, I thought it would be worthwhile. What do you say? I could scout for you? I've also been known to give great advice and find things."

I could taste no lies in its statement and frowned. If it couldn't fight, then what use was it? A scout was okay, but when there was nothing to find, what use could there be? And once again, it was all too eager to help me.

I glared at it for a moment longer as it hopped from foot to foot. That last statement about finding creatures it liked and following sounded like the truth, so I glared at it then said, "Find any hidden treasure in this room, and I will consider allowing you to enter my service."

"Kill all of the enemies and I would be happy to do that for you."

"Let's go, Azlo." Nadir stood straight and walked past the raven, waiting for me to join her before muttering, "I will keep an eye on it while you fight."

She healed all of my aches once more as I prepared myself for combat.

This area was a wooded one of sorts, with a single copse of trees that stood in the center of the floor with simple earthen and sandy ground all around it. There were pieces of glass that stuck out of the ground at odd intervals, but other than that, there was nothing outside the unusual norm to consider.

Then monks stepped from the copse of trees and two small sparrow-like birds lifted from the center and sang a song of their own as they began to fly in my direction.

I could make out their levels as I stared at the five of them, and shuddered.

Tengu Lvl 9

I cracked my neck and sighed, with nothing to do other than attack or wait for one of the groups to get to me, I roared and sprang forward into a sprint.

The Tengu cried out in unison and copied my run. I didn't have my hammer in my hands yet, but as the birds approached above me, I ripped the dagger out and slashed in their direction. They separated and, as they did, a massive bolt of electricity seared the sky and speared the ground I rolled away from.

My voice rang out, "Nadir!"

"I have them, get the Tengu."

As soon as I was close to them, I lashed out again with the dagger and they all scattered and grouped up on me. As one was about to try to lash out at me with a foot, I shifted to my fox form and then back quickly to get under the leg. I twisted and stabbed him with the dagger, the blade biting into his ribs from behind as wind slashed into it from the swing.

The others were not so easily fooled, and I had to let the weapon go in order to defend against them.

Their punches and kicks were only dull aches and throbs in

the grand scheme of things, as far as the damage went, until the one of them that fell died and the others grew stronger.

A soft crackling made the hair on my arms stand on end before a fist covered in electricity slammed into my back and sent me reeling forward, only to be caught and shoved to the ground.

I shifted forms and skittered out of the way of two falling axe kicks, then doubled back and shifted into my fox-man form. Claws flashed and cut skin before I reached up to my hammer and clutched it in my hand. Once they were close enough to try to crowd me again, I willed it to grow in my hands and whipped Shaper into the closest one's chest.

It cried out and tried to breathe, but the hammer spun in my grip and the spike slid into its throat after that, killing it.

The other Tengu screeched in unison and their crackling fists went from looking like they were covered in static to true lightning and their feet began to crackle as well.

"This is getting annoying." I breathed and looked at the three of them, wondering who to attack first when I got an idea. Mobility was important to them, and I had recovered a good deal of my mana while I had worked on the blade of the dagger, so I had a trick up my sleeve.

I willed Shaper to get smaller, to the point that I could competently wield it with one hand and when I was close enough to them all, I acted. I willed the dirt beneath their feet to soften to the point that it became quicksand and clutched at their legs and feet.

They panicked, squawking and crying out as it pulled them lower. I didn't make it terribly deep, just deep enough that I could act. I stepped back and Shaper grew until it was a great hammer again and I swung like I was trying to break the world behind them.

The first one, I clipped in the head and broke its stringy neck. The second dipped backward and I missed, while the third only struggled and cawed before shoving its hands at me and a bolt of lightning arced toward me.

I whirled Shaper in front of me and let the wooden handle protect me as the head attracted the energy and slammed the spike into the caster's throat toward the feet, crushing the ribs and forcing it lower into the sand.

The last one screamed and lashed out, electricity spiking into my body hard enough that it flung me dangerously away and into one of the trees behind me. I didn't know when we had gotten that close to the copse of trees, but it hurt.

I growled, noting that I'd lost fifty-five percent of my total health in the fight.

Rather than getting into an up close and personal fight with the remaining, powered up Tengu, I turned and went to retrieve the dagger that I'd collected and began to slash at it from a distance. It blocked slash after slash, but eventually began to flag and waver. As soon as it did, I made Shaper shrink and threw the hammer at it behind three crossing slashes of wind that it fought to block.

One of the slashes landed, slicing a big bloody cut from shoulder to nape just before Shaper slapped it in the head. It teetered for a heartbeat and I surged forward, clawed hand at my hip before I skidded to a stop at the sandy ground and my hand shot forward.

Blood shot from the wound as my hand slipped through the rib cage and toward the heart, my blood thundering through me as I grasped the Tengu's heart and yanked it back out of the bony cage that held it.

The Tengu coughed up blood as I crushed the heart in my grasp and threw it to the ground with disdain, blood flecking the sandy earth.

"Wait," Nadir ordered and I stilled as her energy washed over me, my wounds closing and my HP rising to full once more. "That was reckless."

"I have few options." I had to admit, if I weren't trying to test my limits, I would have had Nadir assist me with the fight. Rather than arguing with her as she looked to be prepared for, I simply said, "I would like for you to assist in the next fight, if you can. Limit yourself so that I can still learn, but your assistance would be appreciated."

She bowed her head and said, "Very well."

I grunted. "Don't do that." I turned and called, "Raven! We kept up our side of the deal, now it's your turn."

The raven appeared in one of the branches of a tree within the copse of trees and opened its wings. "So it is! The bad news? There's nothing really here." I narrowed my eyes at it, and it did a bird-like shrug of sorts and stated, "I never said there would be. But if you want something valuable, lightning glass can be a highly prized component to crafters, so that's of value, yes?"

"It is, but that's skirting my desire." The raven stared at me. "Follow us to the next floor and you can prove yourself there."

We traveled to the boss room beyond the trees and were surprised to find that this was less a room as it was a cave.

At the back of the cave was a large, shadowed alcove and in it were two hatefully glowing yellow eyes. A hissing cluck greeted us as a monstrous form slowly emerged from the darkness.

Cockatrice Lvl 10

"Oh, this is going to be hard," Nadir muttered under her breath. "Bite can cause petrification on top of poisoning. They can breathe fire, and are hard to kill."

"If you need to step in, or have advice to kill this thing, I'd be amenable."

"Some legends say that making it bite itself will turn it to stone, or that looking at its own reflection will kill it," the raven called over the continually growing sound of the creature hissing angrily. "I would advise cooperative fighting for this, as most aren't any taller than the knee of your typical peasant."

I resolved to make a shield when I got the chance. A reflective one as well.

It reared back and the raven bellowed, "Fire!"

I seethed and pulled the dagger from my waist and sliced at the air in front of me where the flames licked and ate the oxygen. The wind slid through the fire and forced it away, but it seemed like the wind blades weren't as sharp as they had been.

It worked in my favor for now, but if it wasn't a viable defense, there was no point in carrying it.

The slices battered the flames aside as my mana assisted with Flame Manipulation keeping them from closing and hitting me or Nadir.

"On your right!" Nadir barked and I put Shaper between me and the tail that slipped through the fire to mitigate the blow as it sent me skidding to the left of the room.

I bellowed, "You want to distract it?"

"Fine, but don't get bitten!" She pulled out a weapon that I hadn't seen in years and launched an attack of her own. It flashed and the cockatrice screamed as its front leg fell to the ground.

Blood poured onto the stone floor as it snapped at her with teeth that reminded me more of a viper than of any bird I'd ever seen or heard of. The scales around its head shimmered and I could feel a pulse of warmth in the air.

The raven and I called out in unison, "Fire!"

Nadir heaved her axe into the creature at the same time I threw an enlarged Shaper at the thing's head but the weapon didn't hit nearly hard enough. That was fine.

It was enough of a distraction that it wasn't able to move out of the way in time to avoid Nadir's strike, or my attack.

I leaped into the air and stabbed the dagger into the cockatrice's throat where the scales turned into downy feathers. Blood gushed from it as I twisted the blade savagely and yanked it down toward the throat, dropping from my perch.

Blood splattered onto me, but other than a surprisingly cool feeling from it, I felt a revulsion that made me shiver as it fell to the ground.

It wheezed and fell to the ground and heaved as it tried to stand again but fell. I grabbed Shaper and hefted it, only to bring it down with all my might.

Nadir stopped me, her fingers flicking my attack away like I'd hit the side of the anvil and the hammer bounced aside.

"I want to collect some of this creature's material components so that I can either experiment with them, or make potions to ensure nothing can make good on the things that this creature can."

I blinked at her, seeing that it was clearly immobilized if not actually dead.

I kept my hands on Shaper, just in case it so much as shook the wrong way.

She pulled teeth, blood, saliva, feathers and even some of the scales and sinew from it before she put all of it into her inventory and then collected more.

It took the better part of an hour for her to be completely satisfied and as she stood, she motioned to the cockatrice. "It's regenerating slowly. I think the dungeon didn't know what it got itself into with this one. But until it's fully dead, we cannot move on from here."

I grimaced and looked into my inventory for a moment, unable to find anything that would serve well as a mirror. "Do you have a mirror with you?"

She shook her head and I sighed, perplexed. It was incensing that something of this irritating of a magnitude would be here within a dungeon.

I frowned. My breastplate wasn't completed, but it was just rough enough that I could use it to act as a mirror if I polished it, but that would take time.

"Can you keep injuring it while I work on a solution?"

She smiled. "Indefinitely. Do it right."

I nodded once and took out my items, but the raven cleared its throat. "There's a secret wall over here, if you need it. It looks to hold some things that could prove to be of value to you."

I frowned at it and followed it to a wall inside the 'cave' that the cockatrice had come from. Sure enough, there was a wall made of an illusion of some sort that held a single small chest within it.

I checked it for any sort of traps with some lockpicking tools that Rowland had suggested one day. "I donae like 'em, but donae mean swift fingers be a bad thing dealing with the wrong sort, aye?"

That had made me laugh as he waggled his eyebrows and made a show of moving his eyebrows jokingly.

I missed him already.

I picked the lock, taking about ten minutes or so to get through it, then looked inside. There were coins and moder-ately-sized chunks of ore that I wouldn't be able to clearly iden-tify without a good source of light, but I could be patient for that. The coins were only three gold and some change, nothing that would make anyone of my station overly happy.

There was a weapon inside as well. It was another dagger, this one made of bone and stone, it looked like.

Petrified Limb

+9 to attack

55% chance to partially petrify whoever the wielder injures with this weapon. The longer or more often the blade is introduced to the body and blood-stream, the more effective the petrification.

There was no created information for it, so I assumed it was created by the dungeon as a reward. It was a good one, for certain. The blade might even work against the creature outside the cave if we didn't need the blood to move on into the dungeon.

I checked the rest of the chest and found nothing else, so I left it and went back out to what I was doing. I put the breast-plate up to myself and began the process of fitting and ensuring that it would be snug enough with the clothes I had on. I would need to modify it with leather or thick cloth to ensure the beating it took was mitigated more.

For now, it would work for what we needed.

I measured it loosely to my figure based on the assumption I would gather the materials for it to be the best it could be.

Once I heated it and began my work, time faded away as I was enveloped by the work before me then put it back into the forge before setting up my oil quench.

It was just a large barrel that had been treated on the interior not to leak the liquid inside, and enchanted not to catch fire as well.

Once it was up to temperature, I pulled it from the flames as the elemental watched me, and dunked it into the oil.

Flames crackled out of the oil as I let the item sink and cool rapidly. This would give me time to get all of the materials I would need to sand and polish the piece's interior to act as our mirror.

Sanding was easy enough, and then there was the paste that I had to use to continue to polish it. The whole process took hours of work and when I was finished, the ground around the floor boss was drenched in blood.

Nadir looked completely fine as she read a book and finally looked up at me as I came closer. "Finished?"

I nodded and grunted. "We're going to need light bright enough to make it see itself."

"There is time yet before it recovers enough to be able to see." She closed her book and looked over it, then sighed. "It's been long enough that your mana should be recovered a good amount and mine is plentiful. I am going to cast a minor healing on it after we make enough light to speed things up."

I nodded and we got to work. She cast a spell that made flickering torches appear around us, and I used Elemental Manipulation to make the spectral light converge together above the cockatrice, making the mirror glow with enough light that I could see my own reflection in it, albeit hazily.

Nadir put a hand on my shoulder and said, "We can kill it again if needed, so that you can perfect the sheen of the metal, but we have to try."

She reached down and placed a finger on it as a pulse of mana left her and entered the creature's head. We backed up and I held the breastplate up to its face. It lifted its head and blinked before a horrible guttural gasping groan escaped from its gullet.

My breath caught in my throat as it began to shake and writhe until its eyes filmed over and turned a patchy white color. Once that petrification was complete, the neck relaxed and it fell to the ground.

Nadir reached out and took both of the eyes and put them into her inventory before taking her blood-stained fingers and smearing them on the exit. The doors opened and she looked back at me. "We can rest if you need it, but I suggest moving into the stairwell and have something to eat before continuing on."

I dipped my head to her and collected my tools, putting them away before picking up the breastplate and doing the same.

We ate on our way down the stairwell, just something to keep hunger from gnawing at our bellies, and finally, once we reached the door at the bottom, we noted it was much larger than the others.

Nadir lifted her hand to stop me touching it and opened her book. "This is the final boss of the dungeon. But it was only two floors above us, most dungeons are larger."

"Maybe it has something to do with how strong or weak this dungeon is?" My observation was mild, but I explained a bit more cautiously, "It's out of the way, in an abandoned village on top of a mountain, and it doesn't look like there's been anyone here recently."

"There's not been, I'm afraid. This dungeon is also fairly young too. The creatures were strong because of the emotional attachment to the area by someone or something stronger than it." The raven stared around, then looked at me. "Have I not proven myself?"

I glared at it for a moment, then sighed. "You have. What

name shall I call you, and what are the terms of this binding from where you stand?"

"All I want is to watch over you both." The raven shook out its wings and stared from me to Nadir. "An interesting adventure is all I seek. I'll help you as I can, and all you have to do is let me tag along."

I stared at him for a long moment, unable to help the feeling that it just wasn't telling me something, before looking over at my sister. "I couldn't taste any lies. Did you feel or taste anything?"

Nadir shook her head. "I think they genuinely believe what they're saying to be the truth." She folded her arms over her chest and added, "That makes them both naïve and potentially dangerous. There's no way to really stop them, other than forbidding them to be near us."

"So the only way to keep an eye on me is to keep me close!" The raven genuinely seemed proud of that point as its eyes flashed from my face to hers and then back again.

I glared at the little beast and sighed softly. "Fine, you can come."

"Yay!" Their wings fluttered excitedly. "You won't regret this!"

"I know I won't." I grinned wolfishly and the raven audibly gulped.

CHAPTER FOURTEEN

Me again! You love it when I'm telling the story, don't you?

This boy... I grumbled to myself as he stared me in the eyes with the confidence his mother wielded effortlessly. "I bind myself to you, by name and by calling, to serve you to the best of my ability."

"And?" he goaded gently. Really, he was just ensuring I repeated the statement as it was, but I was so annoyed because this was an oath I hadn't expected to work. If it did, I was okay, but if it didn't, it would be noted. Luckily, he was unbound to another Fae, so there was a chance that I could pull one over on him.

"I do hereby bind myself to the name..." I stared at him for a long moment, hoping that he would change his mind, but he just stared, so I sighed and said, "Midnight."

Saying the name made my skin crawl and my feathers ruffle on their own, so I just tried to keep my disdain to myself as I could, but even I had to admit it would be evident to the blind.

Warning!
You have given your word and bound yourself to

royalty of the Unseelie Court. Breaking this bond or your word in any way outside the service of your new master will result in the dissipation of your being and the accumulation of power for them.

However...

That made me frown and blink as I read on.

Your new master has an obligation to uphold your safety and use your skills to their maximum advantage given. They are duty bound to protect you as you are them; they cannot abuse you or your abilities without risking their lordship over you. This bond is sacred to both ruler and the bound—treat it as such. All parties have been warned.

I frowned more, and if it weren't for the beak I currently wore, it would have deepened to the point my lips would hang from my face.

She said it would be hard, watching over them—she didn't say it would be this hard.

Still, this allowed me proximity without the boy questioning me, and the girl was ignorant of my being near her. She had always been ignorant of me. I'd seen more of her than her own mother ever had, and was proud of her for her skill and knowhow.

Oh well. "You know, this next fight could be really hard."

They both looked at me as I hopped forward and shifted my wings. The boy asked, "How so? What can you tell us?"

"Remember the bird you saw on the way in?" They blinked and the boy nodded. "That."

"You are sure?" Nadir frowned at me and I nodded. "How do you know?"

"I can feel it waiting nearby. One of the things I have going for me." They continued to stare at me then turned to one another.

Nadir spoke first. "There is no way you can fight something like that on your own."

The boy actually grinned at her and then said, "I'm not

alone, am I?" He patted her shoulder and turned to me. "Let's go."

They walked in as the corpse of the Lightning Roc rose from the ground, shambling corpses of goblins scrambling under foot. The roc screeched a horrible, pitiable cry, almost as if it was mourning something.

The goblin zombies' shrieking gave a chorus-like feeling to it. As if they added to the larger creatures' frustration and pain, it brought a hollow ache to my own bird-like chest.

"That's huge," Azlo observed in an underwhelming kind of way. For such an observant and bright boy, he had a way of letting himself speak too soon sometimes.

"It is." Nadir nodded once and pulled her favored weapon out. It was her father's first truly enchanted weapon. He'd named it Storm Caller and it had been made from materials collected from the creature they faced now.

She held it in one hand, the mass of bones before them both rising to full height as she took a deep breath. She closed her eyes and growled to her brother, "This one is strong. At least a level higher than you. I have read nothing like this in my book. If you will let me, I will end it before it can be a threat."

"You can help, but I want this. I need the power too." Azlo cracked his neck, almost making me gag at the crunching noise, and stepped forward as he made his own weapon grow larger. "Keep it busy while I deal with the goblin zombies."

Nadir tensed her muscles and jerked her shoulder before grunting. "Very well."

Azlo launched himself forward and into the squadron of undead goblins before him, hammer leading the charge as he bellowed. Both of the children looked to have a severe hatred of the little creatures for some reason, Azlo's hammer decimating the force he battled with an ease that was surprising, to say the least, a number of them falling with each swing of his mighty weapon.

The gigantic roc that tried to fling itself into the air had a difficult time working against Nadir, even with her sometimes dropping to the ground to pick off one of the smarter zombies, odd as that thought seemed.

Rotting flesh failed to keep its composition as the heavy weapon blasted exposed bones to dust and congealed blood was hardly an issue as the prince stormed his way through the slowly falling crowd in a whirl of metallic hatred.

It took moments for him to finish with his prey and turn to the roc as it continued the one-sided battle with his sister and that was interesting to see, as his face became a mask of confusion. From the looks of it, those creatures gave no experience, but he was less concerned with that and more concerned with the Roc.

"It looks kind of like…" I fluttered closer to him and he just shook his head, focusing on the fight. "I'm going to go ahead and try to keep it grounded so we can kill it!"

Azlo took no more than two steps before the flesh on the ground slithered up the legs of the undead skeleton before them and began to make a gross-looking version of what the creature could have been previously.

Mother's Remorse Lvl 13

The wing that Azlo would have attacked lashed out and struck him and Shaper away from the massive creature, sending him rolling through the discarded and flesh of the fallen.

He rolled back onto his feet and snarled before sprinting back toward the enemy. Nadir's power flooded him and he was topped off on health before he leaped as high as he could with Shaper's spike presented.

The spike pierced the wing that had slapped him away, and the dungeon boss screamed in fury before lifting the injured appendage and spreading it to try to get the boy to leave it be.

Nadir growled and whipped her axe at the beast, the blade slicing through the creature's neck with ease, killing it where it was about to take off.

"Nadir!" Azlo called in disbelief as the giant undead bird fell to the ground dead.

"It was too tempting, Azlo, my apologies." She didn't want

to say what she was really thinking, I knew. She had seen the mana radiating from it that was going into the ground. It was about to summon an army of the dead, and she had stopped it before they were overrun.

She would have been fine, but it would have been more than her brother could handle at his present ability.

A chest appeared where the creature fell, shrinking into the ground and dissipating into nothingness.

"Open the chest, Azlo." Nadir sighed as the boy just stared at her with naked disappointment. "It's the least I could do for stealing your fun and level."

He just rolled his eyes and opened it, pillaging what was inside. "Looks like a sword, bones, a crystal of some kind that has no status, and then seventeen gold."

Nadir frowned. "Stats on the sword?"

"Basic stuff, but it looks like it has an enchantment to make it harder?" He frowned and examined it. "Something called diamond crust?"

"That should be interesting to use at least, right?" He shrugged noncommittally and put the items in his inventory. Nadir turned her sights on me and asked, "Can you sense any hidden rooms or anything here?"

I blinked and closed my eyes, casting my sense out. There was the dungeon core itself, which was only about ten feet or so from where we were, six feet down in the ground, which I mentioned and then frowned. "Nothing else at the moment. The place isn't old enough or strong enough to have access to the minerals and veins of ore that surround it. If it were better established, then the dungeon would be able to grow stronger. Sorry."

Nadir looked at her brother. "You can take the core if you like."

"What use would I have for it?"

She shrugged. "I thought it could make an interesting material component for a weapon or item you could craft. They have a way of naturally pulling mana into themselves."

"That would destroy this dungeon, would it not?" He lifted a brow and stared at the two of us and I nodded, so he added, "Couldn't that be dangerous?"

"The extra space would be concerning if we were to just take it and leave, or put it in your inventory. As long as we leave with it out in the open, it would be fine." My explanation seemed to be enough for him and he had me show him where it was.

The boy had to dig manually as the core fought to keep all alien magic away from itself and to hide. Unfortunately for it, it wasn't permitted to move from where it was when someone was inside the dungeon. It had to watch through proxies or monsters.

Usually they hid themselves in the rooms with the most devious traps, or the smarter ones hid in the easiest floors to keep themselves safe, but this one had been one of the former and hid with the strongest monster.

The core was a small rock-like crystal with amber and jet streaked markings that Azlo grinned manically when he plucked it from the ground.

"It speaks!" He laughed and looked at it curiously before tossing it to Nadir. "It keeps threatening me to put it back or it will kill me. I have to make it into a weapon. Or maybe I'll make it into a shield and let it take a beating for me?"

Nadir shook her head and grunted. "Whatever you decide, make sure you don't let it speak to you this way. What foul words come from this thing."

She tossed it back to her brother, and they began the track upward and out of the dungeon. Without being attached to the dungeon by touch anymore, any and all attempts to reach out to its surroundings were fruitless and pointless. The core was taken. Once they exited the domain it had once claimed, it would take all that energy back into itself and be terribly exciting as a material component.

I had to say, things were looking exciting already.

CHAPTER FIFTEEN

Once the three of us had cleared the entrance to the dungeon unmolested and recovered, it was easy to see how so many competent adventuring parties could have fallen victim to the very dungeons they delved.

As soon as we stepped from the dungeon with the core in hand, there was a voluminous, violent, venting sound as the mana was sucked back into the material in my hand.

It began to warm where it was until the entrance was gone and the bones that had stood as a means to denote the entrance slowly becoming less stone-like and more decayed until there was only a wisp of true bone left.

I collected that, then put it into my inventory along with the core.

"Where do we go now, north?" Nadir nodded at my question and I glanced over at Midnight. "Do you happen to know of a way we could travel faster?"

"You could always try to summon an elemental for it?" The bird shrugged, then frowned. "Or another Fae creature. Did you not go through the ancestral dungeon?"

Nadir stared at it for a moment then answered, "No, we

have time before that happens to do something of our own, but trying to get a mount was why we had gone into this dungeon in the first place." She grimaced and said, "Summoning other Fae would be messy just to have mounts."

"There are whistles one can obtain, for an exorbitant fee, that will summon a mount that will bind to your soul if you want?" Midnight closed their eyes and sniffed the air. "It's too hard to smell anything with that massive spatial fissure so close."

"Even with the bindings and barriers?" The bird nodded and Nadir grimaced and said, "We should probably avoid it then, just to be certain. There will likely have been cities erected in the area as well to take in the refugees."

"Some, but none close." The raven fluttered to the northern wall of the room and passed through the stone, forcing us out into the windy plateau in order to follow. We found him perched nearly horizontally on the stones below the plateau, looking northward. "There are some small towns on the edges of the battlefield where all the demons were slain; demon blood has a way of making things a little more barren and dangerous. Some of the creatures that roam the plains around the barrier are a little more brutal and mindless than their cousins in other places."

"Mindless?" I raised a brow at that. That was usable.

Nadir nodded and we were off down the side of the plateau without a word to each other.

———

We found the barren area near the barrier, the vast purple expanse of it cutting into the sky for what looked like miles around. I knew better than that, but still, the sheer size and density of it was impressive. Even from this distance, I could see that the thickness warped the image of what lay beyond in a way that kept people from prying too much, at least from where we were.

It neared dark on the second day when we decided that

making camp would be a good idea. Nadir walked the area of our camp, setting up a string trap that would be easily avoided by intelligent creatures.

I worked on my chainmail for a time, adding links, heating them as I finished so that they formed the mesh that I needed them to. It was slow and delicate work at times, but when I was finished, it would prove worthwhile. Certainly, I could have had armor made for me, but how else would I learn? This was a great training exercise.

It was well and truly into night when the first animal came toward us. Some kind of giant lizard of some sort. Not exactly an iguana, from the books that I had studied about the animals in the Prime plane, but it was more streamlined. Almost like a monitor of some sort, the purple tongue that flickered forward tasting the air around the camp was long and slim, but insistent as it searched.

"That one?" Nadir asked and I shrugged. If it wasn't suitable for a mount, we could always kill it and use it as bait for something better.

Nadir walked out of our tent and stared at it. "Level twenty Blight Lizard. I think I could tame it for myself, but with it being so much stronger than you, it would likely try to kill you any time you touch it."

"Can you check to see how fast it is?"

She nodded and rushed at it with a hand outstretched, the creature hissing and slapping her with its tail as she grabbed it and pushed it backward to the edge of my being able to see. There was a rather loud hissing noise and then a snarling hiss and all fell quiet.

Nadir walked back covered in blood and hit me with a soft smile. "It was faster than walking, but too foul-tempered. We may not find anything for you here, but I think I might have found some creatures in the outskirts that I wouldn't mind trying for."

I looked down at the links that I had in my lap. "Need me to help at all?"

She shook her head. "Just have Midnight watch over you."

I nodded and the bird Fae took up a post above me, watching curiously as I worked, my fingers and small hammer working diligently and dexterously.

Finally, they couldn't keep quiet and spoke. "What is it that you hope to become with your class?"

I stilled, wondering if this probing question had alternative ends. "What do you mean?"

"I've watched you for a time, Forge Sorcerer, and I have to say that the class seems interesting. But the abilities you have, while seemingly intuitive, are far from it." Midnight hopped down closer. "That flame elemental you have in your forge is stronger for being near the enchantments that keep it strong and fed longer, yet you add more food to keep it happy. Smart."

I stayed quiet for a time and finally it said, "I suppose you meant to try to find an earth elemental to affix to that armor? Likely to give you some defense, right?"

"And?" It was hard to keep the challenge out of my voice as I growled that at it. "So what if I meant to do that?"

"How many elementals can you call into one item?" That was a rhetorical question, it had to be, because I didn't even know. "Not sure? As creative as you are, you could be making this armor with the wind elementals in mind."

I frowned at the bird and it croaked before continuing, "Evasion, even flight are possible if you get a strong enough one and the right kind of enchantment, or spell."

"I don't know any spells." It was even harder to keep the annoyance and bitterness out of my tone there.

"I doubt that." The bird smiled with its beak and tilted its head at me again. "You manipulate the elements well for someone only used to a couple of them."

That made me still. "How long have you been watching us?"

"I'm under no obligation to reveal that information." I stilled again and turned to actually affix Midnight with my gaze and he laughed. "But I will tell you because I want to—for a while now, ever since I learned of your existence."

"Why?"

If a bird could shrug, they had just done so before answering, "The children of strange outworlders, a Fae queen and an orcish... bath attendant? Come on, there can't be too many more interesting things to look into than that, can there?"

I narrowed my gaze at it. "Why are you telling me this now? It makes you sound bad."

Midnight blinked. "I wanted to. I find your class fascinating, and I want to help you succeed so I can see where it goes?"

"Why does that sound more like a question than a statement?"

Midnight cawed, laughter coming from it again. "Because I request to be able to assist you. If you were to tell me to leave it alone, I would happily do so at your behest."

"What do you know of crafting like this?" I stopped working and stared at it. "Of the trappings of my class?"

"That the sorcerers of old were much less confined the way you are." The bird hopped onto the ground to look more closely over my work. "They were powerful in their rights. They channeled a more specific element type, better and with greater mana reserves, but this allows you greater diversity."

Inwardly, I seethed, but outwardly, I just dryly stated, "While limiting my ability to do anything." With careful thought, I added, "I cannot even cast spells."

The raven blinked at me in surprise. "Oh, that's not good." It blinked at me then frowned to itself before saying, "Permission to change forms, sir?"

Curious, I allowed it with a simple, "Granted."

The bird form shimmered and turned into a rather lanky, tall man with a bald head and a jacket of black feathers that dusted the ground at his feet. He knelt and looked up at me, ghostly purple eyes questing.

Other than his eyes, his features were no more notable than a passerby on the street or a no one in a city.

Finally, he asked, "The elementals you bond to, have you never thought about forming pacts with them?"

Pacts? Pacts were things that the powerless used to borrow power from the powerful. Some of the Fae took great delight in forming pacts with strings attached in ways that formed webs that ensnared the 'beneficiary' in ways that made it impossible to make the power their own.

They usually ended up being nothing more than glorified servants with no will of their own. But part of my class already allowed me to make them with elementals for the weapons I made, so why would they suggest something that was already a feature I could use but haven't been able to yet?

But here Midnight was saying that I could possibly do that?

I looked at the ground when he looked up and stood. "Prepare to defend yourself, master. Something approaches."

Grimacing, I tossed down my work and held Shaper tighter as I glared out into the darkness into the fetid yellow eyes of whatever creature stared back.

CHAPTER SIXTEEN

Whatever it was padded over the line with the bells attached with an unnerving ease as it stared at me. There was a scented musk to it, and as it entered the dimly-lit area of the camp, I could see what that musk was—lizard blood and viscera trailed down its jawline and onto its chest.

The fur around its head was stained crimson as it stopped growing lower along its chest where a scaly, sickly looking abscess-covered skin was.

Barren Hound Lvl 21

Its pale and gross-looking skin was unnerving, but it still had muscle that was clearly defined, and along its legs were thorn-like protrusions that grew from its flesh all the way to its paws, where they looked thickest and dripped with a yellow pus.

That could have been the source of the scent as well.

"Midnight, get Nadir if you can."

The bird took off, running closer to the beast than he should have, which gave me a precious distraction that I needed to charge around the tent away from the animal. It barked continuously as it gave chase until I got to the inside of the tent toward the middle of the camp and stood my ground.

The hound skidded to a halt as it found me, then barged into the tent where I rolled out of the way and then shut the flap to secure it. No one could open it except the ones who were tied to it, so this should theoretically be able to hold it. Anything destroyed inside would be fixed when the space was shrunken down and restored. I breathed a sigh of relief that was quickly snuffed out by more barking and growls coming from the ebon night around me from several directions at once.

Chill speared down my spine and I rolled backward, letting my feet fly over my head so that I could stand again. One of the hounds that had found me had flown over me and just missed, some of the pus from it splattering my shirt and making it stink.

I whipped Shaper into the creature's rear leg, barely doing two percent damage to its health bar, and it whirled on me just to be attacked by another as two more entered the fray and tried to get to me. There was no way I could open the flap and get them all in.

"Nadir!" My call was punctuated by me trying to attack the hound that ventured too close to me, only to bat away the hammer and tackle me to the ground.

Claws pierced my flesh as I fought to keep the slobbering creature from biting into me, but it was much stronger than I was. I just *knew* that disgusting pus would be leaking into my wounds. Healing was going to be terrible.

Seeing that the two squabbling with the one that attacked me after exiting the tent were beginning to back off, there was little room for something to go wrong, and I was running low on time.

I willed my hammer to shrink, then shoved the head into the hound's gullet and willed it to grow, fast. The weapon grew and the spike shot up through the hounds upper jaw and into the brain, disabling it, but it wasn't fully dead. There was a paralysis symbol under the health bar that let me know it wasn't a threat, at least for now.

One of the other hounds grabbed my leg in its jaws and pulled me back, the tendons straining and popping as I fought the stronger enemy. I willed Shaper to shrink once more, but it was stuck and blood coated it, making it slip from my grasp.

I reached down and plucked the wind dagger from the sheath on my hip, stabbing at the hound that bit me, only to be grabbed by one of the others on my shoulder. My grip slackened, so I tossed the weapon up slightly, grabbing it by the hilt and blade. The pain was annoying, but manageable as I slammed my weapon and fist into the nostril of my second attacker.

Minimal damage all around, but it was Nadir appearing over me with wild eyes that made my heart stutter.

Her tusks bared, she roared and, with a swipe of her fist, all of the hounds fell as her mana surged into me.

My wounds healed, but the ones on my chest burned painfully as the pus and rot were cleansed and pushed out of my body.

I grunted a terse, "Thank you," as she beat the hounds to death with her bare hands.

She finished a few seconds later, and looked me over with her hands and eyes, much more intensively than I cared for.

"You'll recover, but you'll feel weak for a bit." She turned and found the hound that I had injured. "Kill this one and you should level up. That will help your recovery."

I nodded and slowly crawled toward the hound on the ground, blood still seeping from the grievous wound in its head.

I pulled Shaper from inside its broken jaw and willed it to grow just large enough that I could stand with it helping me.

I shrunk it, then hefted it over my head and swung it downward with all the strength I had remaining. It thunked against the animal's skull and a crack began to form. I hit again, and again, then turned the weapon and began to drive the spike into the skull. After three more hits, it finally gave way.

Level up!

I blinked and a rush of energy ran through me. Two levels. I'd gained two levels from that, but it made no sense to me. The animal was almost twice my level.

"The creatures here give less experience," Nadir explained, her eyes narrowed at the area around us. "I found the creature I want, but it's being shy. Is there anything else I need to take care of?"

"There's one more in the tent." She nodded at that and walked inside. There was a yelp, and then she tossed it outside; it still drew breath, but it was heavily injured.

"The blade will cut it if you wish to collect more experience." I nodded in her direction as she moved off. I limped forward and fell onto the hound, stabbing it through the eye. It died and experience flooded into me.

Once again, it was less even than the creature I killed just now. Did the experience get exponentially worse the more creatures we killed here?

I pulled out the forge I kept in my inventory and set it on the ground before speaking, "Pop?"

The forge grew and I called again, "Hello?"

The flame elemental inside peeked out and watched me. "Yes?"

"I wanted to see about making a pact with you, if you wouldn't mind it?"

It stared at me and frowned. "I'm not big like the others. You would be better off finding another."

"What if I were to give you all of these?" I motioned to the five corpses on the ground. "I just need a small amount of power. A simple spell. Just something to give me a slight edge."

It stared for a moment longer, then sighed. "I *am* hungry…"

It came out into the open and took the first body, fire blooming all over it like orange flowers that seared it to the point where only ash remained. Then it hopped to the second body.

I lost track of how much time had passed before Nadir came and pulled me into the tent to rest. The elemental had retired to the forge and shrunk back down, but asked me not to put it away, so I didn't.

Rather, I rested and recovered, allowing myself to meditate longer than I might normally to get myself back to full capacity.

Once I was back to myself, I came to and took the forge from the tent into the morning light.

When I grew the forge, I spoke softly. "Pop?"

It was warm, but dark. There was nothing inside other than coals and ashes that I had to stoke back to a healthy glow.

"Hello?"

I gave up trying to call it after another ten minutes and just returned to doing what I had been doing last night. More links attached to the breastplate. By the time I was finished with the lot that I had, I was more than halfway done with the attachment to make it whole.

Heat flared around me, then fled, so I turned to the forge to find it filled with flames once more. "Pop?"

"Yes?"

"Did you think about what I asked you?" The flame left the forge and joined me in the open.

"I did." It looked down at the ground, then back up at me. "We need to form the pact, but I don't know how."

"Midnight!" I called, and the rustling of feathers let me know that he was with us. "How can we form a pact?"

"You'll need to make an outward sign of the pact to create a seal." He plucked out a feather and stared at us. "Something that shows the bond."

"Something like a bangle?" Nadir asked softly.

"That could work," Midnight confirmed.

I nodded and pulled out the metal that we had gotten from the dungeon.

Touching it, I could feel it was something denser than iron, but not something so specialized as Fae iron, or an alloy of some other make.

It would serve if all I needed was just an outward symbol of the pact.

Using Shaper, I beat the dirt off the ore. Though it was more pure since it was a chest reward, there was still dirt on it.

The dungeon had to have pulled it from its surroundings in order to fill the chest.

I melted it down in the smelter and formed the ingot as naturally as I had done so many times before.

The bangle I saw in the metal would fit my arm perfectly, the top and outer portion of it engraved with the crown of the Flame Primordial. The same one that burned inside the very same forge my father created.

It took the better part of three hours, hammering and chiseling to get it to look just right, but when I was finished and quenched it in oil, I was proud of my work.

I looked it over then pulled the small amount of leather that I carried to attach it, but the elemental stopped me. "I will bind it to you."

"What are the terms of our pact?" He reached out to take the bangle from me, holding it in its warm hand.

"Feed me, and become stronger." The elemental shrugged. "The bond to your forge is nice. I would prefer to remain there."

"I can do that."

He added, "Please, don't replace me in the forge."

I blinked at him and smiled. "You do great work. I wouldn't think of it."

"Then I'm okay with you borrowing what power I am capable of giving you." The flame elemental stepped closer and placed it on my left arm. "Let this trinket made by your own hand serve as the catalyst for our pact. While you, Azlo, serve me, I will give you the power that I can as your patron, and in your service to me and my people, that power may grow in ways unknown. Abide the tenets of our agreement, and I shall faithfully allow my strength to be your own. Do you swear to do this?"

"I do." I knelt down so that he could place the bangle against my skin and heat warped it until it was crimson, but there was no pain. As galling as it was to be the servile one in the pact, I had to hope that the other end of the deal was good for him. The pact could be annulled if both parties wished, from my understanding of some of the pacts my mother held. Serving someone, to me, was annoying, but as it would give me more power, I had little choice.

The glowing grew and grew as it even overtook the two of us until finally it stopped, and I could see again. The bangle was complete, held together by metal, as it was thinner now but wrapped wholly around my forearm. The symbol of the flaming crown carved into it was filled with roiling flames that looked to be contained almost as if by a shield of glass, or something mystical.

But perhaps the most curious thing of all was the elemental itself, who was now considerably larger than it had been.

"What happened to you?" Wonder invaded my voice as I took the sight in. There were streaks of blue running through him now, his eyes an intelligent white as he blinked and smiled.

"I'm bigger now. Not necessarily bigger than my former caste, but not as I was." Gone was the timidity that had been the norm when speaking to my increasingly familiar fragile flaming friend, replaced by an air of confidence. "I'm stronger too. But I feel like there's more power to be had?"

"What do I call you now?"

The elemental considered something to itself, then responded, "Duke Forger."

What have you done? the winds whispered as Seraestar's curiosity clashed with her cautious, carefully laid plans for the prince and his sister.

CHAPTER SEVENTEEN

The elementals stared at each other with ranging emotions, all of them. There was joy, rage, sorrow, curiosity, and even disgust.

"Had we known that he had the ability to become a warlock, we would have just given him the power to do so with our strength!" The wind primordial seethed, standing in front of his throne in their meeting chamber. More than a few of the lesser elemental primes, beings of mixed natures and more than one elemental aspect to their composition, mirrored his outrage.

"Because it wasn't supposed to happen!" Seraestar bellowed, losing her composure over herself. This had begun happening more and more when the gods realized that the Stolen Ones had awakened on their own planet on the other side of the veil. "He was supposed to remain pure, until he could become my cleric!"

"Games among gods matter not to the children of this world." The Flame Primordial crackled as he stood and stretched out. "I am proud of my wayward child becoming something more than the others. He is a new caste, some kind of sub-royalty of sorts."

"I don't care if the machinations of the gods matter to the

mortals—I care that there is a rogue magical being doing things that are unheard of."

The water primordial watched with mild interest. That she was revealing so much of her hand here among those she thought beneath her and the other gods was just so telling for her. More so than the norm, at least. Which had to mean that something big was going on betwixt the gods.

She motioned to the void and light elementals with her head, then flicked her gaze at the goddess beneath them as she raged wordlessly.

She wondered what they thought of all of this and that was about as much as got across to them. They were ancient by elemental standards, and until recently had no reason to interact with the mortals, but now they were just as entrenched as the rest of them.

The void whispered to her through the shadows at her back, "She fights with her brothers once more, and though she fights destiny in some fashion, she battles foolish mortals as well."

The light around her head crackled and the feminine voice of the other filled her ears, "Having someone she can only partially influence means part of the game she will play is up to chance. She hates chance." There was thoughtful quiet and then she added, "I sense that she will try to force our hand on this and, if so, we will be forced to stand united."

"We will," the Water Primordial stated as she stared down at the goddess who looked to be collecting herself. She raised her voice and spoke with authority, "We will not stop our children from forming these pacts."

The goddess stiffened and turned a baleful glare her way. "You already gave your blessings to the other mortal who yet still lives. As such, you cannot do so again."

"This is true," the Earth Primordial rumbled, surprising all of the other elementals. He was slow to anger, and usually more candid with his thoughts. The only ones to make him talk really being Zeke, then Azlo.

The rumbling from him surprising even more as he spoke again, "That distinction means nothing to our children."

"You have control of them!" Seraestar asserted, throwing her hands out beside her. "Tell them to leave him alone, then tell that freakish one to dissolve the pact."

"No," the primordials answered in unison.

She growled her frustration and snarled, "You would *dare* disobey the goddess of magic itself?"

"You need allies, goddess," the water elemental informed the glaring goddess. "With our children assisting the boy, he stands more of a chance than you baiting him to your service through piecemeal gifts of strength or how to use his power."

"You already know of a way for him to obtain spells through his primary class, don't you?" The Wind Primordial's disdain was evident in his tone.

"I do." She crossed her arms and frowned as the other occupants in the room stared at her. "If you think I mean to tell you so that you can tell him yourselves, you are more foolish than I thought."

"Then it will have to be gained as our children can give it to him." The Wind Primordial released a sigh as if he had expected this outcome. "If you wish to keep mages and the like alive to follow you and feed your Dominion, you need our power flooding the world to bring balance to the forces below."

Seraestar grumbled to herself, then shook her head. "I will win him from you and have him dissolve it himself if I must." She stared ahead. "I know that my telling you not to interfere will fall on deaf ears, and I do need your assistance with maintaining the magical world—but I will have my revenge for your disobedience."

The Water Primordial's eyes narrowed at the threat, but there was nothing she could do in that moment without a more severe loss in the end.

For now, the machinations of the gods would be for them and the gods to take care of themselves.

I clenched my fist as I stared at the notification in front of me as the spell I had gotten from the Duke wrote itself into the bangle on my forearm.

Congratulations!

Spell obtained!

Flicker Flame — Caster can summon and throw a small, weak flame at a distance equal to 5(Strength Stat). Cost: 10 MP.

Class Unlocked!

Warlock Class obtained — Your pact with another being of power greater than your own, or of a differing plane of existence, allows you to tap into powers previously untenable to you.

That made me frown. So I had a class, sub-class, and now a secondary class?

Would that affect my ability to do better work with my original class?

Class Ability: A choice to make.

Strengthen a previously meshing skill, or obtain a class specific spell.

The only 'spell' I had to strengthen was my Elemental Manipulation. Having *another* kind of spell at my disposal would be better, wouldn't it?

I stared at the notification and there was another that came to light.

Make a choice:

Strengthen previous skill: Elemental Manipulation

Or

Gain one of two spells:

Buster Beam

Or

Slip Step

The spells weren't explained in the slightest, but I could imagine what they did based on the names alone.

The beam would likely consume a large amount of mana, or have a large cooldown, so that made it more of a risk that I wasn't interested in at the moment. The other would have to be some sort of movement spell, but that would work well with my fighting style, would it not? Being able to move out of the way at the last second to avoid a strike would be amazing. How many injuries could I have avoided if I had only had that?

There was no telling how much stronger my manipulation skills would be with the boost to them from this, so taking it was just as much a risk as Slip Step. For now, building a good dual-class synergy between the two, Forge Sorcerer and Warlock, would be better for me in the long run.

I chose Slip Step and the notification disappeared, only to be replaced by an explanation of the skill that confirmed my thoughts on it, but it made me smile for good reason.

Innate Warlock Spell Unlocked!

Slip Step — The caster moves to any space within one foot in any direction with nothing more than a whim. This spell will grow as the caster grows without cost. Cool down: 30 seconds.

I thought about the spell and suddenly stood a foot to the right of where I'd been and the countdown timer until I could use it again appeared in the lower right-hand corner of my field of vision.

I grinned and thought about casting Flicker Flame, the small globe of embers gathering in my hand instantly. I threw it away from myself, the spell arcing and landing near where I had thought it would hit. It was pretty easy to use, if a bit weak. It barely scorched the grass as it was.

"It's my hope that the spell you got from me will grow with the experience you sacrifice to me as you go on." Duke Forger cleared his flaming throat and motioned to the mobile forge nearby. "I'm going to go ahead and return. Being outside the forge makes me anxious. Will you be making anything else today?"

I shook my head. "No, I think I'm going to be practicing

these spells I've gotten, and then I'll be working my links for a bit. But thank you for being my patron, I truly am grateful."

He just ducked his head and pressed himself back into the forge to become the flames within them.

"Excellent work, Highness," Midnight croaked from where he watched. "The spells both look interesting to me."

"They are indeed. Where is Nadir?" I noted her absence a few moments ago, but as I was busy, I couldn't spare the energy to ask outright.

"To collect the bounty she caught. She will return soon, I think."

I nodded and returned my focus to the spells I had just learned. Slip Step was an interesting conundrum. I could almost blip my movement with it, meaning that if I was mid-stride when I used it, I had a higher likelihood of slipping up. But if I stopped to use it, there was no way that I wouldn't be giving away the spell the first time someone saw it.

I was patient and persisted, pushing myself to use it while just walking and moving. It was easiest to use it while moving forward and after ten minutes, I figured out how to do it and maintain my steady stride by just maintaining the stride itself.

Doing so while moving laterally was a lot trickier. While stumbling for the umpteenth time in fifteen minutes after that, I heard the heavy breathing of something closing distance on the camp and pulled out Shaper.

"It's me, Azlo," Nadir called, and I smiled as I saw what it was that she rode.

It was some kind of hulking warg. It had tusks and massive red-stained fangs, as well as long canines that made it look like a saber tooth. Its brownish fur rippled as it moved, the glorious fur along its head and shoulders almost tall enough to hide Nadir's mass as she rode it. As it entered the camp, the beast eyed me hatefully and began to growl, but Nadir reached out and smacked it on the nose, making it yelp.

Nadir spoke in a tone that was chastising, and then down-right terrifying as she held its face. "That is my brother, and if you so much as sniff in his general direction in a manner I don't like, I will eat you." She glared at it a moment longer before calling me forward. "Let her sniff your hand, Azlo. The sooner she gets used to you, the easier it will be for her to recognize you as not food."

I rolled my eyes at that and did as she said, putting Shaper away so I didn't appear to be any more of a threat than I could have been.

Dread Warg Lvl 25

I sighed at the fact that this thing was so much stronger than me anyway. I needed to spend the points I had for my level up, but with the new class, I wasn't sure how I wanted to do it yet. I would need to ask Nadir if she had any books on the subject later. For now, we would need to be leaving this place to avoid another night in a hellish fight that we could otherwise avoid.

That and the seemingly diminishing returns from killing the creatures here too.

"What have you named her?" I asked as the softly growling warg snuffled my hand. I could have sworn I saw teeth just before Nadir grabbed a fistful of her scruff and pulled, eliciting a whine that made me worry for the creature.

"Oh, I'll just call her Dread." She ruffled the warg's fur a bit and that seemed to calm her and make her relax enough to wag her long tail.

"Did it work, though, or did you have to do something else to her?"

Nadir blinked at the question and then her eyebrows rose. "Oh! You mean the Unseelie Binding? Yes, it worked perfectly. It was still a battle of will though. I had to beat her into submission at the end there, and that was after tiring her out too. It would have taken less time if I had gotten her last night, but things happen as they do. I have her now."

I nodded. "Good to know."

The Binding was a way for the Unseelie to begin making non-Fae creatures act progressively more Fae. Mother didn't do it while she was on the Prime plane because she had multiple dozens of Fae creatures bound to her already, and that took serious willpower to handle.

At the edge of one's being, they could feel the brushing of another who was bound to them. As it was, I had two such bindings. Duke Forger, and Midnight. Midnight being Fae was a different sort of feeling. More natural to me than the other, but the Duke's was also growing on me.

If I did so, I would be required to find myself a mount that would slowly take a shape befitting the Fae who bound it.

For Nadir and Dread, the creature would likely become more savage or stronger. There was no telling for me until it happened.

I could only hope I would find as powerful a mount to bind to my will. Chances were high that I would not be choosing any of the creatures who frequented this place.

"We will be leaving as soon as I get the tent secured." Nadir sat Dread down and went inside, leaving the massive warg to stare at me as if I were a walking stick to fetch and maul.

I turned, careful to keep an eye on her as I packed up my gear, the forge, and the links, then picked up my discarded materials for the armor I was making.

After that, I felt a chill down my spine and whipped around to see that Dread stalked closer, and I roared at her, "Sit down!"

The warg blinked at me and growled, before Nadir poked her head out of the tent and growled, "Dreeeeead!"

The warg sat on the ground, then laid down and put her head on her paws, eyeing me with more than mild distaste.

"That played out better than you thought it would, didn't it?" Midnight observed from where he sat atop the tent watching. I hadn't noticed his return, though I had known he was close by.

"It showed I was willing to at the very least make myself known and that I wouldn't back down." I smiled ruefully to myself. "Not my fault it also got my sister's attention."

A few moments later, we were on our way. Dread didn't like my riding her, but she was more than accommodating when

Nadir made her wishes known and fed her some of the meat she had mysteriously accrued overnight.

It took us all day on the sturdy creature, but by nightfall, we had reached the northern edge of the barrens, careful to skirt the barrier as best as we could, since Midnight reported that was where the strongest creatures holed up and attacked anything that they could.

"Do you know anything about the diminishing returns for experience from the Barren creatures?" Nadir's question confirmed my theory and that it had affected her as well.

"Something about their proximity to a hole in space siphons their god-given power and makes them slightly different." Midnight fluttered in the breeze for a moment then continued with open disgust in his voice. "That lack compounds when it enters you and eats the experience you should be due."

"Could be why so few people dare hunt here," I observed. With how careless those hounds had been last night, there was no way they cared about proximity to hunters or potential danger. Just food.

"That would make sense," Nadir grumbled and pushed the warg on for a short while.

Finally, she stopped and said, "Dread needs to sleep, and with her being so intent on you if I'm not watching, she will be outside. So you should stay inside, Azlo."

"Makes sense." I frowned and asked, "Do you have a book on the classes available to mortals? I received a new one I wish to learn more about."

"Warlock?" I confirmed with a nod and she dug into her satchel of books for the book she wanted, pulling out a large tome. "Here you are. This is all the information I have on classes and then some. Every warlock is different based on their patron, so there may not be too many specifics, but it should help you make an educated selection for the free points you have."

With that, she went outside to work with Dread, feed her, and wash her down. There were many methods to taking care of a new bond, one of them being proximity. The only reason she was with me at all right now was necessity. When I found mine, I would likely spend a lot of time with it to ensure that we were fully connected before leaving it for any period of time.

While she was gone, I flipped through the pages until I found the chapter that made me groan aloud and I *swore* I could almost hear Nadir snickering from outside.

Im-pacted by another? You may be a Warlock. The ins and outs of an outside source of power.

I rolled my eyes and read on.

CHAPTER EIGHTEEN

I grumbled to myself mentally, *This book makes my head ache. If I have to read one more passage written with a pun at heart, I think I might need to find this K. Rout person and throttle them with the nearest animal bone.*

The book told me that a warlock's abilities and power scaled with Charisma as well, so putting points into it wouldn't be untoward.

There was really nothing to do so far as multi-classing either, as a person's level was actually the level for the class you were. So I was both a level thirteen sorcerer and a level thirteen warlock for all intents and purposes.

"That makes no sense with how the spell Slip Step works." I closed the book and set it aside. "If that were the case, the spell would be stronger in some way."

"Have you spent the points for the levels you earned yet?" Midnight asked curiously, his beak over my shoulder. "I was reading further down the page and it says to do that."

"Oh." My cheeks burned slightly, but I corrected myself and simply went into my status to spend the points that I could.

As it was, Charisma, Strength, Intelligence, and Dexterity were the highest stats I had, and seeing as I had been getting beaten up quite a bit, I decided to spend the six points that I was free to spend on Constitution. The other two Chaos Points went to Strength.

I rolled my eyes, wondering if that had been fair at all. I needed more health.

Name: Azlo Erebos
Level: 13
Strength: 30
Dexterity: 26
Constitution: 23
Intelligence: 27
Wisdom: 17
Charisma: 30
Unspent Attribute Points: 0
Unassigned Chaos Points: 0

With that, I frowned and focused on pulling the information on Slip Step back up, but the information remained the same, until I noticed that the words shifted and now instead of one foot, it was three feet.

I smiled and had to wonder if that was something to do with the fact that my Charisma was so high? If that were the case, it would be my Charisma score divided by ten that judged how far I could move with it.

Excitedly, I began to test the new distance and found that while traveling in a straight line, I still had a pretty good grasp of how to not skip a step while using the spell.

"That's an interesting spell you picked up." Nadir tilted her head. "Does it cost you much?"

I shook my head. "Not at all." She watched me and I just waited out the cooldown before doing it again, appearing three feet to the right. She started and sat up as I said, "It just takes getting used to if I want to use it while moving."

"That's an excellent skill to have close up." She smiled at me as I sat down and prepared for the next part of my self-training. "What will you do now?"

"Well, the other spell I have is Flicker Flame, but I want to see if I can manipulate it with Elemental Manipulation."

She watched me as I summoned the dimly glowing globe in my left hand and focused on it with Elemental Manipulation active. With a little focus, I could change the shape of the flame, minutely, but it wasn't enough to truly increase the amount of damage. At least, not with what I felt.

"You might be able to add flames around you to it," Nadir tried to offer helpfully when I sighed with frustration and flung the spell into the brazier in the middle of the room. "I don't know if it will break down the further it gets from you, but it would be worth a try for some added damage. If anything it could be even more useful up close."

I nodded, as that did seem like a possibility to me at first. I could only hope that there was a solid way for me to gain spells as a sorcerer based on what the goddess would tell me eventually.

Or show me, hopefully. I grimaced at the idea of her doing something like what Mother said most gods did, making mortals chase them for answers and promises of power to bring them into the fold. I had no intention of becoming anyone's cleric or priest.

The thought alone sent a shiver down my spine.

I stared at the floor for a moment, then spoke. "What do you hope to find with the orcs of the north, sister?"

Nadir considered my question for a short time before answering, "Myself." My head whipped up so that I could look at her as she stared uncomfortably into the brazier, where a small flame crackled into life. "I wish to find my heritage, Mother's heritage, and cling to it so that I might at least come to have a sense of self that cannot be taken or claimed by my former master, or the court."

I opened my mouth to assuage her fears, but she just leveled her eyes at me and gave me slight shake of her head. I shut my mouth, and she instead said, "I know what you and everyone else would likely think, but I cannot not do this. I have to know."

There was no mulling it over on my part, no decision to make. "You have my support."

She nodded once, a sigh escaping her lips. "We should rest. We can't really stop in any of the towns as we are now, and not with Dread."

"Maybe I should go into one and see if there is anything of note for my quest?"

"That wouldn't be a bad idea." She frowned, then pointed to Midnight who had made a perch for himself among the wooded slats in the rafters. "Or we could have him go and listen in?"

"I will go, but getting into most buildings serves as a problem for me and one of my kind." The raven blinked at me and dipped his head. "I will bring back information and places of interest, if this is your will?"

I nodded and the bird disappeared in a rain of feathers that quickly vanished before even touching the ground. "That has to be an interesting skill to have."

Nadir's eyebrows raised as she nodded her agreement, then said, "His presence is familiar."

"Because he's been watching us since childhood." She frowned at that and I just added, "He spoke the truth, sister. He watches us, and I don't know if his reasons for being with us are as certain as he has shared, or if he's as weak as he leads on."

"He would have to be powerful in order to hide his presence from not only the queen, but my master, Winterheart, and many others."

I agreed, but refrained from commenting, opting to just go back to trying to manipulate the spell in my hand. It did either of us little good dwelling on a creature bound to my will as it was. The nature of the oath he was under would also keep us safe from any sort of reprisal, or I would gain power from any kind of betrayal he tried to make happen.

Wouldn't be the first time it happened, or the last.

———

MIDNIGHT

Clever of the boy to stop speaking as he had, playing his hand close to his chest. I ruffled my feathers excitedly as I waited for the clone I had sent to the village to come into the area. Luckily, I had power of my own and the skills necessary to keep myself hidden.

I closed my eyes and allowed my consciousness to merge with it and saw what was there to see.

For a village on the edge of the barren lands of the barrier, it was decently fortified with a tall wall made of stone with thick wooden beams supporting it from the inside. They also had sections of wooden stakes dug into the ground facing oncoming attackers.

The planner for the village was obviously intelligent enough to know that not every attacker would come for doors.

The layout was standard for humanity. Center of the village held the important villas and governmental buildings that were clearly labeled with signs in a standardized way.

The largest of the buildings was stone as well and had symbols engraved around the base and top of it.

Defensive wards enchanted into the building and attached to a three foot by five foot sunstone. The design of this one was primitive from what I'd grown accustomed to in the Fae Realm. It was designed to pull in ambient mana and heat from the sun to power the enchantment on the building.

The storage for it would see to it that the building was protected magically for at least some time. As to how long? It depended on the duration of the attack, size of the force against it, and the power of those attacking it. If it were Nadir?

This building would crumble in a matter of hours if she kept a level head.

Less if she was angry.

The humans below were a dirty sort, hardy and hard-working looking. There were other races mingled in, but it appeared the humans weren't comfortable with them. Not entirely.

The humans' furtive glances as they passed were telling, and though I could see Mana clinging to some of them, they were not the majority. But most of the humans I saw were powerless, non-magical beings.

I flew closer, getting into the shadows to listen to things, one of which was a popular-looking stall outside of a larger building. There were seats that belonged to the establishment.

Patrons sat and ate or drank alone or in groups, but it was one such secluded group that interested me. Their conversation back and forth under their breaths as they glared at anyone close enough that they could have been heard. Rather than just ferry the information back, I decided to give it to the two royal children in real time, though I would give it as if I had heard it earlier.

I split my mind and allowed my now-corporeal form to fall between the two, speaking as if I were trying to recall things. "A group of humans with one dwarf among them speaks at a local eatery called the Hub. They're muttering about some happenings in the locale they find bothersome."

The boy leaned forward and began to notate things in a small booklet he pulled from his inventory. Where he had started this was interesting, noting things down instead of trying to remember it all, but I was distracted at present and needed to relay the information.

"There's too damn many of 'em," the dwarf said with me mimicking his disgusted tone. He was a blond one with a short beard that looked frazzled. "Donae sit well with me. Disgustin'."

"Craglim, that's enough open hostility," one of the humans began with a droning tone. "The governor will see to it that they learn their places before they fall, do not fret. All we need do is wait."

"When are they moving in again?"

"Don't know." The human rolled his eyes. "They're coming from the northlands and they have to avoid the orcs."

That revelation made Nadir sit up straighter as the blond dwarf growled, "Damn beasts kill anythin' an' everythin'. Only thin' worse'n a orc be a mage."

Both Azlo and Nadir grimaced at that assertion but remained quiet as the conversation devolved into plans that meant little to me in the grand scheme of things. But what caught my eye next was that there was a boy carrying a letter to the table, which I passed on to the children.

The human speaker snatched the letter as the child continued on and slid his finger under the seal with shaking hands. He read the first few lines and a smile crept onto his face. "They've managed to hole up in a network of badger tunnels and a ruined village for now. They want us to prepare the Dizern for their arrival, then come and get them to bring them in. The governor has gone on to make other plans ready where he is needed."

"So how do we prepare the village for them?" Craglim asked as his hand dropped below the table.

"Magic has to go." The human smiled cruelly and, with that, Azlo launched himself to his feet and roared.

Startled, I lost connection with my clone and looked at him. "What is it?"

"That's it! That's how we get in!" He punched his hand and grinned. "True Sight is rare here, yes?"

Nadir and I both nodded so Azlo continued, "So all we need to do is appear human, come in and make a fuss about one of the local mages. Get them to recruit us and we're in."

"You would think that they would have a way to get around that." I frowned, wondering if they likely did.

Azlo shrugged. "If they do, we kill all of them and go looking for this 'governor' character." He smiled. "Let's perfect our glamour for this; I would prefer to be much more ordinary-looking, but perhaps have a scar or something that makes me look mysterious but approachable for a homicidal psychopath?"

Nadir snorted and rolled her eyes. "Show me what you have and we will work on it."

CHAPTER NINETEEN

Journeying to the village only took another two days as we traveled by mundane means rather than by warg. Nadir had sent Dread off on her own to hunt and grow stronger, using the bond that she had made for them as a means to track her and call her back if Nadir needed her.

The two of us walked in our dirtiest clothes, covered in blood and grime from the dungeon. It was to cement that we had indeed been fighting their way here.

The destruction and barren land around us cemented in my mind that the fight here had been much too brutal for what had happened. What creatures had come through this place? What had they wanted to do? Why was it so bad that the gods themselves had to call upon outsiders to fight their battles for them and then allow them to be taken from them?

Maybe next time Seraestar comes to me, I can ask? Movement to my side caught my attention and almost startled me, but it was only Nadir in her glamour.

The two glamours we wove around ourselves were for siblings, the female one Nadir wore was basically her if she were in orc form, but with dark skin and brown eyes, lighter scars crossing her arms from 'years of fighting' for a mercenary band that fell recently trying to raid the barrier ruins.

Mine was close to hers, scars as well, but more on my chest and shoulders, with one bisecting my left eye just for flavor.

I carried a mace-sized Shaper on my hip, and the dagger in my hip sheath, while Nadir carried Father's axe.

By the time we got to the front gate, we found the half-closed wooden doors to the wall stymying the flow of any traffic that could have come in, or stopped any monsters coming. Guards stood there, but they were barely armed and didn't care about the straggling people who meandered into the village.

They glowered at us, but since we looked capable, I was sure they would leave us alone. Midnight flew overhead and kept watch for the subjects that could take us to whomever was in charge. He didn't find anyone right away, but my keen hearing picked up on the clanging of a hammer.

"That will likely be Craglim," I grumbled to my sister as I set my course for that noise.

Rowland had told me about him once. Hated anyone not dwarven, which was concerning, considering he was working with humans and taking orders from one. Did that mean he hated mages worse?

All I knew was that he was a 'bleached arsehole and a shite smith' from Rowland and that was all he would say about his family other than Vilmas and the boys. Vilmas, on the other hand, had called him more names than I was certain she entirely understood the meanings of, and had growled that if he ever came back to Sunrise, she would hang him from the wall and use his testicles as target practice for the knife throwing Vrawn had been showing her.

The thought of it brought a smile to my face, though I did have to wonder how useful he would prove.

We wandered for ten minutes and finally found the source of the clanging hammering and waited patiently while he finished the piece he was working on. He was a master crafts-man, that was for certain, but he was no Rowland who had reached Grandmaster by now.

I watched him for a while longer and noted that while Rowland would infuse his body with mana to make his weapons, Craglim did not. Which was odd to me. I didn't either, but that was just because I wasn't good enough to do so yet.

"What ya want?" the surly dwarf growled as he put the ingot he was working on back into his poorly-made forge. "Donae do shows an' such."

Nadir had told me that greeting him as a dwarf would likely have been a bad idea with his hatred of outsiders, so instead I said, "Looking for work. Our band of... problem solvers was attacked in the barrens a couple days ago."

He didn't so much as look at us before saying, "An' ya think a blacksmith would be able ta tell ya where ta find some?"

"Most of the smiths we've known have been some of the smartest in the places we've gone," Nadir rumbled with her arms crossed. "If you're selling weapons to people, they likely know how to use them, or have use for those who do."

"We have a little coin we can give as an incentive too." I pulled out a couple silvers and flashed them before cupping them back into my palm.

He held out his palm so I put one there and when he finally looked up at me. "Rest if it pans out."

"Excuse me?" someone hollered. A studious-looking man with sideburns that went down to the bottom of his chin waved as he strode forward. "Yes, hello. My master needed you to complete the weapon that he ordered *today*. You don't have time to be taking on new work."

He had nicer clothes on and carried a wand on his hip.

This couldn't have gone better if we had planned it ourselves. I wanted to smile at our good fortune. "Can you not see that a professional is at work? Who are you to bogart his time, huh?"

"A paying customer!" the man answered imperiously. He

pointed at me and growled, "What sort of brutish brigand would be able to pay this man for his time anyway? Not you. This man is making something of import for my master, and he will do so or we will—"

He didn't finish the statement as I leaned closer and snarled, "Or you'll *what*?" I turned my head and spat on his boot before looking back up at him. "Or were you threatening him?"

Craglim's beard twitched at that, but something much more telling was that as he glanced at the young mage, his eyes went dead and there was something there beneath the gaze that Mother had trained me to look for—malice. He didn't like the mage, and the report we had gotten from Midnight lent even more depth to this. He hated him. His knuckles popped as his grip tightened on his hammer, the man's blathering not falling on deaf ears in the slightest.

Most smiths didn't care if their customers were needy, they had to be if the weapons were useful, but this one looked like he was ready to kill his, and me and Nadir would use that to our advantage.

"Magic users are all the same." Nadir sneered. "Can't pick up a sword, so they just try to wave a wand and make all their wants and needs appear. Fuck the little man who makes things happen with the sweat of their brow or the blood from their flesh."

The man grimaced and pulled the wand. "Now see here, you miscreants!" He leveled it at my chest, which was smart since I was the closest.

But he also wasn't actively casting a spell either.

I grabbed the wand, snatching it away from him, and broke it over my knee in one smooth motion.

"Pointing a weapon at someone without them offering any sort of physical harm?" Nadir gasped mockingly as she leveled her axe at the man. "Looks like someone is *asking* for a beating."

Sweating and breathing heavily, the man swallowed and stammered, "Y-you wouldn't dare!"

I shook my head and tossed the two halves of the wand on

the ground. "No, we came here on business." I grinned wolfishly, pointing to Craglim. "But I would gather the price of the item your master wanted just got steeper for wasting this man's time."

Craglim smiled genuinely, his short blond beard fanning out along his chin as he did. "Oh, aye. That it will. Ya run 'long now—got hammerin' to do. Unless ya wanna pay three times what it be worth for threatenin' me clients?"

The man turned heel and walked away as quickly as he could, likely without running.

Craglim looked considerately at the two of us. "Clever work, that." He sighed and pulled the ingot out of the forge, the red turning to a blue as it had almost gotten too hot.

"Can't stand an uppity mage," I grumbled in a way that I hoped was convincing.

"Can't stand them at *all*," Nadir corrected with a growl.

"Aye." Craglim coughed into his elbow and looked around. "Cannae abide 'em meself, either."

He might need some convincing to help get the ball rolling, I thought to myself. "I've heard that there are some people out there standing up to them. Some even fighting back when their oppression is too much."

Craglim raised an eyebrow at that and ran his hand through his hair once before I muttered, "Killing a couple would keep the others in place, wouldn't it?"

Once I said that, he walked inside as the metal cooled slowly and came back out with a paper that he handed to me. "Come here tonight after dusk, got someone with work possibly in mind who might have use o' yer skills. Cannae say he won't test ya, but that's up to him."

I nodded my gratitude and flicked the other silver into the air for him to catch, though curiously looked at me. "What's this for?"

I smiled at him. "I have a good feeling about this meetup."

Craglim's teeth flashed white and he nodded before turning back to his business.

We walked off before looking at the paper. Scribbled on it was an address that Midnight spoke about, "That's near the place that they met last time!"

I nodded to myself and grunted. "Go, surveillance only, and if anyone is there, I want to know who. I need to know that building inside and out."

Nadir watched as the bird fluttered off to do as bidden, then she turned back to me. "What's with that?"

"If we have to kill them, then we will, but I will know all points that could be used against or for us."

She nodded. "Good idea."

I smirked. "I know."

We went to the place that Midnight had mentioned that served food, and did some light enquiry there. There was some work, odds and ends, but nothing that would interest the two personas we'd adopted for this.

We ate while we were there, listening into the conversations around us, but there was little of interest. The residents who spoke loudest talked about being annoyed at the current political environment. The leadership of the village kept them in the walls all the time, and anyone not pulling their weight was treated poorly because their skills weren't immediately useful.

This was the perfect type of place for someone to bring in a Fae representative to start making changes and deals.

My eyes narrowed. "You don't suppose that this governor could be Seelie, do you?"

Nadir stilled. "I don't know." She frowned at the thought of that and considered it for a few moments before answering fully, "I don't think that they would willfully choose to set an enemy loose that could come against them just as easily as anyone else."

I let my lips fall into a thoughtful frown before countering, "Unless they thought that they could control it."

"That's a fair statement." She sucked her teeth, irritated now. "We should keep an eye out for any Fae activity."

I tapped the table at her in agreement and waited for dusk

to fall as patiently as I could, given how excited I was to get to the bottom of this and potentially finish my quest.

CHAPTER TWENTY

Midnight croaked under the table, "They're meeting now."

It was approaching dusk, and I wondered what they could be discussing, but the Fae bird spoke again. "They seem interestin', an' they apparently hate mages an' need coin." It was the Fae's impression of Craglim that almost made me laugh. "Thinkin' they could be useful, if for nothing more than fodder."

"You said they were covered in blood and scars?" the human asked, obviously sounding skeptical. "How fortuitous is it for them to show up *now* of all times."

"Things get messy out in the barrens all the time, Maldev," the other, quieter human muttered.

"You're suggesting that they were already in the area?" the human, Maldev, retorted hotly. "That out of all the places they could have gone, they end up in Dizern? It seems a setup. What if the Hooded Council knows about our movements?"

"The what?" I muttered under my breath. What kind of stupid naming convention was that? Hooded Council. Sounded pompous.

"Someone to look into." Nadir had a small booklet out and penned things down. "Continue, Midnight."

"They stopped talking at that and just stared at the man until he looked cowed." The bird blinked and hopped onto my leg. "They know you're coming. And I think one of them muttered something about a test?"

I grimaced. "So they're keen on wasting our time?"

"If it doesn't pan out, we have the name of another organization to look into, at least." Nadir smiled softly as she said it. "I think we will be above any test they give us, and that we could avail ourselves well. But I find myself... concerned."

"Why so?" Midnight wondered when I said nothing.

"They're an organization on the run from orcs up north, who have people who hate mages amongst them." She flipped a page back in her notebook and said, "'...Prepare Dizern for their arrival.'" She blinked slowly and then looked at me. "'Magic has to go.' Azlo, they mean to either round up all the mages in this village and put them in chains, or to kill all of them. Their leader isn't even among them."

"I thought of that as well." I tapped the table for a short moment, then whispered, "What if we offer this place to the Queen? We help them *round up* the mages, then kill them all and have Mother send an envoy to help them all recover?"

"And further grow the Unseelie's influence in these lands." Nadir finished the thought for me and nodded. "That would be a good idea. And your quest would be solved with that, considering all you need to do is figure out their motives, destroy them, or just hamper their abilities to carry out their plot."

"There is that as well." I stared at the table, not having considered my quest in that matter. Just the court and our influence on the Prime Plane. I glanced up at the sky. "Very well. When it's time to begin killing them, we need to come up with a signal of some sort."

Nadir gave it some thought then shrugged, suggesting, "Murder them all?"

That made me laugh and she just smiled her same soft

smile. "That could work." I motioned to Midnight. "Their levels? The ones in the room?"

He thought for a moment. "Low twenties was the top I saw. They're skilled in some ways, I'm sure, but if surprised and both of you are fighting, it's reasonable to say you could take them."

Nadir dipped her chin and then said, "What about the group of reinforcements coming to hold the village?"

"We kill them too." I smiled, thinking of all the experience we could get killing them all. "From the report Midnight gave, they're ragtag at best, tired and driven. They won't be thinking of a resistance to their plans if they're on the run from orcs. When, though, will be dependent on what these people decide to have happen."

"So here we are, the consequences of their decisions come to see how long it will be before we decide how to show ourselves to them?"

I snorted and actually guffawed for a moment while others around us stared, openly concerned or confused. Some were annoyed but I didn't care. That was perfectly summing up what we were to be—the consequences of bad decisions.

The light continued to flee the sky as we sat and waited, then I spoke. "Lead the way, Midnight."

The bird fluttered from beneath the table and up onto the nearby building close to the alleyway we needed to enter.

Carefully, so as to be inconspicuous with the rest of the nightly strollers, we walked toward where he led us. We were being followed, of course. We'd had a watcher since the little boy who delivered the letter to Malvern had found us where we ate our food.

It had been just alright; some soup with too little seasoning and nearly-stale bread.

We moved to the door with the number that matched the number on the note and knocked three times. The scent outside was less than thrilling, and the inside wasn't great either. I wanted to ruminate on it but something moved on the other side of the door.

There was a gruff, muffled answer and movement before Craglim opened the door and nearly shouted, "What?" He realized it was us and smiled. "Oh, good. Come in."

Inside was destroyed. Like, the interior of the place was just demolished. Walls were busted, cracked, and in dire need of patchwork to even keep cockroaches in. The furniture—what could have been mistaken for it, at least—was debris and so many wood chips and splinters on the ground. All what Midnight had shown us.

There was mildew, dust, and more than just the scent of urine floated in the air. That made me question his reporting skills.

"Smithing always seemed like more of a paying skill than this. I have to say I'm disappointed." I couldn't keep the observation in line with how I had seen Rowland and his family making money hand over fist.

"Ain't my place, boy," Craglim growled and moved on the one clear enough path through the detritus without another word.

I shrugged and followed along, still cautious and observing to see if anyone was watching us as we entered. With there being gaps in the walls large enough to glare through, it was possible we were being stared at and watched for ambush.

I took a deep breath and counted some of the scents that wafted into the room from the far side of it. There were at least four, but with the rank stench of the debris and mildew in this room, it took a toll to get that much.

Nadir caught my eye and held up five fingers as she was walking. To others, it would look like she was just taking a step, but to me with the look on her face, I could tell she was showing me how many she had scented.

Not for the first time did I wish that I could speak to her mind to mind, but that was not in our skillset.

We walked into the next room and found the other people waiting there to be a little lacking in the hygiene state of things, their scents strong and musty. And they were chained to the wall behind them in a manner befitting prisoners.

Looking at them, there was a distinct look of near-frenzied worry in their gazes as they knelt in their own urine-soaked clothes and waste.

"Seems an odd place to inter prisoners," Nadir observed haughtily.

"Only place we care to put their kind." Craglim spat on the ground, the spittle bursting and hitting one of them on the leg. "These ones were most vocal about the non-mages in the area acting uppity and 'above their station.' Kept pushing and imposing. So we fought back."

Glancing at them, I could tell that only one of the five had any magic, while the others were just normal. I blinked and stared at them. "So what's the plan for them?"

"Local magistrate has been taken in by them, so there's no such thing as a fair trial for a mage here—*we* have to be the law." He lifted his hammer and brained the mage that was among them, the skull crushed instantly. The other prisoners balked as the body fell to the ground, twitching for a heartbeat before stilling with blood slowly pooling. Thankfully, the man had been gagged so the groan he let out was more muffled.

I stared at the carnage and the dwarf glared at me. "They all die tonight. That bother you?"

"Doesn't seem to bother you at all," Nadir observed dryly as she crossed her arms. "We prefer to go after monsters and bounties; murder charges are no fun."

He grimaced at her. "Is it a murder charge, or a mark by someone sullied by magic?"

I snorted, remarking, "Legal system doesn't give one stray fuck about either."

"No one is going to know, and in order to be counted on for what is to come." Craglim's beard shook as he spoke insistently. "All future endeavors and pay, you'll need to prove you can be counted on to act."

I looked at Nadir and wondered what to do. These were just

humans. Their only crime was being near a mage, or claiming to be able to perform magic.

I sighed and, before I could decide for or against, the nearest human stood and shook off the bonds, pulling the rag from his mouth. "Too long to decide."

The others stood up as well, doing the same. So it had been a ruse and we had fallen into it handily. It wasn't as if Midnight had been in here to confirm who we saw, or that they had all been involved. I was going to have to try to figure out a way for him to get involved like that.

"So if you aren't ready to join the cause because you're too queasy about ending lives..." The original speaker said as he offered an attempted I-have-no-choice-style shrug.

Nadir gave a subtle nod to me as I rolled my eyes and then I surged forward, gripping his throat in one hand and lifted him bodily off the ground.

The others shouted and began to hurl snarled curses my way as I spoke calmly. "My 'queasy' behavior could have saved you. But I guess this is fine. Sister?"

She smiled and shook her head. "You need the experience."

I grunted and steeled my grip before crushing his windpipe and whirling on the others. They were strong for humans, certainly, and the dwarf was strongest among them, which was unsurprising.

Most dwarves liked to fight, drink, and create things. Not always in that order.

So killing another before he was on me was easy enough, his hammer swinging for my chest as the other human fled. I dipped backward, hammer glancing against my shirt but not the bulk beneath as I kicked out. My foot caught his knee and shoved it backward as his swing rotated his hip.

With the legs firmly planted as they were, the leg I kicked buckled in on itself and he fell down.

I sent a Flicker Flame into his beard as a distraction and then pounced on the human attempting to flee.

This one I just punched in the back of the head at the base

of the skull as hard as I could before spinning and stalking back toward the injured dwarf.

"Midnight." The whispered Fae's name under my breath made it appear next to me in raven form. "Do you see the corpse of their leader here?"

The bird glanced around. "No. Nothing of value either." He tilted his head down at the dwarf. "But him? He knows things. Can I eat him?"

I blinked at him and my brow furrowed. "You can eat things like him?"

"Magic creature!" Craglim snarled and spat like a wild beast as he swung his hammer in my direction. "Fiends! Charlatans! Disgustin' thin—"

The bird didn't wait and fluttered down onto his head, shoving his beak into the fighting dwarf's left eye.

He bellowed as the Fae bird snatched out the orb and then shifted until the majority of the body was humanoid with massive feathered wings. Craglim stopped moving and only began to scream as the creature devoured whatever it was he was consuming directly from the dwarf's eye socket.

It was a sight and sound that would never be far from my conscious or unconscious mind for many years, I was sure.

CHAPTER TWENTY-ONE

MIDNIGHT

I watched as my clone devoured the dwarf's knowledge, skills, and ideas, then turned my attention to the children.

While we feasted, Azlo began to dig through the pockets of the corpses and found something within some of them. Papers for orders or something, from what I could read from this distance.

Nadir, on the other hand, was more interested in the mess around all of us. There was nothing of note to me, but when Azlo whooped excitedly, she reached down and grasped something, then pulled.

It was an entrance of some kind to a stairwell that I hadn't been able to sense at all, which was concerning to me.

Still invisible and hidden, I fluttered into the room below and began to look around, only to be caught off guard by movement to my right that closed in on the now-lit entrance.

Through my clone, I bellowed a warning. "Mage killer!"

The children were instantly on alert and the weapon in

Azlo's hand swung fast enough that it clipped the woman surging up through it to attack Nadir.

The woman grunted as she beat on the orcish woman in front of her. I could see the aura of magic around her being savaged as it flared.

The more Nadir went to use her magic, the faster the woman's fists collided with her.

Azlo's hammer swung at her chest, but she just ducked it and let the swing through hit Nadir.

Except, it didn't. Azlo had swung full strength, but Nadir had stopped it with her palm as her eyes flashed red.

There it is! It was so hard to stop the glee I felt as I watched her rage flood her being. This alone was worth the annoyance of having to deal with a mage killer.

Nadir bellowed and launched herself at the woman attacking her.

Her left leg raised to kick the massive woman, but Azlo was there attacking with his weak flaming crap shot.

The brief flicker of flames against her forearm flustered her just enough for the furious orcish fighter to grasp the foot that flailed past her side.

Nadir growled and swung her into the rubble as hard as she could, not too difficult considering that she was so much stronger than a normal person. The woman's spine cracked but Nadir didn't stop.

She lifted her own massive leg and brought her foot down into the attacker's stomach, making the woman's shout of pain cut off instantly as she fought to keep conscious. I would eat this one too, if they let me.

"Why did you attack us?" Azlo asked, but his sister just lifted her leg once more and rocketed into the woman's guts. She screamed then, wetness soaking into the leggings she wore as Nadir ground her foot into her flesh. "That's enough, sister."

Nadir said nothing as her red eyes found her brother and flickered, and as the woman grabbed the orc's leg, the crimson returned and Nadir's lips pulled back in a savage snarl.

Nadir kicked once more and Azlo tried to tackle her, only to be picked up and tossed away with minimal effort on Nadir's part.

It was time to speak up. "Azlo, she's not going to allow you to stop her. This is her—the real her. The side that her master tried to beat out of her, then hid when he realized that it could be useful."

He gasped as his breath returned. "What do you mean?"

"She will likely want to tell you herself. Just know that you aren't the only one with another class."

The boy grimaced as Nadir's foot fell again and this time the woman she accosted didn't make any noise. Her body just shuddered as she lay there, eyes glazing over.

Sourly, I thought, *There goes my next meal.*

The woman was dead, but the rage in Nadir was something else entirely. The corpse was crushed entirely before she was done doing what her rage pushed her to. By the time she finished, her eyes were back to normal and she realized what she was doing.

She blinked and frowned, then sighed and looked into the air as she said, "I'm sorry."

"That doesn't explain it." The boy spoke softly as he looked around, then continued to dig into the mage killer's pockets. "But with the noise we made, it wouldn't be too far out of mind to know that guards will likely be on their way now."

Nadir listened for a second, hearing what I did—hushed tones discussing something outside, far enough to be safe, but close enough to see what was going on.

Humans. Disgustingly curious lot those ones, morbidly so at times.

"Search her pockets and see what you can find," Azlo ordered softly. There was no tone in it other than to do what he said. He was showing his royal lineage and training that way.

Interesting thing to fall back on, boy. Training will always prevail, it seems.

They worked in unison, stripping the corpses of useful items before getting themselves underground where the girl shut the door behind them. With them doing so, I had time to look about and found why I wasn't able to see in here or find the room. Runes.

Runes were carved into the walls and powered with blood. This was old magic. Older even than me, and if someone didn't want mages or magical creatures to know of where they were, this was how they did it. I would need to be more cautious for them in the future.

————

AZLO

The room below was a larger, well-cared-for one. This one had furniture, a large table, and several cots for people to sleep in.

It honestly more resembled a simple bunker than a meeting place. And there were even people sleeping with all the noise that had been upstairs the whole time.

Was the mage killer a guard for these others? Looking around at all of them, there was no way we would be able to kill all of them stealthily enough so as not to wake the others unless we got started now.

In total, there were seven others in various states of dress. Some wore nicer clothes to sleep in, one of them wore rags, and the other was nude for some reason. That one was the one I killed first.

I covered their mouth with my right hand and drove my dagger into the base of their skull at the spinal cord like my assassin-style training dictated. Mother had shown me herself in small blades classes when the instructors failed to show me the quickest way to neutralize an enemy. The spine was always a safe bet and severing it here was the best way to truly kill someone quickly and efficiently.

Level up!

I grimaced at the interruption and continued to move from

bed to bed, killing all of the sympathizers where they lay. Luckily, no one woke until the last died. He must have sensed something was wrong or smelled the blood. Either way, it took Nadir a single punch to end him.

"I forgot the queen taught you assassin's arts."

I nodded. "She had no way of knowing what I would become, other than king." I motioned to the corpses around us. "What better way to prepare for an attempt on my life than knowing how to take one in that way? If I know how I would come into a room to kill a target, I can better judge the precautions I should take."

"An excellent training method."

It had been. Though I had lived a sheltered life for the most part, it had not always been easy. Mother had been a brutal and expectant taskmaster, and her training of me had to be above reproach at all times. If I failed, I did not fail again.

I had only ever failed to meet her expectations twice and only in one matter. The thought of it made my skin crawl to the point I had to shudder, then urge myself on. "Search them and the place to see what we can find. There has to be correspondence here that we can use to get to the main force."

We worked silently for a moment before finally Nadir spoke softly so as not to chance the investigators above hearing us. "I'm sorry my rage made me lash out at you."

"Hardly." I snorted, still digging through one of my victims' pockets. "You just tossed me aside like so much wheat."

"Still." She sighed and pressed her hands to her forehead. "I thought I had tamped control of that, but seeing her attack me like that was just too much."

"She hardly could have killed you, Nadir."

She shook her head and stated coldly, "She was attacking my master's legacy."

I stopped digging in pockets and glanced at her. "His what?"

"His legacy." She sniffed and looked over at a wall. "There's something here." She pulled her arm back and shot her fist through the wall before pulling it back. The wall was false and there were items inside it. "Good. I'll take all this for now."

"Keep explaining, please."

She grimaced and sighed. "When I received my levels, his power—his legacy—joined that and is now a part of me." She came to the desk at the end of the room with me while I picked through it. There wasn't much. "Unfortunately, it takes time to absorb it into myself. While it's there, it's an aura that can be attacked like the aura of magic around a mage. She was attacking it."

I frowned and reasoned, "So then that's why you entered a rage."

She nodded once and I grunted. "I suppose attacking someone's power directly is a good enough reason to become enraged."

"It is." Midnight chirped. "This would also be a good time to feed your pact."

I frowned and looked around. "Corpses?"

"That will feed a flame," Midnight assured me and tilted his head. "There are searchers above. They are not keen on outsiders."

I grimaced, but summoned the forge, calling softly, "Duke Forger?"

"Yes?" The flame elemental poked his head out of the door in time to see me motioning to the dead. "Oh, that's nice."

He left the forge and began to pull the bodies into it, one by one without burning them. Once he was done, he looked out at me, "Thank you for feeding me more. Please, continue."

I nodded to him and, as I watched, lines appeared on the side of the forge that corresponded with the number of corpses that Duke Forger took into the forge.

He saw my curious glance and said, "More sacrifices, and I may be able to imbue more power into the forge, and your creations with it."

I nodded, thinking of the power I could obtain, then brushed those thoughts aside and continued on before Nadir asked, "Should we leave here and return to the outskirts to look through our collection?"

"No." I glanced over to Midnight and spoke softly. "You've found another way out of this room; take us to it, then take us to the one who leads these ones."

Midnight closed his eyes, then nodded and fluttered over to the area in the back of the room. "This way, there's a door hidden by a mechanism in the wall." It sounded like he wanted to say more, but didn't and I didn't pry. Less now could mean more later.

I looked for the spot on the wall that could have activated the mechanism, but failed to find it. Nadir did though, grabbing one of the sconces that lit the room to try to give us more light. As soon as she touched it, there was a metallic hissing and a portion of the wall sheared to the side silently.

It opened into another below-ground-level room, but this one looked to be a simple basement for a business or something to that effect as there were casks, boxes, and other items just stored here. They were all well out of the way, but it was still concerning not to be able to see the whole space as we moved through it. We reached back through the space and used the sconce to close the room behind us before moving on.

Up the steps to the room above, a room occupied by a sleeping couple was all that separated us from our exit. I walked over them with ease, much more nimble than my sister, but she managed to get over them before one woke and she hit him in the jaw with a punch that made his lady friend awaken and gasp.

Nadir hit her with her other hand and both were out cold then and there. She turned back to me and muttered, "They will tell the guard that we were here. We cannot stay here much longer without running the risk of having to cull the entirety of the village."

I nodded my agreement and followed Midnight outside.

He flew above us and led us nearly to the other side of the

village to a shack that could very well have been a hovel. "Are you certain that's the place, Midnight?"

"I am," was all the bird would say as we watched it from the nearest alley.

"How do we handle this?" The question was more for myself than Nadir, but she took it seriously and put a hand on my shoulder as if she wanted me to stay. "You can't be preparing to go in there on your own."

"If there's another mage killer in there, they will obliterate you." She pressed harder into my shoulder. "Stay here so I don't have to worry about you, brother."

I grimaced and sighed. "Fine, but be safe and thorough."

She smirked at me and managed a brief, "Always," before loping over to the shack and disappearing inside.

There was no sound, only her dragging a body out behind her with blood on her hands.

Alarmed, I bolted closer to her and she waved me away. "He was dead when I got there, something is wrong."

Midnight chuckled. "I'll say."

I glared up at him and growled, "What haven't you told us?"

"Those investigators that you avoided?" I nodded and he flapped his wings once as he added, "Those weren't guards— they were mages."

A breeze wafted by my face, carrying the scent of copper and blood with it, as Midnight chittered then said, "Seems like they're on the warpath."

CHAPTER TWENTY-TWO

"Anything on him?" I didn't wait for Nadir's response, just digging into the man's trousers myself, not finding anything of use. "We need to leave unless we want to stay and murder a lot more people than we planned on."

"Change your glamour to be different enough that we won't be suspected, but normal enough to be considered safe." Nadir changed hers to get rid of all her scars and her bulk, almost becoming a man herself. I changed mine to get rid of my scars, allowed my hair to grow slightly, and then filled out my stomach a bit to look paunchier and less threatening.

I began to look around and finally asked, "Which way do we go?"

Nadir just pointed further north and spoke quietly. "Midnight said that the force they were expecting was coming from the north where the orcs' lands would be. We should head that way."

Nadir frowned and thought for a second then added, "There are tribes of wanderers who attack the outlying lands fairly regularly. There would be some places that they avoid, though."

"If we found a more current map of the area, do you think we could plot a possible location out?"

Midnight cleared his throat and stated, "I recall relaying something about a system of badger tunnels and a ruined village northward of here, if that helps."

I nodded once in gratitude and looked to the sky in the direction of the north. "There's not much we can do here in favor of figuring out where the head of the snake is to cut it off."

Nadir agreed and we were off in that direction a heartbeat after.

We cleared the wall with ease as all the guards that should have been on duty were too busy dealing with the falling out within the village to care about two strangers leaving. From the looks of the wagons and carts leaving from that side of the place, we weren't the only ones.

It was as good a cover as we would get, and once we reached an appropriate distance from the village, we stopped for a brief lunch and to look over the documents and things we'd collected from our various victims. We made about two gold, all of which I gave to Nadir to hold onto as she had the bulk of our money.

There were documents denoting things about their organization, but nothing of what they called themselves, or who was in charge outside a figure called the governor.

Nadir grunted and laid back on the ground. "I keep running across things that advise members to be wary of magic of all kinds." She took a deep breath and let it go before asking, "You?"

I glanced down at the document in my hand and read, "'Trust not a mage, lest you be turned into a …'" I squinted as the word swam with the blood that speckled it. "A frog?"

Nadir's knuckles popped as she clenched her fingers at her sides, fists hanging there as she mouthed, *A frog? Really?*

After a moment, she cleared her mind with a sigh and grumbled softly, "So it seems like whoever it is that is behind this is just praying on superstition and malicious intent between the skilled classes."

"And they aren't having to work very hard at all." I looked through what appeared to be a charter of signatures from those in the village who hated mages and wanted to put them in their place where they belonged. Or in the ground. Once more I read aloud, "'A mage told my momma I was gonna be ugly on account of my lips if they didn't heal me proper, and my momma says I'm the handsomest boy ever been, so I didn't need no damn magical treatment.'"

"I want to burn that place to the ground." Nadir once more had to rein herself in. "For that sentence alone, I would burn it all down."

I snorted and rolled my eyes at her anger. "We need to be careful." She frowned at me and I explained as I tapped the charter in my grip. "An organization with nothing spelled out to their members means that more people feel as though they are in charge of leading it in the direction they wish, however they wish."

"But there's still a hierarchy." Nadir frowned further as she thought about it and then pointed at the book. "That's the proof, isn't it?"

I nodded. "Proof one exists, but this far from their head-quarters or true mission; they let the fodder act how they please." I hated to admit it, but, "This is how the Fae courts operate, by and large."

She looked at me in disbelief so I explained further, my tone shifting a bit more to that of an educator than her brother. "Both courts and the 'free' Fae know that the ruler of their designated court is the law. Their whims and desires hold sway over all things, but for the most part, so long as the Fae pay tribute, muster for a fight, and heed their rulers, they are mostly left alone. They know who holds the swords at their backs, it's just their actions that see it either plunged into their back or into the chests of their foes."

"What about the Seelie?"

I snorted. "They operate on the notion that vanity and trickery are power. So long as they don't try to trick or outstrip their king, they can do as they please." I'd hated reading those books and accountings from the spies we sent to them, but it was what we had. "Much the same as us."

"Do you think it could be the Seelie behind this?"

I glanced at my sister, wondering the same myself. "I don't know. With this simple and nearly ineffective charter, I'm not entirely convinced that it's not them. But we can't know until we investigate for sure. All we know is that they want the mages either under heel, or dead."

Quest completed!

I blinked and almost panicked as the quest information populated for me to read once more.

Rumblings of Magical Malfeasance — The Primordial Elementals and the Goddess Seraestar have requested that you investigate a series of deaths believed to be linked to various individuals or organizations with motive to hate magic users and beings such as elementals. Find them and either figure out their motives, destroy them, or hamper their ability to do what they do. Reward: 30,000 EXP, further support from the goddess herself, and possibly untold aid from the elementals. Failure: Nothing aside from what may come from inaction.

Partial requirement for completion met!

I looked up to Nadir and discovered she held a shred of paper and she muttered, "True Children of Brindolla."

"That makes no sense, though." I grumbled and looked back at the incoming information.

Part of their plans for Dizern have been thwarted thanks to your efforts! Reward: 5,000 EXP and untold aid!

I grunted as the same quest presented itself to me, but as it was already accepted, there was only more that we could do. So this was a nearly unending quest until we either did all the things, or destroyed them completely.

The ground rumbled briefly and I wondered what it could be until I saw a large herd of sheep running toward us from the south. Nadir and I got out of the way and watched as Dread chased through with one of the poor creatures in her jaws.

"Dread!" Nadir snarled and the beast looked none-too-pleased to see her either. "Drop it!"

The warg sat back on its haunches and tossed the dead sheep on the ground with a nasty belch that fountained some wet tufts of wool into the air.

"Gross." A breeze thankfully carried the scent away from me, and I looked further toward where we would be heading. "Looks like the plumes of gasses from the swamplands ahead."

"A few days north to it, yes." She smiled to herself as she stared longingly. "The easterly portion of the continent that high is just plains to the north where the high elves hide. On the west, you have the swamps and bogs that then turn into plains and finally icy mountains."

"And the orc lands?"

Nadir grinned. "Span all three."

———

Darkness fell that night and for the first time in weeks, I heard whispering.

I opened my eyes from my trance and saw nothing. Worried, I blinked and still, nothing, but as my eyes adjusted, I could see the stars above and around me.

The ground was barren of all life. Not even the sparsest of grasses grew here.

"Welcome to the Null, Son of our Loves." I recognized the myriad voices as the Shadow Primordial as it reached out to me. "It is here that we will present our reward."

"Where are we?" It was too hard to hide the worry and wonder I felt, let alone keep it from my voice.

"The Null." The shadows around crept closer until finally I could see three distinct figures standing against darkness.

One wore a cape, the hood over it hiding all features from view. The second was a figure of incorporeal form; there was no face, just a medium-sized gaseous figure floating morbidly in place.

The final one looked like an infant, the head grotesquely large but the eyes black holes as it watched.

It spoke, mouth moving in a manner that disjointedly looked like it should have been speaking but the voice was too fast for the lips to keep up. "It had been some time since anyone dared visit us here, but there had been one of late who touches on the power to come."

"You said I was to be rewarded here?"

The baby and hooded figure nodded, and then there was the sound of movement near me. "We note that you need a mount. Your mother found a whistle in the dungeon that is ancestral to your people, and you have yet to visit it."

The gaseous figure floated forward, the voice ghastly and hard to figure out while the meaning flooded my being, *So we offer one that will be transport and transport only. Unlike our children who await you in the shadows for your summons.*

Though I was here for a reward owed, I couldn't keep the sarcasm from my tone as I watched them. "I could use them at any time. There's a mounting resistance against mages on Brindolla."

The hooded figure spoke with a hauntingly deep voice. "The quarrels of humanity do not carry weight in the Void, sweet child of Darkness Beloved."

"But your quarrels..." The pregnant silence by the baby head was enough to allow me to believe what was said.

Speaking of humanity was something a god, or something those far removed from their influence, would do. So their interference was being regulated by the gods somehow?

"Is it a..." I paused and narrowed my eyes as I stressed the next word. "*Magical* reason that you can't concern yourselves as much as you might like?"

"No. The Void will claim all eventually." The baby head shrugged.

The ethereal form spoke after that, *But if you desire to know why we do not interfere more directly, it does involve the goddess. Were it truly up to us, we would send the host of our children to allow you your strength, weapons, and more.*

"But she forestalls us for her own means and ends." The hooded figure assured. "Until such time as you *find* or summon one of our children, allow us to give you the mobility denoting one of your prowess and potential."

"And your station," the baby head added.

Something touched my shoulder, and it was as if shadows had come alive, given form and the ability to move. *This is Kestral, and she will allow you to ride her. She, like many shadows, is governed only by her will. The shape she chooses to take is hers alone, but she will also take council from you, should you deign to give it.*

I turned to find a massive mare, at least sixteen hands tall, staring down at me with eyes as white as the snows back in the Unseelie Court. I reached up subconsciously and she lowered her head to put her nose into my palm.

That single touch was enough to ignite something, as the shadows she was made up of fell to the ground with a soft, hissing splash that faded as she swallowed my smaller shadow with her own. After a few frantic heartbeats at the surprise, my shadow returned, though it was slightly darker.

"Whisper her name, and she will come to you." The hooded figure stood straighter. "We have tarried too long here, and the residents grow curious. Be free of us, child, and remember that you have our favor."

The others melded with the hooded figure as it turned and flew at something that crested a ridge and shrieked, a bone-chilling cold invading my being as it stared in my direction.

Something jostled me, and I opened my eyes to find Nadir shaking me. "Azlo? Are you alright?"

Even as I knew the terror gripping my still-beating heart, I just stood up and went outside of our tent, whispering, "Kestral."

Sure enough, even under the cover darkness, my shadow lengthened and she appeared.

I reached up and stroked her glorious mane as Nadir joined me. "Is she...?""

"A reward for the quest." I dismissed her, though I sorely wanted to ride upon her back. "What about you?"

She looked almost ashamed. "Don't want to talk about it." I frowned at that, but she said, "I went through what I found in the wall. A ledger of minor weapons supplied, simple swords and maces. A bag of coins, some of which didn't appear common, and then small game pieces. Nothing of any overt value or reason to keep."

There was no argument as she turned and walked back into the tent. If she wanted her privacy, I would respect that. Though I wondered who would deny her part in all this, if that was the case. Surely, they hadn't seen her gifted power and denied her, had they? And the bounty from the wall; why had they hidden all of that?

Until she decided to share that with me, I was as clueless as I was before I'd asked the question.

CHAPTER TWENTY-THREE

"Kestral!" She leaped from my shadow at my feet once more in the morning and stared at me, her long, flowing mane fluttering in the breeze as she stared down at me.

"A rather intimidating mount." Nadir whistled as Dread growled at the shadowy figure. "Is that all she can become?"

"She can change her form, but it's mainly up to her." I patted her shoulder as she stared down at me. "I think she's beautiful."

"She is, but she's a target and paints us in a poor light if we're trying to be less distinct."

I nodded and muttered, "Do you think you could take the form of a more... *normal* horse?" I quickly offered some flattery. "You know, because someone who sees you is obviously going to try to attack us to take you if all of your beauty is bare to the world."

She blinked her snow-white eyes at me before flinging her mane, and her visage shifted until she was a gray donkey a little taller than my chest.

Nadir guffawed hard enough that the donkey twitched an ear in her direction in irritation. "Thank you, Kestral, I appreciate you doing so for me. I will endeavor to make certain your sacrifice is not in vain."

She lifted her muzzle and huffed, allowing me to climb into the ebony saddle on her back as Nadir did the same with Dread, though the warg kept throwing sidelong glares at the donkey I rode upon. I had no doubt Kestral would defend herself if the lupine creature came too close. Even as a donkey, she carried herself regally and with pride.

Odd as an image, yes, but it was still interesting.

We rode on for the next few hours, needing little in the way of rest as Midnight scoured the countryside for any place that could be where we searched for.

On the second day, he surprised me by landing on my shoulder and telling us, "Stop."

"What's wrong?" I frowned at him and he ruffled his feathers.

"They're en route here as we speak, but it's a bit of a dicier situation than that."

Nadir called over to us, her warg frightened after getting too close to Kestral once already and receiving a bloody nose for it. "Are they embattled?"

"Yes, but not how we would prefer, I think." We both glared at him and he just said, "The orcs are hunting them, yes, but there are other humans chasing them as well. These ones are mages."

"So it's essentially a three-way running fight?" The bird nodded and I sighed. "This is a good chance for you to meet your people, no?"

"No." Nadir grunted and grimaced. "They could mistake me for trying to aid either side, or as an invader. It would be too much to risk."

"What do you suggest?" It was difficult not to be frustrated over all this. Who were these mages, and how were they on this group's trail so fast, especially when we were just beginning?

"We should look into the mages as well," Nadir said, startling me from my brief reverie. I blinked at her and she shook her head. "Something is weird about how quickly they're getting to them."

I gritted my teeth before nodding along with her. "True enough. We should get to where we can watch them, then pick at whoever is winning."

"Oh, it's a bloodbath." Midnight chuckled darkly. "The mages are massacring the non-mages, and the orcs are killing anyone they can that isn't an orc."

He was quiet for a time and then pointed his beak northwest. "That way; we should meet them soon if you ride all out. Then you can decide how best to proceed."

Nadir grunted. "Fine. Azlo?"

"I'm in, let's go see what we can learn."

We rode northwest from where we had been, but not all out so as to avoid as much of a fight as we could for now. If we had to join in, we would, from the set of Nadir's jaw, but it would need to be agreed upon.

MIDNIGHT

The children only rode for an hour before they found what lay in store for them. Truthfully, I'd found their hideout on the first day, but there had been a small scuffle amongst the leadership before one of the menial laborers among them disappeared for a day and a half. Curious, I had let events play out as they would, deigning to relay what I knew to the children when it was most pertinent.

It was only this morning that they brought back a host of mages all wearing the same color and kind of cloak, as if it were a uniform.

They had laid into the warriors of these supposed True Children of Brindolla like a smith hammering iron.

It was thanks to the three mage killers among their number that the others had managed to run at all, the spells focused on the swifter fighters as archers fired uselessly into barriers of mana.

The only reason that the mages hadn't completely overrun them was the orcs having come upon their flanks where they harried them mercilessly. It was carnage.

Orcs' weapons sailed through the shields meant for weapons of man and the men died to magic that they feared. Honestly, the group that seemed to fare the best was the orcs, who fought without fear of reprisal. When one orc fell, their mount would fight on as two more orcs would replace their fallen comrade with the fury of kin that others may never understand.

The savagery was enough that it even made me wonder if the two royals below would be alright among them, or if I should stop them again to avoid the worst of it all.

What I hadn't been prepared for was the boy seeing something that made him urge his mount forward with Nadir trailing behind him.

He looked mad, like all of his faculties were just free in that moment.

I dove down to the girl and called out, "What the Hells is the boy doing?"

"Seelie!" she snarled in return. "There is a Seelie Fae hidden among the humans."

I blinked and stared ahead at the scene, still seeing nothing. "And he means to take on all sides to get to them?"

"We both will!" Nadir roared and charged in, her axe flashing in the sunlight. She looked almost as crazed as the boy.

Is it too late to tell her I don't want to do this anymore? I was really just griping at this point, excitement getting the best of me as the boy neared the fray and stood on his mount's saddle with the dagger in his fist. *Oh, don't tell me...*

He did it. The prince actually *jumped* from the saddle onto the woman he had targeted, stabbing her three times before she realized what was going on. Then I felt the tug that I hated—the boy had said my name.

I blinked and fluttered next to him, hating the pull but not stealing any more mana from him than necessary to make me appear. "Yes?"

"We need information faster than we have time. Can you devour her, and tell me what she knows?"

I blinked at that. *He learns faster than I thought, and is much more annoyingly adept, like his Mother.* I answered aloud, "I can, but if I get hit, that means I won't learn as much."

"If you can do so and relay it to me, then do it now. I will get her away from the fighting so you can feast." He grabbed the struggling woman under the jaw as she began to shriek to her compatriots around her, dragging her from the worst of the fighting as I tried to land on her face for my impromptu meal.

One of the humans bellowed, "Jaska!" The woman struggled harder and the man rallied two of his friends to come forth, only for Nadir to ride in and bowl them over. Her axe swung twice and three heads thunked onto the ground.

I was jealous of her strength instantly, but being busy holding onto the struggling Seelie so that she couldn't swat me away was an ordeal of its own.

Finally, Azlo gathered from my lack of feasting that I needed some interference and he grabbed her around the neck with his arm and wrapped his legs around her upper arms, snarling, "Hurry up!"

With no preamble, but no less gusto, I began my descent into her memories.

Flashes and glimpses here and there of the Seelie Court, their proclivities for hiding their flaws with gaudy fashion and even more extravagant illusory magic. There were very conspicuous gaps in her recollection that started when a man I couldn't recognize walked into the room with her and another dozen or so agents. I recognized the reverberating name that her mind screamed as she was trying to mentally fend me off—Oberron. The Seelie king and the one whose existence was a threat to the children's court.

I continued to eat, devouring skills and lessons on the Seelie and how they operated, what little I could before something jostled me hard enough that I had to come out of my meal to ensure I wouldn't be killed for humbly eating my food.

"No, you imbecile, you can't have her back!" Azlo savagely kicked the knee of the aggressor backward and it snapped like a dry twig.

Back in I went, more knowledge, this time, much more useful.

I committed several names to memory and then the plans as best as I could before something hit me and knocked me away.

Jostled and angry, I turned to see that it was one of the orcs that had hit me. I fought the urge to kill the beast where it stood, but the boy got to it first.

He hit it as hard as he could with his massive hammer and snarled as he whipped the weapon over his head and crushed the still-struggling Seelie woman's chest, likely splattering her heart.

Then he hit her a second time, crushing her skull, the most obscene act of defiling them and the lies their beauty enforced. This was the ultimate way to disrespect the Seelie.

This was going to make dealing with the Unseelie and the Seelie much more interesting, considering she had been the Seelie King's niece.

CHAPTER TWENTY-FOUR

AZLO

My sister roared as another orc made his way at her, falling to her axe as she attacked and defended herself. The Seelie was dead, that was certain—the brains and blood I flicked off Shaper assured me of that.

The humans had all fallen and there was hardly anyone left standing among the mages as well, but they made a grandiose show of fighting the orcs off as the few better ones crafted a spell together.

They finished with a flourish that opened a gate that all but the two mages holding the barrier up before the onslaught of orcs crossed into. The defending mages turned to flee when the gate closed, just before they could enter it.

The orcs were on them in an instant and from the sounds of their victory cries, I doubted there would be survivors.

"Nadir!" She turned to me and blinked. "Can we make it out of this without needing to kill all of them?"

"I will challenge one to combat for the right to speak to their leader." She shifted her stance and eyed all of the orcs circling us. "You will likely need to prove you are capable of defending yourself as well."

I grimaced and focused on the orcs around us. Their median level was in the low-to-mid-twenties. That didn't bode well for me, though I was capable in a fight against someone close to my level.

I shrunk Shaper to a more reasonable size and held it at my hip before calling out to Nadir, "Ready whenever you are."

She pulled herself up to her full height and let the human glamour fade, tossing away a ring on her left hand with it. An interesting act, but I did my best to ignore it and remain calm enough to seem like it should have been a surprise.

The orc closest to her stomped forward and bellowed something that she returned with just as much vigor. Her skin was just as green and her bulk as impressive. He backed down, if only slightly, for a second, and someone else shoved their way through.

This one was larger and calm, for some reason, pointing from himself to her as he spoke in a deep, guttural tone at her. He seemed genuinely reasonable.

"He says that we fought well," Nadir called as she cautiously walked closer to me. The same man called out. "He hopes that we will provide a good fight before death."

"Can you challenge him?" She shrugged and I frowned. "I thought we were going to challenge them."

"I thought they would give me the option." She frowned then called out to the leader in orcish. He retorted and then she smiled. "I can challenge them. It just may or may not mean we survive."

"So win." It was simple to do that, especially for a monstrous fighter like her. "Then we get to live."

She snorted and said, "The fight doesn't decide that, it's to decide on whether they will hear us out or not. They could still just decide to kill us."

I rolled my eyes and then one of them called out and bellowed something at me, pointing as they walked forward.

"Your nonchalance has offended him." Nadir pointed out with a smirk. "He wants to kill you for your impudence."

I blinked at that. "So then if I kill him, I'll be okay?" I amended that question. "Or on my way to being okay?"

She looked to the more talkative orc and spoke, then nodded after his response. "You've been allowed to fight before his champion and I do, so if you win, they'll consider you strong enough to be mine."

I grimaced at that and she shook her head. "Like property."

I frowned at that and shook my head slightly. "Orcs." I shook my shoulders out and checked my weapons before glancing at Nadir. "Rules?"

"Fight to the death, and don't dishonor yourself. Other than that, fight well."

I heaved a sigh and glanced over at Midnight. "You know how to reach my mother, correct?" He nodded and I added, "Go to her and tell her about what we've found, then return to us."

"I would like to see this fight." I was about to order him away, but he stalled me with his wings spreading. "If I go without news of your health, she might kill me for my impudence."

I grimaced and then sighed. "As soon as you know, you'll go."

It wasn't a request, just a statement made as I walked forward.

"I don't know what your name is, but thank you for allowing me to prove I'm more than a corpse waiting to be killed." I did my best to sound reverent as I said this in the Prime Realm's common tongue. I wasn't meek enough to be daunted by taking the life of someone who would gleefully take mine.

That had been beaten out of me by my instructors as a child.

The orc took my stoic statement as Nadir translated and spat on the ground, his whole body shaking as he brandished his spear toward me.

I pulled out Shaper and sighed as I settled into a stance that would let me defend and attack.

The orc did have some skill, his broad body and tall build allowing him added reach with his spear, which he used to great effect. His opening salvo was a leaping stab that would have pierced my chest if I hadn't rolled forward.

Once I was close enough, I snapped my left leg out and kicked him in the side of the knee. The orc held up much better than my previous human opponents, his strength likely on par with or just above my own.

Then I swung Shaper. The hammer hit the knee I struck with a meaty thud. The spear sliced my left upper arm. It was a good hit, and would have stopped my swinging the hammer if it were as heavy as it should have been.

My left hand slapped the haft for the spear away as the orc bellowed and swung with Shaper growing in my grip. The weapon connected with his meaty shoulder, which popped sickeningly out of socket.

The orc roared in pain, switching hands with his spear to attack me.

Once again, I slapped the haft of the spear away while twisting to slam Shaper's spike into his hip with another meaty squelch.

There was a gasp and I twisted, slipping my hand into his mouth and grasped his tongue, yanking it out as hard as I could.

The muscle didn't want to give it up, but I pulled harder as I let go of my weapon to strike with my right.

My fist connected just before I reached down and grabbed the dagger from my belt. The orc slammed a fist into my chin that made my vision flicker, but I held strong, at least until the other fist connected with my chest and pushed me away.

The orc man snarled, his voice and the sound slightly askew as his tongue was probably looser. He tried to speak as I climbed to my feet, his hands on Shaper where he tried to pull the weapon out.

The weapon came out a little bit, just enough to distract

him. I pulled the wind dagger and charged him, releasing two dull swipes of the wind blade. The orc's spear took the first and then the other zipped through it, slicing his flesh slightly.

Then I was on him, dagger glinting with a dull sheen as I stabbed it into his throat. The blade bit harder than I thought it would, slipping a bit from my grasp.

I adjusted my grip and slid the weapon from where it was to the other side of his ear away from myself.

He slid to the ground from me, slumping forward when his knees hit the earth and then he fell onto his face.

The orcs shouted and raised their voices in a chant that eventually raised the hair on my arms and the back of my neck.

I collected my weapons as the bird cawed once before disappearing, and I knew Midnight was obeying my orders.

"They like the brutality of it." Nadir spoke to me over the chanting. She smiled at me. "You fought well."

I grunted and felt the experience rushing into me. It was enough that I was almost ready to level up again with all the others that we'd had to kill. I could check later. There were a lot of dead here.

Maybe I could let Duke Forger have all of them?

I blinked, thinking quickly as the sun continued to lower toward the horizon. "Nadir, ask them if I can burn the dead for them as a show of pride in their victory and ours."

She frowned at me, then turned and asked the question. The response was cautious and uncertain, but she translated a message of general, but halting consent.

I gathered the dead as Nadir spoke to the orcs. They maintained a safe distance as I worked. It took me the better part of half an hour to get all of them close together, and once I had the dead all piled on top of one another, I bent and took a breath.

"Duke Forger, I ask that you come forth and claim these sacrifices for your power."

I pulled the forge out and a spark of blue flame burst from

it, shooting into one of the bodies where it ignited against the cloak.

The flames spread faster and faster until a twenty-foot tall pyre of now-green flame bathed the world around us emerald.

The crackling and crumbling of bone was fascinating, but the orcs began to chant again, someone beating a drum that they must have had to pull from their inventory.

The leading orc called to Nadir and motioned to the circle forming near the pyre. She nodded and another orc came forward to fight. This one was a massive specimen that reminded me of her a little bit, at least in build.

I wondered if she would be okay for this fight, considering he only brought his hands into the ring with him.

Nadir stepped into the ring with him, twirling her axe only to plant it haft down into the ground behind her. She shifted her hips and shoulders experimentally and did an awkward squat to loosen up.

I raised a brow as she did so and wondered just what the hells she was thinking.

———

Queen Maebe sat on her throne, half-heartedly attending a telling of what preparations had been taken by the minor nobles she employed to cement her hold over her lands farther from the Unseelie capital.

I watched her for a time before I presented myself to her once she was alone with a flourish of feathers and grace.

Her tone held surprisingly little ire as she stared at me. "What are you doing here?"

"I come bringing news from my master." I took great care to stare at her as I spoke. "He wished that I speak to you and tell you of his and his sister's findings."

Her eyes widened and she lifted her hand imperiously for me to speak.

So I did. I told her everything, and then filled her in on who her son had just murdered.

There was pride in her savage grin. "Excellent to know, but I do not think this slight will be without reprisal." She tapped her fingers on her arm rest before growling low in her throat. "As to the names, I have heard of some of them. They are neutral Fae likely used to scout for her, or to be summoned as a means to recruit them. Give him one of them, and Nadir another. They must begin assembling their forces if they are to be prepared for *his* vengeance."

She stood and began to pace the ground and then thought of something and reached into her inventory and pulled out a satchel. "This is for Azlo. Take it to him with a word of contentment from me. He has proven his worth of this prize for felling a foe of this magnitude. Should he kill more and survive, he may earn more—I speak as queen, do this for me, Ai—"

"I am that no more, Majestic Shadow." I bowed my head in contrition before lifting it to stare into her gaze. "Not for some years have I been that. I am now simply Midnight."

She arched a brow at the new moniker then nodded once and made a dismissive gesture. "Fly to them and keep them safe if you can, *Midnight*. This is his will."

I grunted, knowing that damn well better than anyone on the face of this planet—these planes of existence on this side of the Veil. She didn't need to tell me.

Lowering my head once more, I shifted from the Fae Realm to the Prime Plane and fluttered closer to where the fight had begun for the girl below.

I would watch for a time and let the boy think it took me longer to go and return so he wasn't wasting my time or his resources. Mainly my time though.

CHAPTER TWENTY-FIVE

AZLO

I watched as Nadir closed the gap between the other fighter and herself with measured strides. She ducked a soft jab and countered easily with one of her own that the other orc just let land on his chest.

The smack from it was audible just before the cheering started. The orc snarled and attacked her, trying to grab her arm for a throw, but Nadir dipped away. Her nimble steps flowing one to the next like she danced to a favorite song as she struck him twice more on the way out.

They were softer strikes, nothing that would do more than be blows to this man's pride if nothing else. I worried she was doing this on purpose until I could see his eyes flashing the same as hers had.

So he was a berserker too? She was feeding his rage, but why? She could end the fight so much faster if she just went straight for the kill.

She toyed with him for a time and finally he lost his mind, roaring at the top of his lungs before launching himself at her.

She braced her legs and set her stance before elbowing him directly in the neck, her whole body twisting behind the technique to add extra power.

Blood drizzled from the orc's broken jaw, the grinding sound weird to me. I'd heard and had a broken jaw before; this was nothing like it. Could it have been the tusks grinding against the other teeth?

The orc didn't seem to be too fazed about his jaw, turning back to lash out at Nadir, but she was already on his left, stringing a series of jabs and crosses together that hit her opponent on that same spot she hit before.

She picked into him and his defense as if she knew exactly where to take him apart at the seams and when her last, most powerful strike slammed into his temple, the man fell to the ground unconscious.

Rather than making some kind of cheer or noise of reluctance, the crowd simply waited as Nadir bent down and hefted the large man up into the air and threw him at her weapon.

The body hit the axe blade and knocked it over. Blood began to pool around the wound as the still-unconscious victim didn't stir. She flipped him into his back with a brutal kick, and he lay there with the axe at an odd angle in his chest and collar bone.

Nadir plucked the weapon from the wound and twirled it once before it arced overhead and sheared the orc's head from his shoulders. She reached down and gripped the skin on top of the orc's large head with her finger tips and lifted the head skyward, bellowing a challenge that the other orcs returned in kind, some of them even stepping forward to fight her themselves.

The man she had been speaking to before held up a horn and blew into it once, the horde of green-skinned warriors crying out with it, then falling to a knee.

All except one, that was. He stepped through the crowd carefully, as though he knew that knocking over any of those beneath him would likely hurt them. He was larger even than the one Nadir had killed and as he moved with the grace of someone who had been fighting a very long time, there was another sense of surety to him.

He spoke, and I was surprised. "Allow me to speak to you both, as our time here nears an end." He looked to both of us and motioned to the pyre burning behind us. "We can see that you are not from either group of fighters, and that you only fought us in honorable combat shows that you mean us no harm, at least outright. I ask. What is it you wish?"

He blinked at us as Nadir watched him carefully, he tilted his head. "If you wished to leave here unharmed, you have proven to us and to Uk'Beth that you are worthy to walk his lands. Even you, human."

I frowned at that and looked down, realizing I still wore my human glamour. I would need to reveal myself or keep it set this way for a while now.

"Have I proven myself orc enough to walk with you to your home?" Nadir asked, defiance in her tone. "How many more do I need to kill to prove I am?"

"Uk'Beth smiles on you, sister." The orc stood straighter. "I am Urtan, son of Ragul, shaman and chieftain of my people. If you wish to come home, we will welcome you to march with our band so that you can seek out my father and his blessing."

He cleared his throat and spoke lower. "I do not promise that he will grant you what you wish, or that he will not test you. I can only offer you, a fellow warrior, a place amongst my men."

"And my brother?" The orc looked at me in shock as Nadir motioned to me. "He is here to support me, and I will have him with me in this."

Urtan frowned and offered a tentative, "Humans do not find themselves well-liked among our kind." When Nadir didn't back down, he looked to me. "I saw that she had some sort of ring that released an illusion, do you have the same?"

I released the glamour while I fidgeted with my hand, though instead of appearing as an elf, I stood in my fox-man form, though I still used a glamour to hide my natural celestial lineage and appeared as a black fox. Several of the orcs behind Urtan gasped and looked to their leader for guidance, though more than a few hands flew to weapons out of instinct.

"I can sense that you are not of this plane." Urtan was cautious now.

"I am not, though I am of her blood all the same." It was all I would say on the matter for now. "Do I need to spill more blood for a right to walk among you?"

"You will be asked to fight for almost everything you wish," he confirmed. "But as you made abundantly clear, you are at least worthy to travel with us, for now."

"Then let us not waste time." Nadir turned and threw the head in her grip onto the flaming bodies that slowly cooked and crackled under the attention of the flames. She leaned down and did the same with the body at her feet, then I got the idea and lifted the body of my own opponent and did the same.

The fire consumed all of them, though I would need to let Duke Forger eat them wholly before I could return him to the forge.

No, I will be able to return to you if you leave me here. His crackling voice echoed through the core of my being. *Once I finish, I will find you. I just wish to enjoy this meal in peace. Thank you for it, by the way.*

I nodded and she looked to Urtan. "We will join you on your march home."

He nodded. "Very well." He motioned to the man with a horn who blew two short toots with it and all of the orcs rose from their kneeling positions. "It will take us three days to get there from here. We were on patrol and happened upon the old village these cowards hid in."

———

We marched for hours throughout the day, eating handfuls of whatever we had that took no time to prepare as the orcs had no intention of stopping any time soon.

They kept their distance from us, though more than a few of them glared at us. Some of them even waggled their eyebrows at my sister and spoke in hushed tones, which almost made me challenge them.

I glanced over at her and she blushed and looked away. I had to know. "Can I kill them for that?"

She shook her head. "It's no different from the nobles' daughters and sons who vie for your attentions in court, Azlo. They don't know that our senses are sharper than theirs."

I blushed, remembering all the times that some of them had whispered what I assumed the orcs had been saying to each other in confidence to me directly. My mother had overheard and said nothing, but Vrawn did not stand for that at all, and dressed the young elven woman down immediately.

She hadn't cared, staring at me with a soft smirk the whole time, but I knew she didn't want me—she wanted power. Influence.

I had no interest in any of them.

Though there had been passing fancies and crushes, swiftly crushed by ulterior motives and political machinations, it was difficult to ascribe to the fact that I could end up marrying to produce an heir someday. I grunted to myself and pulled myself from the reverie as something warm drew my attention.

An orc stood close, Urtan. "We will stop soon for the evening meal. There will be a great bonfire to ward off animals as this will be the last time we have the luxury of such." When I frowned at him, he explained, "The swamp we travel to has many pockets of flammable gas that could spell disaster."

I had to ask. "Urtan, you speak common so well. Why is this?"

He lifted his chin and jutted his tusks out proudly. "I am a shaman as well, and as such, we learn the languages of the dead we summon as spirit guides. I have killed and spoken to many humans, Fae, and other creatures. I speak and understand many languages, as does my father."

I nodded and switched to Sylvan. "Then you can understand us if we speak this language?"

He blinked at me. "What language is that?"

"Not elven, it's Sylvan, and we both speak it," Nadir answered. "Don't worry, we won't use it unless absolutely necessary."

He nodded, then shrugged. "We do not care whether you do or not. There is no language orcs speak that is meant to be hidden behind ignorance. If you do not speak our language, you will be ignorant, and we will prevail." He turned to me and smiled. "The same goes for the languages we don't know. If you use them, we don't care. We will win anyway."

I chuckled. "You have to appreciate the bravado."

"Bravado means an attempt to impress." Urtan spoke softly, staring into my eyes. "This is true. I attempt to impress upon you that you are surrounded by people who would kill you if you stepped out of line. While we do not observe conventional rules of hospitality or care whether something is rude to others like you would, we do recognize when we are outmatched."

He leaned back and grinned. "While many of our kind also wouldn't care about that, I assume you would, considering your lower level."

I laughed at that, allowing it with a nod. "It is a concern, but I would happily take as many of you with me as I could before I fell."

He raised an eyebrow and his grin only widened. "You would make a good orc."

We continued on into dusk where we stopped near a large tree that they cut down to use as wood for the fire that they meant to have with several cooking fires around the larger one.

While the others cooked their food, I wandered closer to the massive fire and waited by it. I linked more of the links for my armor together, the piece coming more and more into completion. If I spent the whole of the night working on it, I could finish it.

The fires around the area grew hotter, suddenly, almost unbearably so, as a figure stepped from them.

It was Duke Forger. He smiled at me and I pulled out the forge he lived in to let him in as the orcs began to scramble for a fight.

Once he was gone, Urtan stomped over to me with a retinue of his men. "What manner of creature was that, and why did it not attack us?"

"It was a fire elemental, and we are bonded." He stared at me and even then I could see that he was uncertain, so I smiled at him. Though it wasn't a comforting smile, I said, "He doesn't like to fight, but he gives me the ability to do so. I figured it wouldn't bother you for him to come to me if all of you were so strong."

The massive orc jutted his jaw forward and exposed his tusks once more. "We are strong."

"Then him returning to me is no problem." I continued to work on my links, and after a moment of intense scrutiny he left, though some of the orcs stayed closer to watch over me and make sure I wasn't being clever.

They passed out food, giving some to Nadir, but not me. That was okay. I had my own.

As I ate, I read over the notifications that I received from Duke Forger.

Congratulations!

Your pact to your patron (Duke Forger) has grown stronger!

I smiled at that, then pulled the forge out of my inventory, noting that all of the markings for the sacrifices were gone and in its place, a marking for something different. One I didn't recognize.

It is for you to imbue more magic to your pieces. This will allow the forge to pull in ambient mana to assist you in empowering your items more.

I mentally thanked him and grinned. There looked to be

new fittings that suggested I could attach a pan to pour the mold of a weapon or piece of armor into. This would help me streamline making something so that I didn't need to take so much time—great for traveling.

I decided to stay awake and watch over Nadir, much to her annoyance, but I needed to finish my project, so she acquiesced and went to bed in a bedroll she pulled from her inventory.

With her out of the way, I began to finish the chest piece.

CHAPTER TWENTY-SIX

The orcs didn't appreciate the noise that I made making the finishing touches on my chainmail backing, but I didn't care because they left me alone.

I attached the chains to both sides of the piece, and smiled as the information was visible to me at last.

Half-Chain Breastplate
+3 defense, no decreased maneuverability.

I skipped over the other information because I knew who had made it, and smiled to see I was now a level 27 Smith. Still a layman, but improving. I would hope to be improving sooner rather than later with more projects coming.

I had plans, but they would require some patience and more than a few sacrificial items used to increase my level.

As I looked over the armor and blueprinted several items I wanted to make, the sun rose and I smiled. Others would be exhausted, for certain. Especially the orcs who had to listen to my tinkering.

Nadir woke with a smirk and raised a brow at me. "They're all muttering about you keeping them from getting good sleep."

"I was busy and there was a good watcher." It wasn't a lie.

Midnight had returned to me and kept watch over all of us as the night progressed, though he complained of a headache that came with plane hopping.

She raised an eyebrow until the raven Midnight landed on my shoulder and croaked a hello to her without words so as not to alert the orcs that he was more intelligent than what they could handle.

Once there was a brief breakfast, the orcs tore down their bare camp and marched on. Those that had been nearest me overnight plodded on over the course of the day and into the increasingly moistened earth and then the dregs of the swamp.

It wasn't long into the dampness and unpleasantly scented copses of trees that the sun became no more than a feeble dream and one that I wished for readily. This place stank, and with our sensitive senses enhancing every suctioned step and stinking draft of air swirling into the insufferable place, I understood why there would be no stopping here.

There was nowhere *to* stop should there have been a need to in the first place. One of the more nimble orcs led a march of no more than two abreast through the area on the driest and most stable grounds possible.

Even then, it was impossible not to find yourself grimacing as the sickening and disgusting goop swirled over the lip of your boot and down to your toes.

I *longed* to clear this place and leave so that I could at least change my socks.

We made it through the first half of the swamp with no more issue than one of the orcs needing to be pulled from a section of deeper mud that bordered the walking path our guide had navigated us to.

The second half was another story. Monstrous mosquitoes larger than Midnight plagued the band of warriors as they trudged through the area of their nests. If it weren't for Nadir's skills as the Healer, more than a few of them would have ended up diseased like some of the creatures we'd found lying strewn about that section of the swamp.

There were lumps that moved around beneath the mud and muck that, when stabbed with a spear, no longer moved but never came up to counter, either.

Then there was the bog witch.

———

MIDNIGHT

The orcs found her first, but not before she had struck and grabbed one of them, yanking them into the water.

I watched in curious interest as she stuffed her crooked, malformed arm into his throat and pulled his stomach up and out to begin feasting on it with a piercing cackle.

The orcs' response was to start throwing javelins at her, but she and her prize simply splashed into the water and out of the effective range where she would eat what she liked then come back for more.

I landed on Azlo's shoulder and muttered, "She's got a taste for flesh now, and all of you are in her territory. She will keep hunting you all until you're out of her turf, or she kills all of you and eats you."

The boy grunted. "Most hex-bred creatures are the exact same way." He frowned, sniffing the air. "She's not one of ours, must have been born here on the Prime plane. If we can't get to her on the water, she's got us pretty much at her mercy."

The boy has about three feet of movement that he can use once every thirty seconds that is nearly instantaneous. I grimaced at the water and muck around us and sighed. *I doubt that it will be able to get me more than a passing or glancing blow. She has to be in the level twenty-five to thirty range to have been able to take an orc that size away and kill him easily.*

The bog witch screeched and attacked once more, the orc it chose managing to club her on the shoulder before she nabbed him.

"I think it would be a smarter idea to run, at this point."

Azlo looked at me as I checked her position relative to him; he was safe for now. "If you flee fast enough, you can leave and come back stronger."

"If we flee now, Nadir may not get to meet the people she wants to, and will look like a coward. That's not an option."

"Then you have a higher likelihood of dying." It was so hard to keep from pecking the stubborn little princeling that almost missed the movement under the water. "That's it. That's how we can do this!"

He frowned, looking at where I pointed my wing. "What?"

"Those things moving below the surface of the water? Those are elementals."

The boy frowned and leaned toward the water. "I can't sense anything."

I rolled my eyes. "If you were a magical creature being stabbed at by anything above you, would you move?"

He shook his head and frowned. "Fine."

He leaned down and spoke to the muddy water. "Hello? I can't hear you if you don't talk to me—we could use some help." I watched as the orcs continued to stab at the swamp around then and amended my statement. "I could, at least."

A small head poked out and burbled something that the boy seemed to understand, then ducked back under the water.

"Please?" Azlo asked. The small head never returned, but he held out the armor he made and spoke clearly. "If one of you will help me, I will help you. I can try to make you stronger. I know that you've heard of me. If I don't do something, a lot of the orcs here and possibly me are going to die and put the elementals in jeopardy."

A large, misshapen hand reached out of the water and pulled itself up out of the muck. There were vines and twigs sticking out of it, but it was easily much larger than Duke Forger.

It burbled at him and he frowned. "I don't know if I can do that, but if I can help you do that, I will try." He pressed the armor forward, asked, "Again, will you help me? We can discuss a potential pact later."

The eight-foot-tall elemental reached out and touched the breastplate, the object drinking in its power until the creature was gone. Vines wove between the links and the metal took on a more copper-like sheen as bits of oil began to wear on it, then solidified to a muddy brown color.

The bog witch struck again, slashing her long, clawed fingers down an orc's face, leaving a grizzly, savage row of lines blooming with blood. Then she noticed the magic around the prince and shrieked excitedly.

He grimaced as she slumped into the muddy muck and disappeared. I shouted to him, "She's coming for you and that armor, Azlo. If she gets her hands on you, you'll be in trouble."

The boy grimaced and set his feet while pulling his dagger in his left hand and Shaper in his right, but in a more manageable size.

He stood at the ready and when she screamed out of the muck beside him, he faded from view and stood on the water behind her.

His blade flashed in the sunlight and the witch screamed, trying to clutch at her wounded shoulder, but the boy whirled and sprang in the opposite direction she faced.

The best way to kill any kind of hex-bred is either magic weapon, silver, or fire. He had two of those three.

He left the dagger in the wound where she could just barely touch the end of the hilt and put both hands on Shaper as she turned to engage him.

An orcish javelin sailed through the air that she caught and hurled toward the prince, only to have him knock it aside with his hammer before he snarled at her, "Come on!"

She screeched again and leveled her hands in front of her, shoving forward as magic swirled around her fist, the muck rising like a wave in a storm to push the intruder away. I half-expected to find the prince wading out of the muck on the other side. Instead, he appeared on the other side of the attack and charged her.

Another three weapons swooshed through the air at her from behind before another, ghostly creature lifted itself from the ground and grasped her ankles to pull her into the water.

The witch bent and two of the projectiles splashed into the water harmlessly, but the last one speared her calf as Prince Azlo crossed the distance with savage determination etched into his features.

The specter clawing at the witch's feet and ankles kept her just distracted enough for Azlo to clobber her in the face with his hammer fully enlarged.

She sailed off the muck and onto land, screaming as the orcs rained down heavy blows with mortal weapons, but luckily, Azlo sent a ball of Flickering Flame into the wounds that formed in her belly and chest.

There was a wheezing gasp and she screeched, a rippling wave of energy pushing everyone but Nadir away. The orcish woman pulled out a weapon I didn't recognize from her inventory that she used to cut the creature's head off with a resounding roar.

The witch died and I could see the ethereal energy that was *experience* flooding those who fought. Mainly the boy, one orc, and Nadir.

It was interesting to see, as it always had been.

"Fox!" Urtan snarled, stomping to the front of the group of orcs. Azlo looked at him in surprise. "What is your name?"

The boy frowned and said, "Azlo."

"You are a brave warrior," Urtan asserted and lifted his chin. "I will tell many of your courage and prowess. Come. We go to our village."

Interesting how combat forces the shaman to lose a bit of that intelligence, or at least some of his vocabulary.

They began to move again, the orcs carrying the witch's body along with them to show to their shaman chief.

The trek was long with their need to stick to drier land, but it wasn't as eventful as the middle of the swamp. By the end of the following day, the group cleared the thinning trees of the swamp and rested for the rest of the day into the following morning. Even the children took turns resting as they would.

That level of vigilance was taxing on the mind and body, especially in ones so young, even if they had been trained to maintain said state of mind since the time they could walk.

I closed my eyes and allowed my clone to take over as I rested and digested the information I needed. I would tell the boy what I had when I woke.

———

My trance ended and I stretched as I stood and went to my inventory for my new piece of armor.

"You can come out now, elemental." I set the armor on the ground so that the massive elemental pulled itself out of the breastplate and sat on the ground in front of me. It stared at me curiously and burbled to me before watching me for a time. "I remember. You asked me if I could help you to become a pure elemental, and I said that I would try to help."

The creature nodded, and tapped the armor. "Yes, you're welcome to stay in the armor. I was wondering, though, if you would like to form a pact with me." I held up a hand as it continued to observe me and clarified, "Not to serve me, but for me to technically serve you. I think it would be more of a mutual thing."

It blinked at me, slowly closing one eye then the other. Finally, it burbled again and disappeared back into the armor. I sighed and quietly muttered, "I understand. Thank you for wanting to think it over."

A fluttering of wings drew my attention back away from the thoughts of more potential spells and I found Midnight kneeling next to me in humanoid form. "Risky, what is it?"

"I need to take you away from here for a moment. Do I have your permission to invade your mind so that I can give you information?" He didn't look at me as he asked the question, just affixed his gaze to the ground and stared. He must have been able to glean my discomfort, because he muttered, "I cannot harm you or defy your will without a *very* good reason. With this spell, I can safely pass this information without drawing attention to either of us and you will need it. I swear this on our bond."

I felt the oath lock into place around our bond and a marking appeared around his throat almost like a tattoo. "Fine. Do it."

He reached up and touched my forehead, then disappeared.

I closed my eyes and the information he wanted to pass to me flooded my mind. I felt a blood vessel under my eye rupture and something oozed from my nose, but I *knew* now.

"If I summon this creature, how likely are they to fight me?"

Midnight, now in bird form, grimaced and clacked his beak before saying, "It is likely. This one is the least prideful and spiteful, but not necessarily the weakest of the names I now hold access to. I also passed along some other knowledge that I gained access to that I am certain you will like, though from who it came from, I doubt you will enjoy it."

He cleared his birdie throat before I could close my eyes to think on what he'd alluded to and a bag appeared before me on the ground. "Your mother wished to reward you for killing the Seelie you found." Before I could speak, he clacked his beak and turned to stare at me. "She was not normal Seelie, but their king's niece. He will likely not abide her death long without sending someone to return the favor for you."

I frowned, heart beating a bit faster at the prospect of the Seelie coming for us directly, but that was just an eventuality that I had merely sped along.

Midnight spoke again. "She said that she is proud of you for that—not her words, but it was my interpretation and that matters." The corners of his beak lifted and he nudged the bag. "This is from her. It's probably something really nice, so feel free to open it."

I stared at him and he just grumbled, "Or not…"

"Go and tell Nadir what you just told me, and do the rest of my mother's bidding." He muttered to himself as he flew off and I looked over the bag before me.

I opened the bag and turned it over in the air over the ground in front of where I sat. Three chunks of ice as large as my foot fell out and *clomped* onto the ground and against each other before the area around them began to cool comfortingly. Then a note fell out.

I lifted it and turned it over to read.

My beloved son,

This is a gift I have had prepared for you since I found out about your interests all those years ago as a boy, and have never given them to you for fear of disheartening you from your interests by my interference. If you have received these, it means that you have earned them, and that is a feat that not many outside those of true skill can do.

I hope that this Ever Frozen can be useful to you in your crafting, and that you will have cause to further deplete our coffers as you grow. I love you as far as the stars are from me in the night sky.

Mother.

I blinked at the words and their meaning, before speaking the name of the items, "Ever Frozen." I touched them and they were painfully cold to the touch. I wondered how I would be able to use them, but it was something I would likely need to reach out to Thogan for. Or go to Djurn Forge. I had always wanted to go there, if I was being honest with myself.

It was one of the last bastions of dwarven culture, and the way that Thogan described it was just too enticing not to want to see for myself. Some day while we roamed free, I would go there and meet the clan I had been born into thanks to my father. That was one of the only good things that he had done for us outside just getting our mothers pregnant and though I was grateful for it, I would never *ever* say that aloud.

The thought of it alone made my mouth dry and left me wanting to gag.

I put the prize into my inventory and thought carefully

about the Fae I could summon. If it didn't want to come to me, it would take my mana and potentially some of my health with it. Better to attempt it with Nadir nearby to keep me from being killed. If I had learned nothing from my mother, it was most highly impressed upon me that 'pie' moments needed to be done with those of real power nearby and typically with medical aid and healing spells at hand.

Father had a deplorable talent for getting himself and others into trouble with those thoughts, and I could not risk my mission and Nadir's with my negligence due to curiosity.

With her walking toward me uncertainly, I was curious to see if that would have happened sooner rather than later.

CHAPTER TWENTY-SEVEN

MIDNIGHT

The girl had taken her gift that Maebe had given me, though more as an afterthought than anything else, before summoning the worm-like being that answered to the name I told her.

Both were strong in their own rights, the gift a weapon that Maebe thought the young woman would like, and the worm covered in scales and poison. Luckily, the majority of the orcs closest to her were asleep or they would have panicked and attacked. She made it take a less threatening form, and sent it off northward to scout for trouble before she looked back at me.

"You've been watching us for a long time." It was a statement, sure, but it held something else. I nodded. "Why?"

"Curiosity, mainly." Omissions were clever things. When I offered nothing else, she frowned. "Why do you care?"

"I find myself wondering how much you know." She watched me steadily as I continued to stare back. "I know that Azlo hasn't said anything, likely because voiced distrust is a sign that whatever you're hiding needs to be hidden better, but I know something else. Lies, even ones of omission, have a way of biting you in the tail. When that happens, I will be there. So, how much do you know, bird?"

I grinned a birdie grin and simply sighed. "Everything, Nadir. I know all that I can know." She frowned deeper and I spoke with mirth. "Do you remember the first time you slipped the spell that druidess put on you to keep you from shifting shape? I do."

She had been in the middle of a sparring match with her master and was being walloped with his cane when suddenly a wolf-cub stood there and attacked him. She'd bitten him and he was forced to teach her how to control the shifting. She'd been five years old at the time and drawn blood rather easily.

She blushed and stared at me for a time and I finally decided to take pity on her and said, "I know." I held a wing tip up to my beak and made a shushing noise. "I may not have always been watching, choosing to just keep tabs here and there to see if my interest would still be sated by watching, but I know. Knowing what I do, I swear that I will remain silent on it. Not even the prince can divorce me of this information without the *strictest* line of questioning, so I wouldn't go making it look like I'm too untrustworthy to him, unless you want that out there in the open for who knows what to see and use against everyone, catch my drift?"

She stared at me with her face fighting between visible outrage at my blackmail and curious distrust, and I just flew to her close enough to speak softer but far enough to be safer. "To be honest, I've always liked you more, Nadir. I can understand you. Can sense what you feel and almost see how your mind works behind those deep eyes of yours. Watching you grow with that monstrous schedule you had? You've kept my interest this whole time."

She grunted and seemed to decide something on her own, then turned to where her brother would be and began to walk in his direction. "Why do you really watch us, and who sent you?"

I scowled to myself. "Was my answer earlier not good enough?"

She smiled. "No."

I chuckled at that, clever. "Suffice it to say that I am here because I have a vested interest in watching over you. Who will tell your story to the masses? Who will report things to your parents?"

"We will, when we decide to," she answered me and stared ahead. "You avoid the question."

I grinned a birdie grin. "And I will continue to do so until telling you more is of benefit, or less a consequence than it is now. Please, I swear to you that you can trust me." She seemed even more cautious, so I cleared my throat. "I *did* just swear to you that you can trust me, and I'm not a pile of feathers on the ground yet. So you can obviously smell I don't lie in this, right?"

She must have received the notification of my word given because she just nodded once and walked on with me on her shoulder.

Once we arrived to where Azlo now stood, he smiled at us both and said, "You look close. How did you rest?"

"With both eyes closed." I grinned at the boy and Nadir actually laughed at that. "Have you tried it yet?"

He shook his head. "I wasn't going to be so brazen as to think an unknown Fae would be willing to consult with me without taking as much as they could, unless they were curious like you were." He looked at Nadir and asked, "Would you be willing to assist me?"

She smirked. "What kind of sister would I be if I wasn't?"

Azlo slowly nodded his head, steadily steeling himself and muttered the name, *Bladthirn,* under his breath as he fell to his knees.

He convulsed twice before his health rapidly bottomed out, Nadir's regeneration spell doing well to keep him hovering just above *0 HP.*

Finally, his mana began to drop and then a woman stood in front of him. She looked much more elven than any other Fae creature I had ever seen in person, much more so than some of the oldest ones I had ever seen on my galvanizing days in the Fae realm, slaking my curious nature.

That meant one of two things. Either she was powerful enough that she should be considered royalty in her own right, or she was unbelievably old—which could also be taken as powerful. Had both the king's cousin and I been wrong about who this was?

She glared down at the boy and pulled a long, barbed spear from behind her body that had thorns on it as she watched him. "I do not take kindly to those who call on me that I do not know."

"I was under the impression that since a Seelie spy knew your name, you might know some of what they have planned for the mortal realm," Azlo muttered as Nadir's healing spell continued to lift his health bar away from death. "Am I wrong?"

She did not keep her derision out of her tone as she spat. "I do not associate with the Courts, boy—who are you?" She frowned as she sniffed the air around all of us. "Why do you smell of mildew and cold?"

"I am Prince Azlo of the Unseelie Court, and I am accompanied by Princess Nadir, Healer of the same Court." Azlo slowly stood to his feet so as not to provoke an attack from the stronger woman. Nadir watched her hatefully, but even I doubted that she would be able to take her. Close as we were, I couldn't make out any information about her, who she was, or what level she was at all.

That alone wasn't always a concern among the Fae, as they had a tendency to value privacy and carried items to obscure or fudge that information. Hers was just outright gone, which was terrifying if you knew what I had at my disposal to peek on most who didn't want to be spied on.

Azlo continued his explanation with a nod. "We simply wished to see what you know, and if you would, I would like to make a bond with you."

The woman lifted her toned chin and chiseled features

higher and simply said, "No." She narrowed her gaze at Azlo as he was about to object. "I do not know how a Seelie whelp knew my name, but I do know that you are not strong enough to be worthy of serving, and I have no time to babysit children. My own interests far outweigh the coddled youth of our realm and their targeted tantrums."

She leveled her spear at Azlo's throat and growled, "Summon me before I deem you worthy again, and I will kill you where you stand. This is a threat."

Azlo swallowed and sighed. "I understand having things that you need to do that outweigh the needs of trivial beings." The woman's spear drifted slightly closer, so he hurriedly said, "Please, hear me out. I am a crafter and I need time to work on my own projects. Having to spy and constantly worry about those around me eats into my ability to do what I need to, and I need to know more of my craft as well. If I had someone as strong as you in my corner, I could accomplish so much more than without."

She frowned and lowered her spear, holding out her hand to touch the weapon he had on his hip, Shaper. She touched the blade at his waist and snorted. "Dungeon made and the other was made by you, but not enchanted by you." She touched the breastplate and her frown deepened. "This is created by you, but there is a being within it."

Confusion ate at her for a millisecond before she stepped back. "Again, I say no." She lifted a hand and her gaze went from lividity to one of tepid respect. "The path you walk is interesting to me. Call me when you grow strong enough to withstand my ire, and when you master your skills."

She lifted her hand and suddenly was gone.

———

AZLO

"That was... harsh," Nadir observed and I had to admit that it was. "Should we try another one?"

I shook my head. Though my mana returned steadily, I was mentally exhausted from almost dying and though I was tougher than that, the thoughts in my head wouldn't let me devote the necessary focus to allow summoning another potential threat.

What she had said had interested me greatly, though. She was interested in my path. Which meant she had to have some kind of interest in crafting at the very least, right?

Could she potentially train me at some later point? With her strength and the right tutelage, I could become a legendary smith and be a real force to reckon with.

That was enough to make me want to start on my next project right away, but with the orcs watching us so closely, and trying to keep a low profile for now as we headed deeper into their territory, making something just wasn't going to happen.

I rested and recovered, blueprinting some potential weapons and items I wanted to make that might be able to offer me some different powers based on the potential elementals that I could find, while the orcs continued to gear up to leave. Once they were up and ready, we began the trek once more for their tribe's lands.

"We will only need to walk two more days before we come into our tribal grounds, and from there, you will meet my father," Urtan proclaimed as we moved. Nadir was off tending to those who might have accrued any wounds that they would be too proud to mention after the fight, so we were alone. "Our village is strong, and there are many there who will be happy to enter into combat with you, should you seek a challenge."

His pride at that was almost enough to make me smile, but I was curious. "Does your village have a blacksmith?"

Urtan frowned at that question and closed his eyes as he walked, veering for a dozen paces or so before he reopened his eyes. "Yes, we have three of them. They are very skilled in the way of metalworking and crafting, but they are different than what my spirits tell me of your own crafters."

I nodded, then asked, "How so?"

"I do not know exactly." He frowned and shrugged. "They cannot tell me, as I do not understand myself."

I frowned at that but when he couldn't describe it to me, I allowed him to talk to me about the many orcish women in his village who would find me lacking physically, but if I proved myself well enough, one might take me as a consort. "This is an honorable thing, as orcish women are the strongest women there are." He puffed his chest out and grunted. "This is a desirable trait to have in a mate. All an orc male can hope for is a strong woman to bear him strong children."

"If the women are so strong, then how come the chieftain is a male?" The question didn't sound as petulant as I thought it would once I stated it.

The massive warrior took it in stride and grinned. "Father is strongest, and his power lends him much wisdom to lead our people into the coming Fall of Night."

"What's that?" I asked as Midnight clenched his foot on my shoulder. He had previously discussed that with me. When he squeezed, it was because he needed me to ask a question for him so he could learn something that might help us in dealing with all of this.

He blinked at the sky and lifted his hands almost reverently. "Orcs worship the strongest god, Uk'Beth, the patron god of warriors and those whose martial might is the pinnacle of their being. To fight is to find the truest portion of one's soul and temper it to become the strongest version of oneself." He sighed and grunted before letting his arms collapse to his sides. "Uk'-Beth told the orcs many years ago that there would be a warrior born of us, and that they would usher in a new Tagor."

Tagor? I blinked and he stopped me from asking him anything. "I do not know this word in your language, but it means time of plentiful-ness."

My eyebrows lifted in understanding and I nodded slowly. "How will you know them?"

"Uk'Beth said that the Black Wolf would fight the shadows one day and prevail before they turn their fangs on the skies to help Uk'Beth and his people claim the world as it should have always been." He smiled and closed his eyes as if he was remembering some joyous memory. "Then the Tagor above can begin as well."

I frowned at that and blinked to myself as my mind raced. *Is Uk'Beth going to start a war among the gods too?* I looked over at Nadir and frowned deeply. *She's a black wolf, but that couldn't be, right?*

As much as that would annoy me to truly know, I had other issues to contend with as a large party of orcs moved down the plane in front of us.

"Are those people here to welcome us?" I glanced over at Urtan as his tusks flashed in the light.

"Bad welcome." He turned his head back to the orcs arrayed behind us and shouted a command before he clenched his fist and his mana aura flared around him.

Summoned spirit warriors, a dozen orcs wearing spectral armor and armed with ghostly spears.

Nadir appeared at my side and pointed. "If they wear that blue and green crest that looks like an eagle, kill them. It's a rival tribe."

I blinked and stared, seeing a swirling crest that resembled an eagle mid-flap on a chain hanging around most of their necks and embossed on most of their bits of armor or weapons. It was easy to tell them from the orcs I traveled with, but I hoped that it would be even easier once battle joined.

I took out Shaper and made sure my armor was tight before snarling and charging the orcs that charged us.

Urtan and his spirits charged next to me, their legs pumping but their stride looked so ethereal and unreal that it was almost jarring to see the ghostly dead orcs running near me. One of the orcs from the opposing side led the charge and met the spirits, only to be speared so perfectly that his momentum hoisted his body over the orcs behind us.

From there it was pure chaos.

It almost felt like any orc that saw us from the rival tribe took my presence as a personal affront and made it their mission to attack me. I danced around spears, cleavers, and even fists with minimal damage as Nadir came in after me like an angry dragon in a room full of ceramic plates, glass, and the one person who stole from them.

Blood flowed and it was worrisome with how it muddied the ground, but with the mud it made, I was able to walk better than my opponents.

My hammer rose and fell as I roared, first in frustration but soon in glee. Killing all these orcs meant that I could feed Duke Forger again and there were a lot of corpses to be had.

My great hammer plummeted toward an orc with his back toward me, but at the last second, I noticed he didn't have the crest on his person. Grunting, I threw my left shoulder into it as it swung, just missing his head and shoulders as the momentum pulled me forward and over the haft of my weapon.

A spear stuck me in the calf, and I seethed angrily as I used Slip Step to move away. The spell pulled the weapon from my body without any more pain, letting me turn on my good leg and crush my attacker's chest.

Snarling came from nearby and a massive dire warg, spikes jutting from it like a porcupine, careened into the fray as it attacked the orcs who traveled with the party we had arrived here with.

"Nadir!" Healing energy whipped through me as I whispered, "Kestral!"

The shadowy mare surged from beneath me as I jumped into the air and rode her toward the slavering beast that held Urtan down on the ground, his spirits hacking at it with their spears to no avail.

I was almost to him when all his spirits vanished and he snarled, his eyes glowing a bright blue for just a fraction of a second. He clenched the dire warg's thick waist with his legs and twisted savagely. I could hear a soft pop from where I was and the warg fell to the ground with a piercing yelp.

I stood in the saddle and jumped from the shadow mare's back onto the spiky beast as I swung the spiked end of Shaper toward its spine.

Another spear caught me in the hip and I managed to get grabbed by another orc before I could finish the arc of my swing. They pulled me down and tried to wrestle Shaper out of my grip. I fought them, lashing out with my elbow and even casting Flicker Flame into one of their faces, but another set of hands gripped mine before I could get loose.

One of them punched me hard enough in the face that I saw my health drop by a fourth and snarled, "Damn you!" I cast Flicker Flame again and this time managed to catch his clothes on fire.

He patted his clothes and the fire stopped where it had been. Suddenly, Nadir stood behind my assailant with her axe slashing, and moved to the ones holding me as another bout of healing energy roiled through me.

I grasped Shaper's haft and yanked it from the corpses clutches and attacked the warg as Urtan still struggled with it, his movements slowing ever so slightly as the battle raged on.

I swung as if I were about to drive a spike into a tree and plunged the spiked side of the weapon into the dire warg's shoulder. I yanked it back out, then while it struggled to free itself from Urtan's clench, slammed it back into the beast's neck. The blow rocked both the beast and Urtan, who dropped from his precarious perch. I could see its level now.

Dire Warg Lvl 23

And its health was almost gone. I grit my teeth and pressed my advantage, pulling myself toward the beast with my right hand on Shaper and yanked the wind dagger from my waist. Closer now, I plunged the blade into the warg's neck four times before it began to flag visibly, but someone grabbed me and pulled me away.

I turned to find one of the orcs we had been fighting with, one that I had managed to save. He pulled me back and flung me away as something grazed my left foot and he grunted.

I landed a few feet away to find that he had been stabbed in the leg as the warg's spikes had ejected from its body as it died. The orc fell to his knee and one of the orcs attacking us went for him. I snarled and used Slip Step to put myself in the way, throwing my shoulder into the spear aimed at my helper's throat.

The attack went wide, slashing someone else's tendon as I whipped around and slit the attacker's throat and grabbed the orc who saved me beneath one of his arms. I pulled the man out of the fray as far as I could without taking a spear in the gut for it, but the attacks were still coming and it wasn't long before I was targeted again.

This time, it was orcs trying to tackle me and drag me down to the ground. I hopped over one deftly and stabbed another as I fought my way back into the battle and toward where Shaper had been. I dipped under the outstretched arms of one orc and kicked another in the knee, only to have my foot bounce aside from his superior musculature.

The orc's fist plummeted into the side of my head, catching my cheek and jaw with my temple and spun me around easily as I fell. Suddenly, Nadir flashed across my vision. She streaked into my attacker and the sound of horns in the distance made orcs shout in triumph.

The fight raged as I struggled to climb to my feet, woozily stumbling forward toward what I thought was my weapon. It was the butt of a spear that I took to the clavicle and a snap let me know that the bone was broken.

Healing energy surged through me and the bone snapped back into place painfully as my vision cleared. The butt rocketed at my face and I turned my head hard enough that my spine adjusted loudly to avoid the strike as I grabbed the weapon and pulled.

The momentum of the strike and the fact that I yanked on

it as hard as I could threw my attacker off balance long enough for someone else to topple into him and knock him to the ground. I stomped on his neck and chin as hard as I could while I twisted the spear in my grasp and stabbed down.

The blade speared through his trachea and I twisted it so that it would sever the spine as I stepped away. The ground began to shake as a massive herd of warriors came sprinting toward where we were.

"Nadir?" I bellowed and she just looked up and roared, her fist pumping in the air.

"The tribe comes, Azlo!" Urtan bellowed with a victorious smirk on his face. "Kill all you can, but stay near me, both of you."

I grunted at him and began to lob Flickering Flames into the faces of warriors fighting a little too well on the opposition's side, distracting them enough so that others would be able to make cleaner finishing strikes.

When the orcs from the tribe arrived, the remaining force from the rival tribe died. There was nothing more for them in this place than to be slaughtered where they stood with the amount of bodies that had come.

I leveled up with the sheer number of dead that I had helped kill as they were stronger than me level-wise.

One of the larger orcs who could have been Urtan's twin walked up to the other orc and put his forehead against the shaman's. The two men hugged and smirked at one another before the orc turned and growled at seeing me and Nadir.

Nadir spoke for herself, motioned from herself to me and then back; all the while they all listened intently.

I heard Urtan mention my name while speaking to the new arrival to our small group. The orc grunted and lifted his chin, so I returned the gesture, jutting my lower jaw out.

He raised a curious eyebrow as Urtan snorted and hid his face. Nadir looked at me cautiously, as if trying to decide why I did what I did, but I just maintained eye contact with the other man.

"If you continue to stare at him that way, Azlo, he will try to fight with you," Nadir explained and stepped between the two of us. "Exposing your tusks is a way to show strength and spirit. Staring them in the eye is a good way to show that you either don't respect them, or don't see them as a threat."

I narrowed my gaze and growled, "Bold of him to treat me that way."

Nadir laughed and shook her head. "We all watched you get coldcocked by that spear, Azlo."

My cheeks heated, hidden by my glamour and I muttered, "It was a sneaky hit!"

CHAPTER TWENTY-EIGHT

AZLO

It took the majority of the rest of the day to get the bodies together to drag back to the tribe's property and then put together a little 'funeral' pyre for these ones as well. Duke Forger was highly pleased to eat even more corpses and relished them. As he consumed, I could feel the bond between the two of us growing.

While he feasted, Urtan brought the horde of orcs to the foot of a great hill with a long hall that stood high above. As the orcs grew closer to this place, they began to call and chant something. Drums beat as the warriors began to step rhythmically to a beat that they hammered through the air and as the beat came to a pitch, the doors opened and out strode a mammoth of an orc.

His tusks framed his face, hair grew from his head in a shaggy mane, and his arms were covered with it as well. One of his eyes was milky white and bisected horizontally.

The orcs' simultaneous roar at him deafened me to the point that I dropped to a knee at the shock of it, holding my ears with both hands.

A hand gripped my shoulder and pulled me painfully to my feet, I glanced over to see Nadir's glamour-covered hand gripping me. She stared down at me. "No outward weakness. I don't care if you can fight well, they will view it negatively."

Blood dribbled from one of her ears as she spoke to me, and I realized that all the noise affected her too.

I assumed that this had to have been the leader, but Urtan spoke first. "Father, chieftain of the Spirit Mountain Tribe, our patrol was successful and we killed many humans, mages, and orcs from the River Hawk Tribe."

"I see you, my son. Come to my side and tell me of our guests." He was quiet for a short amount of time then smiled. "Or stand and proclaim their right to stand among the chosen."

Urtan strode forward three steps and bellowed louder than I'd heard him yell before as he waved his hand to Nadir. "A sister from the realm beyond called Nadir, she seeks her people and felled our second strongest warrior in honorable combat with her hands. She threw his body at her axe and cut him down. She slaughtered many of our enemies on the way here, and protected her brother with fervor. Her glory is much."

The orcs with us bellowed a return to Urtan's call and some even shouted about her fighting and healing them.

Ragul watched and nodded as they called.

Then Urtan bellowed a second time, silencing the rest. "I bring you a Sylvan warrior from another realm, Azlo, he fell our fifth strongest warrior and he wields his hammer as well as any orc a spear. He courageously fought a Bog Hag that has killed many orcs, and a number more of this hunting party. He fought and killed many of the orcs of the River Hawk Tribe, even killing their prized dire warg stud."

I blinked at that. *They used that thing to breed stock?*

The orcs behind us bellowed together and began to call out about my fighting and crafting abilities. How I could walk on water and the blood of their enemies.

Urtan roared long and hard before clashing both of his fists together on his chest. "These two warriors are skilled and fought with bravery and strength that both is orcish, and close to it. I, Urtan, vouch for their strength, and petition the chieftain to allow them to stay in the village as guests, if not as tribesman."

Ragul stared, unblinking, down at all of us for a time before calling out, "I hear you, shaman, and I hear your cry of honor. The call of bravery. I see the spirits of the dead that cling to their very arms and legs, fueling them." He lifted his hand and the orcs began to sway to the point that even I felt like joining them. "I can smell the blood that coats your weapons and armor, and I can *feel* the passion of your convictions."

He lifted his arms and the orcs who milled about around the group of warriors lifted theirs in return. "But what say we to those who wish to taste the *thrill* of life after victory?"

"Feast!" Those who raised their hands repeated their assertion. "Feast! *Feast!*"

Ragul nodded and snarled, "Feast!" He clenched his fists and pounded his chest with them before calling, "To celebrate the death of unworthy foes, and the fall of brave brothers and sisters, we feast."

Orcs brought out blankets and pots with food cooking in them, breads that lay flat against their palms, and meat to cook at the fires that sprouted from all over.

The orcs from the war party broke apart as various members of the tribe came over to claim them and pull them to their cooking fires.

Several came to claim Nadir and even me, but Urtan puffed out his chest and claimed us. "Guests of the chieftain."

As we moved, I caught up to Urtan and asked, "If I hadn't killed the hag, would I have been able to eat with all of you?"

He grinned and shook his head. "Your sister would have had to feed you from her own food."

The disappointed orcs milled about closer to all of us until the chieftain came down from his hill and opened his arms.

"Brothers, sisters, who am I to keep you from feasting with your chosen warriors? Come, feast with us and hear tales of glory."

The orcs by us cheered and began to bring out piles of food on clay platters and plates.

There was succulent pork with butter and garlic, vegetables that had been steamed in clay pots that smelled divine, and even a fried bit of meat that reminded me of venison. Then they brought out the potatoes.

These were everything from stewed, cut and seared with honey and garlic, mashed with butter, and cut with pork and other various things.

I'd never tasted such decadence in a simple root, and if I didn't know better, I would have called this bribery to get someone to stay here.

It could have worked if it weren't for our goals. *My goals.*

Other than growing stronger and trying to improve my skills as a crafter, it was hard to really define my goals other than trying to prove I wasn't just my father's son.

"You look as though much weighs on you." The eldest orc, chieftain Ragul, watched me curiously. "Does the food not agree with you?"

I bowed my head respectfully. "The food and hospitality so far have been beyond reproach. Thank you for your concern."

The orcish man grunted and pulled a large hunk of meat from the bone spinning over the cooking fire on a spit. He tore a hunk from it, avoiding his massive tusks as he did so with his teeth, then he passed the hunk to me. "Orc tradition to share meat with an interesting guest."

I watched as he ate it, following suit. The meat was a bit undercooked, but nothing that would kill me. The blood pooled in my mouth and I fought to swallow it all as he watched me intently. Once I had no more food in my mouth, he smiled and nodded his head as if all was right.

"I hear you are a craftsman and you are a healer?" Ragul glanced from me to Nadir, "What brings you to our lands?"

"I want to learn about my people," Nadir explained. "My

mother was raised by humans, and I was raised by Fae. This is my way of discovering who I am through who my people are."

Ragul nodded and looked at me. "I'm here to support my sister." I lifted my gaze to stare him in the eyes before looking around. "I also seek knowledge of how to better work metal. Smithing, creating metal weapons and armor, is my passion."

His voice rumbled in his throat as he grunted. "Passion is important, as is supporting family." He lifted his hand dismissively into the air as he said, "Crafting not so much to me. Fight our smiths for the right to learn from them, and I will allow it as a reward for killing the bog hag."

I dipped my head in gratitude and he grunted again. "Urtan, my son, regale me with tales of your battles!"

Urtan jumped to his feet and beat his chest as he went through the process of explaining everything he went through before having found us. It was a lively retelling and I even found myself laughing along as he came to some funny deaths.

We watched and laughed and even called out in protest as he spoke, Nadir having to translate for me. It was an amusing time spent with warriors of this caliber and people who understood them.

We ate and some drank well into the evening where the majority of the village, save for a few of the stronger orcs standing guard, fell asleep where they were.

In my trance, I played through some of the things I'd seen and wondered how the smiths here would fight.

―――――

I opened my eyes and found six orcish children leaning in close to me, staring at me tentatively. The biggest one flinched and stood up, his fist flung toward my cheek haphazardly. I let the strike land, the minuscule amount of health it took away cute more than anything, and tilted my head to the side at them.

"Is something wrong?" I blinked as they continued to stare

at me until their apparent leader stepped forward and pointed at me, barking an order. "I can't understand you."

"He's telling you that you're not that strong if they can sneak up on you." Urtan chuckled to himself and pointed to the lead boy. "He is a promising young warrior and one of the smith's sons."

I raised an eyebrow and stood up, shifting my footing so that I could lean down and stare into his eyes. He was only up to my chest, but he was broad for a child, broader than I was.

He jutted his chin out and leaned forward to stare down his nose at me when I dipped forward and grunted, "Boo!"

The boy startled and leaned too far back to recover himself and fell onto his rump. I turned around and shifted my form to my fox form, kicking some dirt at him before I romped forward.

The children immediately squealed and gave chase as I frolicked through the slowly stirring adults, some of them attempting to catch me as well until finally Urtan called a stop to the game and I shifted back.

He grabbed the large boy on the arm as he went to run by him and pointed to me, then to himself as he spoke. Once the boy finished gawking, he ran off hooting and hollering as Urtan shook his head.

"Come." The shamanic orc motioned that I follow him as we jogged after the boy. He led us to the outskirts of the village, but not so far as to be one of the homes on the outside where thick smoke already rose with the morning light.

We walked to the house as the boy, panting and red-faced, dragged a massive orc out of the home behind him, yanking and pulling like his life depended on it.

This orc was about seven feet tall and at least three feet wide, maybe more as he followed the boy with a soft grin on his face. He saw me and his smile faded slightly as he grunted at Urtan.

Urtan spoke back and they conversed for a moment before the man looked me up and down, saying something almost dismissively. Urtan nodded to himself and said, "He will not fight you until you are stronger. He said to train with the other smiths first."

"I can do that." It irked me to have to do so, but I would learn how I could. I hadn't seen anything breathtakingly different from their weapons anyway.

I turned with Urtan and he walked me through the village as Midnight flew overhead and watched us, the bird banking on the various air currents above us. I would have him memorize the layout of the village for me if I could—if he hadn't already —so that we could travel easily should we need to.

We walked for ten minutes to another home on the outer ring and found another orcish man cutting wood outside with a small hatchet. He looked at me curiously, then to Urtan and the two spoke a few brief sentences.

"If you want, he will fight you to see if you are worthy of his time." The man spoke again, then Urtan added, "But he has work to do so this will need to be quick, the first one to fall from their feet loses honorably."

I shrugged. "I agree to that."

I approached the man as he continued to split the wood in front of him until I was close enough then tossed the hatchet at me.

I caught it, the balance of it blade heavy and suddenly my footing got wobbly and he was shoving me over. He smiled at me and shook his head, saying something to Urtan as he helped me back up.

"He recommended his teacher, Fjlak." Urtan's nose wrin-kled in disgust. "She is... how humans would refer to someone without manners?"

"Rude?" He nodded and I frowned. "Is that frowned upon in orcish society?"

"She cares for nothing of honor, or perseverance through battle," he translated for the other orc. "But she is a good teacher."

"If she will have me, I don't care about niceties as much."

Urtan nodded at that and off we walked.

CHAPTER TWENTY-NINE

The cave we stood outside was weirdly located due to the fact that in the beginning foothills of a mountain where we currently were, there shouldn't have been any until you traveled a little closer to the mountains themselves. But here we stood in front of a cave carved into the side of a larger hill.

"I thought the orcs here were nomadic?"

Urtan frowned at me and grunted. "Humans assume this because we move to different hunting grounds every year, letting the ground and nature reclaim their place and replenish the numbers of our food sources." He smiled and lifted his arms out beside him almost as if in praise. "When that time comes, we will break down our homes with fire and from the ashes, new life will grow forth."

I frowned. *That makes you nomadic though.* I just ignored it and he snorted. "Yes?"

"We have areas we go to in a rotation, and we do not wander aimlessly." He pointed to his face and said, "Orcs have to read faces well in order to understand our tongue. You do not hide your expressions well against us."

I blinked at that. "I guess as I spend my time away from

Court, with those of my own hobbies and know that my face makes them uncomfortable, I assumed the same of all of you. I've let myself grow lax in schooling my bearing and let myself be seen. Forgive me."

"Do not worry." He grinned and looked down at me. "You are small, weaker than me. Of course I would see through your face to the heart of your mind."

I stayed quiet and carefully stared forward.

He nodded and bellowed something into the dark entrance of the cave. There was a sniffle from inside and a large woman shuffled out, scowling at the light as she continued to scoot hunched over as she was.

She glared at Urtan and grumbled something to the man before looking at me. In Sylvan, she asked, "What do you want, Fae?"

"To learn." I pulled out some of my materials and she just sniffed at them and growled under her breath.

"You don't have the skill to work with me—no one does." Urtan leaned closer and spoke again in orcish and she just laughed once, harshly, before saying, "I don't give a warg shit what your father said, I don't fight for the right to work with me. I care about skill, results, and m—"

I pulled one of the Ever Frozen chunks out of my inventory and said, "Materials, right? I have some. Rare pieces that I intend to work with once I learn how to incorporate them into my work. If you don't want to work with them, that's fine." I watched as she crept closer to the edge of the shadowed entrance to the cave to observe the blue and white hunk of material in my hand. The way her eyes shimmered curiously and the way her nostrils flared, I knew I had her. But that wasn't enough. "I'll just go through the materials I have with trial and error and see what I can do on my own."

I turned on my heel and walked away, making it about ten strides before she called, "Wait!"

I didn't stop, instead looking over my shoulder and calling out to Urtan, "Can you show me where I can set up my forge,

Urtan? If I have to fight for the space, I suppose I can do that."

The woman appeared in front of me and glared down at me. "First lesson, I speak and you listen." She put her finger into my face as she loomed over me and narrowed her eyes in a glare. She went to open her mouth again but I just stepped around her.

I spoke while keeping my gaze forward. "First lesson—don't waste my time." I turned and stared at her as she slowly turned to get a good look at me. "I don't care what you think you know, I will waste all these materials to spite you for wanting to waste my time. I'm too weak to teach? Fine. I'm not skilled enough? I can respect that."

I pulled the hunk of Ever Frozen out once more and held it aloft above my shoulder and snarled, "But avarice is not something I care for." I smiled after that, changing my tone. "I can work with it, but I will not be jerked around again."

I put the item away before turning to find her close enough that I could feel her breath. "I want to shore up my weaknesses as a crafter whose life depends on his ability to make items with the materials he finds." I glared at her as she returned my stare. "If you take me as a student, I will share what I don't intend to use to make things for myself, but I will not be treated like peasant garbage because I don't know the orcish methods of smithing."

She glared at me for a long moment, unflinching and unblinking. She sniffed and said, "You have other things, I can smell them on you." I nodded once, just a dip of my chin as I continued to stare at her. "Don't want your time wasted? Fine. Come with me."

She turned and stomped to her cave with me following a little further behind. As I walked past Urtan, he grinned at me and nodded his approval because he had known what I'd done. I'd used her facial expressions against her. That was how she was so rude, she had no bearing.

And even if she knew that, all she could do was try to kill

me to take what I had and that would be fruitless because I wouldn't allow it. I had a backup plan this time. If all else failed, I would summon the neutral Fae I had nearly died to and allow her to run rampant on her. Sure, I would die, but then at least Fjlak would be gone too.

I followed her into the cave and darkness crept over me like a glove. On the inside of the cave after the darkened entrance there was a pause of sorts, like walking through a barrier, and then I was in a room that wasn't a cave in the slightest. I was in a temple with a large effigy of the god of crafters, Fainne, rising high into the air over the altar—a forge and an anvil with a hammer that glowed with a holy light.

Fjlak turned and glared at me. "Smart of you to bait me like that. I don't fall for things easily, but I'm sorely looking for new materials to work with, and you arriving here means I don't have to go on an expedition for at least as long as you have interesting things to work with." She turned back and walked over to one of the many work benches that rose from the stone floor at her feet as the hunching she had been doing faded. She went from looking like she could have been ancient to looking like she was no older than Vrawn was. "What?" She looked down at herself. "What, you've not seen a glamour before?"

"I've seen it used by Fae." She stood there watching me steadily and I just gave up that train of thought and instead said, "Do you want to see my materials first, or do you want to show me how to work things the way you do?"

"You know the basics of smithing, that's fine to start." She grunted and motioned to the table. "Put what you have here."

I did as she said, putting the materials I had onto the table, while keeping the most important to myself. One of the horns Winterheart gave me, a tooth, Kayda's large tail feather, her talon, and one of the Ever Frozen hunks.

She stared at all of it and picked up the other tooth before whispering, "Where did you get the tooth of an ancient white dragon?"

I grinned. "An ancient white dragon."

She narrowed her gaze at me, saying, "There is a white who rules the peaks of the mountains behind us. If you want to be a smartass, I will send you to collect materials from her."

I raised an eyebrow at that. *A white dragon who lives here? I wonder if she has a mate? Would Winterheart want to sire hatchlings of his own? Could he?*

"Where?"

I chuckled again, inwardly. "The Fae realm. It's never just a matter of what you know, but also who."

She glared at me and asked, "Could you get more?"

I shrugged. "If I were to ask nicely, certainly."

She frowned at that and then pointed to the feather. "I've never seen anything like this, what's it from?"

"One of the rarest birds in existence," I answered and stared back at her. "Don't ask. I cannot tell you if you don't know. Suffice it to say that she is exceptionally powerful and will kill on accident."

She stared at me for a long moment before dropping it and poring over the other materials. "All high quality."

"It has to be, I assume."

She nodded once. "It has to be." She touched them and smiled. "Lower quality cannot be beaten from these materials like imperfections from an ingot. No. It has to be better than good quality to enhance the weapon or gear you make."

She tapped one of the feathers twice. "This? This is good quality. We will start here."

She reached down and plucked the chest feather from the table and then lifted both chunks of Ever Frozen.

She smiled, and it made her look even younger. "This is a type of ore I have never seen before, but I understand the use of it from dealing with its opposite in magma."

She took all of the materials to the altar and prayed for a short time before coming back to her forge.

"The way to forge an item with items like this is to melt it, or make it firm for the opposite of itself." She put them on the table by her forge and began to build a fire.

"Is this something that would greatly benefit from more magic?" She glanced over at me and raised a brow. "I have a forge that can imbue the items I make on it with more magic."

"My altar is blessed by a god and the forge with it, but I'm curious."

I pulled out the forge and Duke Forger watched curiously from within as Fjlak looked over the enchanted tool.

She touched it cautiously as she observed every detail she could. "This is…"

I nodded, not needing her to tell me how exquisite she was about to call it, then she said, "Not magical enough to warrant the use over my own tools." She turned to me and arched an eyebrow. "But interesting nonetheless."

She patted it and went back to her table and forge to continue building her fire.

She also pulled out a cord of wire and began to make measurements of the feather as she waited for the proper heat from her flames.

"For something like this, we will need a core made of a highly conductive material." She thumped the feather and grinned. "This will serve nicely as a core, but that means we need a mold to hold it and the metal." She turned back to me. "You have a preferred weapon you want to make?"

"Something with a bit more reach than my current weapon, though with the ice and the feather, I assume that you know this weapon will be heavily influenced by ice magic?" She nodded, so I continued, "Elemental affinity isn't something that I will shy from."

I showed her Shaper and she took it from me gently, respecting the craftsmanship. "You have two here. If you have more, I suggest using them in order to give you said reach. With these two chunks and the feather, we could add an additional ore type to give the weapon some increased strength, but without more, it would only really make a longsword."

I frowned and said, "Very well." I pulled out the last chunk of the Ever Frozen and set it on the table, then pointed to the dragon tooth. "Will we be using this one?"

She shook her head. "No, we will use wood and appropriate leather for the hilt and grip." She smiled and said, "Second lesson: too much power can only be controlled and not created —too much of a good thing in a crafting makes for a terrible base."

I frowned at that and put that fact into my own words as a way to confirm I had it right. "So, if we were to make a weapon with multiple materials that do the same or similar things, or even of too high a quality, it could weaken the weapon overall?"

"Yes and no." She frowned for a moment in thought, then explained, "If I were to put all of these items into crafting the perfect weapon, it would be an amazing weapon to have, but it would never be able to be further perfected. Either with enchantment or by other means. So the best, most suitable materials for the job are always the right idea and should be the norm, but piling things in just to do so is wasteful and can be detrimental. Does that make sense?"

"I don't fully comprehend how it can be detrimental."

"So, say I have the feather as a core for the weapon, and the ice as the body." I nodded along as she spoke. "If I were to use the tooth as a core? It would be exceptional, but as a handle? It's a waste of a fine material because you would have to shave it down to use it without cutting yourself on it, and it would serve so much better as a weapon in its own right."

That seems fair enough. I watched as she worked and found that her process wasn't all too different from that of a normal smith's. It was just more… *wild.*

The aspects of it were simple enough to observe and close enough to what I could do to make it replicable.

I would have preferred to do things the old fashioned way, with drawing out the ingots myself but I could heat a casted weapon and beat the impurities out of it that way, if necessary. There was also the fact that this was entirely new material to me and Fjlak so I didn't know if there was anything I could even beat from it.

She smiled. "Heat's good. We can start the smelting process and get it poured soon."

"How soon?"

She looked over at me with a smug grin. "When it melts in about twelve to eighteen hours."

CHAPTER THIRTY

I rolled my eyes once more as she continued to look over the weapons and armor that I had created and everything I'd brought along, like the wind dagger.

Six hours into the melt for the ore, and she had said two sentences to me the whole time, uttering things to herself so low in her language that I couldn't understand that I just assumed she would have been happier if I weren't there.

Finally she stood with a grunt and a crackle in her lower back that almost frightened me. She glanced back at me and tilted her head in a manner that I took to calling me closer, so I obliged and she pointed. "This is garbage."

She picked up the wind dagger and looked like she was about to snap it in two in her massive hands. "The enchantment on this is detrimental, it needs to be sharpened after so many uses or the wind that it exudes is nothing more than a gusty breeze that won't cut."

That was more a confirmation of what I had already surmised, but at least this way it was a good way to recognize that my instincts had been correct. "It was dungeon made."

She sniffed. "I know—I find myself wondering why you

would continue to carry a faulty weapon like this that requires constant maintaining to be of mild use. The damage isn't even that great." She swung it as if that would explain anything and a line of air slipped from the dulling edge. "See? You could dodge that with ease! Garbage."

She pointed to Shaper. "That is much better, and the enchantment on it is interesting as well. I take it this is what you use to smith with?" After I nodded, she smiled. "A good thing. Here."

She handed Shaper to me and I put it away on my hip, hanging it in the ring that held it. Next, she took up the armor. "Why half-plate armor?"

"I wanted something that would be lighter and easier to don and doff than platemail, but sturdier and more physically resistant to damage than just chainmail."

She nodded. "Why isn't it enchanted?" When I opened my mouth and had no answer, she frowned and motioned to it. "I know that it is now thanks to the elemental that lives inside it, but otherwise there's nothing to it. So why not enchant it?"

I stared at her for a long moment and frowned myself. Was that even really a question? "I am a blacksmith."

She snorted and rolled her eyes. "Forge Sorcerer." A shiver rolled over me as she continued to stare at me. "You can use magic. You didn't know about wild smithing before now, so you couldn't use that, I understand, but you could have enchanted your weapons at the very least."

"How did you know that?"

She motioned to the sky flippantly and spoke again. "Why didn't you enchant anything?"

"I'm a smith. Enchanting is beneath us."

"Enchanting was invented by the dwarves," she stated and pointed at the statue of Fainne. "He wanted perfect weapons, armor, and accessories. His breathing life into the dwarves was his enchantment."

The anger in her statement confused me. "What would an orc know of Fainne's will?"

Her nose and brow wrinkled angrily. "What would a Fae know of smithing?" She stared at me expectantly but when neither of us spoke for a few moments, she spoke again. "This is the holy ground of Fainne. I would meditate on that question if I were you, child."

"But there are better things that could be done w——"

She held up a hand. "If you are going to disrespect my knowledge, I have nothing to teach you until you do as I wish." She pointed to the foot of the god's statue. "Go."

Regaining control of myself and my tongue, I bowed my head and did as instructed, going to the foot of the statue. Once there, I just laid my hand against the stone, trying to feel the craftsmanship of it before I closed my eyes awkwardly, thinking, *If there is insight or knowledge to be gained, I ask that you grant it, Crafter of the Ages.*

I turned and rested my back against the stone to feel closer to it and began to meditate on the sentiment.

———

All I could see was darkness. Similar to the darkness of the void that I had seen in the Null until there was a faint *ting, ting.*

I blinked and there was a light that sped forward so fast that it was hard not to flinch at the attack. But it wasn't one. The light was a flame held in a forge all too similar to that of the forge in the building we were in.

"Open your eyes, lad." A gruff voice spoke to me from the other side of the forge. I blinked again and opened my eyes, the rest of the room spinning into sight. This room was exactly the same as the one I had been in, but it was in worse condition.

There was debris and waste, shavings and dust on the floor.

The speaker, Fainne, stepped from the shadows of the forge and pulled something misshapen and glowing cherry red from the flames. The tinging returned as he hammered lightly on a small being that resembled a dwarf.

"So, you want knowledge." He grunted and then stuck the dwarf into the flames once more. "Insight."

The god made of pure mithril stood as his children did, broad of body and muscle, a bulbous and strong gut that would hold much ale. His beard was gold, and his eyes cut from emeralds the deepest shade of green. He was bald, and through his beard I could see his consternation-filled grimace.

"I am but a humble smith."

He chuckled and shook his head. "And the son of one of the most gifted enchanters of the mortal age—I know because I helped him reach his potential."

I blanched. My father had met Fainne?

He raised a brow and laughed again, using his tongs to grasp the project he worked on from the forge and said, "Come, work with me."

I could have wept at that and rushed forward to attend the god's will. He softly hammered the dwarf, beardless and small as I watched. "Are you making another race?"

He guffawed. "Nah, not me." He smiled lovingly down at the things and said, "It's a child. I forge every newborn dwarf."

He looked the tiny figure over before shuffling to a small workbench where he selected a small chisel. Placing it on the figure's cheek, he smacked it on each side of the child's face on the cheeks.

"Dimples that'll drive all the ladies crazy one day." There was a love, deep and profound, in his eyes and tone as he spoke and showed me. The child was adorable. Truly the work of a god, as all children were.

I couldn't help beaming at the tiny creature.

"Would you like to hold him?" I flinched and he chuckled at my worry. "Not now. But someday, when you make the pilgrimage to Djurn Forge as many dwarves do on the Way."

"You mean...?"

He turned and gently placed the child into a bath to quench. "Yes, child. You will venture to Djurn Forge." He walked around the forge to sit on his anvil and pulled a jug of something from the air. "I dare say it's how best you would proceed on your path in keeping up with your skills, though meeting one of my priests was fortunate as a turn of events."

He took another long drought of his jug and smiled briefly before sighing in delight. "I do enjoy these sacrificial kegs they send me."

I frowned and then thought of the kegs the dwarves buried, usually the best or the first keg of a mead or ale they made. Their brewers were dangerously good at what they did.

"Excuse my impertinence, Exalted One, but is what she said true?" He raised a questioning eyebrow at me, so I explained, "That your children invented enchanting?"

He smiled to himself and set his jug down. "That's not what I call what I do, that was more a means to an end, but in their fervor to craft like me, the first dwarves did invent a rough approximation of the enchanting you know today." He frowned. "The elves and then humanity found different ways to enhance it and make it what it is, but it *did* begin with our people."

"Our people, Your Grandness?"

He blinked and stared at me flatly. "Stop with the Fae flattery, lad, it does nothing for me. Just call me Fainne."

"As you wish." I bowed my head and he just snorted. "Please forgive my ignorance, but why do the dwarves not enchant now?"

He sighed tiredly and looked at the ground. "My fury." He grunted and stood, rubbing his golden beard with his dirty hand before shuffling to a large shelf. He motioned to it, row upon row of figures stood on it, metal shapes in the relief of dwarves in various states. "This was the fall of their magical prowess."

He picked one up and closed his eyes. "My children, led astray by a stranger's whispered knowledge, sought to create life that only the gods were permitted to make."

He hugged the dwarf in his hands to his chest and there was real pain in his voice as he whispered, "I had to do it. I had to end them."

He cleared his throat and put the figure back. "After that, the survivors turned their back on magic, all but the most fervent of my subjects, certain clans who created things that relied on magic and the like who knew my heart and will the best." He lifted one, an old woman with many rings on her fingers. He grinned broadly, his teeth silver gleaming against his golden beard. "This one taught your father much of what he learned of enchanting and gave him hell."

That made me smile. "Is she still alive?"

He shook his head. "Unfortunately, she passed in her sleep next to her love. But she would have loved to meet you."

"I would have loved to meet her and hear how she tortured him." I knew her name. Mother and Vrawn often laughed over how the woman had tormented him and forced him to remain humble.

"So that is why dwarven smiths disdain enchanting weapons."

"Aye." His simple response was unsettling to me as that meant I would have to do something I hadn't cared for. My work would likely suffer. "Enchanting is just another way to make a powerful item more powerful, it gives a weapon more reach, or an item more depth. Though, after your father proved that I did not hate the magic they feared, I dare say that some of them have begun the process of learning."

He waved his hand and racks of weapons and armor appeared, all of them carved and enchanted. "Some enchant garbage to make it useful, or lean on enchantments to correct a mistake or flaw. Do not lean on an enchantment to make an item special, but allow it to enhance it."

I blinked at that, and found that knowledge frightening, but as a crafter, I was more excited to try it than fearful of it. Though his mention of my father irritated me.

"Especially as the Forge Sorcerer."

That made my stomach flip as he turned his gaze from Shellica to me. "Your weapons hold much more promise than anything created even by grandmasters, and yet you do not fully utilize everything available to you." The room warmed considerably as my cheeks blazed in shame. "That armor you made could have guided that elemental if you had bothered to enchant it in the first place."

I remained silent, so he just sighed tiredly and shuffled toward me until he could stand in front of me. "My *beloved* sister asked me not to interfere with you after we designed the class that you took. She seems to think that you would be convinced to become a servant of mine and she wants you *real* bad."

He just shook his head and waved his hand in the air next to his head. "I don't need any more priests or clerics or whatever." He put his hands on his hips and grinned broadly. "I just want to watch someone create something truly awesome."

He turned to me and touched my shoulder, the weight of his hand almost enough to make me bend at the waist like some huge burden.

"Stop fettering yourself and your creations with being closed-minded, lad." He patted me affectionately. "You know, your da was a dwarf. At least, he was accepted as a dwarf, by me especially. I can bless you as I did him. Make it so that your will can be etched easier into your craftings."

I thought about it, then asked, "Was my father a good crafter?"

Fainne laughed. "He was shite, lad. Creative, and found ways of making things that were truly awe inspiring at times, but he was not of the type to use his hands for much more than wielding an axe." He cleared his throat and chuckled. "Among some other lesser things, but he was of the honorable sort, and that meant more to me than his failures as a craftsman. He gave depth to his friends' creations and even some others."

I nodded, dwelling on that a moment. "I feel like if I refuse, I might upset you, Fainne, and that's not something I want to do."

He stilled and raised an eyebrow at me before narrowing his gaze and asking, "Why would you refuse?"

"A craftsman should make with his own hands, right?" I

looked down at my own hands, calloused with the years of working with weapons and a hammer at the forge. "If I accept your blessing, I will wonder if I truly earned the weapons I've made and with that, I think I might doubt myself and my craft. I'm better than that. Better than my father."

He laughed, softly at first but it grew so thunderous I almost fell to my knees as I worried the building would collapse. "Refuses the blessing of a god to hone his craft, bah!"

He turned his whole body and grabbed me into his massive hands, pulling me into his grasp in a hug unlike any I had ever known. "Would that you had been born a dwarf in more than just name, lad, I'd have taken you as my apprentice for that alone!"

He shook me affectionately as he continued to guffaw and finally sat me on the ground and stared down at me. His palm dwarfed my face as he beheld me like he was seeing me for the first time. He nodded to himself and turned away before walking back to his anvil.

He leaned down and scraped his hand around the base of it, scraping together some dust and etchings of his previous works. "I task you with this quest from a god, lad."

He came to me and grasped my left hand in his and held it gently as he dribbled grit and metal into my palm. "Take this to my child in Djurn Forge, name's Granda, and he'll know what I want. He's a wee bit old, but he's a better smith than most, even Thogan."

That made my jaw drop. "But…"

Fainne just snorted and laughed. "Aye, I know." He finished dribbling his waste into my palm and closed my fingers. "Even a legend can be outshone by someone who forsook their own growth for the good of their students. Go."

He ruffled my hair and guffawed as he shoved me backward. There was a weightless sensation before I opened my eyes and blinked.

I looked down into my clenched fist and there it was. My mission to take something to Granda in Djurn Forge.

CHAPTER THIRTY-ONE

Fjlak had decided to leave me alone once I came back from my meditation and prayer, allowing me to find a small satchel to put the debris from Fainne in and digest what had just happened.

I stayed quiet for hours, allowing the experience to ruminate within me as I dwelled on the fact that the goddess I had thought was trying to manipulate me was truly trying to do so. *Chances are likely good that she already knows how I could obtain spells of my own without needing to form a pact and she just doesn't want to share until she has my soul bound to her service.*

That would not do at all. I would not be bound to a goddess and used as a pawn in her war for supremacy against her siblings after the latest threat to her kind had passed.

But what could I do in order to stump her and keep her complacent with me long enough to amass power of my own?

While I continued to beat my head against the problem at hand, I decided that I couldn't avoid earning her ire forever and resolved to push it off as long as I possibly could, owing that she was immortal and therefore time meant little to her. Outside something killing a god, there was little that would affect her perspective of time unless something spoiled some grand design of hers, in which case I would be as prepared to deal with it as I was now. No point making a mountain from a molehill if she wasn't going to force my hand now and wanted to make me come to her.

The gods and their pride.

Glancing up, I found Fjlak watching me, so I stood and bowed my head respectfully. "My sincerest apologies for my mistake and disgraceful questions, Fjlak."

She observed me for a short time longer quietly then grunted and nodded me forward. "Your training was woefully misrepresented to you by those other smiths. We have much to catch you up on and I am not a patient woman." She smiled. "Come."

True to her word, Fjlak was not a patient instructor in the slightest. "Pick up the pace, Azlo, your lines are fine but your pacing is shit!"

I sighed mentally, having learned the hard way that outward shows of annoyance were met with equal parts sarcasm and prolific violence toward my work.

The wood I had been carving a sigil into when I sighed at her pestering had been roughly grabbed from beneath my chisel and snapped over her knee to be done again.

Now, I kept it in and simply asked, "I thought this was about perfection? I don't run a smithy to support my livelihood or a village, only my own fighting and protection."

She snorted as she watched me from three feet away at her forge. "Because spending days on subpar work as a smith is useless and wasteful—especially when said work needs to be enchanted to be useful."

"And taking it to an enchanter to be taken care of isn't always feasible," I grumbled to myself, more out of annoyance than anything else. If I could have someone else do that work for me, I would be set and could focus on just getting my own work taken care of.

"As an elf, you have the lifespan that most crafters would kill for. Imagine what I could become if I were blessed with the years you had?" She snarled a swear word in orcish that I was becoming all too familiar with upon hearing it only a few short hours ago. "This is melting nicely, but the heat needs to be upped again."

She went to the pile of wood that she had and pulled a few more logs from it, then came back and tossed them into the forge and went to a small shelved area to find something.

She came back with a small canister of something in a thick metal cup. "Here we are." She tossed it into the flames and they burned a darker color for a moment before the heat of the room shifted the temperature hotter. "Fire drake saliva, it works wonders and makes flames all the hotter. Too bad it's hard to get."

That was an interesting thing to have in a forge, and it made me wonder if there was a way I could get my own. "Where did you find it at all?"

She picked up a skin that had lay on her workbench and peered over at me as she took a long drought of it. She sighed after her drink and wiped her mouth roughly before answering, "Protected drake sanctuary. Remember the white dragon I told you about?"

I nodded and she waved her hand for me to keep working. "Well, she went a bit... off after a Sylvan egg-eater ran off with her clutch and began adopting drakes and wyrmlings of all colors. She's actually managed to raise quite a few dragons herself. She's repopulating their race as we speak, and it's both wonderful and terrible."

I fought the urge to whistle at the news. Dragons were really only as rare as they were because they fought each other, the mages of old, and sometimes even the gods if they took offense to what their chosen ones did. Father and Mother had fought a dragon once, a black one who was poisoning the ocean at one point.

The dragon's hoard had funded a great deal of their adventures.

"So how did you manage to get some of the drake's saliva?"

She smiled and said, "Made a deal with the dragon. I would keep the orcs away from her home and children if she supplied some materials for me occasionally." She chuckled to herself and admitted, "Though I do send the odd party to her now and again to give them food if the winter hunting is scarce."

I took umbrage with that for Winterheart's sake and that of his pride. "White dragons are the perfect winter hunters, she would have no trouble feeding herself."

She blinked at me and scowled. "Fool, I meant scarce for the *orcs*."

That horrified me as well. "You knowingly send your people to their deaths?"

She snorted and took my work to check over. "Orcs care about strength and balance. If you have no food, everyone shares what little they have so that the balance is fair. Starving people are weak. Strength is important to remain safe from rivals. If food is scarce for our tribe, I will send a group of hunters into the mountains to 'hunt' and feed the dragons. In return, the stronger remaining orcs have more food to remain safe for the winter."

She held up a hand and stopped me. "And the dragons hunt in our lands less because our 'tithe' goes to them willingly. I do not do this out of cruelty, I do it out of necessity."

"Do they know?" She frowned at me curiously. "The orcs you send there. Do they know there's a dragon there?"

"Of course they do, I'm not evil." She tossed the wood I had been carving on into the flames and handed me a new piece. "The orcs hunt for the dragon herself! If they came back with that much meat, the tribe would grow fat off her and strong as well."

"Because fed orcs are happy orcs." I rolled my eyes and she

paused to stare at me. "What?"

She snickered. "What you just said is ludicrous." She laughed again. "Orcs grow stronger when they eat stronger foes. Orcs seek out strong meals when they are pregnant, and kill strong opponents to take some of that strength for themselves and their young. If an orc were to eat a dragon's meat, the strength of that dragon would invariably become the orcs' own."

I laughed at that and she just watched me, so I had to stop myself and confirm, "You don't seriously believe that, do you?"

"It's a racial trait." She stated it coldly and stared me in the eye as if daring me to say anything. "Why do you think that bog hag was brought with you, proof?"

I nodded and she snorted, shaking her head. "We ate it at the meal last night, boy."

My stomach nearly dropped and it was so hard to focus after that. Was that part of how Nadir was so strong?

I would have to try to figure that out eventually.

"Work for a while longer and then you can come and help with this sword when it's done. You'll be doing most of the work, and get to enchant it under my watchful gaze."

I nearly groaned at that, but figured it was better than nothing.

I did as she said, working at carving the engraving I would be using on the sword. At least she had me practicing that first and foremost since it would be the most practical thing for me to have at my disposal.

The wood moved readily enough out of my way as I outlined with a slim blade. The charcoal I had would be dulled on the wood, so I just used a knife to draw. Once I had my design, a snowflake, I picked up the chisel and began to carve into the center of it, following along the lines that I'd drawn up.

I worked steadily, much to Fjlak's irritation, but it was difficult to argue with progress. I'd carved the same thing for hours and as I grew more comfortable with it, I'd grown more proficient at doing it.

I still didn't know how my father had done it so well, but if he was good at it, I would be better. I would be better than him at *everything*.

Which left me with a conundrum. Technically speaking, there was no limit to the number of crafting classes one could use, but as the crafters' levels climbed and their abilities began to catch up, they ran into more plateaus and thus had to work through those. While I could always make things to bring my enchanting up to par, it meant that my smithing might suffer from the inattention.

"Pay attention!" Fjlak bellowed as my chisel scored outside my lining. She took the board and tossed it into the flames with an exaggerated sigh before turning back to me and crossing her arms. "What?"

I blinked at her and decided not to insult her intelligence. "I wondered how my smithing might suffer if I focus on enchanting as well."

She frowned and considered it for a moment before shrugging. "You won't know until it happens. However, as you level up your skills in both professions, you'll be able to use skills both would have."

She turned to the forge and leaned against her stone workbench. "Wild smiths can add more monster materials to their projects to bring out the power of the materials in new ways. Enchanters can make use of less mana as their skills improve, to the point where it costs them precious little to carve and engrave, as well as to imbue their work with magic."

She smirked and touched an item on her table. "Some of the best can put multiple enchantments on an item that will feed into each other but aren't the same." She turned to me and then frowned. "We also don't have any idea what your class as a person and fighter will add to your crafting capabilities."

I frowned to myself then looked up at her. "So my potential could be nearly limitless?"

She nodded and stilled before grinning widely. "It's time."

CHAPTER THIRTY-TWO

The Ever Frozen in the large tub looked almost like the clearest and bluest water I had ever seen in my life as it bubbled and waited for us to use it to make something.

We moved to the work bench where we began the process of making the mold for it. The sword would be longer than I was tall, and thick. It would be heavier than I was used to, and I wondered if I would have the strength necessary to wield the monstrosity.

"Okay, we need to pour the metal in." She motioned to the side of the tub closest to me. "You grab that side and when I tell you to stop, pull it back up and set it back on the flame."

I nodded and grasped the side of the tub without needing gloves and she paused. "Perk."

She grunted and nodded to the mold. "Slow, and let me lead the pour."

She did as she had said she would and lead the pour, the molten, water-colored metal slipping from the lip of the tub and into the mold where it settled swiftly. "Stop!"

I grunted and barked a brief, "Hup!" as I pulled the tub

back away from the item and set it back onto the flame of the forge to keep the metal molten.

She went to the bench and came back with Kayda's tail feather and held it aloft in the air. "Fainne, bless this sword and the hands who make it with your strength and wisdom so that it might be as close to perfection as we mere mortals can make it be."

She hummed a soft tune as she lay the feather into the cooling metal in the mold then grabbed the tub once more. "Pour the rest of it in, Azlo."

As soon as the metal touched the feather, there was a hissing and a wave of cool rushed through the room so fast and wild that the flames in the forge were snuffed out.

Fjlak laughed almost maniacally as the metal continued to move and settle into the mold and rapidly cool with the pour of the feather and the properties of the metal merging.

This was exactly the power I expected of the smiths I knew and I wanted to live in moments like this and thrive as I knew I could. I would make powerful weapons and armor and trinkets until the day I could no longer hold a hammer.

As the metal cooled and settled into the mold, we watched it, the clear cast of the weapon slowly turning to the metallic blue that it had exhibited before, but this time I could feel and see the feather within it. It was *perfectly* centered within.

"What do you feel from it, Azlo?"

Fjlak's voice startled me slightly and I shook my head as if coming out of a stupor. "I… I want to carve out the feather so that it's even more visible, but not so much as to sacrifice the integrity of the weapon."

"We can make a bevel on each side so that the feather is clearer. An excellent observation." She smiled at me in a manner that didn't look exactly like *her*, it felt almost like Fainne peeking out of her eyes and she was just the catalyst. "What of the enchantment? Don't forget the one we practiced, but what do you think and feel of it?"

I frowned, calling back knowledge I thought useless from all of Xiphyre's lessons and sighed. "That the one we're going to use is fine, but the material sacrifice we would put into it would be nearly worthless."

She frowned. "I doubt you're leveled high enough to be able to use those."

I nodded. "I'm not—but you are. And you're not about to let this weapon be anything less than perfection and I don't want it to be either, so we're going to need to make a trip for that to happen."

She frowned and I just offered a contrite smirk. "Sorry, but we'll be visiting that dragon friend of yours after all." I stared down at the weapon in front of me, then glanced at the tools I had been using to carve the enchantment sigils then smiled. "But I have another small project in mind for us before we leave that I would request your guidance with."

———

MIDNIGHT

Nadir looked elated. She'd never been around so many people before, let alone feeling like she wasn't some kind of pariah or even worse—a savior.

Whenever there were war practices among the other combative apprentices in the palace, the human children included, they would gaze at her as if her very presence precluded them from death or illness. It did to an extent, as her master's teachings and his powers made it possible for her to heal almost anything, but the emotions behind it were far from what she wanted to be given.

Here? No one knew. She was just another orc thanks to her glamour, and the challenges of orcish life were well within her means. She could fight nearly anyone, she could cook, hunt, or fish. She could protect.

She could just be free. No expectations from anyone to hold her back. But what about Azlo? Her hands clenched and she began to rub her thumb against the side of her index finger anxiously.

Ragul spoke to her from his own path behind her as she meandered through the main road of the village, breaking her from the spiral she was about to enter at the thought of not being with her brother again for her own wants. "Tell me, Nadir, what is it you truly wish for from our people?"

She smiled. "I feel like everyone has been asking what I wish for lately. All I want is to meet my people and just exist with them for a time. To see who they are and be more like them."

Ragul nodded to himself. "And what if those people were afflicted with an illness? Would you stand with them?"

Nadir stopped and I had to switch to another rooftop to watch her face before she smoothed herself over and answered, "I believe I would."

"What if that affliction were mages?" Nadir raised an eyebrow at that and turned to look at the older orc. He watched her steadily, reading her facial features. "Would you hunt them with your brethren?"

"Are you not yourself a mage?"

He shook his head. "Shamans are priests to their gods and the natural world, so we are holy creatures." He stared at the girl curiously and then finally said, "Mages have made the creatures of this world soft. Uk'Beth has deemed it necessary that they be eradicated so that the era of the warrior can begin."

"I thought you were waiting for the Wolf Who Ate The Stars to appear to you and your people to begin any sort of great change?"

He chuckled. "A common misconception of those who are fated to bring change is that they need to *wait* for the signs." He shook his head and grunted. "Orcs do not wait, we are a prepared people. We will begin until our fated leader is born to us, and we need strong warriors to bring about that change."

Nadir looked uncomfortable, something that I hadn't seen of her in some time, since before her master had bequeathed his power to her. "I have magic as well. Does this make me the enemy?"

Ragul stared at her with confidence. "The power of a healer is innately a gift from the gods. While many are foolish and support the enemy, Uk'Beth smiles upon you with your strength and skill." He shuffled closer and put a hand on her shoulder as if he were a proud uncle. "I know that he sees you as a warrior of much skill, and his blessing upon you is proof that you are fit to walk with us upon the rest of the world."

That made Nadir pause. "The rest of the world?" He nodded and she frowned. "The orcs may see the rest of the world as inferior, but they've never marched on anyone who didn't earn it or attack first. Why attack the rest of the world?"

"Because Uk'Beth demands change!" The older orc held up his hands and splayed his fingers out toward their surroundings. He clenched his fists and beat them on his chest. "When the enemy of the gods was slain by the pretenders, they left a hole in space and time that allowed something to creep in. Something that the gods squabble over. With our people driving the others to defend themselves, the gods can fight amongst themselves without being disturbed."

Nadir nodded to herself and finished his thought in a way she thought led to her understanding. "And it's a fight that Uk'Beth believes he can win."

He nodded once to confirm her statement and leaned close enough that I had to fall from my perch once more to get close enough to hear what he was saying.

"The hole leads to a place where the gods could go to gain more power and take their strength to another world." He straightened and stood before her in a way that made her look up at him as he was beaming proudly.

"And if Uk'Beth makes it there first, he gets to remake the place in his own image, right?"

For the first time, Ragul appeared uncertain. "I do not know. But I do know that he wishes to liberate the people there."

"And the orcs are content to just serve as fodder for a war they have no true part in?"

He frowned. "All orcs serve Uk'Beth, and he gives us strength and his visage as warriors. We are his chosen people." He took a deep breath and sighed as if he were thinking of how to speak to a child. "As such, we will be fortunate to fight for the warriors of this world and of the new world when Uk'Beth triumphs."

I watched with growing curiosity as Ragul motioned to the orcs around them and then back to Nadir. "We stand together, and we will win, but we need all of us."

"And what of the other tribes?" Nadir watched Ragul as he considered the question, almost looking like he could have ignored it until she added, "Surely there can't be a unified force against the rest of the world—all of those mages—without unity. If you can't even unite the tribes, how can Uk'Beth have the orcs do all that he expects?"

He motioned for Nadir to walk with him and I followed along with them, keeping up with a new form I chose to do so. Maintaining my… stealth surveillance was difficult in new forms, but I would manage. **It's a cat, okay? How many stories do you know of have talking cats in them? Probably not many, so let me just tell the story, alright?**

"The other tribes see us as usurpers to the powers that should have been their own. With two shamans, we are stronger and closer to Uk'Beth." He smiled at another orc and nodded to them as they passed then spoke on. "We prepare and build ourselves up for the good of the mission to come. We send out warriors to scout and push against humanity and the other races, to include our useless, true-nomad cousins who mate with elves."

It was so hard not to snicker at that, but as a consummate professional, I refrained.

"They believe that it was ordained that we should await the birth of the wolf who would devour the sky." He caught her gaze, the slight correction to her previous statement evident before he continued. "They believe that our preemptive strikes paint us as a target before we are truly ready and that is hubris on our part."

She frowned to herself. "And you only mean to begin the changes you can before the wolf arrives, so that the way is paved."

A sigh of relief. "Yes. Heartening that you understand." He came to stand before a large building, one that appeared to be something more than what it was. "It's why we have this place."

He opened the door and led her inside and what was there was incredible—terrifying, but incredible.

Children trained against automatons of sorts that had wands in their hands. Magic flared around the wand of the closest one as it was aimed at the child before it. The small orcish girl, probably not yet old enough to have been walking and talking more than a year, held a wicked-looking dagger at the ready. The magic built and built until finally it blasted and the girl dipped beneath it and then back up, scoring a slice against the wooden body of the automaton.

Where did the orcs come across these things? The fact that they existed on this plane of existence at all, on this side of the veil, was surprising.

"We collected these from some mages who populated a tower in the mountains some time ago on one of our raids." He watched as the child reset and did the same thing again before another child stood in front of the wooden creation. "Practiced *dueling* against them. As if it would prepare them for a real fight. Now, we use them to breed mage killers."

Concerned, Nadir turned to the man and spoke softly so as not to distract the children. "I thought that was a special class."

"It can be, or an assortment of classes working in conjunction." He watched as the boy hopped over the spell and scored a slice against the wood before resetting. "The only thing that matters is developing the skill to see the building of mana around your opponent and tearing it apart. These new warriors will be able to do so."

Mage killers. The idea of them wasn't outside the norm, but training them and *breeding* them in order to fight the vast majority of their enemies? The ones hiding behind magic that they thought would protect them because they were used to the status quo. Even with average people trying to stand against them and rising up, they were still so certain that they had the power to protect themselves.

Also, why hadn't they joined the human mage haters? Was it that they didn't want to work with weak humans? With everything they had shown her before, that had to be the case. But to me, if the goals aligned, why not?

I glared at the children and watched as the magic hit one in the leg and they limped away, but other than a broken leg, the child was fine. *And they may not be able to protect themselves after all.*

"This is horrifyingly callous." Nadir surprised me and there was true outrage in her tone. "Training children to fight like this without a healer is hardly the way to make real change. Setting them up to fight automatons that can't move and change a spell on the fly is setting them up for failure."

She walked out into the training grounds and pointed her hand at the child limping to the back of the line to get some help. Her hand glowed and the children snarled savagely before attacking Nadir.

The girl glowed briefly before she began her own attack, enraged by the use of magic.

The adults in the room bellowed commands but none of them could reach the children as they sought to kill the mage.

Nadir simply withstood the assault and slung the smaller orcs into their handlers arms before turning back to Ragul. "They won't be able to stand before a mage of more skill than a poor warrior. A middling level caster will *kill* them."

Ragul nodded sadly. "Some may fall. But it is an eventuality we are prepared for. The price it takes to prove our belief to the god of our kind." He pointedly stared at her. "Your god."

"I worship no gods." Nadir's voice didn't quiver as she spoke; the Fae were devotedly atheist despite the proof that gods existed.

"Yet." Ragul spoke calmly and almost cajolingly as he gazed at her. "The call of a warrior is loud to all, but orc kind always fall back to his service eventually. If you want to truly understand your people, you should learn their religion."

He paused at that and then followed her gaze to the children who still fought against the orcs holding them. "They hate and fear magic because mages hunt our kind. The mages kill what they want indiscriminately and then do as they please. Those with unholy magic must be stopped before they turn their sights and cruel experiments on us as they once did the beast kin."

That made Nadir pause as the man ushered her from the building, her eyes darting back and forth. "You mean…"

"The very raid against that tower was a raid to recover missing orcs." The explanation said a lot as to why the tribe was so adamant and fervent to go along with their god's supposed plan, but it wasn't all adding up. "They were experimenting on them. Torturing them with spells that they wanted to try."

Nadir turned her head away, knowing that the words he spoke aligned with books she'd read as a child. Mages normally grew bored and *pressed* the boundaries of what was acceptable, but to find that they had kidnapped her people and experimented on them?

Anger threatened to boil over within her, I could see it in the hard lining over her body and the way she cycled into the breathing that her master had taught her.

"Will you help us, Nadir?" Ragul asked as the voices of the children inside returned to normal levels. "You seem to know much of fighting casters, perhaps you could assist our training for all ages. With your help, we could make true change. Change the way our god meant it to be done! And while you help us, you could grow closer to the family you've never known."

My eyes widened. *Oh. Oh this conniving* prick! *That's how he's gonna get her? Well, we'll just see about that!*

"Allow me some time to dwell on it?" Nadir's reticence surprised me more than his cunning. Was she falling for this swill? "My time is not my own. My brother and I are required for things to go well in places abroad, and being a part of some grand coup was not in the plans."

Ragul spread his hands in a non-threatening gesture of goodwill. "Of course. We wouldn't want your brother to think you capable of being on your own, would we?"

The insult wasn't lost on her nor me, but he quickly found a means to escape before she could make him explain himself, someone nearby to extricate him from the awkward conversation as if by design called and he fled. *The creep.*

Sourly, I watched Nadir as she continued to the village and watched the orcs move amongst each other in a manner that struck me as feigned, but to her and her continued uncertainty, it was genuine.

This is going to be terribly difficult to break her of, this need to fit in with someone. I watched her pause and watch some orcs shearing a warg and passing the fur to someone else before they slaughtered the animal and butchered it. The teamwork practiced and easy. *Better tell the boy of my thoughts and soon.*

CHAPTER THIRTY-THREE

I packed the tools into the satchel that I had never expected to use in my lifetime, then put that into my inventory and shrunk the forge to put away as well.

"You're certain this is what you need to do?" Fjlak hadn't necessarily been trying to change my mind on going to visit her white dragon friend so much as she had been trying to impress upon me how foolish it was for the two of us to go there.

"I know white dragons, and I think I can get her to do what we would need her to." I knew exactly what I could offer her in order to enlist her assistance as well, if she would act the way that Fjlak described her. If she acted *half* as she described, we would be fine.

Once I was finished packing, she grabbed a few items from shelves across the room and sighed heavily. "Then we will be leaving now."

As soon as we were out of the shadows of the temple, we stood in the entrance to the cave as if we had crossed no distance whatsoever. Spatial magic at its finest.

"We will be gathering what supplies we need on our way

there if you need any." Fjlak observed me and I just nodded once as Midnight alit on my shoulder. "Is that bird yours?"

"In a manner of speaking." She grunted at my answer and began to walk away toward the mountain range behind the hill she inhabited. "Midnight."

He dipped his head. "Prince Azlo." He stood and watched the scenery around us as any bird would, affecting the air of a prey bird looking for predators. "Nadir is in danger of being taken in by these people, the chief the worst among them. He means to try and lure her to his peoples' cause."

I raised an eyebrow and almost stopped following the orcish woman in front of me. "And that is?"

He shrugged and grumbled, "Oh, you know, world domination at the behest of their god." That made me throw him a dirty look but he stared at me with one eye and in a deadpan tone said, "This is no jest, Highness. They mean to kill as many mages and make as much of a mess of the world as they can so that their god can attack his siblings and gain control of the tear in the wastelands."

"For what reason could they want that?"

The bird grumbled to himself and shuffled his wings uncomfortably before answering, "I hypothesize that there is a place within the tear in space and time that can be used as a hub to other worlds. If the gods can take control of it, then they can go through and find a world potentially all their own to remake in their own way."

I was silent for a time and Midnight cleared his throat. "They're training mage killers, Prince Azlo. They may not have the numbers now to be a threat to the people of this planet, but once they get their chosen one in their grasp, the tribes will rally and it will be a matter of time before civil war takes this continent."

"The matters of the mortal races only mean much if they will interfere with our holdings in this realm, our allies and interests. Or within the Fae realm." I brushed my fingers over my cheek as a snowflake fell from above, the clouds beginning to build and swirl. "And I am certain that they will move to the cities of man as soon as they possibly can, which means that our interests in Zephyth would be in jeopardy."

"Sunrise would be in danger too, though it's harder to find, but if Nadir joins them, then she could lead them to it."

I froze where I was and plucked the bird from my shoulder. "Nadir wouldn't do that."

He stared at me, unfazed. "Ragul would see to it she felt obligated to so she could be with her kind."

"Stay with her. I have a short trip to take to see a white dragon about assistance with an enchantment, and then I will return to assist in dissuading her from this path of destruction." He blinked at me and I sighed. "I will be fine, Midnight. My sister needs someone who knows her to watch over her; do this for me and for her."

I tossed the bird into the air and began the process of donning my half plate armor. Once it was on, the gift from the elemental made itself useful and my stride over the steadily cooling and sloping ground no longer faltered.

Midnight flew next to me for a short time, maybe mere moments, until a strong breeze forced my eyes shut for a heartbeat and then he was gone.

Ten minutes later, I caught up to Fjlak and stayed with her the entirety of our trek to the mountains themselves. It was not as hard a walk as I thought it would have been, and that was cause for concern. "Were the mountains always so close?"

She grinned and said, "No. Part of my abilities as a Cleric of the Mountain, and my affinity with the Way, means my stride and those who stride with me find themselves moving faster."

I raised my eyebrows. *There's a good reason to be a cleric right there!* "Interesting to see that there is such a perk for those who practice divine worship." I frowned and then asked, "Can you use it while mounted?"

She grinned, her tusks showing with the expression. "Somewhat." She thought about it for a moment then shook her head. "No, and the second I am not on the ground, it will be as if I never walked, so the distance will return to normal I think."

Onward we walked, her feet sinking only a little more into the snow gathering at the bases of the twin peaks before us. The stone rose high into the air, the snow-capped tips hidden in the swirling banks of clouds growing ever darker above us. There were multiple pathways here, some well-worn featuring ropes to tie to in case of travel, others that would have been hidden to most.

Fjlak closed her eyes for a short time and pointed to one of the hidden pathways leading into the mountains and above toward the peaks. "First we must rise and then fall into a valley under her power. The cold here grows much more brutal, will you be alright in that?"

I fought not to be disrespectful and snicker, instead offering a small bow of my head. "Long have I fended off the frosts and frigid airs of others whose powers dwarf my own. I will be well, thank you."

She snorted and grunted. "Whatever." She dug into her inventory and pulled a grouping of furs that she had obviously sewn together to act as a brace against the freezing air here. "Stay with me and do not speak until I introduce you."

I nodded serenely and followed along behind her into the slowly rising rock path before us that sliced between the mountains' bases. The cold cloying the area was almost enough to remind me of home when the wind gusted past us, and I expected to be able to smell the white dragon as I had as a child, but there was no sense of that coming to me so easily here.

As soon as we began to clamber along a section of the path that had given way to a fall toward a freezing rivulet below about forty yards or so, the orc turned toward the stone and searched for a handhold. She found one and growled triumphantly, "Come!"

I smirked to myself, happy to oblige as I gripped the stone and pulled myself up the side of the mountain behind her. Here and there she would pause to collect her bearings and find a better path for herself, but eventually found places to shove her whole arm into a crevice to rest herself.

It seemed to me that her abilities applied only when she actually walked with her feet on the ground, as she had a much more difficult task ahead of her here. As we continued to cling to the mountain's bony flesh to climb higher, I found myself pointing out spots for her to get to and after the fourth time, she snarled, "Just go ahead of me, boy!"

I laughed and said, "As you wish, Fjlak." My fingers nimbly gripped the stones next to her feet and I moved around her, giving her a wide enough berth so as not to be a threat to her position. "Where do I go?"

"Straight above, you'll find a ledge." She grunted and sighed. "There's a rope on it that should be there. Once you get to it, toss it down and I will climb up to it."

I nodded and pressed onward, grips and holds growing more and more sparse until finally I could see the ledge she spoke of. There was a cave carved into the side of the mountain.

My left hand's fingertips searched for a hold to bring myself up with, my grip with my right alright but nothing to warrant complete carelessness. The lip of the cave was only ten feet from where I currently clung to the cold stone and I wanted desperately not to fall.

The nodules and crevices that I had found plentiful before were sorely missed as I found a bare grip that I didn't fully trust with my left hand. My right lifted and I found one there before my left leg slid into a gap that I'd had my arm in previously. Seven feet now.

"Hurry up!" Fjlak's voice bellowed from below. "Cold!"

A cool flake of snow chose then to land in my hand and I grimaced at what that would mean for climbing.

Pressing on, I was four feet from it now and seeing nothing that would even *remotely* qualify as a grip, let alone a safe one. *If the bird were here, he could have easily flown up and just dropped the damned rope for us.*

Pondering as I could with the wind whipping at my clothing and threatening to pull me from the face of the mountain I scaled, I pulled Shaper from my belt and lifted it toward the lip of the cave. I willed it to grow and as soon as it was large enough to touch the side stone and air, I pulled back so the spike would catch and act as a bolster for me.

Cautiously, I shrank it and pulled myself along with it on some of the more unsavory holds.

Crack! One of the stones under my palm shifted and tore away, my heart fluttering like a flag in a storm as my right hand clutched my hammer for dear life.

Shaper shifted backward slightly as the stone fell away, whipped aside easily by the wind and I pulled myself up onto the hammer's haft a bit more and fought to keep the weapon from slipping from the lip of the cave any more than it already had.

Shrinking the weapon a bit more, I could reach the mouth of the cave and pulled myself in, using the spike on Shaper to pull myself in further.

Sure as she had said it, there was a large length of rope tied to a stake bolted into the ground with strips of metal with enchantments on them.

I kicked it over the lip of the cave and it plummeted downward until it grew taut.

Not even a moment later, the older orcish woman stood in the opening to the cave with the rope tied around her waist. She looked down upon me and raised an eyebrow. "Tired?"

"Mentally." My answer made her laugh at me and I took a soothing breath before claiming to my feet. "I will be fine. Let us continue."

She shook her head. "We rest here tonight, then we

continue on in the morning." She looked around and motioned to the fire before her. "Can we use your forge to warm me up?"

I shrugged. "It depends on the elemental within. If you feed him, he will warm us. Though I would like the time to create picks if we mean to continue climbing at all."

She snorted and rolled her eyes. "No sense of adventure?"

I shook my head. "Adventure is often mistaken for life-threatening happenstance, that I do not believe in on a funda-mental level." She raised an eyebrow at me in challenge. "Yes?"

"You're on your way to ask a white dragon—a notoriously feral breed—to assist you in creating a weapon that you want to enchant with nothing physical to offer her." She rolled her eyes and added, "You could have fooled me, boy."

I grinned. "I said I don't believe in it—not that I wouldn't do it." I sat, back against the wall with my burning legs flat against the blessedly cool ground. "I just don't believe in being dumb about it."

Fjlak chuckled and motioned for me to get the forge out, so I did. "Duke Forger, we wish to bask in your presence and warmth. In return, Fjlak, Blessed by Fainne, will offer you food."

The elemental spoke from inside the forge. "Alright. Are you making anything?"

I cast an expectant gaze at the orcish woman who blinked at me and said, "What?" When I frowned at her, she just huffed. "All I hear is a warm fire, but I'll toss a log in, sure."

"Will I need to make anything for this next leg of the journey?"

"Oh!" She pulled herself into her furs and comfortably said, "No, likely not. The way forward is carved into the mountain itself now. She carved it."

I almost stood as I demanded to know, "Then what was the point of the climb to get here?"

She laughed as she pulled a log from her inventory to toss into the hungry elemental's clutches before fixing me with a teasing grin. "Easy food falls and makes itself known on the way down."

I blinked and found it hard to eat some of the hard tack I had with me suddenly. Unusual for me, but these were some seriously new experiences.

Fjlak chuckled darkly and growled, "Splat! Breakfast!"

CHAPTER THIRTY-FOUR

We crawled through the back of the cave; more like a tunnel, really. The exit to it was larger than the orc by a few inches, which meant I had no trouble getting through the exit while Fjlak had to suck it in in some places to squeeze through.

That went a long way toward soothing my irritation with her and her nearly endless jokes about falling to our deaths and becoming dragon food. She was the one who almost didn't make it!

Now she was huddled against the cold once more and shivering bitterly as the frost nipped at her. I stretched laboriously and felt myself loosening well under her scorn-filled gaze and just took it in. She may have been able to pervade my mind with images of dragons nipping at my corpse, but I could remind her of something she didn't have, and that was youth.

Through the carved out hollow in the mountain we tread, carefully picking our way through the series of pathways and loose rubble until she took my hand and pointed to a drop.

"No one ever takes the drop, because they assume it's a trap."

I blinked and raised a brow at her and wondered, *Is it?*

"I assume that means we need to go that way?" She shook her head, then pointed at me. "*I* do?"

"If we both approach her, she will assume that I brought you for something rather than as an introduction." She shoved me toward the hole in the side of the mountain. "This way, I get to her and she will come to you *with* me."

"What if she's too hungry to care about waiting?"

She snorted. "Then I'll be dead and you'll be not too far behind, boy. I mean to see her first, and I'm only going to tell her that you asked me to bring you to her."

I nodded and set my jaw as I put myself closer to the drop and then hopped down into it. The stone swiftly gave way to ice as the hole became a slide that disoriented and swirled to continue confusing the trapped prey.

The slide bottomed out into a large cavern with icy walls decorated rather lavishly with the claw marks of the poor sods or animals foolish enough to have been trapped here. Hunks of ice with limbs inside that reminded me of my mother's collection of entombed and frozen foes truly reminded me of the home that I had left behind.

Here I stayed for the better part of two hours, exploring and finding discarded weapons in various states of disrepair and breaking down. If anything, I could melt down some of these metals and reuse them.

There were few—if any—perfectly preserved animals among the dead, some smaller ones here and there like birds that may have been caught in a gust of wind and then turned to ice over time as they perished due to the temperature of this place.

Then once their corpses were caught up in the blast for a bigger being, they were left behind. Beautiful reminders of the fragility of life for those not strong enough to fight certain death.

There was a large portion of the cavern that held the least dead, and far enough above it to make climbing out nearly impossible was an outcropping reinforced with ice.

Without a doubt, this was where she would come from to survey her trap to find what morsels she could. What made me wonder was that the blood here was non-existent.

A memory of when Granduncle Winterheart had been teaching me to bathe myself fluttered to mind unbidden. *We white dragons sometimes prefer our food frozen, so that there is a savory* crunch *that is just a bit more than that of the snapping of bone. While I do enjoy a wonderful cooked meal, hatchling, I do also so adore the simplicity of devouring a frozen foe.*

He had then stared me in the eyes pointedly as he said, "Be certain to reach all the way behind your haunches, hatchling, there are times when we move and the ice we forget to gorge on gets caught in our scales."

Smiling, I decided to wait where she wouldn't see me right away and sat to begin sharpening the wind dagger I carried as it had dulled to the point that it was nearly useless other than to clean the dirt from under my nails.

Two hours passed and I thought I heard movement above me on the ledge. "You said he would be here!"

The growling voice was decidedly feminine, though there was a tinkling sound from it. The room was no cooler for her presence either; that wasn't a good sign for her. It meant she was younger than an ancient dragon.

I called out, sheathing the weapon I had been tinkering with. "He is!"

She peered down at me with her eyes narrowed dangerously. "Fjlak says you have come to be introduced to me. The others she sends here become food—speak."

"I am Prince Azlo, Prince of the Unseelie Court in the Fae Realm, son to the Lady Darkest and soon to be heir to the throne." Once I could see her fully, I glanced over her, knowing Fjlak was probably staring at me. The old orc gave nothing away, and the dragon once more filled my vision.

She kept her scales well groomed, looked well-put-together and strong. Her stomach hung low as well, so she had eaten recently, but Granduncle Winterheart had always impressed upon me that the state of a female dragon's stomach and her hoard were key factors in finding a desirable mate. "I come to you seeking aid in making a fang for myself, and I request your breath to do so."

She scoffed, her beautiful fangs flashing at me in the dim light of the cavern. "You *dare* come to me seeking my resplendent breath?"

"I come not just asking for something with nothing in return to you, Cold One." I bowed my head politely and made sure I had her gaze when I spoke again. "I offer you the attention of a potentially desirable mate—powerful, and the owner of a magnificent hoard."

"*Lies!*" Her snarl shook the room and the temperature dropped to the point that even in her furs, Fjlak shivered. "How dare you?"

"I do not lie, Death Given Wing, I merely offer my family to you." I spoke quickly, "I have a granduncle who has yet to sire a nest of eggs, and while he dotes on my mother and I, I feel that he regrets not having hatchlings of his own."

She glared at me distrustfully. "I have heard of no white dragons who have no mates."

"He resides with my mother in the Unseelie Court—if you would but aid me, I will see that he has the opportunity to come here to meet you."

"And if he is not desirable to me?" The ridges of her brow shifted and she lowered her head to consider me almost casually. "Do I eat you?"

I almost laughed, but it would not have been a welcome response to her attempting a threat, so I merely shook my head. "No, my offer was just the attention of a potentially desirable mate, not that you would be able to mate with him."

She considered it for a long moment and the entire time she clicked her claws against the ice in a thrumming rhythm that would have grated on my nerves. "Where is this '*fang*' you spoke of?"

"We would need time to prepare it to receive your mighty

breath, but I would only ask for a short time." She nodded and I smiled. "Did you want him to come first?"

She smiled coldly, not hard for a dragon whose nature was akin to the very ice around us. "No, because if I do not like him, I will kill you both and collect the weapon for my own hoard."

I bowed my head. There was no deal, so therefore no power to steal, but her attacking Winterheart, or me in his presence, would be a death sentence.

A rope fell and I found the dragon holding the top of it so that Fjlak could join me and assist in carving the engraving into the icy weapon. While I pulled out the chisel that I had made specifically to engrave items with, I smiled.

Enchanter's Claw

All items engraved with this chisel will be easier to score and become more receptive to mana, enchantment, and materials used.

Chisel created by Layman Smith Azlo and Grandmaster Smith Fjlak Faultbrand

In my hand, the metal-capped dragon's fang fit perfectly as I began my carving into the frozen metal on the ground. We had to put small chunks of ice beneath it to keep it stable so that I wouldn't mess up the engraving, but it worked well enough.

The chisel moved through the Ever Frozen slowly, almost as it warmed up the material to the point that it became liquid and moved aside. A flash of inspiration occurred to me as I carved and in the tips of the snowflake I carved, I wrote the Sylvan symbols for freezing, cold, strength, and sharpness. I didn't know if it would do anything, but we would certainly hope that it did. I carved them small enough that they would look alright and be nearly indistinguishable without an in-depth inspection with a lens of sorts.

"Alright, that should be well enough, I believe. Let me see it?" She leaned over the weapon and scowled at it, her fingers running over the symbol as she inspected the lines and frowned.

"Here and here, flesh out the lines again, they're a little too shallow."

I did as she ordered and fixed my mistakes as she watched over my shoulder, her breath on my neck making it difficult to focus well, but I did my best.

She looked it over again and grunted. "Good, let's get this done."

We walked toward the opening above us and I called, "Oh great Frost Wyrm, we are ready for your magnificent contribution to my meager making."

She stared down at me and a slight flick of her scaled lips smiled. "You flatter well, princeling."

I grinned up at her. "My granduncle ensured I was raised well from the time I was a hatchling."

That caught her interest and she lowered herself down from her ledge. "Oh? Tell me more of this dragon who raised you."

"He is the least temperate being where we live. Why, his existence in my proximity is the reason that your *thorough* cold and beautiful lair doesn't freeze me solid where I stand!" I spread my arms and smiled. "He is ancient, his understanding of the cold unsettling, and his scales are the very rime that could freeze the oceans."

A low, rumbling growl emanated from deep in her throat. "I find myself eager to make his acquaintance."

I stood the weapon in front of me, the blade presented broad-side toward the dragon and held my hand on the back of the weapon as Fjlak stood behind me. "We will feed it mana and, on our say, give us a blast of your breath, just a small gout of it."

The dragon held her head high. "I understand."

Fjlak and I began to feed mana into the item together, slowly so that it wouldn't over fill and lessen the enchantment. "Get ready!"

The dragon reared her head higher, craning her neck as her softer underbelly scales glimmered and glowed with the magic power that built in her throat. I could feel the mana edging toward the right amount, and Fjlak bellowed, "Now!"

Freezing cold breath that smelled like ozone to me rammed into the blade of the sword and then raked to the far side of the room where it froze another several feet of ice onto a wall.

Fjlak, shivering so hard her teeth chattered stammered, "N-n-n-a-ame it, buh-b-oy."

I held the weapon in my hands and felt the cold just *radiating* from it and spoke softly, "I'll call you Glacial Fang."

"Seriously?" The dragon raised a ridged eyebrow at me. "Are naming conventions truly not your strong suit?"

I frowned at that and muttered, "That's what I felt would be a great name for it."

"You speak Sylvan, elvish, and draconic, I'm assuming, so why not something in those languages?" Fjlak's joining in on the teasing made me even more self-conscious.

I closed my eyes and grumbled, "I'm still learning!"

Fjlak rolled her eyes and took the weapon from me. "Well, I'm not. Override!"

My eyes widened as she kept her hand on the blade and closed her eyes. "Your new name will be now and forever more: Grim Feather."

The dragon nodded her head. "Suitable, there is no mention of an element, as that is the sign of weakness."

I blinked at her. "How so?"

She snorted. "If someone wields a hammer called 'Flame-tongue,' do you not expect to find it a fire-attributed weapon? You can prepare for that. At least this way, the weapon is less likely to be a giveaway."

I threw my hands up and then at the great sword. "It's a gigantic block of ice!"

The dragon snorted, a gust of cool air ruffling my clothes as she admired it. "A rather pretty one as well, if I do say so. Look at that magic playing along the side with the feather visible. Lovely." She turned her gaze back to me as I went to touch it and firmly placed herself between me and the weapon. "You will uphold your end of the bargain now."

I glanced around the room and spoke with resignation. "If this is where you mean to receive him, I don't know that he will fit." She frowned at me and I grinned. "He's a pretty big deal, and requires a little more space than is available here, unless you want him shapeshifting into something a bit smaller?"

CHAPTER THIRTY-FIVE

MIDNIGHT

Nadir sat in on a meeting between the chieftain and the various elders of the tribe as an observer as concerning reports of a missing patrol came to their attention via concerned family members. They were supposed to have been patrolling the eastern lands of the tribe's hunting grounds no more than a day or so out by this point.

"There has been no response from the other tribes, their banners not raised in the way that is the norm after an attack on a rival." The speaker, one of the older women in the village who I had seen in the back of the mage killer classroom watching in the shadows, stood and nodded to Ragul as he considered her statement. "We would do well to send out scouts to find out what happened to them."

I grimaced and just rolled my eyes, already having my clone go to the area that they were supposed to be in, since we could cover more ground quickly than the legged orcs would be able to.

Nadir tapped the portion of the table in front of her absently before asking, "And what if it's something else?"

"Our warriors will meet whatever it is in battle and defeat it or fall." Urtan stood next to his father and beat his knuckles against his chest as he lifted his chin. "This is our way. You have seen what the orcs do, Nadir. Do you wish to join us in this?"

She smiled, her tusks flashing as many of the others in the room watched her. "I would love a good fight."

"Then perhaps you would like to go and investigate what has come about?" Ragul's voice made her flinch but there was an odd note to his voice until he added, "Urtan could accompany you, to ensure you do not enter into another tribe's territory."

She smiled. "That is not necessary." She lowered her voice and her mouth moved silently before a massive shadow appeared behind her. "Report."

The orcs stood in unison, shouts and cries to begin battle causing guards to flood into the room they occupied when Ragul snarled, "Quiet!"

Nadir raised her voice. "This is a Fae creature loyal to me. I sent him to survey the territory with the group in case anything happened and so I could learn more about orc tactics."

She turned back to him and said, "Speak."

"Seelie accompanied by..." The creature paused and lowered its voice. "The Hunt."

Nadir gasped at the same time my clone caught wind of something. I closed my eyes and willed my consciousness to it and blinked as I glanced around where I flew.

Miles and miles away, almost near the area where the patrol should have been, there was a dark cloud in the sky that I swiftly realized was the Wild Hunt itself circling over the corpses of the orcs that had been patrolling.

Hounds baying made my feathers crawl as I watched one of the larger ones tear open the stomach of an orc with his eyes shot out with arrows made of shadow. The intestines it pulled out looked like the most grotesque string of *not* sausages I'd ever seen, and it almost made me stop flying toward them.

But if I did, I wouldn't be able to accurately assess their numbers and that was a necessity for reporting purposes.

This was not *alright.* The fact that the only creatures moving down there other than the hounds were the Seelie picking at the items the orcs carried was highly concerning. It meant that the Hunt swirling like an angry thundercloud above them was massive.

There were at least ten Seelie, and three of them were strong enough that the Unseelie would be duty bound to send some of their own here to fight them and kill them if they could.

This close to the children... the queen may well send her most trusted fighter to protect them.

A hissing noise made my blood run cold as a soft *snick* made my wings fold and drop toward the ground, my vision fading. I came back to my real body as I hit the ground, my spelled clone fizzling out as the darkness roiled forward with the Huntsman at the head.

I fell. The height of the fall would've been concerning if it hadn't been for me falling right into Nadir's lap.

She grabbed me and spoke softly, "Midnight, what happened?"

"Hunt." I heaved, fighting to catch my breath. A clone dying like that, brutally as it happened, was painful to the caster even though it was just a spell.

She shook me again and I grimaced. "The Wild Hunt and the Seelie have come!"

Nadir snarled and stood. "The tribe needs to prepare for battle—now."

Ragul frowned at her. "Are these 'Seelie' threats?"

"They are mages bringing magic warriors with them." She seethed. "The Wild Hunt is one of the greatest enemies not just to our Court, but to warriors as a whole."

Ragul considered her quietly, then motioned for Urtan to

go. "Warriors meet warriors in combat, and if they fell ours, then we should repay them in kind."

He stood himself and put a hand onto Nadir's shoulder. "Warriors who fight together grow closer." His face was serious as he looked down at us both. "After this battle, you will be one of us. And your decision will be easier."

I mentally roared, *Sonofabitch!*

This was going to get bad, quickly. Azlo needed to get back to his sister quickly, or he was going to lose her to these zealots.

AZLO

I closed my eyes and let my breath fall from my lips. "Queen Maebe, Darkest Night, and Mother, please hear my plea."

The air around me made a crackling noise and I *felt* her presence and attention on me, curious and waiting.

"I request your aid in accomplishing the goal laid out before me, and completing a request: please send Granduncle Winterheart here through a portal, as I have someone here who is eager to meet him." I took a deep breath. "He will likely be pleased to meet her as well."

I could almost hear her tone take on salacious lilt as her voice breathed into my ears, *"Her?"*

It brought a grin to my face.

"Very well, Prince Azlo, allow me to collect the requested party, though his payment for this request will fall squarely upon your shoulders."

"As you wish, Mother."

"Who are you talking to?" The dragon's head jutted into my eyeline and stared at me with accusations in her gaze. "Why could I hear another voice from someone who is not here?"

"It was the one who currently holds his chain." Not an outright lie, as she did have a chain with his name on it that she had used *once* to chain him up outside after one of my more...

physically educational tutors ended up disappearing while on a walk after a particularly painful lesson.

We ended up waiting for two hours, long enough for the dragon to begin glaring at me as she loudly demanded to know when he would be here.

I just maintained that the time between realms moved differently, and he would be here as soon as he could be.

Twenty minutes after her latest threat to eat me, about three hours total waiting, a fissure yawned open near us.

Winterheart in his misshapen humanoid form walked through with a blizzard-like freeze accompanying him.

"Where are they, dear boy?" He growled as he swept into the cavern. The air froze around us, making it painful for most normal people to breathe.

I glanced over at where Fjlak fought to breathe and put a hand out to keep him back. "Granduncle Winterheart, thank you for coming to meet me here."

"Anything for my favorite hatchling." He reached out and stroked my cheek affectionately. His eyes wandered and he wondered aloud, "Where is your sister? I wished to see her before you both left, but she seemed to have been avoiding me."

"She is currently with her people in a village below this mountain, not too far away from here." He grunted and turned his sight to the others. "This orcish woman is an impromptu instructor for my smithing skills, Fjlak, and this is the dragon... uh."

I blinked, realizing at last that I didn't know her name at all.

Winterheart stepped forward and took a deep breath before looking around and deciding something. With that decision made apparent as he began to grow at an alarming rate, almost to the point that the cavern wouldn't be able to hold his massive bulk along with the dragon hostess and we mere leg-bound things.

He expanded until he could no longer grow and maintain distance from her and then there was a massive *crack! Pop!* Winterheart's tail punctured the icy wall that she had just made thicker and then his head clattered into the stone above us where chunks of icy stone fell as a result.

"I am Winterheart, companion to the Unseelie Queen, Guardian of the Starred Children, and ancient white dragon." His voice deepened and resonated around us as ice built along his jawline only to break with each movement of his maw as he spoke. "I am the Blistering Cold and Hoarfrost given wing."

Fjlak's friend stood on her rear legs as her wings flared wide. "I am Gertinax, Snow Terror, and Matron of the Drakes of Mount Sorrow Fang."

There was a shimmering around her and a clutch at my heart as she spoke her name. It was her true name. This was dangerous knowledge for her to give away, but I was glad to have it.

Granduncle Winterheart tilted his massive head. "Drakes? I have yet to meet any of those—I take it you do not eat them?"

Gertinax snarled savagely, spitting out a simple, "No."

Winterheart nodded along and then looked down at me. "You promised that I would meet her, little one. What is it that I can do to assist you?"

"I offer this opportunity to both of you." I fixed my gaze to Gertinax. "To you, I offer the attention of a prospective mate who is powerful enough to sire and protect your nest."

I turned my attention to Winterheart as the female dragon sputtered and looked away. "To you, I offer the chance to leave a legacy more appealing than having the children of others to dote on." The ancient wyrm cleared his throat carefully and lowered his head to look me in the eyes from a foot away, but I put my hand on his chin to still his tongue. "I know that my sister and I are the pride of your hoard, but I think you would make a wonderful father and any wyrmling would be lucky to have you."

Winterheart eyed me closely for a heartbeat and sighed, his cool breath ruffling my hair and clothes. "I am old, Azlo, very old. I do not have long in this world, or even our realm. My time is coming."

My heart, normally steadfast and resolute, suddenly ached. Winterheart had loved me dearly and openly for as long as I had lived, and some of my very first memories were of him looking over the edge of our crib to see that we were safe in his massive hoard.

This was usually followed by Mother and Vrawn coming to collect us to return to the royal chambers where we had been unceremoniously stolen by the crafty dragon, but those memories were warm and fondly held.

"I would take you as a mate." The sudden interjection by Gertinax made both of us pause, and we turned our heads in unison to her where she lifted her chin. "I see how well you have raised the Fae, and while that does not matter much to myself as a dragon, as a mother, there is nothing more attractive."

She stepped forward and narrowed her gaze. "I have given my power to the child in order to create a weapon and in meeting you, I see a future." She looked to me. "I see our deal as concluded."

Gertinax spread her wings and lifted her head until her neck was fully extended so that Winterheart could see all of it. "I ask you, Winterheart, are you so old that you would deny the hopes of a child who loves you so?"

Winterheart's eyes widened and he looked down at me. "I always did have trouble denying my hatchlings, and a soft spot for this one." He smiled, his fangs bared for all to see. "If it means so much to him, then I see no trouble."

There was a rumbling along the ground and I could see Winterheart beginning to grin. "You did manage to find a beauty, did you not?"

Fjlak chortled at that, falling to her rump on the ground and holding her ribs. She laughed so hard that even Gertinax looked down at her with concern. She tried to speak. "Ha... haha... oh the flirting of dragons... Ahah..."

Even I found it a little unbelievable and I'd been the one to try to make it happen. Granted, for more reasons than I had let on.

If this plays out well, we might be able to gather even more strength to the Unseelie Court via Gertinax and her brood.

Winterheart growled, "I have a request for you then, Gertinax, if you would hear me out?"

"Make it quick. I have drakes to feed, and we must begin setting up a nest for the brood."

The ancient white dragon shook the ground with his chuckling again. "I belong with the Unseelie Court. They are a part of my lair, could we perhaps move there in order to protect what both of us hold dear? If you have a hoard, we will ensure it is taken there."

Her wings flared wide once more and she allowed her head to dart forward as she spoke, teeth clacking together. "I will raise my eggs where I am queen, and that will be here." Gertinax obstinately stood her ground.

So we would need a common ground and a bit of a workaround? "I think if there was an agreement to assist in times of need, Mother would be able to assist in putting a portal here so that you could come here and visit as often as your heart desires."

"I am certain that my beloved niece would do this for me if I were to ask it of her." He took a deep breath and stilled, his eyes closing slowly as he hefted his massive head further into the air than was possible for those of us he dwarfed. He took a deep breath and exhaled slowly, ice forming and dripping from the air above where his nostrils flared as he growled low, "Seelie."

CHAPTER THIRTY-SIX

AZLO

"Are they edible?" Gertinax asked excitedly, much to my surprise and Winterheart's. When we turned to look at her, she looked away, stating, "Eggs require nourishment and I have not eaten in a week or so. It would be good to have food readily available for me and my drakes."

"Then there will be food." I glanced at Winterheart. "How far off would you say they are?"

"Three day's hard ride from the village of orcs your sister has lost herself in. I can smell her from here, there is... doubt in her aura." He looked down at me and frowned deeply, the scales on his face clattering at the attempt at facial expression past what most dragons would call distaste. "Has she been eating well? I know I did not get to teach her to be a very good dragon, but we must eat well if we are to maintain confidence in our actions and selves."

I almost laughed. "I'm sure she's been eating fine, but with the Seelie approaching, she may not know they're coming." I whispered Midnight's true name and summoned him to me.

There was resistance, but only because he was asleep when he appeared. "Midnight?"

"Why is he here?" Winterheart snarled and put his head closer to me.

"This is Midnight, my subordinate and scout."

Winterheart shook his head and spoke softly. "That is Cieth, part of your father and an Airy. That he is here means that he could be spying on you."

Midnight's eyes snapped open and the raven shimmered as his humanoid form came to the fore. "You never could keep a secret, could you, you tottering old coot?"

Anger bubbled beneath the surface of my skin, my cheeks reddening and my fists clenched as I asked, "Midnight—Cieth —whoever you are, what is the meaning of this?"

He looked at me and sighed heavily. "The name I gave you belongs to the host whose mind broke when I introduced myself. The body is still tied to it. I've been watching over you and your sister since the second you were born, because the two of you are special to him, and by no fault of my own, me." He ran his hands over his head and then glanced at me with eyes that no longer resembled the ones that were usually on his raven form, but those of a large predatory lizard's, like a dragon's. "I was the Beast half of your father, Zeke. My presence was always meant to be kept a secret to protect you as a last resort, but when you two started to do things a bit more recklessly than I would have liked, I stepped in and introduced myself under the guise of my host." He pointed at Winterheart, who growled menacingly. "*You* were sworn to keep that secret by the queen!"

I blinked and turned to Winterheart and gasped softly at the realization that he could die if she found out, but if he swore an oath of power to her, she would already.

"I swore an oath to never tell them who you were while I walked the grounds of the Unseelie Court, or until such a time as it became necessary to ensure the children were safe." He held his head high, clearly victoriously in his mind. "I am neither at court, or even in the realm of it, and your presence without being hidden is a cause for concern."

"It doesn't matter!" I shouted finally and both of them turned to me. I pointed at Cieth. "You lied to me, how is it that your power is not mine?"

"I told you half-truths and made oaths as Cieth, the being who resides in the host whose body you have control over. I was never in any outright danger so long as I was careful. And annoyingly, you and your sister are smart, so I had to do so much more than I wanted to." He held his hands up to stave off my outrage and fury. "There is more going on here than you can know, but please understand, I am drawn to you to protect and watch over you. It's more my decision than anyone else's will, and the Wild Hunt is about to ride for the village your sister is in, so we need to be moving yesterday."

"How can I trust that you aren't lying?"

"Because I've never outright lied to you before, and because you killed the Seelie King's favorite niece in that fight with the orcs and mages—*unprovoked*, if I might remind you." He frowned and then said, "Also, because the orcs mean to try to get your sister to join *them* in cleansing the planet of mages and magic users that aren't beholden to Uk'Beth, and that's another part of the quest you've been given solved."

Sure enough, I received another notification of gaining experience and a reward for it.

"And she's thinking about doing it."

I closed my eyes and took a deep breath, knowing what I wanted and what needed doing.

I hated to do this, but there was no time like the present. "Gertinax." As I said her true name, I walked past Winterheart to stare her in the eyes as she blinked at the oddity that was my will brushing up against her own. "I need you to take Fjlak somewhere safe for just a moment, because Granduncle Winterheart and I are going to make it so cold here that an ice elemental will be summoned."

Gertinax growled low in her throat, her will flaring against mine, but I battered her back with better control. No one had fought me for control of anything like this, but I knew how to win. The only people who could beat me for control in a battle of wills were Mother and Winterheart, and the latter only because he had been trained by the one who trained Mother.

She took Fjlak in her foreclaw and lifted off the ground and into the entrance to the cavern that she had come from.

Once she was gone, I glanced at Cieth. "You and I will discuss this later, and I do mean that we will be discussing it at *length*, but for now I need to get to work."

"Wouldn't have it any other way, kid." He just crossed his arms and stared at Winterheart. He just shook his head as he leaned against the wall of ice behind him. Finally, he spoke again, this time to the ancient dragon. "She's still going to kick your ass though, you know that, right?"

Winterheart sniffed at the air. "I care not what happens to me so long as my children are safe." The dragon turned his massive eye to me and his gaze softened. "Forgiveness is not something dragons ask for, Azlo, but it is something a Grand-uncle would beg of his beloved child."

I sighed and put a hand on his massive jaw. "I know you meant no harm, but he has a point. Mother will not be pleased."

"I have weathered more than her fury, and she knows I would not break my word to her lightly." He sighed and glanced after where Gertinax had left the cavern. "She will not care for that having been done to her, you know."

"I know, but it needed doing. This sword will be more powerful, and me with it, if I can manage to summon an ice elemental to reside within it." I stared at the weapon, knowing that it would be less than perfect for an elemental, but that didn't mean it wouldn't be an apt host for now.

But before that, I had to be sure we weren't going to return to find the village occupied by enemy forces.

"Cieth, go and ensure that the orcs aren't overrun before we get there, and keep me updated as you can." The man turned and paused, so I growled, "What?"

"Do not call me that in front of Nadir, please." He turned back toward me and stared me down. "You may control the body of my host with his true name, but not mine. I can leave it and inhabit any creature or form I please with my half of our remaining power and all of my own. I am not a tool you want to lose, boy."

"We have work to do, Cieth, just do as I ask." He continued to glare at me until finally I snarled, "Fine! I will not speak your name again until we have the conversation I wish to have, but you will do as I ask as recompense for your half-truths and the convenience of my knowing you better now. Go!"

He turned and faded from sight, so I turned to Winterheart and pointed at him. "I need you to make it *very* cold now, before I have to petition Mother for aid for our work to be done."

Winterheart chuckled. "As you wish, my boy. Hold on to your scales."

MIDNIGHT

Flying as I wished was much faster now that I didn't need to maintain any semblance of secrecy, since being an Airy made me naturally faster as I flew. Before, if the boy could find me or somehow see me doing things outside the norm for a normal Fae creature, it would have been bad and led to questions I wasn't prepared to answer. Returning to the village mere hours after he summoned me to him rewarded me with a pleasant, but disconcerting sight.

The orcs were as prepared as they were willing to be based on the threat of casters coming to their village in their lands. Which was an all-hands level of threat that they didn't appear to care for in the slightest. Orcs milled about closest to the edge of the village nearest the threat, carrying their best weapons and painting their bodies with colored paints.

The mage hunter children had been given armor to protect their smaller and weaker bodies, but mainly at the request of Nadir, it seemed, as she oversaw them putting it all on. It was really only hide armor which served to help marginally. A margin, to me, that seemed almost silly to bother with.

Against the might of the Seelie and the Wild Hunt, they would serve as little more than flies to swat away when they became annoyed at the best. At worst, there would be highly qualified illusionists among them who could manipulate the battleground and force them to fight themselves.

The bastards could do that easily.

Nadir stared at the children in front of her and dread filled the pit of her stomach.

She closed her eyes and muttered, "Lady Darkest, Sweet Sickle of Ice, please hear my plea." The wind along the plains below whipped into a frenzy, then the air around her grew noticeably colder as her shadow lengthened. "The Seelie and their hounds come for the prince and I for slaying Seelie in fair combat. Children are being put on the front lines and while I am powerful, I cannot protect them all and slaughter the Seelie scum and the Wild Hunt on my own. Please, send warriors to aid our battle, or at the very least to protect the children."

The chill came and with it a whisper, *"Let us see what you can handle, though I do have an agent in the area who will be willing to assist you as they can."*

Nadir frowned and as I was close enough to hear her response, I frowned as well. Maebe was never one to allow harm to come to children; she would move the heavens and earth before she allowed any harm to come to an innocent child.

That made me suspicious. She couldn't have possibly meant Winterheart, could she?

The whispering cool wind returned and this time it whispered into my ear as I flew above Nadir, *"I am placing you in charge of keeping my children safe. I will be sending Eve and one other Fae to corral the small orcs, capable fighters I am certain they will become. If they are to come into danger, you know what to do."*

I rolled my eyes and responded with a terse, "Yes, my queen."

"Do not be cute with me, Airy." Her voice held little in the way of veiled threats. *"I already know that Winterheart cleverly worked his way around his vow to me about you. Their safety is paramount, am I clear?"*

"I may not have been there when they were created, but I know how we felt about them, Maebe." I could tell my using her name without her title bothered her from the way the air chilled around me and my feathers began to crackle slightly with frost. I snorted. "If you think this pathetic chill bothers me, you have no idea what I'm capable of. I will watch over the kids. Ensure that your Fae know I am on their side. I would hate to have to kill them too."

The wind around me died as soon as I was finished speaking, though the chill clung, much to my enjoyment. I missed my body and my mountains. Hopefully, the children would go there someday.

I focused as Nadir made her rounds among the orcs and then eventually toward where Ragul and Urtan stood with the tribe elders. As they were distracted, I went behind one of the larger tents and cast my host's cloning spell, the body and our consciousness splitting apart so that I could cover both children. It was tiring to do so, but seeing as though the Hunt and the Seelie were still at least a day or so off, and the former wouldn't move on without their Seelie watchers, we had the time necessary for me to rest as the clone flapped into the air to watch for Nadir and the boy.

We watched over the proceedings below as Nadir explained the idea of the Wild Hunt to the orcs around her to disseminate to the ranks. It wasn't pretty to us, but the orcs took the information really well. As a matter of course, it seemed to us, the majority of the massive green warriors looked even more excited for the battle to come. Some of them bickered with each other and boasted that they would kill the most invaders, a few of them even going so far as to make *wagers* on who would fell the most!

These poor fools.

I had Zeke's memories—not only his, but my own from my own encounters with the Seelie and their dogs, the Wild Hunt. This was a practiced force meant to ride down anything that the Seelie ruler deemed unworthy of existence in the Fae Realm, and while he couldn't send them to meddle in the affairs of the Unseelie, he surely sent them out to ride against the free Fae.

To be unaligned without the power to protect yourself or hide meant to constantly live in fear of the Wild Hunt and her riders. To fear the unerring accuracy of the Huntsman and his bow, the only miss to have been recorded in history having been Storm Company as they had been swept away by Maebe before the arrow could take its target.

The Wild Hunt ran rampant otherwise, hunting and killing those who crossed their path to 'keep their skills sharp,' the unaligned Fae whispered in hushed tones and at the time, I didn't believe them. Watching a family of red caps who I thought strong enough to keep themselves out of trouble and harm's way being hunted down like a pack of rats before a barn cat. The hounds barely left anything behind to be recognized after the Huntsman shot each one of them dead with an arrow the size of your average spear.

Watching the roiling darkness in the distance knowing that, and what the contents of those ominous clouds were capable of, there was nothing but trepidation in my heart for the battle about to come. I only hoped that Nadir and Azlo would be able to pull through with what brewed on the horizon.

CHAPTER THIRTY-SEVEN

AZLO

Heartbeat slow and steady as the tundra-like frozen air continued to whip through the cavern as snow began to collect on the floor in drifts as the ancient wyrm continued to allow his very presence to exude into his surroundings while I meditated.

Cries of confusion from the drakes in the area outside the cavern prompted me to call out with my eyes closed. "Rein it back in, Granduncle, we need it all in here or they could go elsewhere, and we would need to hunt them down."

"Ah, forgive me. I never get to play like this, Azlo, you know that." He laughed a little as he pulled his power back toward himself like a physical force that you could just touch and manipulate. "I can feel the magic in here growing more dense, is this what you need?"

I allowed my eyes to open and felt the surroundings with my own powers. I could feel it too, and he was right. "Close, just a little more." For another hour, we waited as the snow built and covered the frozen corpses and parts along the floor until finally I called out, "Primordial Elementals of Water and Wind, please heed my call. Send your child unto me so that I might request their aid!"

Nothing came. The chill of Winterheart's cold around me was the only comfort I had in this moment. Wondering how I was going to be able to fight the Seelie with a weapon I couldn't control, and it was hardly perfect.

I only had fledgling fire magic, a trash-quality wind dagger, and armor that would allow me to move easily on top of mud, water, and the ground. Those things would hardly allow me any kind of advantage against the Seelie, and would barely even leave a scratch on the Wild Hunt.

I turned my mind inward, fortifying myself to go through what I needed to. Hours. We had hours to prepare for this, if I was being generous and if we had no issues getting back to the village in time.

"Winterheart, will you be fighting the Seelie and Wild Hunt with us?"

I turned to find the dragon comfortably laying behind me with his eyes drooping, preparing to fall asleep as he continued to grow ever more comfortable with his surroundings and how chilled they became. Beneath him, I saw movement and froze where I was, watching cautiously—hopefully.

"I am not who you thought would be coming, child of our Beloveds." A shadow flitted from beneath his mammoth wing and then stood from my own shadow. This one was as large as the swamp elemental that had come and bonded with my armor. "We are here because the others are too cowed by the goddess to come for fear of her... dissatisfaction."

The soft, hissing voice emanating from it lowered and took on an almost gleeful lilt as it watched me. "*We* are the Void. We do not care for that usurper and her threats, so we make our own rules. Do you have a receptacle I can reside within?"

I hefted the blade at my feet where I sat and spoke calmly. "I only have this, and it's heavily aspected to the cold and to freeze things." I allowed the uncertainty to poison my voice as I continued to say, "I cannot say what it would do with you in it, if it will ruin the weapon, or if it will harm you."

The creature chuckled. "I can tell you that the cold of the Void is *much* more to worry about than this, dear child."

I frowned at the familiarity, but the creature truly didn't seem to hold any malevolence toward me. However, I had to know. "Did you ever work with my father? Or Mother?" The shadowed figure stood taller, but they remained silent, so I asked, "Are you and the Primordials one and the same?"

The elemental crouched again and blinked, the lightless eyes only becoming more lightless in doing so, before answering, "I never worked with them, but they and the others, Balmur of the Fleet Foot and Yohsuke of Tainted Blood, are known and also liked by us. As to our reference to ourselves, it is no more than how someone refers to one's self. The Void is the Void. We are but fragments of the whole, though I am smaller and weaker than they, I am still Void."

The tinge of disgust that the elemental said the word 'I' with, lent to the statement more than the explanation itself. "Very well, if you would like to bond with this weapon, I will allow it. But before doing so, would you be willing to form a pact with me to allow me some of your strength?"

"We would be *delighted* to form a pact with you." The shadow swept over me and with it came that same semblance of there being nothingness surrounding me. "What terms would you like to ask for with this pact, hmm?"

I frowned at their sudden relaxation as to what I could possibly want. "Do you want to be able to wield the very shadows around you as our beloveds before? Do you wish to bring the full crushing might of the Void to bear upon your enemies, crushing them?" There was a slight gaseous giggle with that one. "Tell us what we can give you."

"I was thinking more along the lines of what would the Void expect from *me*." There was a brief pause and then the shadows almost receded for a heartbeat, quivering, but I couldn't tell with what emotion. Was it excitement? Glee? Fear?

"We know that the end of all things comes, our very own mage holds sway with our magic and the magic of another, and yet we love her still." The shadows swirled around me some more, the motion slightly nauseating to watch, but I dared not look away. "Death does not feed us, or excite us, as it is inevitable, but the life that comes with it can be beautiful."

There was a soft pause. "The creation of things is also interesting to us, the end of all things."

That made me frown. "Do you want me to create things for you?"

The Void around me paused the swirling motion and formed a dome as it contemplated. "Yes. Yes, we would like that. What would you recommend?"

I blinked, uncertain, wondering how I could possibly offer the Void something that they would like to have.

"Maybe something that you could wear as an elemental? Or a better item to inhabit?" I touched the sword and frowned. "I should have made this one with an elemental in mind, but I didn't have the foresight at that moment to make something that could truly guide and wield the power you offer."

"Then you will make us armor, a weapon, and accessories fit for us and us alone." I frowned at that and they lowered their tone. "Is this an issue?"

I shook my head. "No. Actually, I was trying to think of the types of materials and effects I could make in armor for you. I have somewhere to go after I get done with the fight that's coming, and that's to learn from the people in Djurn Forge."

"We are not familiar with this place, but if you are going, and to learn how to make things, we will go with you." The swirling stopped once more; it had begun again with the elemental speaking. "We offer you our power, vast is it is and vast as it will become, to you should you follow our accord."

I nodded and frowned. "I don't have anything that will be able to work as an outward show of the pact that we share."

"Your father had markings of our bond etched into his skin,

and your mother wears the stars on hers." They closed in on me. "If you would like, we would take something of the same."

"I have midnight skin and stars present on my body already. What more could be an outward show?"

The swirling miasma of the void closed in around me further as the hissing voice made an offer. "We could take something different."

———

MIDNIGHT

The darkness of the impending strike from the Wild Hunt and their Seelie handlers ebbed closer and closer, leading the orcs into an almost frenzied state of excitement. Fights broke out among some of the more boastful that were soon broken up, and it took me coming to Nadir to break her from her own nervous excitement at what was coming.

The line of her body and the hardness of her stare at the sky said it all—the Seelie would pay for coming forward and interrupting her time with her people.

I landed on her shoulder and spoke in a hushed tone. "Azlo is coming. He has a new weapon, and Winterheart is here as well. I don't know what you plan to do with these people, Nadir, but their holy war isn't yours, and they don't stand a chance against the host that rides with the Huntsman."

"They are warriors, Midnight, and as such, they will fight and defend their lands. I cannot force them to take a knee while Azlo and I fight the Seelie." She glanced around, pausing to allow some of the wandering warriors to pass us by before she said, "I will make my own choices as to the religious zealotry I allow around me."

I scoffed. "You can't be serious." She turned and her eyes met mine from inches away and a chill ran down my spine as she turned away. I pleaded with her, "Nadir, they don't care about you. They will use you just as surely as anyone else would, and toss you aside as soon as you don't fit what they want you to be. You will be nothing more to them than cannon fodder and a body to step over for a god who could care less about you *or them.*"

She glowered at the sky, her hand falling to Storm Caller absently as the dark clouds waded closer. "And I will be strong enough that no one will be able to step over me, Midnight." She picked up the axe and sighed as a chill came over her. "I don't care what their god wants, I want to learn about my people."

"And if that knowledge brings consequences further reaching than your own misguided curiosity?"

As soon as I said it, I regretted it, but she made damn sure I knew she was talking to me. Her massive palm slammed into me fast enough that I couldn't do more than squawk indignantly as she gripped, and her grasp tightened menacingly, the malice in her voice edging on homicidal. "Then I will deal with those consequences as I would any other before me, in the same manner I would for those who feel it necessary to interfere with my own free will—violently."

She tossed me into the air and snarled, "I have been forced to think of the good of others and the Unseelie my whole life, and will have to again as soon as this timer runs out. I will live this time for myself, and no one will tell me otherwise." She stared at the axe in her hands. "My father may have had a mission, but he still lived the life that he could, and in that life, he promised mine to someone else. I will live as I want for now."

I cleared my throat and did my best to sound sympathetic. "And what of your brother?" She frowned at that question and stared up at me with slowly worsening anger in her eyes. "I doubt that Azlo means to stay with the orcs with you forever. I think he means to go to the clans under the mountain and learn to smith from the people he adores."

She opened her mouth to speak, but a commotion rose behind her and we both turned our gaze to the hubbub, only to find that something moved from the mountain in the distance at a disturbing pace.

"Who is that?" Nadir asked and despite my current upset with her, my own curiosity piqued.

I closed my eyes and focused, then opened them and allowed my skill, Crow's Curiosity, to let me zoom in on the approaching figures.

It was Azlo all but carrying a woman whose legs worked next to him like she was trying to run alongside him. As they grew closer, the woman grew old and weary-looking and they slowed down significantly, Azlo's stride maintained but less urgent.

He huffed and smiled at his sister. "So glad I got here before you all took all the fun!" He coughed slightly. "That was a bit rough, do you have a flask on you?"

"You don't have yours? Where's Winterheart?"

He frowned and took his out of his inventory and shook his head.

"What happened?"

"We went to see a white dragon about her breath, and he remained behind for a little bit to take care of a… transaction, of sorts." He looked away, abashed, before taking a drink of his water and capping it with a sigh. "Magic water never tastes that great."

He pulled out some food and started eating it in front of her, asking, "What's the situation here?"

"It is what you see, Azlo…" She grabbed his chin and forced him to look back up at her as she firmly reiterated, "What. Happened?"

He blinked and stared up at her as I landed on the ground next to her and saw what she was talking about. His left eye was changed; the white of it was completely black and devoid of color except for the iris itself. "Oh, this? I can see just fine."

"That's not the answer we were looking for, Prince Azlo, and you know it."

Both the prince and his sister glared at me, and I huffed.

"Fine! I'll go scout the enemy or something." I fluttered into the air, leaving my clone invisible behind the boy to make sure that I could hear everything they said as I flew off.

"It's the mark of the pact I just made with the Void." He kept his voice low as he ate, knowing how the orcs around him would react poorly if they overheard anything.

Nadir frowned and then her eyes widened. "The Void? As in the Shadow Elementals?" He nodded. "That's great! What was the pact that you made, and what did you get?"

He swallowed his bite then belched softly before answering. "I agreed to make them armor, weapons, and accessories, and when I do, they will wear it." He shrugged and though my clone couldn't see his face, I could hear the skepticism in his voice. "They like it, I guess?"

"And what did you gain?"

He grinned. "A lot. A lot more than I did with Duke Forger, but this one is… wild." He stood up and held his hand out, a massive blue great sword appearing.

"Take her." He let Nadir take the weapon and she gasped. My clone turned around the boy and beheld the weapon for itself.

It was beautiful, shot through with a darkness so deep it could have siphoned away the light around them easily, but that didn't take from the details etched into it or the detract from the feather floating inside it, forever encased in ice. It was Kayda's feather, Nadir would have recognized it anywhere.

The handle, almost three feet long and large enough to wield well, was covered in a beautiful soft purple leather down to the simple pommel. I had to admit, the length of it made me wonder how it could be wielded but that wasn't for me, seeing as I had no hands in this form.

I ordered my clone to hop onto the item, my identification spells not working on it without physical contact. As soon as I did, I fought the urge to whistle and turn around to look at it with my own eyes.

Grim Feather

+15 to attack, + 7 to damage

Frost Bite — Every successive attack landed on an opponent will cause the wounded party to take additional cold damage, and to slowly lose feeling in their affected limbs. Wielder is immune to the cold of the weapon.

Shadow Tether — This weapon is bound to the wielder and will return to their hands at will.

Boreal winter comes with every swing of this blade, the cold clasp of crackling death ebbs ever closer.

The clone didn't get the chance to read the information about the makers of the weapon because Nadir passed it back to her brother. "This is an amazing tool, Azlo, you should be very proud."

"I am, but I wish I could have made it better, or done it all myself." He sighed and with a soft *whoosh* the weapon disappeared. Nadir made a motion at it and he smiled. "Weapon skill for wands. It's called Ready Grasp. With it, I can have any weapon in my arsenal at my beck and call with a flick of my wrist and a bit of will. I'll never be unarmed again."

"Amazing!" Nadir grinned at him and clapped him on the shoulder. "I'm happy for you. And the pact ability?"

Azlo's grin grew even wider as he said, "I obtained two new abilities. Well, really one was an ability or skill, and the other a spell." He looked around, noting that several of the orcs watched them furtively, some of them looking uncomfortable with him there. "Better to show you in the fight, but I got a skill called Gravity Shift that allows me to change how heavy or light something is as long as I'm touching it. The other is Spectral Pull; that's the spell."

"And that does?"

He laughed and said, "Exactly as it says, it's a grasping spell that pulls either the target to me, or me to it, it just depends on what I want." He smiled and rubbed his hands together. "And all for the low, low cost of ten mana up to thirty feet and five more for every ten feet, to a maximum of however much mana I have. I just have to be able to see what I'm grabbing."

"Did you spend your last level?" Nadir's question made him pause and she frowned. "Azlo, you cannot do that, you need to remember these things!"

She looked to the side of the village, then toward where the darkness flowed toward them and the orcs. "Take care of it now and meet me at the front lines, we will lead the charge."

CHAPTER THIRTY-EIGHT

AZLO

I shifted uncomfortably until she looked away, as I didn't want to tell her that I'd actually neglected to allocate two levels worth of points. I wouldn't correct her for that though, and began raising my stats.

I chose to put six points into Constitution, since the coming fight would be harder with the Wild Hunt involved. The chaos points I had went into Wisdom by themselves.

Name: Azlo Erebos
Level: 13
Strength: 30
Dexterity: 26
Constitution: 29
Intelligence: 27
Wisdom: 19
Charisma: 30
Unspent Attribute Points: 0
Unassigned Chaos Points: 0

That left me pretty well rounded for the coming violence.

My Strength was plenty high enough for me to be able to properly fight with Grim Feather and Shaper.

With my wand skills coming in handy, it would be much easier to fight in a new way. The spells I had would limit me some, but it would be easier to gain more power now this way, at least.

I glanced up at the clouds as they gathered and pressed toward us, the wind whipping around us.

My heart thudded in my chest as I called a warning to Nadir, "They're here!"

The whistling of something piercing the air streaked toward the village. An arrow the size of a spear slammed into an orc three feet behind me, and I couldn't help but jump at the sound of the impact. The squelching sound of the orc trying to move and call to his friends was enough to turn my stomach sour.

I risked a glance back and saw the orc trying to grasp at the bloodied projectile piercing through her back, pinning her to the ground. She groped at it with hands that couldn't close properly and she fought to speak, but her lungs had been sliced.

I had no particular attachment to these people, but the fact that the Seelie and their lap dogs were here to interfere with Nadir's bonding time, even if it was slightly tainted by the people trying to coax her into servitude for them and their god, infuriated me to no end.

I hefted Grim Feather and twisted my wrist to put it into one of my wand slots before sprinting to the front line and joining Nadir. We ran together, leading the charge against the forces arrayed before us.

The Seelie showed themselves, their illusions building massive, gray-skinned beasts with ivory horns coming from their mouths and long appendages from their faces that had spikes attached to them. They roared, trumpeting cries from their long noses as they hefted them into the air.

They were lies. The army that spread out behind them, archers in gold and silver armor, were lies too. But the spears flying down on the orcs were real and they came from above.

MIDNIGHT

The orcs were not far behind the children as they sprinted toward their most hated enemies. The orcs' war cries were augmented by the wargs that bounded beside them. Even Ragul rode a warg into battle, a staff hefted in front of him as he spoke in a low tone.

At least, it sounded low to me from where I flew above them all.

A tingling came from the back of my ear hole as the boy spoke my host's name, bringing me to his shoulder and ruining my sight of the shaman's skill.

"Yes?"

"I need you to distract the Huntsman, if you can. His arrows will destroy the orcs before they can be of any use." The boy began to run even faster as the void of his dark eye shimmered. "And I'll need you to point out the true Seelie. I can see their illusions, but the orcs can't."

"That's a lot to manage without revealing myself unnecessarily. I can try to do one, and not the other."

Azlo huffed. "Then distract the Huntsman."

A bone-chilling howl echoed around us as the Hounds from the Hunt fell to the earth before the charging children and the orcs. There were dozens of them, their riders and handlers sporting javelins in satchels on their tack and lances on their arms that leveled toward us.

The boy growled and spat, "Go now!"

I lifted myself into the sky from where he was, and put my clone on overwatch for both of them as the front lines closed.

Wargs bounded faster and began to worry and bark at the Hounds, easily a head larger than they were.

As I dodged an arrow from the horned creature on the horse at the head of the Hunt, the Erebos children found their Seelie counterparts.

AZLO

I whipped my wrist out and called Shaper to my hands as my body left the ground and twisted with the swing of my attack.

The Seelie had surrounded himself with 'warriors' whose faces contorted with rage at the sight of me as they drew swords. All of it was a mirage to hide him drawing his own sword to try to shove it through my stomach.

My attack looked to be landing on one of the illusions, and with my hammer, it did. But the now-sharpened wind dagger flicked from my left hand sent a rippling crescent of air at the Seelie swordsman.

The elf blocked the strike, but gave himself away by dropping the illusion.

I shoved the dagger into the sheath and let go of Shaper, letting it fall to the ground as I landed and sprang at the surprised Seelie.

He snickered. "I'll cut you down before taking you back home." He raised his blade lazily to strike me with an overhead chop, but I just held my hand out and summoned Grim Feather with Ready Grasp.

The tip of the blade slid into the pale-skinned elf's stomach, the wound already blanching further before darkening with frostbite.

I grinned as I took the dagger out once more and plunged it into the side of his neck and jerked it back and forth once before using Ready Grasp on Grim Feather again.

The weapon flickered away and settled back against my spirit and I used Spectral Pull to grab Shaper and pull it into my hand. Ten mana slid from my bar as I was only about ten feet from the discarded weapon, well within the thirty foot casting range for the cost.

I glowered around the battle before me, the Wild Hunt

beginning to fall upon the ground to fight the orcs and the spectral warriors who fought alongside them.

The orcs were being slaughtered, but to their credit, they gave as good as they got. There were shadowy corpses on the ground and the war cries of the orcs still sent chills down my spine.

The hunting horn blasted above me as the Huntsman had found his prey. The three Seelie beneath him closed in on me and one of them looked familiar.

"Is that really the Unseelie bitch's brat?" the man called, his stubbled attempt at a goatee almost enough to make me roll my eyes. "We thought it was someone more important!"

It was the Seelie Court's own Prince, Ozmark.

I'd read enough about him to know he was a fool who spent more time courting the ladies at parties than he did studying fighting, but he was a highly skilled mage for his age.

He had a foppish hairstyle, the radiant gold of it just like the paintings I'd seen of his father, his eyes a distinctive amber like honey. He had a narrow face that the Seelie liked, and his reedy arms and legs spoke of his lack of physical prowess.

I snorted. "You had a thought?" I shrugged and began to clap slowly. "I bet your father's *so* proud, Ozmark."

"At least he has a father, orphan boy," one of the others quipped. This one looked nearly identical to the one standing to the prince's right. Long blond hair, thin face, carried swords on both hips, and wore leather armor dyed in the Seelie Court's silver and gold regalia. Their levels were obscured, common for the Fae, but they looked to be about as strong as he did, so I wasn't overly worried.

I just clicked my tongue against my teeth as I began to pace around them to find a better position. "Orphan means both parents are gone, Seelie. I would think with how quickly you were dumped on your head at birth, you'd know that."

The one that had spoken to Ozmark's left stepped away from the others and snarled, "I challenge you!"

I rolled my eyes. "This is a battle, just fight me!" He watched me with marked disinterest, so I pressed. "What makes you think I can't just kill you all now and then move onto whatever enemy I want?"

He whispered something and the neighing of a horse behind me startled me enough to turn to find the Huntsman only a dozen feet away with his massive bow drawn taut.

"I could end you right now if I so chose to, but I value my subordinate's honor. Too afraid to answer the challenge, Unseelie scum?" The prince jeered, then snapped his fingers, and the Huntsman's bow lowered to the point of being away from me, but nearly drawn enough to be able to sling that spear-like arrow straight back at me. "Don't worry, I'll keep my dogs off you while you two fight."

I blinked, sighed, and grimaced as I turned back and pointed at him. "Swear on your power that the Hunt won't interfere and you won't attack me while we fight." He went to open his mouth and I snarled, "Swear it or I kill all of you without care for my own well-being. Three times—swear it."

"I swear on my power that no one shall interfere with your fight upon my order or otherwise." He crossed his arms and stared coldly but with a confident smirk. "I swear, I swear, I swear."

I grimaced and turned back to where the Seelie elf was watching me with his swords drawn and at the ready. If I killed him, the Huntsman would surely strike with the prince's displeasure. His statement would give me the time to argue that his 'order' would be his own will as well, and that would give me his power and life.

I also only had to hold out until Winterheart came here himself to create a little more conductive chaos for me to operate under.

"Fine." I tilted my head to the side and adjusted the bones in my neck before rolling my shoulders to loosen up. I grinned and put Shaper onto the ground before taking out the dagger. "This is the only thing I'll need for you."

He snorted and surged forward, a ring of light glowing from

his chest and then suddenly he had two more pairs of arms swinging swords in an array of attacks that would have been formidable if it hadn't been for the fact that I had True Sight.

I allowed the illusions to *hit* me and parried his thrust with the flat of my blade before planting my foot into his chest to shove him away.

He stumbled backward and regained his footing before coming back toward me for another attack, this time not bothering to cover his attacks with his illusions. Both blades moved efficiently, but they wobbled more than they should have as they sliced through the air.

Most swords had some give, but these blades had more than most. It looked like whoever had forged them had been drinking while they did it. They weren't sturdy at all.

His next slash went at my legs; a step back cleared me from the attack. I stepped back in once the attacks went wide, slicing the back of one of his hands with the blade of the dagger before dancing backward.

I didn't want to use my spells yet to keep myself safe and secrets up my sleeve. However, with these weapons so poorly made, it would be easier to keep them from touching me.

Another thrust, this time with more body thrown in, his hips rotating with the strike as his left arm went back. The thrust was a feint that overextended more than the Seelie meant it to.

His blade scraped over the edge of mine and I whipped my elbow into the flat of it, bending the sword into an angle that would make it useless.

He roared as his other weapon sliced the air en route to my neck, and I ducked the slice. Some of my hair fell to the ground as it slid past and I growled, "I thought this was a fight, not an aesthetics treatment."

The elf bellowed again, but Ozmark snarled, "Herat, enough. What is the Seelie way?"

I grinned, asking innocently, "Death?"

The elven warrior, Herat, spat and threw his bent sword to the ground. "Killing Unseelie."

I took the dagger into my left hand, the blade facing the ground as I lowered myself into a fighting stance. I waggled the fingers in my right hand at him and he took his blade in both hands and sprang at me.

The sword lashed out at my hip, then my arm, scoring a small slice on my upper arm.

He laughed and I just rolled my eyes as I jumped into the air and twisted. I kicked toward his head, but he ducked backward and instead I threw my dagger toward his stomach.

He snatched it into his grasp just as the tip slipped into his skin. He hissed and only looked up in time to catch my fist with his nose.

Blood splattered my armor as his head rocked back. I grabbed him by the neck and swept his feet from beneath him.

He fell to the ground, a soft *crack* issued from his skull, his eyes glazing over slightly. Sighing, I knelt and grabbed my dagger from his grasp, his blood flowing from his hand as the dagger bit the skin there.

I held the weapon to Herat's throat and glanced at Ozmark, his face a mask of fury.

The wind dagger nicked the skin before I pulled it away and the Seelie Prince spat, inches away from me. "Don't toy with him, scum."

I smiled as I whispered, "You heard him, he wants you dead."

The Seelie beneath me hissed and spat in my face, the spittle running down my chin as I stabbed the blade into his neck as methodically as I'd been trained to before leaning back a bit.

I leaned back a bit more, preparing to stand as I cleaned my blade on his cloth shirt, then slid the blade back into its sheath.

The world shook, forcing me to kneel over the Seelie on the ground once more, Granduncle Winterheart having made his entrance.

I turned back to Ozmark with a grin as I stood and the snow began to fall around us. "You ready for your turn?"

The other prince grinned as he snapped his fingers. "I think not."

———

MIDNIGHT

Nadir strode through the battling and confused orcs and dealt death to the Seelie as they came at her, the Wild Hunt's horde being more of an issue to her than the elves trying to figure out what the hell she was.

The girl was livid. The more of her people who fell, the angrier she grew. Her axe rained death on all who crossed her path and her healing magic saved the lives of the orcs it touched but there were only so many that she could save from the Hounds.

The trio of riderless ones she found eating one of the larger orcish specimens turned together to attack her as a Seelie mage began to cast a spell behind them. Six orc children sprinted out from behind her and toward the shadowy hounds as large as horses with tiny war cries.

Nadir's eyes widened and she sprang, leaping twelve feet to intercept the first Hound with a kick to the neck that made it yelp. Her axe flashed at the second who ducked below its friend to get to her legs and sheared half its face from the rest of it.

The third ignored her entirely and went for the snack packs waving daggers at the Seelie caster who grinned as he blasted the closest three with his spell.

Two of them died instantly, Nadir's spell unable to save them from being turned into ash. The third child just barely missed being vaporized thanks to the Hound that slammed into him, crushing his windpipe with a massive, dinner-platter-sized paw.

The spell instead struck the Hound and vaporized the rear half of it. The beast cried out in pain as it tried to drag itself away from the offending mage, only to find Nadir's wrath.

The three surviving children threw themselves at the Seelie caster only to be kicked aside. Nadir healed the one that had fallen to the now-dead Hound and turned her attention to the Seelie before her.

He sneered. "Annoying little creatures abound here, scum."

Nadir just glared at him as she gripped her axe so hard her knuckles popped. He began to weave a spell when the orcish children laid into him again.

He slapped one away when the other two attacked his flanks on opposite sides. He stepped away from one on his right only to be stabbed by the one attacking him on his left.

He wailed, the blade slashing toward his leg again. The slash gashed his leg and the spell faded as the caster's concentration failed, the Seelie's hands flying to his head in pain. The first child stood and bellowed as he sprinted forward and leapt onto the man.

Three daggers lifted and fell into anything the three of them could reach and shortly after, the man died.

The one she'd healed stood and walked over to her with a glare on her face. Knife clenched in the tiny green fist ready to attack when the first Hound stood and began to bark and snarl.

"Nadir!" I called from above, tired of watching her struggle with the children. She glanced up at me as I landed on the Hound and slashed its right eye in the process. "Ozmark is here and Azlo has answered a challenge from one of his cronies. As soon as that fight finishes, the little shit is going to order the Huntsman to murder him like the king wants."

Nadir's axe slashed and slit the Hounds' throat before she snarled, "Where?"

I turned and began to fly toward the scene of the fight as she howled, "Dread!"

The massive warg stomped to her and she caught a thick tuft of fur on her way past to swing onto her broad back.

We flew as fast as we could when something white caught my eye. I glanced and despite my disdain for him, I whooped, "Cavalry's here!"

Massive chunks of ice streaked through the sky as Winter-heart's attack against the Wild Hunt began.

He roared, the fury in his voice tangible to a degree that everything beneath him save for the orcish children froze where they were. Snow plummeted from the clouds above as he made his way toward his chosen target.

But it wasn't him we needed to worry about—it was Azlo.

He stood and faced the putrid pustule called Ozmark and said something. Neither I, nor my clone, were close enough to hear it, but he looked confident to me.

Ozmark glared at him and spoke in return, then snapped his fingers.

Nadir raced under me, holding out her hand, and called, "Azlo!"

The world slowed to a crawl as the Huntsman hefted his bow with ease and drew back his large arrow, the armor giving away little. But his target was close and his aim sharper than ever.

I did something I had sworn I would never do to the boy unless I absolutely had to. I opened my mouth and whispered his true name under my breath.

His whole body flinched, but he didn't fight is as I summoned him to me, but too late. The arrow was loosed and flew at a mockingly swift speed. I shifted my wings into a dive as he appeared with me, my form shimmering as I shifted to catch him in our fall.

While I caught him, I happened to see the second that Nadir's mind snapped. I could hear the whirring in her head as she tried to make sense of her brother having been shot and then just disappearing right before her very eyes. My clone's emergent insistence pulled me from worrying over the boy to watch as Nadir sailed through the air from Dread's back and she lost control.

Her fury awakened, her glamour was gone and so too her orcish form. Instead, the werewolf with skin like the night sky plummeted onto the Huntsman like a comet hitting the planet.

As soon as she touched him, his mantle flickered, a bewildered elven man with fair skin trying to figure out what beast assailed him stood there trying to defend himself.

Azlo gasped, his hand on his stomach where the arrow had found its mark.

"Stay still, boy!" I looked over the wound but had no way to treat it myself and I didn't dare move from where we were to create another target.

The orcs began to chant something as they closed in on the fight.

But what made me gasp was the fact that Azlo began to cackle as he stared dazedly at Ozmark.

The boy looked at his hand and stared in disbelief as it began to shrivel. "What's happening?"

"You swore an oath!" Azlo grunted, then winced as he sat up out of my grasp. "Your friend isn't dead! I just paralyzed him—the challenge isn't done, and your Huntsman attacked me *on your orders, oathbreaker.*"

Ozmark shrieked shrilly as golden power enveloped him and began to swirl with a lavender energy that then streamed into Azlo. The boy shook at the contact and shivered but seemed to be on the mend.

Grunting, I broke the arrow and pulled it as his wounds began to heal slowly.

The other boy with the Seelie Prince spoke something and then tossed a stone behind them. A portal opened and his guard dragged the still-shrieking Ozmark through it as his features began to melt and grow more and more grotesque.

As soon as they were through, Nadir stomped on the ground and a wave of magic-shattering energy burst from her at its epicenter. The Huntsman's mantle shattered and left the man there on his nightmarish-looking elk mount with matted fur and craggy skin that made it look almost undead.

He spoke softly, too softly to hear once again, and then a small band of orcs crashed into him. They pinned him to the ground before Nadir raged at all of them and began to toss them aside, her claws digging into their flesh like a hot knife cutting snow.

"Child! Be still!" Winterheart roared and landed, the distraction from both the orcs and Nadir searching for her enemy enough to allow the leader of the Wild Hunt to limp away and fly off on his mount. As soon as he was out of her range, his mantle returned and he summoned his bow once more.

He aimed a shot carefully that looked like it was going to arc toward the lupine woman, but instead he angled it down and shot at the ground below him.

A fissure opened up that he and his recovering riders plummeted into without stopping before the fissure closed and left nothing of the battle but the fallen orcs and remaining Seelie casters.

Some of the orcs chased them as Azlo slowly, limbs still shaking like a newborn deer, stood to his feet. "Nadir!"

His call drew the girl's attention. She huffed at the air and stalked forward. He started to walk toward her when Ragul and Urtan appeared on both sides of him and passed him to intercept her.

Ragul raised his voice, his tone holding a fervor that scared me, his words not making sense as he spoke orcish.

Azlo frowned and grabbed Urtan's arm. "What's he saying?"

Urtan turned to the smaller man and, with a grin on his face, translated. "The Wolf who's swallowed the sky has come to us at last. Our time has come. Uk'Beth is good."

My stomach dropped and as I watched, I could see it dawning on Azlo as well. Nadir *had* been what they were seeking. But why?

CHAPTER THIRTY-NINE

Ragul and Urtan had insisted that once Nadir calmed down and was herself again, she would be taken to his chieftain's longhouse to rest and recover while they took care of the battleground. Once again, I offered to help with burning the corpses that I could, but they said that could wait.

The guards outside stood between Nadir and I and her new-found adoring fans. They were fervent that they needed her and she needed them, her blessing would be able to cleanse them and make them stronger warriors or something.

Once she'd finished looking me over, she sort of sat there at the table in a fugue state.

I tilted my head to try to see her face, her glamour no longer necessary to hide who she was from the orcs around us. There was a tightness there that hadn't been there before. "Are you alright?"

She blinked and looked up at me and then to the angry, puckered scar that had been left behind on my stomach, just slightly discolored from the healing that absorbing the strength from Ozmark had given me. "I'm fine. I went toe to toe with the leader of the Wild Hunt and won, even if I didn't kill him."

"What did he say to you?"

She frowned and bit her lip, odd considering she had her tusks. "Something about 'old blood,' but he didn't speak Sylvan or even Elvish. It was something different."

"Well, whatever it was, I bet we see less of him after that. Ozmark as well, considering the next time he's close to me, his life will be forfeit and I'll take all his power." I thumped the table angrily. "Who would have expected them to carry such a valuable item on them like that?"

"We should have, but I was too busy worrying about you and my…" Her words trailed off as she fell back into silence.

"You were going to call them your people, weren't you, Nadir?" Midnight spoke in a low, soft tone from his perch on Ragul's high-backed chair. He had been quiet until now, and I had a major bone to pick with him, but at present I was more concerned with my sister.

She nodded, then lifted her head and looked at me. "I plan to stay, Azlo."

My heart dropped into my stomach. I hadn't expected that so fast, but she didn't let me dwell on it too long. "They mean to hunt mages and try to distract the gods so that Uk'Beth can sneak through whatever hole is hidden in the barrier in the wastes." She clenched her hands and then relaxed a little before explaining, "I think if they see me as their"—she gulped and looked like saying the word would make her vomit—"savior or leader, I can help them realize their mistake and stop this madness from erupting into a true civil war."

"I have a quest to go to Djurn Forge." I cast my gaze down at the table before me and muttered, "I'd hoped we would be able to go and meet our clan together before I could go finish it with Granda."

She reached out and took my hand. "I can't worry about you and the orcs at the same time." She offered me a sympathetic smile. "I think if you have Midnight with you, you'll be able to make it there, and then possibly get into touch with what your class needs you to become. The dwarves would be able to help you better than anyone here."

She gripped my hand and softly added, "Better than me."

"Nadir…" I opened my mouth to argue but I couldn't. We should be able to stay together. We *should* do this as siblings. But we couldn't. "We came here to this plane to grow. And you can't do that with me here, can you?"

She refused to say anything, but her grip on my hand eased before finally she pulled it away and it hurt so bad to realize the truth that had been staring at me this whole time. If she had to worry about me, she was going to fall and lose something that she finally had for herself. Something that no one else could touch and control but her.

I had to respect her wish, but I knew what she meant when she refused to speak. "Neither can I if I have to rely on you to come to my rescue all the time." I grimaced and said, "I depend on you too much for my own good. If I'm to be effective on my own, or for our people, I need to be able to do things for myself."

She nodded once, her lip quivering enough that I worried she would cry. I didn't want to see that. She sniffed and smacked herself, the loud clap enough to summon one of the guards outside who grunted something at her.

She waved him away and he left as she said, "You aren't a burden, Azlo. You're capable, if a little reckless. That stunt with tricking Ozmark was dangerous, but it paid off. You should be proud of that, but caution will aid you." She smiled at me. "The queen will be proud of you, and I know I am. Without a legacy to aid you, you stood against so much. And you're becoming *you*."

I laughed once, harshly. "We will see how much of me is left when I have all these pacts."

"We will, but I need you to know this one thing." She took my cheek in her hand, then smiled sadly. "I love you, brother. And I will miss you every day."

I frowned, then thought of an idea. "How quickly do I have

to leave?" She shrugged. "If I can stay for a few days or so, I can make something for us."

She smiled. "Oh? Something for me?" I nodded and she grinned. "I will get you as much time as you need, so make it well."

I nodded and stood to leave the building, the crowd outside calling until they realized it was me, then hushed. I went to find Fjlak and told her what I wanted to make.

She grunted, then spoke as if recalling something. "Should be fine. I've made similar before, though it will be severely limited and you'll be doing all the work."

I nodded. "That's fine. I only have one function in mind."

————

MIDNIGHT

For the next two weeks, the orcs praised and mourned their fallen. They feasted and told tales of their glories and battles, then at the end, they allowed Azlo to assist them in setting their bodies ablaze.

As the flames danced and flickered, and the orcs sang songs and wrestled, the siblings met once again under my watchful gaze.

"Is it done?" Nadir's excitement was almost equal to her worry as the boy nodded and handed her a small bundle of cloth. "What is it?"

Azlo motioned to it and just said, "Open it."

Inside was a simple ring with no adornment on the outside strung through with a thick piece of leather to strap it around Nadir's broad and powerful neck.

"I just need one thing to make them work." Nadir watched as Azlo pulled out an identical ring that hung from his neck, then took her hand and poked it with a small pin.

Blood welled up and when it touched the ring dangling in front of him, the metal dyed red, then turned a burnished copper color. He did the same thing with his own finger but with her ring.

"Now, when we hold them in our hands, the other will grow warm and we can feel each other's heartbeats." He smiled and looked at his sister. "Like when we would cuddle as children, remember?"

She laughed. "I remember you biting my leg a lot."

He just snorted. "And I remember you trying to kick me out of the basket Granduncle Winterheart would watch us in."

"You cuddled more than any creatures I've ever heard of!" I grumbled from above them. Boy and girl both tossed me a nasty glare and I just shook my wings out. "Well, it's true. Inseparable you were, and now look at you—both of you leaving the comfort of the other to tread your own paths. I must say, I am very proud."

"Bold for a Fae creature to say aloud," Nadir observed mildly. I wasn't going to correct them on my non-Fae lineage. She still didn't know who I was and I wondered if the boy would tell her.

If he did, she might not let him go, or worse—to him—she might leave to come with him and sacrifice her wishes.

I'd heard him grumbling about that to himself when he wasn't sure I was around or not.

I stared off to the mountains where Winterheart and his new lady friend likely still tried to conceive a clutch and grimaced. Why should he be so lucky while I had to watch such a grotesque display of sibling affection? Oh, to be free again.

They took my indifferent silence as consent for them to speak to each other again and this time, it was sadder.

Nadir looked pained. The same look she had worn throughout the many meetings and ceremonies to explain her role in the orcs' future. The look of a sister worried for her brother.

Azlo wore a look that mirrored hers. But old habits die hard. "I'll miss you, but this is for the best."

His bearing a mask he wore to hide the sorrow and ache

was firmly in place. Nadir, not trusting herself, nodded once, grunting.

"I'll leave in the morning, though that's really only a few hours from now." He sighed and I almost did as well. "I'll go make sure all my things are packed and then I'll meet you at your tent to say goodbye?"

Nadir smiled. "That would be nice, Azlo."

They parted ways, the orcish girl off to her new friends, their cheering and deference as she walked among them only mildly uncomfortable now that she was beginning to get used to it.

Then the elven boy, off in the darkness among the stars with the fires of civilization behind him, left alone to collect his tools and small tokens the tribe had given him. Fjlak had said her goodbyes days ago, ordering him to be safe, mainly because of her god.

In a few hours' time, I would watch them part, their worlds splitting to a degree that neither of them knew what would be coming next. But I knew one thing was for certain.

Their paths would cross again, and how that happened would be up to fate, the gods, and their choices.

The sun rose slowly, blinding radiance building a tower of colors on the horizon—a new day. A new adventure laying itself out before them both.

I closed my eyes and grumbled as I flapped my wings and hefted myself into the painting-like sky. "Dwarves? This is going to suck!"

ABOUT CHRISTOPHER JOHNS

Christopher Johns is a former photojournalist for the United States Marine Corps with published works telling hundreds of other peoples' stories through word, photo, and even video. But throughout that time, his editors and superiors had always said that his love of reading fantasy and about worlds of fantastic beauty and horrible power bled into his work. That meant he should write a book.

Well, ta-da!

Chris has been an avid devourer of fantasy and science fiction for more than twenty years and looks forward to sharing that love with his son, his loving fiancée and almost anyone he could ever hope to meet.

Connect with Chris:
Facebook.com/AxeDruidAuthor
Twitter.com/JonsyJohns

ABOUT MOUNTAINDALE PRESS

Dakota and Danielle Krout, a husband and wife team, strive to create as well as publish excellent fantasy and science fiction novels. Self-publishing *The Divine Dungeon: Dungeon Born* in 2016 transformed their careers from Dakota's military and programming background and Danielle's Ph.D. in pharmacology to President and CEO, respectively, of a small press. Their goal is to share their success with other authors and provide captivating fiction to readers with the purpose of solidifying Mountaindale Press as the place 'Where Fantasy Transforms Reality.'

Connect with Mountaindale Press:
MountaindalePress.com
Facebook.com/MountaindalePress
Twitter.com/_Mountaindale
Instagram.com/MountaindalePress

MOUNTAINDALE PRESS TITLES

GameLit and LitRPG

The Completionist Chronicles,
The Divine Dungeon,
Full Murderhobo, and
Year of the Sword by Dakota Krout

Metier Apocalypse by Frank G. Albelo

Arcana Unlocked by Gregory Blackburn

A Touch of Power by Jay Boyce

Red Mage and
Farming Livia by Xander Boyce

Space Seasons by Dawn Chapman

Ether Collapse and
Ether Flows by Ryan DeBruyn

Dr. Druid by Maxwell Farmer

Bloodgames by Christian J. Gilliland

Unbound by Nicoli Gonnella

Threads of Fate by Michael Head

Lion's Lineage by Rohan Hublikar and Dakota Krout

Wolfman Warlock by James Hunter and Dakota Krout

Axe Druid,
Brindollan Affairs,
Mephisto's Magic Online, and
High Table Hijinks by Christopher Johns

Skeleton in Space by Andries Louws

Dragon Core Chronicles by Lars Machmüller

Chronicles of Ethan by John L. Monk

Pixel Dust and
Necrotic Apocalypse by David Petrie

Viceroy's Pride by Cale Plamann

Henchman by Carl Stubblefield

Artorian's Archives by Dennis Vanderkerken and Dakota Krout

Vaudevillain by Alex Wolf

www.ingramcontent.com/pod-product-compliance
Lightning Source LLC
Chambersburg PA
CBHW021436240626
47153CB00001B/177